Cupcakes at Carrington's

Alexandra grew up in Brighton and left school at sixteen to run away to London with dreams of being a writer. On realising that she needed a proper job too, she went to work in an office.

Throughout her twenty-year corporate career, she survived many dull meetings by writing a scene or two, until she could bear it no longer and collapsed in a heap and begged her husband to support her while she lounged on a chaise and waited for the muse to arrive. He's now living in hope that she'll become rich and famous so he can retire to sun himself by an infinity pool somewhere exotic.

After escaping office life, Alexandra won a competition run by *The London Paper* to write the weekly City Girl column, an exposé of working life in the City of London. She wrote the column for two years before giving it up to concentrate on her first novel.

Alexandra lives in a rural village near Brighton with her husband, daughter and two very shiny black Labradors.

ALEXANDRA BROWN

Cupcakes at Carrington's

HARPER

Harper
An imprint of HarperCollins*Publishers*
77–85 Fulham Palace Road,
Hammersmith, London W6 8JB

www.harpercollins.co.uk

A Paperback Original 2013
1

A catalogue record for this book is available from the British Library

ISBN: 978-0-00-748823-0

Set in Birka by Palimpsest Book Production Limited,
Falkirk, Stirlingshire

Printed and bound in Great Britain by Clays Ltd, St Ives plc

MIX
Paper from
responsible sources
FSC
www.fsc.org
FSC C007454

ACKNOWLEDGMENTS

As a child growing up in Brighton, I have happy memories of wandering around Hannington's, a magnificent department store on the corner of East Street. It was a place where nothing bad ever happened or so it seemed to me. It smelt of Revlon lipstick and Chanel perfume (the glorious old one). It exuded luxury, from the Art Deco tearoom to the attendant in the Ladies powder room; even the open gilt-caged lift fascinated me. So my first thank you goes to Hannington's, I couldn't have written this without you.

Kate Bradley for laughs, chats, tears and being everything I hoped for in an editor, but most of all for making my dream come true. SCREAM.

Penny, Claire, Jaime and all at HarperCollins for their support, talent and patience.

Jackie Collins for giving my teenage self an escape when I really, really, really needed it, and also for tweeting me last year. FAINT.

Lisa O'Carroll for giving me my first break and liking my writing enough to actually pay me proper money to write a newspaper column every week for two years.

My wonderfully kind and generous author friends, Victoria Connelly, Miranda Dickinson, Elizabeth Haynes, Sue Hunter, Lola Jaye, Chrissie Manby, Jacqui Rose and Sasha Wagstaff – your emails, chats and fabulous cheerleading is so very much appreciated.

Caroline Smailes for being such a dear friend, your patience astounds me and the Poundland chat will never ever leave me. NEVER. Not that I'm bothered, of course x

Lisa Hilton and Rachael Hale for reading those early drafts, girls I made it out of the cellar, now where's that paper bag to go over my head? ☺

Carla Berryman for being excited and making me crack up with your 'Loub-for-a-phone' pic.

Jadzia Kopiel for changing my life, you're the wisest woman I know.

My lovely, supportive father-in-law, Dr Brown, for sharing the memories of his family's department store, Brown's in Newtownards, I hope I've captured a whiff of the memory.

Yeeman To, for being a fantastic sales assistant and telling me all about it, your generosity is very much appreciated and any exaggerations or fabrications are totally down to me.

C and L for bringing my beautiful, vivacious and funny daughter, QT, into my life while writing this book.

QT for making me whole again, I love you sweetheart with all my heart xoxoxo. Oh gawd, I'm going to cry.

My husband Paul, aka Cheeks, for 'knowing' it would happen, for the plot brainstorming sessions and for telling me what happens next when I had no idea and just wanted to run away and stuff my face with cake. I love you, now go and get me a cheeky box of macaroons . . .

And you lovely reader for picking up this book and actually buying it. I really really hope you love it, that it makes you laugh, that it makes you cry but most of all you tell everyone you know just how fabulous it is, and yes, I have no shame but then would you if you once did a running bodyslam at the hottest actor on earth, only to fall flat on your face and have the whole thing posted on YouTube by someone who is no longer a friend, natch?!? Hmm, exactly! ☺

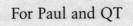
For Paul and QT

1

It's Tuesday morning in Mulberry-On-Sea, and Eddie is glaring with disapproval at my New Look heels as I step inside the staff lift and close the metal concertina cage door.

'You know I just saw Sam outside. That cupcake queen totally blanked me,' he says, preening into the mottled mirror on the lift wall.

'Oh you know Sam. She probably had her mind on other things like giant macaroon mountains or gold glitter sprinkles.' The mention of Sam highlights my rumbling stomach so I make a mental note to pop up to her café on the fifth floor, Cupcakes at Carrington's, for a red velvet cupcake with butter cream icing. My favourite. Mm-mmm. And a good catch-up on all the gossip of course. Sam overhears all kinds of stuff. When Cynthia from the florist down on Sunray Crescent was having it away with Trevor, the town sheriff, she was the first to know. Trevor's sister is a regular in the café and blabs all the juicy details to her mate over a cream horn and a steamy hot chocolate. 'I take it you had a good weekend?' I add, glancing at Eddie in the mirror as I bouf up my shoulder-length brunette bob. Last night, I used those giant sleep-in rollers, but after getting caught in a sudden downpour on my way to work, it now looks more floppy spaniel ears than big hair fabulous.

'Yes, so-so . . . went to an impromptu *Sex and the City* themed party on Sunday,' he replies, in his best diva voice.

'And let me guess, you were channelling your inner Samantha?' I laugh, shaking my head. Eddie adores her character.

'Of course.' He waves an imperious hand in the air before turning towards me. 'And I'm so glad I took Monday off. The pornstar cocktails were divine, but there's a limit, even for me,' he says, clutching the side of his head.

'Never mind the pornstars, tell me about the men.' I'm keen to hear about another one of his scandalous weekends, if only to take my mind off the one I spent alone.

'Oh, wall-to-wall Carries of course,' he sniffs.

'*Aaand* . . .?' I smile, fishing for more information.

'*Aaand* what?'

'You know . . . your "Smith" – was he there too? Come on, tell all, you know you want to.' I give him a playful nudge of encouragement. He hesitates.

'Nope.' He looks away. 'But it'll be Valentine's Day in

six weeks or so. And . . . well, if he doesn't want to spend it with me then it's his loss,' he adds with a flourish, before pulling a face.

'I thought you two were totally loved-up?' I say, steering the conversation away from the most romantic day of the year. It's not that I don't like being single. I do. Sometimes. And I'm only twenty-seven. But Valentine's Day can be tricky. Especially when everyone else is bound to be whooping it up with ten-course taster menus followed by cosy strolls along the seafront under velvety moonlit skies, and I'm home alone with a bar of chocolate to keep me company. And unless my love life takes a serious upturn – I'll be doing the same again this year. I think of the last Valentine's Day I spent with Brett nearly two years ago, it was our third together. I'd felt happy and loved-up, blissfully unaware that I was going to be dumped within a few weeks. He left me for someone else – a tall blonde with big hair and a sylph-like figure compared to my average height and bootylicious curves, as Brett used to say. My heart constricts a little, but I'm over him. I force myself to concentrate on Eddie's love life instead.

'So did I.' Eddie shrugs.

'So what's changed then?'

'Well, not returning my calls for starters.'

'I'm sure it doesn't mean anything. He'll probably call you today,' I say, knowing how sensitive Eddie can be.

'Maybe . . .' He looks away.

'So what do you know then, Ed?' I ask, quickly changing the subject. Eddie is the boss's boy assistant – his BA. Unusual I know, but Walter Davenport, who's the managing director of Carrington's department store, where we work, didn't earn his nickname 'The Heff', as in Hugh Hefner, for no reason. Whisper has it that after Walter's wealthy heiress wife found out about his dalliance with yet another girl less than half his age, she imposed a lifelong ban on him having female PAs. This cued the arrival of Eddie, who is a voracious gossip queen. Rather fittingly he's privy to all kinds of useful – and indeed sometimes useless but delicious anyway – snippets of information.

'Well you know me, never one for gossip,' he says, perking up and smoothing an already immaculate HD eyebrow with his little finger, while I try and resist the urge to smile at his blatant delusion. 'Anyway, enough about me. Although admittedly it is a scintillating subject.' He pauses momentarily and places a hand on his pristine fitted jacket, as if he's pledging allegiance.

'Oh come on Ed. Don't be such a tease,' I plead, now dying to know what he knows.

'*Weell.*' He pauses for dramatic effect and a naughty smile dances across his lips. 'You didn't hear it from me, right?' His eyes dart from side to side.

'Of course. My lips are sealed.' I make a quick zipping action across my glossed mouth before throwing an imaginary key away.

'Seems The Heff has been getting very intimate with one of those über-swanky retail consultancies up in London. You know, the ones where they charge upwards of a thousand pounds per day to tell you what you already know. Twenty-seven phone calls in the last fortnight alone! Methinks he may be looking for a change of direction before winding down for retirement,' he says triumphantly, just as the lift shudders to a halt, signifying our arrival at the next floor and stealing my moment to probe him for more details.

Eddie flashes a warning look in my direction as we simultaneously turn to face the cage door. The Heff is bent over right in front of us, busy tying the lace of his left brogue. Using both hands, I slide the door open, hoping it doesn't get stuck again. Last week I was on my tea break, travelling to the café to see Sam, and ended up trapped on the third floor for nearly two hours waiting for Charles, our Rastafarian handyman, to come back from visiting his sister Esther in hospital and prise the cage door open for me.

'Good morning, or is it afternoon yet?' Walter guffaws. He makes the same joke every day. After returning to a standing position, he strides into the lift and turns to slide the door closed.

'Morning,' Eddie and I both say in unison as we shuffle backwards until we're standing side by side behind him, breathing in the spicy aftershave fumes that permanently beat around his lofty frame.

'Georgina! You're looking delightful today as ever.'

'Thank you Walter,' I mutter, smiling to myself at his dated old-school charm. He's like it with all the girls in the store.

'How's business in Women's Accessories these days?'

'Very good,' I reply enthusiastically, even though we all know sales have dwindled dramatically throughout the whole shop for at least the last year or so. And the new superstore down on the industrial estate hasn't helped matters, either, not when you can get a whole new wardrobe, with accessories, for less than fifty quid in there. 'The new luggage line is doing exceptionally well. We've sold two pieces already. The local designer has delivered a few more of her handmade exclusive silk purses in candy pink, which I'm hoping to sell as Valentine gifts. And I can't wait for the limited edition Chiavacci Kelly bags to arrive from Italy.'

'Jolly good. Keep up the good work. The Chiavaccis could make all the difference. We're lucky to be getting them – only made ten: six in the US, two in Dubai . . . and us.' The Heff slides a hand through his silver hair and, puffing his chest out triumphantly, he starts rocking gently on his heels, stretching his braces out in front of him. I sneak a sideways look at Eddie, who pokes his tongue out and then quickly retracts it, just like a lizard. I try not to laugh as the ancient lift creaks through a few more floors. 'That's us,' The Heff booms, slapping his hands together and making me jump. He flings the cage door open and, like an athlete off the blocks, wastes no time in setting off. I let out a little sigh of relief. Eddie dashes out behind him and then pauses momentarily to look back at me over his shoulder.

'Not a word now,' he says in his perfected stage-whisper voice and blows me a kiss as the lift starts moving again.

I travel down to the ground floor, pondering on Eddie's gossip, trying to fathom out how it might affect me if it were true. What does Walter know? The feeling lingers, making me edgy. These days nobody is changing jobs unless they really have to.

I step out of the lift and make my way along the dimly lit staff corridor that winds the entire length of the ground level. It still has the original 1920s Tiffany glass wall lights. After pressing the security pad to release the heavy fire entrance doors, I arrive on the shop floor. My feet immediately sink down a couple of centimetres into a new plush carpet as I wade over towards my section at the front of the store.

'Georgie Girl! How are you today?' Ciaran hollers in his lovely Southern Irish accent. He's a waiter in Sam's café, and he's calling me from behind two massive bundles of cellophane-wrapped napkins. 'Not like you to be this late – it's practically lunchtime.'

'Ha ha very funny,' I laugh, glancing at my watch. 'It's not even opening time. Anyway, what are you doing down here? Shouldn't you be upstairs making banoffee coffees?'

'What happened, you get stuck in this silly new carpet?' he says, ignoring my banter and placing the napkins down on a counter nearby. He treats me to a huge grin before shooting me with his pretend finger pistol. I like Ciaran – we're Twitter mates and underneath the flirty swagger he's a sweet guy, but he can be so naïve at times, especially when it comes to women.

'Yeah, something like that,' I lie. The truth is I was up until nearly midnight filling in one of those income and expenditure forms for the bank. I'm hoping they'll let me reduce the monthly payments on a personal loan. And then I spent at least an hour lying in bed trying to unwind so I could fall asleep. I must have just slept right through the alarm.

Pinning my gold Carrington's name badge into place, I reach my till point, which I think is the best one on the floor. It's right at the front of the store, next to the floor-to-ceiling window display, giving me a panoramic view of the cobbled street with its white colonnaded walkway, pretty pansy hanging baskets and romantic olde-worlde streetlamps. During quiet times, and we've had a few recently, I love watching all the people milling up and down outside, or huddled in a deckchair enjoying a musical performance on the bandstand opposite. And on a clear early morning, when the town is still empty, I can see as far as the peppermint-green railings down by the harbour and out to the glistening sea beyond.

Carrington's is an Art Deco institution set in a prime

location in the seaside town of Mulberry-On-Sea, where everyone knows us and most of the locals have grown up coming to the store. For anything from school uniforms to wedding gift lists to baby clothes, they all turn to Carrington's.

Tourists stop to take pictures of our impressive powder-blue building with its intricate white cornicing around enormous arched windows. The store is nearly a hundred years old, and not quite as glorious as it was in its heyday, but still a landmark on the south coast. Owned by a family firm spanning three generations, Carrington's offers old-style elegance alongside the latest merchandise.

The shop floor in front of me is lit up like a Valentine's theme park. Red and silver lights are entwined around the original ornate Art Deco marble pillars, which are dotted throughout the high-ceilinged space. Giant Perspex hearts containing merchandise hang on lengths of invisible thread, giving an illusion of floating handbags, shoes and glittery costume jewellery. Even the traditional cherrywood gilt-inlayed panelled walls have twinkly rose-shaped fairy lights draped all over them. The display guys have done an amazing job in replacing all the post-Christmas sales stuff and getting the store ready for our next big seasonal promotion, Valentine's Day.

Even though I'm single at the moment, I still love this time of year. The atmosphere in store is always so fun and flirty, and that makes me enjoy working here even more. All six of the podiums situated by the entrance doors showcase various items amidst scattered rose petals and miniature Cupid figurines, luxury scented candles, thick embossed rainbow-coloured stationery and silky lingerie, drawing customers in, showing a teaser of what's on offer within. All designed to entice customers to touch the merchandise, to place a coveted bag over a shoulder or run a finger across the shoestring strap of an exquisite La Perla negligee.

After all, it's 'all about the merch' as we say, and every decent retail assistant knows that customers who try it buy it. True fact. And there's everything on offer to our customers. Handbags, shoes, cosmetics, all mingled in together with a glorious surge of euphoric optimism. A promise of reinvention, of a better life.

And I just adore the look on customers' faces when they emerge through the shiny brass revolving doors, flushed with adrenalin as they try to decide where their retail experience will begin. Savouring every moment. It's one of the reasons I work here. But my memories of the store go back a long way. I grew up in Mulberry-On-Sea and Mum used to bring me here on Saturdays and we'd shop and eat fairy cakes in the old-fashioned tearoom with its Formica tables and white-pinnied waitresses. We always had such a good time, just being happy together. This was years before Sam turned it into Cupcakes at Carrington's, a cosy café serving red velvet cupcakes and sponge cake with pinkberry-infused frosting.

Plonking my handbag in the little locker secreted behind the glass-topped counter, I rummage around for my mobile. I locate it nestled inside a red payment reminder letter that arrived this morning from the gas company. After flicking the phone onto silent mode, I slip it inside my trouser pocket and quickly shove the letter back to the bottom of the bag, vowing to deal with it later.

The smell of newness mingled with expensive perfume wafts over from the various cosmetics concessions. All three of the security guys are getting into position by the entrance doors. I give Annie, one of the other sales assistants, a quick smile as she plumps up a gorgeous midnight-blue Mulberry tote with rose-gold detailing. As I busy myself placing trays of rainbow-coloured chunky cocktail rings on top of a display cabinet, Betty, our mumsy switchboard supervisor, puffs her way over to me, pulling her hand-knitted cardy in tighter around her rotund frame.

'A rather lovely-sounding man from the Fiat garage called for you,' she just about manages, in between gasping for air and reaching for her glasses that are bobbing on the end of a chain around her neck.

'Oh?' I crease my forehead, wondering why he called the main number and not my mobile.

'He said if you want to call him back he'll be delighted to chat things through with you. I tried putting him through but your extension is engaged.' I swivel around to the phone and see the handset hasn't been replaced properly.

'Sorry Betty, I didn't realise, it won't happen again,' I say, knowing we're not supposed to have personal calls come through the switchboard.

'Don't worry duck.' Smiling, she hands me a pink Post-it note with the return number on before making her way back over to the staff security door.

'So, come on then. Are you buying a new car?' Ciaran says, placing his elbow on the counter and leaning in towards me.

'Oh, err . . . just thinking about things at this stage,' I say, fiddling with my hair. The truth is I can't afford the monthly payments on my car any more, let alone the petrol to put in it. I'm hoping the garage will buy it back so I can clear the finance. And I just wish my last pay review hadn't been quite so non-existent. I'd been hoping for at least a small rise, but nothing. Zilch. In fact, when I work it out, I've probably taken a pay cut, if I take into account the hike in tax and everything else these days. I force the worry from my mind, and resolve to keep all spending to absolute essentials only. Mortgage, food, utilities and the occasional red velvet cupcake . . . I shove a smile on my face.

'Fiats aren't very fast though, are they?' Ciaran says, rolling his eyes.

'Oh, I'm not bothered about all of that,' I say, trying to sound convincing. Better make sure I shift a few more of the high-end handbags just in case the garage doesn't go for it. Two per cent of the sales price of every £2,000 Bottega Veneta soon adds up. And I've got eight of them. I do a quick commission tally in my head and hope for the best.

'So how was your weekend?' I ask, changing the subject. I can see that he's desperate to tell me something, he's swivelling his eyes around like Inspector Clouseau, but before he has a chance to answer, his girlfriend Tina appears. After placing a possessive arm around Ciaran's waist, she flicks her high ponytail, sneaks a smug glance in my direction and turns her face towards his.

'What was all that about?' she pants, desperate not to miss out on a bit of gossip, and not bothering to excuse herself for having barged in on our conversation.

'Nothing, we were just chatting about cars.' He grins. 'Oh,' she says, dismissively. 'Well, have you heard about Emma in Stationery?' She pauses to make big eyes, but before Ciaran can answer she carries on. 'She's pregnant again.'

'But didn't she just come back from maternity leave?' Ciaran says, looking puzzled, and I can't help laughing as he pulls a monkey face. Tina shoots another stare at me.

'She's so lucky. Just imagine all that time off. I can't wait until it's our turn.' Tina tilts her head back and closes her eyes for a moment, as if imagining the whole experience as her very own nirvana before looking to

Ciaran for his response. A fleeting look of panic appears on his face, which is quickly replaced with a half-smile. He opens his mouth to say something else, but she puts a finger on his lips before he can talk.

In addition to being Ciaran's girlfriend, Tina is the accounts manager, or at least that's the title she gave herself. She adds up the sales receipts, checking the money and allocating our commission before someone from the office up on the executive floor authorises it all. But most of all, she bosses people around, especially Lauren, a nineteen-year-old first-job girl on one of those NVQ schemes. Anyway, Tina's excelled herself by making Lauren organise the next Christmas party already. A memo was stuck on the staff-room wall requesting the £15 payment by cheque and our dinner choices by the end of next week . . . and the turkey carcass is barely cold after last year's do.

'Oh I think it's so romantic,' Tina smiles.

'Sure it is. Anyway, got to go, only came down to collect these from the delivery guy. Tweet you later,' Ciaran says, winking at me and grabbing up the napkins before sauntering off towards the fire door. Tina scurries off after him, moaning about his Twitter addiction and how much of a flirt he is. Poor Ciaran! What's wrong with a bit of Twitter? How else would I get to talk to famous people like Cheryl Cole or Mr I Am with his 'boom boom and dope' lines?

2

'Hello. Cupcakes at Carrington's . . . how may I direct your *caaall*?' This throws me for a second. It's definitely Sam's bubbly 'everything is lovely in the world' voice, but there's an East Coast American accent attached to it now.

'Sam, is everything OK?' I ask, tentatively, as I duck into the little recessed vestibule behind my counter. We're not really supposed to make personal calls during opening hours, but everyone does, and as long as the shop floor is quiet and we're discreet, it's all right.

'Oh, thank God it's only you,' Sam says, back in her normal voice.

'What's going on?' I hesitate, and then brace myself for the answer. I've known Sam since school and, despite my abrupt exit halfway through, catapulting our lives in totally different directions, we managed to stay in touch and be best friends ever since. But she has dragged me through some real harebrained escapades over the years. Sam's always been a real foodie, so when Miss Sims retired and some genius here decided the

Carrington's tearoom needed an overhaul, I rang her right away.

At the time, Sam had just been sacked from her personal shopper job at Harvey Nichols because she'd spent more time concentrating on the 'personal' part of her job title than actually trying to sell things to the customers. But her ex-boss had been so impressed with her sterling spending efforts that she'd been given a platinum store card by way of a sweetener. So, after a cash injection from her mega-wealthy dad, Sam made the move down from Chelsea to Mulberry-On-Sea and now reigns supreme over her gorgeous café. It has a honey-hued interior and reclaimed train seats upholstered in crimson velvet, sectioned into booths, so you feel as though you're actually in a real vintage steam train, complete with golden glow lighting from frilly-shaded table lamps. It's very nostalgic in an *Orient Express* kind of way. And the food is to die for – salted caramel cupcakes, rainbow salads, delicious artisan breads and the most fabulous afternoon cream teas you can possibly imagine. Homemade scones piled high with strawberry jam and gooey clotted cream, surrounded by delicate finger sandwiches crammed with every filling imaginable.

'Oh nothing. It's just some guy called Justin. He says we met a few months ago at a club. Well, anyway he keeps calling and texting.'

'Hmm . . . why don't you just tell him you're not interested?'

'Well I tried, but he's being very persistent. Anyway, I'm hoping the other guy calls and I can pretend to be unavailable?' she says, dramatically. 'Hence the screening, this way I can take orders over the phone and still make myself appear elusive and mysteriously hard to get at the same time.' She laughs, seemingly satisfied with her elaborate plan.

'So who's the other guy then?' I ask, feeling confused. The last time we spoke, just a couple of days ago, she was going on about some guy called Steve. Sam changes her men like the rest of us switch TV channels, making it near on impossible to keep up with her.

'Oh my God. I can't believe I haven't told you about him yet. It *must* be love. I'm losing my mind already. He's only "the one". I met him when I was having my monthly dinner date with Dad on Friday, up in London at The Ivy. He was on the next table, and well he's a lawyer, maritime or something, and he lives here but commutes to London. And he's a gentleman, not full of himself like all those shouty Cityboy types, but anyway, Dad knew his boss, so we got chatting and he's absolutely drop-dead, knicker-ripping gorgeous. Not that he's done that yet, but I'm working on it.' I try and push the image of Sam's knickers being ripped from her body, from my mind.

'Are you still there?' I say, having heard about 'the one' a zillion times before.

'Yes. Err sorry,' she sighs, no doubt having lost herself in some fantasy moment. 'What did you want?' she says, dreamily, followed by, 'Oh my God, sorry that sounded so rude.'

'Charming,' I say, feigning mock hurt. 'Just wondered if you're free later for a gossip and to ask if you can keep one of those delicious red velvet cupcakes for me please?'

'Oh sorry hun, none left.'

'*Whaat?* But you must have. It's not even tea break time yet.' I can't believe it.

'A guy came and bought the whole batch for his office Christmas party.'

'But it's January! That's outrageous, why couldn't he have his party at the actual proper time in December, like everyone else?' I say, fighting a sudden urge to hunt the guy down and beg for a cake – they're that good.

'Ciaran served him. You know I'd have kept one back otherwise . . . Talking of Ciaran, have you seen him recently?'

'Yes, he was down here earlier, why?'

'Did he seem different to you?' she says, lowering her voice.

'Not really, why?'

'He's up to something, I'm sure of it. I reckon he's got his eye on someone.'

'Don't be daft. He's with Tina.'

'Even more reason to look elsewhere,' she snorts. 'Why else does he keep disappearing then? And it's not to see Tina, because she's in here demanding to know where he is all the time.'

'I've no idea.'

'Never mind, maybe it's my imagination. Anyway, what delicious delight can I tempt you with instead?'

'I'll have one of those vanilla slices.'

'A *millefeuille*, do you mean?'

'Think so, the one with layers of puff pastry and loads of deliciously thick custardy cream-type stuff inside, topped with combed fondant icing an—'

'Sorry, can you hang on a sec?' I hear the whoosh of the steam from the coffee machine as I lick my lips, willing her to have one left. I'm practically salivating at the mere thought. 'Right, that's all done. I've popped one in a box inside the fridge, what time will you be up?'

'Lunchtime?' I want to use my tea break to organise the Valentine's raffle. With the dwindling sales recently, every bit helps.

'Oooh, can you make it later? I've got to pop out to the cash and carry. How about fiveish?' It's early as we don't close until six today, but I can always ask Annie to cover the last hour. I covered three times for her last week.

'Sure, look forward to it.'

'OK hun. Bye for now. Oh, I almost forgot, you don't mind if "the one" comes along on Saturday, do you? I can always ask him to bring a friend. Just imagine, we could double-date on Valentine's Day – if you like him, of course.'

19

'No. Err . . . yes,' I say, thinking no more blind dates. I've been caught out like this before. Her man of the moment brings along a friend who usually turns out to be the beer-bellied guy with the body odour problem. 'What's his name?'

'Nathan. How sexy is that?' she squeals.

'Mmm. Nice. Well it's your birthday after all, and if he really is "the one" then you'll want him there,' I say, wanting her to be happy. 'But no blind dates, do you hear me?'

'Pardon?' Sam giggles, before ending the call. I drop the receiver back on the phone and peer down at my trousers, only to see that I now look as though I'm wearing a pair of fluffy Ugg boots too.

'What's with the carpet?' I say to no one in particular. It's my boss, the floor supervisor, James, who replies.

'Blame upstairs,' he says, approaching my counter. He's carrying two crystal weights with lengths of silver ribbon attached to crimson heart-shaped balloons. 'Here,' he says, handing them to me. 'Save you having to go down to the basement to organise them.' He's wearing a new slim-fit shirt that nicely accentuates the V of his firm chest. I quickly look away, praying he didn't spot me checking him out.

'Thanks. And I'm sorry,' I say, gesturing to the phone. He waves a hand.

'Ahh, no problem. It's fine if there aren't any customers around.' He smiles casually. I take the balloons, reflecting

20

on how thoughtful he is. His hand brushes mine and he immediately apologises, while a little shiver of excitement pulses through me. It's just such a shame that he's married, and that he's my boss, because he's so hot. I remember when he interviewed me for the job. The sandy-blond hair that kept bobbing into his eyes as he looked down at the questions on the desk in front of him. His emerald-green eyes probing me for the answers every time he looked back up, and the fact that he's oblivious to it – well, it just makes him so damn sexy. 'You OK? You look tired.' He grins, and a warm glow flickers within me. He's the first guy I've felt anything for since the disastrous break-up with Brett. We had been virtually inseparable for three years and his betrayal hit me really hard.

'Thanks a lot. Do I really look that bad?' I say, instantly hoping he'll disagree.

'No. No I didn't mean it like that,' he replies, momentarily patting my arm by way of apology, and I take a deep breath. After Brett left I swore off men completely – I really wasn't interested in going through that sort of pain again – but it's reassuring to know my heart hasn't been completely shattered, and that maybe I'm ready to start dating again.

'So what's with this carpet?' I ask, quickly changing the subject. 'And have you seen the state of these?' Feeling flustered, I peer down at my legs.

'Well, I wouldn't say they were a state exactly. They

look fine to me.' His cheeks flush for a second and he clears his throat. I feel embarrassed. 'Shame about the fluff though,' he finishes, with a gentle laugh. 'Somebody decided to splash out and re-carpet the entire shop. Staff canteen included.'

'What a waste of money. Before you know it we'll be closing down and switching to "online purchasing only",' I snort. The edgy feeling from earlier swirls around inside me again.

'Trust you, always thinking about the bottom line.' He shakes his head.

'Well, I don't see you complaining when I shift all of the high-end stock,' I tease. But the truth of it is that my section of the shop-floor space does make the most money. The others say that it's because I'm shameless and not averse to using my wily powers of persuasion when boyfriends and husbands rush in to buy a last-minute gift. But it's not my fault if they opt for the biggest hobo bag after I let slip how the lucky woman will squeal with delight and love them forever on unwrapping such a gift. All the while discreetly nudging the small version to the far end of the counter, and therefore out of mind . . . as demonstrated by Mrs Grace herself on my induction day. Mrs Grace rocked Women's Accessories for fifty years before retiring and handing the mantle to me. She now helps out part-time in the stock room, as she had to come back to work because her husband Stan was 'driving her round the twist' and spanking all their pension money on his 'filthy birds', which she later explained were actually pigeons.

'True. You're really good at what you do and that's why I need your help this afternoon.'

'This afternoon?' I say, my eyes widening at the prospect of a change in routine.

'Yep, a wealthy customer is arriving to do a spot of personal shopping and he's expressed a particular interest in our high-end designer handbags. Malikov someone or another, I think "his people" said.' James makes sarcastic quote signs with his fingers. 'Six times they've called today demanding to speak to security ahead of his arrival. And then banging on about CCTV cameras and how we must respect his privacy.'

'Malikov?'

'That's right, Konstantin Malikov, a Russian businessman apparently.' James flashes his perfect white smile at me. 'Oh yes, it just so happens that Mr and Mrs Malikov are keen to spend some time here in the south of England whilst their only daughter is settled into Dean Hall.' The mention of Dean Hall injects a flash memory moment of the few years I spent at boarding school before everything changed and my whole world fell apart. 'And naturally they are looking to offload some of their wealth in our fine establishment.'

The memory is instantly replaced with excitement at the thought of my share of the sales commission. James often asks me to help him with the personal shopping customers, and over the years we've developed a strategy, a kind of double act that has reaped some fantastic sales. James looks as though he's about to say something else when a pumped-up version of 'Love Is In The Air' pounds through the sound system, signifying opening time. There's an old dear with a tartan shopper waiting by the door to come in.

'Was there something else?' I ask James on seeing his hesitation.

'It'll keep,' he says over his shoulder as he strolls off towards the escalators.

3

After processing a card payment for a sparkly tear-drop necklace, I turn towards my customer. She's wearing a shiny green skirt that's the same colour as a Quality Street triangle and has the biggest static hairdo I've ever seen.

'There you are.' I've gift-wrapped the item and popped it into one of our special Valentine jewellery bags. Crimson with silver rope handles, and a sprinkle of limited edition Cupid-shaped confetti. 'And thank you very much.' I smile, making sure I maintain eye contact.

'Thank you dear. It's for my daughter, her thirtieth. You know, she was actually born on Valentine's Day, just after midnight, a true gift of love my husband always says. It's so exciting . . . but makes me feel very old,' she chuckles, patting her hair-helmet before stowing the receipt safely in her purse. A lump catches briefly in my throat as I remember Mum. She loved birthdays, always got excited too. I swallow hard and smile. It wouldn't do to crumble in front of a customer. I like to think of the shop floor as a stage to perform on and everything else can be left behind the scenes. Safe and secure. Unlike my foster home, where Nanny Jean used to sigh whenever I walked in the room and her husband would yell 'cup of tea' at me all the time like I was the live-in maid. And as for their brat of a birth daughter, Kimberley, who once told me it was no wonder my real family didn't want me, given how ugly I was . . .

'Well, you must have been very young when your daughter was born,' I say warmly, shoving the memories from my head.

'You're very kind. And yes, I suppose I was,' she replies in a dreamy voice, as if casting her mind back. She pats my hand and smiles before leaving.

The shop floor is really quiet, so I choose a selection of our very best bags for the Russian to browse through and take them up the back stairs to the personal shopping suite before bombing back down to my till. Carrington's is a bit of a maze. The underground corridors down in the basement go on forever and there's even one that runs all the way to the old music hall at the other end of Lovelace Walk, a few streets away. Rumour has it that the original Mr H. Carrington, aka Dirty Harry, had the corridor built especially as a discreet way to 'visit' showgirls, then pay them in kind by inviting them back for secret late-night shopping sprees. Sort of like a free trolley dash in return for sex I suppose. Mrs Grace told me all about it.

Once back, I discreetly tilt the computer screen

and decide to Google **Malikov** while indulging in some online window shopping. I tap the screen to bring up the Carrington's Home Shopping site. As I select the home furnishings icon, Eddie sidles up to my counter.

'God I'm bored,' he says, pulling a sulky face. 'The Heff has gone off somewhere, said he won't be back until the end of the day, so I've got nothing to do. You know he can be so selfish sometimes.'

'There must be something you can find to busy yourself with,' I say, distractedly, as I hover the cursor over the 'Get the Look' tab.

'Nope. Nothing . . .' Eddie pauses and stares into the middle distance for a bit before announcing, 'I know! Let's go to Patagonia and flirt with cowboys.' He widens his eyes and crosses his arms.

Refusing to be distracted, I click the mouse and take a look at a colonial-style bedroom.

'What do you think of this?' I ask, tapping the screen.

'Boring!' he says, dismissively. 'And look at the price tag – more than two thousand pounds. Even with our staff discount card it's still extortionate. Sweet Jeeeesus . . . I'd want my whole flat *and* my next-door neighbour's refurbished for that amount.'

'Oh me too, this stuff is way outside my budget.'

'So why are you looking then?'

'Well there's no harm in taking a peek.'

'Of course there isn't, but tell me something – why *are* you up to your eyes in debt?' he says, placing the tip of his little finger at the side of his mouth and pulling a quizzical face.

'You know why – it was hard when I came out of care, I just wanted somewhere nice to live like everyone else and got sucked in by all those adverts dishing out 125 per cent mortgages like free newspapers at the station,' I say, remembering the sticky cold lino and thin faded towels at Nanny Jean's house, while Kimberley kept all the big fluffy pink ones in her bedroom. And the bank didn't hesitate in giving me the mortgage, even though any idiot knew I really couldn't afford the payments without achieving record sales commission every month for ever and ever and ever. Those were the days when designer handbags were a must-have and my sales commission skyrocketed as a result. I just wish I'd known back then that the boom would eventually bust.

'OK, calm down, you know you didn't even take a breath then. And I'm sorry, didn't mean to upset you and bring it all back.' I pull a face, thinking about the grubby bedsit I wound up in after I was shunted from the care system, with my whole world stuffed inside a couple of black sacks and a jaded social worker to guide me. I was on my own, and the only way to eke out my junior sales assistant's salary and make ends meet was by living on credit cards and personal loans.

'Now, where were we?' I ask Eddie.

'You were just about to buy something,' he laughs.

'Don't be daft,' I say, clicking to close the Internet browser.

'Oh, I'm only joking, kiddo.' Eddie pats my arm.

'So, has Smith rung yet?' I ask, swiftly sidestepping the focus away from my mountainous debt problem. Eddie's the only one who knows about it. He was with me when my debit card got declined in Starbucks one time – it was the day before payday and I was mortified. But Eddie swiftly stepped in and defused the situation by handing the barista a fiver before giving me a hug and a bite of his skinny peach muffin. I ended up telling him everything over a scalding chai tea latte, right back from the start.

'Not a whiff,' Eddie says, looking despondent. He scans the shop floor and after making sure regular customers, Mr and Mrs Peabody, can't hear as they wave at me on their way over to the escalator, he leans in close and whispers, 'Do you think I should call him? Only I don't want to look desperate or anything.' He nervously plucks at the skin on his neck. 'It's driving me mad, what do you think I should do?'

'Mmmm, tricky one. Maybe hold out until tomorrow, if you can. Let him know what he's missing,' I say, feeling sorry for him having to endure the 'will he or won't he call?' agony. He doesn't have much luck with men, and I really thought he'd met a keeper this time.

'But what if it's too late? All I want to know is if he still feels the same way. I'm just not sure any more.'

'Why wouldn't he?' I ask, keeping my voice low.

He shrugs before answering.

'*Weell* . . . not coming to the party for starters, when he'd promised to. And I still haven't heard from him with an explanation. It just doesn't look very positive for a successful Valentine's Day, does it?'

'I suppose not,' I reply, unsure of what else to say. 'But like you said earlier in the lift, it's his loss,' I add, brightly.

'Hmmm, guess I was just being ballsy.' Eddie pulls a face.

'But you definitely don't want to be chasing after him. Nothing worse than hankering after unrequited love on February the fourteenth,' I say. There's a silence, and I can see that Eddie is pondering on what to do for the best.

'Yes, you're absolutely right. Why should I chase after him? He can put his little hoofs into gear and trot after me for a change,' he smirks, changing tack again.

'What are you two up to?' Ciaran appears from behind the Lulu Guinness bag display.

'Nothing much. Why?' Eddie replies.

'No reason. You just look very cosy, huddled together there, that's all.'

'We were just indulging in some online window shopping therapy,' Eddie replies, swiftly. 'Not that it's any of your business.'

'Well don't be spending too much.' Ciaran wags a finger before winking at me.

'We'll spend what we like, somebody has to keep the economy going,' Eddie says, abruptly, and then turns to me. 'Don't they honeybunch?' in a much nicer voice. Ciaran looks towards the ceiling before checking his watch. 'Anyway, what are you doing down here again? Seems like you can't keep away,' Eddie sniffs, glancing in my direction, as if I'm the reason Ciaran's hanging around. But that's ridiculous.

'Meeting Tina. And here she is.' He glances over towards the staff door where Tina is standing with her hands on her hips. After Ciaran leaves I turn to Eddie.

'What was that all about? You know we're not actually buying anything. It's just a bit of fun looking.'

'Oh nothing. I'm on a come-down, and him, with his fake "bad boy" thing going on and his shovel-carrying troll . . . well they just get on my nerves,' he says quietly.

'What do you mean?'

'It's obvious she's only after his inheritance, if he ever gets it! Last I heard his fabulously wealthy parents weren't overly impressed with him working as a mere waiter in a café.' He crosses his arms and pulls an old lady face. 'But he doesn't seem to realise it. See, there she goes again with her little shovel, digging for gold.' I turn just in time to see Tina push her arm through Ciaran's as they leave the shop floor.

'Eddie, that's a horrible thing to say . . .' I begin, but suddenly Tina's relentless pursuit of Ciaran makes more sense.

James suddenly bombs over.

'Quick, follow me.' He drums his fingers along the front of my counter with excitement.

'Why? What's happening?' I ask.

'The Russian bear and his entourage have arrived early and they require fawning. Lots of it. Think *Pretty Woman*. Big mistake. Big. Huge . . . and all that if we don't get up there and FAWN!' James looks charged as he pulls a tie from his pocket and slings it around his neck. Feeding off his adrenalin, I grab the Spring/Summer catalogue and the limited edition Valentine's brochure before hurtling over and asking Annie to cover for me. She nods and smiles before plumping up a gorgeous caramel suede tote with a tassel drawstring.

'Can I come? Could do with a bit of Russian eye candy,' Eddie says, jokingly, knowing really that it's his cue to go. I blow him a kiss as I race after James who is already standing by the staff exit.

'Come on,' James yells. He's holding the cage door of the lift back with one hand and beckoning with his other for me to hurry up. Feeling exuberant, I jump hard into the lift and then instantly regret it when it quivers violently. I look at James but he just grins back at me, totally oblivious to my embarrassment. 'We can chat on the way up,' he says, fixing his sparkly eyes onto mine as he presses the button to take us to the personal shopping suite.

4

'So what will you spend your share of the commission on, Georgie?' James asks, turning to face me.

'Not sure,' I say, knowing it'll go towards the gas bill. 'What about you?'

'Oh, it's got to be a weekend away. I was thinking a few days lazing in the sun. What do you think?' He flashes a smile at me, and I allow myself a momentary fantasy that he's actually inviting me to join him.

'Mmm, I could do with a break. A nice hotel with a pool.' I grin, enjoying the relief the fantasy brings and forgetting my cash-flow problems for a moment.

'Yes. Now you're talking. When shall we go?' he jokes, and we both laugh. 'Now, getting back to Malikov, from what his "people" said, he's prepared to buy a lot of merch, but only if he gets a "super deal", as he calls it.'

'In other words he wants to feel as though he's got a *bargain*?' I say.

James nods. 'Indeed. But, as you know, we only have a very small margin for manoeuvre on the sales price.'

'Leave him to me. I'm sure I can make him see what a

bargain he'll be getting.' I smile, relishing the prospect. James shakes his head. He looks amused.

'So what have you managed to find out about him?' he asks, flipping his cricket club tie over and under until it's knotted perfectly. James has a passion for the sport, which is handy given that he runs Men's Accessories incorporating a little Sportswear section too. And as bowler for the Mulberry-On-Sea First XI team, he spends every Sunday up on the grassy common being admired by the WI ladies who ply him with cucumber sandwiches and cream teas. I remember seeing him in his cricket whites once when he changed into them before leaving work, and it was true he looked pretty adorable.

'Well, obviously Malikov's wealthy. Loves to take a risk; he supposedly sustained a gunshot wound to his right leg during military service, but there's speculation about the authenticity of that claim, according to his Wikipedia profile. He's just returned from his first voyage aboard his yacht, named *He Who Dares*, complete with Baccarat crystal bar and splash-proof karaoke platform, I might add.' I pause to catch my breath. 'Oh, and according to one particularly scathing *Wall Street Journal* article, he's desperate to gain recognition and respect here in the UK, apparently. Trying to join just about every private members' club there is.'

'Is he? But seriously, karaoke?' James says, shaking his head. 'Not sure that's the way to go.'

'Apparently his third wife, Natalya, is the karaoke

queen, or is she one of his girlfriends? Mmm . . . I can't remember now,' I say. He smiles at me again. Feeling awkward, I busy myself by fiddling with my name badge and straightening my top down. He clears his throat just as we reach our floor and simultaneously my phone vibrates. Without thinking, I grab it from my pocket and answer, not even bothering to look at the screen, just grateful for the perfect timing.

'Hello?' I glance at James and pull a sorry face, but as soon as I hear the voice on the other end of the phone, my heart plummets like a bungee jumper from a crane.

'Hi darling.' It's Dad. My head spins. I should have known better than to answer it. I'm usually so careful with withheld numbers. I turn away, desperate to create some privacy. I contemplate hanging up, when thankfully James nods his head towards the Gents loo to indicate a pit stop and disappears inside.

'I told you not to call me at work,' I say, in a low voice, feeling my cheeks warming again as I huddle into the corridor wall.

'I just wanted to know how you are. It's been such a long time . . .' I swallow hard, remembering when I last spoke to him. The strained conversation and the false-ness, just because it was his birthday and I felt sorry for him being all alone. But then it's his own fault, I quickly remind myself.

'Dad, I'm sorry, but I can't talk now.' I snap the phone shut, vowing to be more careful next time it rings.

'You OK? You look like you've seen a ghost,' James says softly, when he reappears.

'Oh, yes I'm fine,' I mutter, doing my best to recover.

'You know if you don't feel up to this I can always do the fawning by myself. You work twice as hard as the other sales assistants.' The way he talks, so kindly, makes tears prick at my eyes. I study the pattern on the carpet and swallow hard before glancing back at him.

'I'm fine. But thanks for your consideration.' The shock of Dad's voice perforating my work day slowly subsides.

'If you're sure?'

'I'm sure,' I say, managing a weak smile.

'OK, so we know that Malikov likes his toys then,' he says in a low voice, thoughtfully bringing us back on topic.

We reach the personal shopping suite and James pushes through the creamy white padded door into the little anteroom that smells of lilies and expensive perfume.

'OK, you ready for this?' he whispers while checking his cufflinks. I nod. 'Great – knew I could count on you,' he says, enthusiastically, and I smile at his praise.

Inside, and standing by the floor-to-ceiling chiffon-covered window is a sturdy-looking man yelling Russian into a hands-free mobile phone. As we walk towards him he snatches the earpiece away and tosses it towards the three enormous men wedged on a cream leather sofa, all wearing identical black suits. The one on the end performs a sudden pincer movement to successfully catch the earpiece. James dashes over to greet our customer.

'Mr Malikov, welcome to Carrington's.'

Ignoring James's outstretched hand, he commands, 'Let's shop,' in a gravelly voice that has an American-English accent. He's dressed casually in chinos with a navy blazer over a canary-yellow polo shirt with a ridiculous paisley cravat. He limps towards the enormous overstuffed circular sofa in the centre of the room, slumps down and rests both hands on a carved, tiger-headed cane that has a ruby the size of a plum wedged inside the tiger's roaring mouth. Lifting his wrist, he squints at a platinum jewelled watch. 'I have twenty minutes before I leave for the opera. Do you like opera?' he barks. James and I exchange glances. Twenty minutes! We better get on with it if we're to stand any chance of securing a big sale and earning some much-needed commission.

'Well, sailing is my thing,' James replies, calmly, as though he has all the time in the world. I smile inwardly, knowing how he hates water, preferring his beloved cricket to anything that might involve getting wet.

'A man after my own heart.' Malikov hauls himself up, grabs James's hand up from his side and pumps his arm vigorously. We're all smiling. So far so good. I feel relaxed. 'And what, *Miss*, do you like?' Malikov says, suddenly and suggestively. He wets his lips before slowly turning a pair of shark-like eyes towards me. I wither under his scrutiny as I rack my brains, searching for a suitable response. It's as if time has stood still. And then, out of the corner of my eye, I see one of the heavies holding out a glass of champagne. Malikov is distracted. He turns to take the flute and gulps it down in one. The feeling of relief is overwhelming.

'So how was your maiden voyage aboard *He Who Dares?*' I ask, steering the conversation away from me and James's faux love of the sea. Malikov's hand is the size of a shovel and with a vice-like grip.

'I see you've done your homework.' Looking impressed, he nods his head slowly. 'Kon. You must call me Kon. It's what the people I like call me.' His gaze lingers for a moment, sending a chill right through me. His power fills the room, practically overpowering the glorious scent from the three Jo Malone candles flickering on a white lacquered table nearby. Eventually Malikov drops my hand and I feel the blood rushing back into my aching palm as I wonder what the people he *doesn't* like get to call him . . . if anything at all.

'OK Kon, if you're sure you don't mind,' I smile, and he tilts his glass up towards me like a tick of approval. 'And how are you settling in to your new home here in England?' I add, trying to relax and get into the swing of things.

'It's adequate,' he shrugs, waving a hand in the air. 'A kennel compared to my home in Moscow.' He juts his head up. 'There I have a house as big as your Queen Elizabeth's Buckingham Palace,' he adds with all the attitude of a movie Mafioso.

'Oh, how wonderful,' I simper, being careful not to overdo it, but knowing the fawning process is the most crucial part of the personal shopping experience. Private customers want to feel special and taken care of. And why not? They're just like any other customer at the end of the day – only with stacks more money, obviously.

'You must come and see it sometime.' He fixes his eyes on me again and I glance towards James.

'Well, I'd have to see what the boss says of course . . .' I venture, playing along with his flirtation. He studies me for a moment, as if peeling my clothes off with his eyes. Then he tugs at the side of his jacket, making it flap open momentarily, and I catch a glimpse of a handgun inside a tan leather shoulder holster. His eyes meet mine.

'I am a businessman, business is dangerous in Russia,' he says by way of explanation. I quickly tear my eyes away.

'Who's your best customer?' Malikov asks suddenly.

'Mr Malikov, I'm sure you'll appreciate that it would be totally unprofessional of me to break any customer confidentialities,' James says smoothly, knowing it's more than his job's worth to name any names. The Heff is very particular about discretion. Only a few weeks ago he had a go at one of the boys in Menswear for sniggering in the canteen after catching a glimpse of a well-known MP in one of the changing rooms. Under his rotund belly, the MP was working skimpy leopard-print Speedo-style budgie smugglers while admiring himself doing a pretend dive in the mirror.

Thinking of the gas bill that needs paying urgently, I launch in. 'I probably shouldn't tell you this . . .' I hesitate, before lowering my voice. James flashes me a warning look but he doesn't need to worry. 'One of the Queen's relatives was a virtual fashion recluse before we kitted him out in the finest menswear, so please be assured you'll be joining an elite group within British high society,' I say, amazed at my own nerve.

'What club does he belong to?' Malikov interrupts, rudely.

'Mr Malikov, I'm not sur—' He cocks his head to one side. 'Sorry. Kon,' I correct myself. 'I've said far too much already. But let's just say he's definitely back on the society circuit now, according to last week's . . .' I hesitate momentarily and flick my eyes over to the pile of glossy magazines artfully fanned on a coffee table for inspiration. '. . . *Hello!* magazine,' I quickly add. Malikov's eyes widen and he nods his head slowly. 'And I could always investigate the possibility of a discreet introduction to him . . . say on the polo field.' His nodding head speeds up at the prospect of mixing in such elite circles.

'What did he buy?' He stares directly at James, who

doesn't flinch. 'Well, I'm sure you will appreciate that Carrington's prides itself on offering a very personal serv—'

'Yes, yes, I know all of that. I've done my checks so you can cut the flimflam. What's the most expensive thing you have?' he asks, waving a dismissive hand in the air.

'Well I know you've mentioned an interest in jewellery . . .' James takes a step towards a glass display cabinet housing Carrington's fine jewellery collection, before he's cut off again. Malikov juts his head forward.

'That's because I own a platinum mine. Won it on a hand of roulette last month. Uranium too,' he chortles. Raising a hand, he bats the air around in front of him before continuing, 'So let's hope there's another war somewhere so demand for uranium from the arms manufacturers increases.' He snorts at his own sick joke, while James and I drag smiles onto our faces.

After showing him each of the bags I brought up earlier and talking him through the quality of craftsmanship, I bide my time as James tells him about the new Spring/Summer collection, prices, styles, and even manages to squeeze in a mention of the Chiavacci bags. A short silence follows.

'No, that is not acceptable. I can go to any shop and get the same prices, so you will need to do better than that.' His chubby paw tightens around the tiger's head. James gives me a look and I'm off again.

'Kon. Of course you're absolutely right. Some of the big stores up in London do have the same items for the same price . . . but I think you'll find this bag here,' I pause to retrieve an exquisite £1,950 buttery leather under-shoulder bag from the display stand, 'is exclusive to Carrington's. The brand manager told me herself when she last visited.' I pause for a moment, give the bag a quick stroke with the back of my index finger so as not to mark it, and lean forward slightly, squeezing my boobs together as I hold the bag out to him. I murmur a silent prayer for forgiveness to the women who chained themselves up so we wouldn't have to resort to this kind of thing. But I can't help wondering if they had to pay their own gas bills too.

Licking his fleshy lips, Malikov's eyes flick to my cleavage and I know I've got his attention.

'And, well, I probably shouldn't tell you this, but Catherine . . . our very own new royal princess,' I discreetly cross my fingers to cover the fib I'm about to tell. But needs must and all that. 'Yes, Kate is the only other person to have this particular handbag. The designer sent it personally as a wedding present, and you know I'm almost certain I spotted it tucked under Kate's arm when she was on the telly the other day.' Malikov's eyes widen. '*And* she was standing next to Her Majesty . . . the actual *Queen*!' I add for good measure, making big eyes and willing my cheeks to stop burning. 'So, I'm sure we can agree on a *super* deal especially for you.' I glance at James, pleased with myself for having mentioned Malikov's specific requirement.

Behind me, the gentle swing of the wall clock pendulum ticks away the excruciatingly long silence as Malikov ponders on what I've just said.

'No. I don't think we have a sale here.' It's as if somebody has slammed on the emergency brake. My heart skips a beat. This has never happened before. 'Is that the best you can do for cash?' He fixes a pair of now sinister-looking eyes on me, and then I get it.

'Kon, I can understand your hesitation. This is a very expensive bag.' I swallow hard. 'With certain . . . more exclusive customers –' I rack my brains for a suitable sweetener before deciding to wing it again – 'we could offer a selection of special promotional gifts.' Pausing to clear my throat, I spot James in my peripheral vision and he looks panicky. 'A purse or two to complement your handbag choices. And a selection of fashion jewellery,' I add, remembering the flashy costume jewellery hidden in the cupboard behind my counter, too garish for our usual customers. The Brazilian jewellery supplier refused to take the items back and, even with the half-price markdown in the Christmas sale, we weren't able to shift any of it.

Malikov's monobrow creases. His eyes dart greedily towards James for confirmation, who nods. 'I'll just pop downstairs and get you a selection of our best purses and bring the tray with the jewellery collection, if I may.'

When I make it back to the personal shopping suite, Malikov and his entourage aren't there.

'What happened? Where's he gone?' My heart sinks.

'I've just got back from escorting him to his car.' James is grinning from ear to ear.

'But what about these gifts?' I say, glancing at the stash in my arms.

'Oh, he said he'd collect them next time.'

'Next time? I take it you got a sale then?' I nod hopefully.

'Damn right,' he replies.

'And?' I prompt, putting the purses and jewellery on the circular sofa before crossing my fingers.

'A Louis, two Balenciaga and –' he pauses to pull a face and make quote signs – 'the exclusive under-shoulder bag that our very own Princess Kate was carrying on the telly.' James laughs and I grin with excitement. This must be more than we've sold in months – it's almost like the boom days. 'Oh, and a pair of Union Jack cufflinks,' James rolls his eyes. 'And get this . . .' James leans into me with a hushed voice, the electricity between us is almost tangible. 'He was hinting at both Chiavacci Kelly bags. And he wants to be treated like royalty.' James and I both smirk at the same time.

'Yes, really sorry about that, it won't happen again,' I say, knowing I overstepped the mark.

'Well, I think we can overlook it this time. Your royal

innuendo sure got him hooked, and just imagine if he buys the Chiavaccis?' My pulse races.

'Oh my God . . . well done,' I whisper back, my mind working overtime to try and calculate my share of the commission. The Balenciagas alone cost well over £1,000 each!

'And it's all down to you.'

There's a moment of silence between us.

'Hardly. I didn't do anything,' I say, loving his modesty. 'You were the one who organised everything.'

'Yes, but you were the one who reeled him in,' he says seriously, as a whiff of his delicious citrusy aftershave teases my nostrils. 'Our dream holiday is definitely on now,' he grins. Then James realises that his hand is still on my arm, and he blushes before taking it off.

'Sorry,' he says awkwardly, and turns to go.

'Don't be,' I mutter, but he's already striding off towards the door.

5

'Three cheers for Ciaran, and Tina of course.' I'm in the canteen and Tina has just announced her engagement. After an initial stunned silence – they've only been seeing each other for a few months – we're all necking plastic cups of Asda buck's fizz, even though it's only lunchtime.

The radio has been switched off and Ciaran is standing in the middle of the floor. 'Guys, I'm overwhelmed. Not only because she said yes . . .' he pauses momentarily to glance at Tina, who's grinning like the cat that's got the whole damn dairy. And it's no wonder. Ciaran hired a suite at a posh hotel in London and they spent the weekend there so he could propose, so Lauren told me. I guess this is what Ciaran's been up to, then, planning the proposal. Sam will be thrilled. As queen of hearts, she loves a good wedding, even if the bride is not her most favourite person.

As we all smile at Tina, and the girls from Lingerie start cooing over the rock that's clinging to her finger like a fridge magnet, someone shouts, 'Yeah, only because the diamond is the size of a sugar lump,' at which everybody except Tina laughs. James is standing next to me. His cup is empty so I make my way over to the bench table at the far end of the canteen to find another bottle. As I turn I almost bump straight into him.

'Looks like we had the same idea,' he says, holding up his plastic cup. I quickly turn back to the table to wrestle the cork from the bottle. Seeing me struggling, he reaches his hand over mine and effortlessly eases the cork free. A froth of white bubbles cascades down the rim of the bottle and I suddenly feel the effects of the daytime alcohol.

'Georgie, stay for a moment,' James says. But our names are being called from over by the salad bar and the moment changes. For a brief second I'm not sure if I imagined the last few seconds, but when I turn around James has gone off to join the others.

'And you will all come to my hen do, won't you girls? It's going to be a-mazing. Ciaran said I can have whatever I want,' Tina smiles, gazing up at him. 'I've opted for a day in the Carrington's spa. I've already spoken to Caroline, the manager, and she said if the board are OK with it, then she's happy to open up on a Sunday.'

'Cor. Can I come?' shouts Gareth, one of the security guys.

'No you can't,' Tina snaps. 'I'm off to get the engagement cake.' She tilts her cheek out at Ciaran for a kiss, and he duly obliges before heading over towards me.

We're all chatting and laughing when Tina starts descending the staircase at the end of the floor. Her spray-tanned face, which I can't help thinking makes her look like she's just run naked through a Ronseal factory, has a smile spread across it, but as her eyes meet mine, the smile fades ever so slightly and her eyes narrow. I quickly nudge Ciaran, who has my upturned hand in his, pretending to have inherited a palmistry gift from his old Irish granny.

There's a huge crashing sound. Everybody turns in unison to see Tina tumbling down the last step of the staircase to land in a heap at the bottom. Victoria sponge cake is splattered all over the banisters and splodges of strawberry jam are everywhere. It's even ricocheted up the walls so the whole area looks like a scene from *Casualty*. I run over to help her in case she's seriously hurt herself, but just as I crouch down and reach my hand out to her she hisses in a tight voice.

'Get off me. I've won. He's mine now.' She yanks her arm away. Her words hit me like a hard slap. I don't believe it. She really thinks we're in some kind of competition and Ciaran is the prize. I open my mouth to protest but the words won't come out. Then she quickly follows with a much softer, 'Oh I'm fine, silly me. I just slipped on the stairs. If you could just help me up, darling,' and I realise that Ciaran is standing right behind me.

'God Tina. Are you OK?' Ciaran asks, the concern catching in his voice. I stand up.

'It's this new carpet – not only a waste of money but a damn liability as well,' I offer.

'Thanks Georgie,' Ciaran says, as he helps Tina up to her feet. She looks at me over his shoulder.

'Actually, I think the carpet was a very good idea. I could have seriously damaged myself if the landing hadn't been so soft,' she sniffs self-righteously. And with that she leans into Ciaran and starts off towards her Lingerie friends, hobbling as though her life depended on it. 'Oh! I almost forgot,' she stops short. 'You'll need to call the in-store cleaners and get them to come and deal with this mess,' she barks in my direction, as if I'm the hired help.

'Sorry,' Ciaran mouths over his shoulder. I shake my head, wondering what he sees in her, when James reappears at my side. He hands me a drink.

'You OK?'

'Sure. I'm fine,' I reply, shrugging my shoulders. We both lean back against the table and his fingertips brush mine as our hands touch the surface, and I suddenly feel distracted and self-conscious, as if everybody is watching us. Mrs Grace catches my eye and gives me a discreet knowing look before smiling kindly. And I know I didn't imagine it this time.

Somebody pops open another bottle of buck's fizz and the cork performs a spectacular arc that just misses the light above, but lands bang on target. The doors at the end of the canteen spring open and The Heff appears just as the cork makes its descent to land slap on top of his head.

'Not interrupting anything, am I?' The Heff booms as he bats the cork away. Everybody stops talking. Eddie appears at his side; he has a black clipboard pressed to his chest. And he's doing his best to look efficient but he keeps staring at his shoes. 'Good. Because, before you all rush off I have some very important news to share. Then you can all return to your sections and send up whoever is on the rota for the next lunch session . . . without telling them what I'm about to say. Is that clear?'

We all mutter, 'yes' in reply. Like that's really going to happen. One of the Footwear girls is already surreptitiously fingering her phone, poised to send a text. 'Right. As you all know, Carrington's has seen a decline in sales of late and I think it is fair to say that unless something is done pronto' – 'Like buy more carpet,' someone mutters behind me – 'we're in serious danger of entering a terminal decline. So to help us revitalise the store, it is my pleasure to announce that Carrington's has today, at twelve noon, secured the services of the country's finest retail guru.' The Heff puffs his chest out, as if he's just, single-handedly, negotiated peace in the Middle East. A collective gasp circuits the canteen.

'She will be assessing the viability of each department with a view to rationalisation. Of course this may alter our staffing requirements.' There's another sharp intake of breath as the news sinks in and we realise what his announcement means. 'Eddie here has all the details,' The Heff continues, and my mind is working overtime. Everyone knows rationalising really means downsizing, which means fewer staff.

I guess in the current climate it was inevitable, with so many shops going to the wall. Tension starts to creep down from my shoulders, slowly trickling around to clutch my heart. If I lose my job then I might as well kiss goodbye to everything. Everyone knows how hard it is to find a new job these days. And besides, I love working for Carrington's. My happy memories with Mum are here.

'Make a note of your meeting time, and it goes without saying that you will all extend a warm welcome to Maxine who will be working here as of tomorrow.' My head feels as if it's bobbing around under water, I can't think straight. I turn towards James and see that his face has paled. He doesn't look back at me. Instead he bows his head slightly and mumbles something that I can't quite hear. Eddie is handing out pieces of paper to us all as The Heff turns around and strides back towards the glass doors.

Immediately, there's a noise. Everyone is talking, and Eddie is surrounded by people all asking him why he didn't say something.

'I didn't know. Jesus, I only found out myself an hour ago and I've been working my fingers to stumps typing out these meeting times at breakneck speed, thanks to that Burberry-clad tapeworm host, Maxine.' He spits the word 'Burberry' like it's a rancid piece of cheese that he's just been force-fed. 'Honestly, if she thinks I'm doubling up as her BA as well, then she can *dream on up into her own skinny arse*.' Eddie grabs a plastic cup from one of the tables and downs it in one, before crushing it in the palm of his hand and letting out a dramatic gasp.

So much for The Heff leaving then. This is worse – much worse. Eddie's face has suddenly turned a violent rhubarb-red colour and there's a hunted look in his eyes, the line of which I follow and immediately see why. The Heff has returned back through the doors and standing next to him is a very tall, absolutely stunning and exceed- ingly skinny woman. I'm pretty certain my hands could span her waist. She's wearing a clinging crimson dress that wouldn't look out of place on Joan Holloway in an episode of *Mad Men*, carrying a matching real Hermès Birkin and standing on five-inch blush patent Loubs to balance out her silicone-enhanced super-bust. And if that wasn't enough, she has perfect, big, flame-red hair.

I manage to stick a smile across my face as I surrepti- tiously push a lock of my own limp spaniel's ear hair back into place before folding my arms across my B-cup boobs. She spreads her red pencil-lined mouth into a dazzling beauty pageant-style smile that I notice doesn't reach her eyes that are bulging like a pair of Buddhas' bellies. No, instead, they are fixed firmly on Eddie, who has now adopted a strange facial contortion that he attempts to hide by busying himself inside his clipboard.

'For those of you who haven't met her before, this is Maxine,' The Heff booms, and attempts a little clap that he quickly halts on realising that nobody else is joining in. We all mutter words of welcome that sound distinctly hollow. I wonder what her surname is. Or maybe she's too important to have one.

'And this is Tom Rossi . . .' and we all glance towards the doors again.

For a glimmer of a second my heart feels as though it might have stopped beating. I feel light-headed. I steady myself against the table and realise my mouth is actually hanging open. I quickly close it and pray none of the others noticed. I see what can only be described as pure unadulterated sex striding towards us. Oh my actual God. This man is a vision. He's wearing a gorgeous suit that I'd say has been stitched lovingly by hand in Italy or somewhere equally seductive. It's the perfect shade of ink-blue and frames a crisp white shirt, the collar of which is undone to reveal a teaser of his black curly-haired and very firm tanned chest that has just the right hint of sheen. His eyes are the darkest brown and nestling in sumptuous eyelashes that make me want to lick them right here and now. I can feel my cheeks warming and my stomach flipping. The last time I felt like this was when I first clapped eyes on Henry Cavill when he turned towards the camera in *The Count of Monte Cristo*.

Every woman in the cinema, and some men too, let out a little gasp of pleasure. I was only a teenager at the time, and raging with hormones that feel as though they've just made a very sudden and momentous return.

'He's joining us from next Monday,' The Heff continues. I quickly pull myself together, remembering I'm at work and that this man probably dates the likes of supermodels and *Made in Chelsea* girls, and only then if *they* are really lucky.

'Pleased to meet you all,' Tom says, with the hint of a *Downton* accent (upstairs, naturally) and the sensual precision of a Ferrari. I glance over and notice that Eddie is positively drooling. He's actually licking his lips lasciviously. But there's no way this man, sorry, this *delicious Adonis* is gay, because if he is then I think I might quite possibly die. Right here next to the help-yourself salad bar.

6

The glorious smell of cakey-sweet loveliness engulfs the air as soon as I push open the door to Sam's café. Instantly I feel my body starting to relax. Every time I come in here it's as though I've entered an oasis of calm, a stark contrast to the bustling atmosphere just a few floors below.

The cosy lounge area has been swathed in decadent plum and rich emerald-green colours, offset with opulent rose-gold cushions scattered all over the huge squishy sofas. Sultry Burlesque-style music is playing and tea lights flicker all around. A projector is displaying a montage of iconic beautiful men across the ceiling.

Collapsing into a sofa by the faux fire, I exhale a long breath and look around while I wait for Sam. She's not behind the counter, so I'm guessing she must be busy in the kitchen. I feel myself relaxing – in through the nose, and exhale out through my mouth. In for six . . . out for six . . . or maybe it's four. I speed up a bit. A pair of small cold hands appear from behind my head and cover my eyes.

'What are you doing, Miss Hart?' I instantly recognise the voice as Sam's.

'Trying to relax. Seeing as I'm early for a change.'

'Relax?' she gasps. 'I thought you were channelling childbirth or something. Did you know that you were practically panting?' She pauses, and then adds, 'Hard?'

'I was not. I was merely trying to invoke a sense of calm,' I reply, trying not to laugh.

'Well, next time you want to relax, pop up here for a camomile tea. Very soothing.' Sam shakes her head. 'Come on.' She helps me out of the sofa. 'Soo, what do you think of my Valentine theme?' she says, letting go of me and running a hand over the back of the sofa.

'I love it. And it's different.'

'Good. My idea of a decent Valentine's Day is sex. S-E-X. And plenty of it. I want decadence. I want tease. And a bit of debauchery thrown in for good measure,' she says, grinning naughtily as she loops her arm through mine. 'Ooh, hang on.' She stops still and beckons upwards with her eyes. 'My favourite is coming up next. Tom Ford. Yes, yes I know he's gay . . . but will you just look at him?' We both stare up at the ceiling for a few seconds. 'Utter perfection.'

Sam steers me towards one of the train seat booths.

'Ta dah!' she says, gesturing towards a three-tiered cake stand crammed with all kinds of delicious gooey-looking cakes next to a big green spotty teapot.

'Wow,' I say, giving her a quick hug. 'You didn't have

to do all this. A vanilla slice would have sufficed.' She gives me a look.

'Sorry. *Millefeuiiiille*,' I attempt and end up sounding like an extra from a dodgy French film. 'How do you even say it?' I laugh.

'That'll do.' She grins, picking up the cake stand and offering it to me. 'So, what's been going on with you?' she asks, pouring me a cup of tea. 'And who's the man?' She stops fiddling with the teapot and gives me an inquisitive look.

'What do you mean, *man?*' I feel my cheeks flush.

'Oh come on. I know that look a mile off. It's the same Ready Brek glow you used to get after the end-of-term disco when one of the boys from St Patrick's had asked you to slow dance. And we must have only been about twelve at the time.'

'Sam, you won't believe the day I've had! The Heff appeared and dropped a bombshell and in the next breath he introduces a second bombshell, only this time it's of the *pure sex* variety.'

'Whoa. Hang on a minute. What do you mean *bombshells*, and *pure sex*? God, I can't believe this has all been going on right below me. How exciting. So, come on, tell all. I want details,' Sam squeals, and stirs her tea. Even faster now. Her natural blonde corkscrew curls are bobbing around furiously.

'Well. The Heff announced it this afternoon, during Ciaran and Tina's engagement toast.'

'*Engagement. Whaat? You're telling me Ciaran got engaged?* Ohmigod. FAINTS. A girl can't handle so many details all in one go. And why didn't he tell me?' she huffs.

'You mean you don't know?'

'No. He bunked off straight after his lunch break, said he had important business to attend to and would I mind? Of course I said it was fine, but he never said a word. Told you so, deffo up to something . . . and now we know. What's the ring like? Did you see it? How could you deny me this for a whole afternoon? It's bad enough he didn't tell me himself.' Sam's puffing for air, she's practically hyperventilating. Always the romantic.

'Well, I just assumed he would have mentioned it. Anyway, I'm telling you now. And yes, the ring is huge. Mega.'

'Oh I bet it is. I can't imagine she would have settled for a Carrington's chip.' I pull a face. 'No offence,' Sam adds, holding her teacup in mid-air. 'Every time she comes in here she manages to find a way to mention Ciaran's inheritance.' This makes me smile. I can just imagine Tina trying to impress Sam, whose dad is Alfie Palmer, owner of Palmer Estates, one of the biggest estate agents in the country. Sam told me Tina practically did a running bodyslam at Alfie when he turned up at the café one lunchtime. It took fifteen minutes for Sam to prise Tina away from him.

'What does Ciaran see in her?' I ask, running a finger across the top of my vanilla slice and popping it into my mouth, savouring the exquisite taste of the almond-flavoured icing. Heaven.

'Oh I don't know. I've tried probing him and he reckons they have a lot in common.'

'Like what? I mean, he's lovely, with the Irish accent and all that . . . apart from that finger-gun thing he does.' We both laugh again.

'Oh that's just a front,' Sam says. 'Underneath it all he's a kind, sweet guy.'

'I know, I'm only joking. But it doesn't change the fact that he's nice and . . . well . . . she isn't.' I shrug.

'I know, but he says she's old-fashioned and wants to be married as soon as possible. And you know how keen he is to be hitched; in fact at one point I thought he might fancy you – he seems to spend an awful lot of time hanging around on your floor,' Sam says, draining her tea before pouring more.

'Don't be daft,' I say, brushing the notion aside. 'But it doesn't make sense to me. Most men, or certainly the ones I meet, would run a mile at the mere glimmer of a bridezilla.'

'I think he feels left out. His family are all married with kids, so I suppose he just wants to fit in. He said every time he goes home his parents get excited, thinking an announcement is coming or, better still, he'll have a bride in tow. Remember, he comes from a tiny village on the southern coast of Ireland. Things are different there. More traditional. Men have wives and children, that's how it is. Anyway, enough of all that, I'll quiz him in the morning. Tell me more about the announcement. No tell me about the *pure sex* bombshell first. That sounds far more exciting.'

'Well, he's called Tom Rossi,' I say, lingering on his name.

'Mmm . . . dreamy sounding,' Sam interrupts.

'He's dark, tall, and – well, I know it sounds like a cliché – but he is *to die for*, Sam. He's very charming, in a proper gentlemanly Colin Firth way, but I'd say he's probably part Italian or maybe Spanish even. Either way he's got that raunchy Mediterranean thing going on too.' I feel breathless and giddy just thinking about him.

'Cor! He sounds lush. I can't wait to get a peek of him. Maybe he'll come up for a coffee and a nice messy cream bun.' We both sit for a moment and imagine watching him lick his fingers clean, or better still . . . doing it for him. 'Who is he then?'

'I'm not sure. He starts on Monday, that's all I know so far.'

'What about James?'

'Shush,' I whisper, quickly, glancing around the café. 'Somebody might hear you.'

'Sorry, but it's obvious he's keen,' she replies in a hushed voice, even though there's nobody else here.

'Hmm, you know he's been acting very strange recently.'

'Really! What kind of strange?' Sam asks, eagerly.

'I'm not sure . . . just, kind of extra-attentive, you know, more so than he usually is.'

'Ohmigod, I knew it. He wants you big time,' she squeals, banging her cup down on the saucer.

'Will you stop it,' I reply, trying not to smile.

'Oh you're such a spoilsport.'

'Please.' I pull a face.

'OK. If you insist.' She sticks her tongue out. 'So, tell me about the other bombshell instead then?'

'Well that's the bad news I've had today. The Heff came charging into the staff canteen, slap bang in the middle of the engagement announcement, and said we're entering a terminal decline and as of today everything changes.'

'So what does that mean then? Your job's safe though, isn't it? I mean, they're not going to get rid of you. You're a fantastic sales assistant. Everyone knows that, and all the regulars love you. I'm always overhearing them saying how helpful and kind you are.' Sam stops licking cake from her fingers and looks me in the eye.

'Ahh, that's nice to hear, but I don't know, Sam. All I know is that a retail expert, Maxine somebody or another, has been brought in to conduct some kind of review. I've got a meeting with her on Tuesday, so I'll guess I'll find out more then.' A trickle of panic starts. I try and shake the feeling off, desperate to keep an open mind.

'Maybe you'll get a promotion, you never know,' she says gently, and I know that she's only trying to make me feel better.

'Perhaps,' I say wryly. The feeling of panic lurches up

again. What if I really do lose my job? Everything I've worked so hard for could disappear overnight. I don't even have any savings – nothing to fall back on – and my credit cards are all maxed out. And then there are the loans . . .

'Well, let's not worry about it until it happens, and I don't for a minute think it will. Now, will you tell me if you like this please?' she says, handing me a miniature heart-shaped sparkly pinkberry cake. 'It's a new recipe I'm trying out for Valentine's Day.'

'Mmm, it's divine,' I say, after taking a bite. I manage to put a smile on my face, although I can't help thinking that it's OK for Sam – she's never been poor, or even had to struggle, how can she ever know what it really feels like? 'Will we still be friends if I lose my job and end up in some dingy dump surviving on Super Noodles?' I ask, trying to lighten the mood, but remembering the early days when I left care, I relied so heavily on over-drafts, even paying by cheque for groceries, just to buy me an extra few days until payday when the same horrible cycle would start all over again.

'Don't be so dramatic. You know that's never going to happen. People don't just lose their job, you know, unless the company they work for goes bust or they've done something really bad, and then it's usually their own fault . . .' Sam's face drops when she realises what she's said. 'Oh Georgie, I'm so sorry. I didn't mean it like that.' She tries to grab my hand, but I quickly pull it away.

'Like what?' is all I can muster. I lean back in the seat. My mind leaps back to the hideous day at school when I was summoned to Miss Braintree's office and ordered to pack up my things. I was on the next train home and in the local school playground the following morning in my ill-fitting second-hand uniform, being slapped around for 'talking posh'.

'Well, you know. That business with your dad,' Sam whispers the word 'dad'.

'But I'm not my dad, I'm me. I haven't done anything wrong, have I?' I know I'm shouting, but the feeling is mounting. I've worked twice as hard to prove I'm not like him.

'No. Of course not. Georgie, honestly, everything will be OK, really it will. You're my best friend and always will be because you're funny, kind, really brave given what you've been through, smart . . . even if you do have a tendency to put two and two together and come up with five on occasion.' She smiles kindly. 'Look, try not to panic. You're going to be fine.' Sam leans forward to stroke my arm and I feel tears stinging my eyes. I swallow hard and silently pray that she's right. 'But if you're really worried then you must cover every eventuality. Why don't you look for another job, just in case?' There's silence while I take in what Sam has said.

'The thought has crossed my mind, but what if Maxine finds out? I don't want her thinking I'm disloyal to Carrington's or lacking in confidence over my position here.'

'She won't. Not if I talk to Dad, discreetly,' Sam suggests. I think of Alfie, her lovely father. During those lonely years at Nanny Jean's I would fantasise that Alfie would come and rescue me. He had even contacted social services and said I could live with him and Sam, but they had not allowed me to as he travels too much and Sam was looked after by a nanny in the school holidays after her interior designer mum ran off to LA with a rock-star client when Sam was just a baby. Said I needed stability.

'Oh Sam, but isn't that cheating?'

'Don't be daft. You've already proved yourself. It's not like you're looking for something you haven't already worked hard for. Let me call him, it can't do any harm,' she pleads.

'I'm not sure. Anyway, I'm a sales assistant not an estate agent.'

'Oh, everybody does it. It's not just *what* you know these days, but *who* you know as well. And besides, you'll just be selling houses instead of handbags. Is simples,' she grins.

'*Weell,* I guess it won't do any harm to ask him, to have a backup just in case, but promise me you'll be discreet,' I say, reluctantly. I can't imagine working anywhere else.

7

It's been ages since I've had a good night out, so after the rollercoaster of emotions I've had this week, I intend to make the most of tonight, Sam's birthday.

After The Heff's announcement, the mood at work has been subdued. I managed to find out that we all have meetings with Maxine next week, but nobody knows more than that, not even James, and we still don't know anything about Tom, or what he's going to be doing. Even Eddie has been very down, although he's the only one who knows for definite that his job is safe. Mind you, he's in a major strop now that his workload has doubled since Maxine got The Heff to agree to him working for her as well. Apparently, her old PA left to work somewhere else, the day before Maxine came to Carrington's, and they haven't managed to find a replacement yet. Cost cutting, she calls it, but Eddie reckons it's his punishment for calling her a 'tapeworm host'.

So after enduring the sweaty huddle on the bus journey from work to Sam's palatial clifftop house, where I cursed every second for economising on the cost of a taxi fare, I press the intercom on her sunshine-yellow front door.

As the buzzer sounds I push the door open and a delicious aroma tempts my nostrils. I'm starving, in a way that feels like my stomach has given up expecting food and actually started eating itself from the inside out.

'*Ceeeelebration time, come on*,' Sam sings, as she comes dancing down the hallway to meet me. She's got a cocktail sloshing precariously around in her left hand, whilst her right hand is busy keeping an enormous turbaned white towel about her head. 'Oh, are you OK? You look a bit frazzled.' She stops singing.

'Yeah, I'm fine. Packed bus with the windows jammed shut and the fan heaters pumped up to max . . . it was like being in a sauna with all your clothes on,' I say, dumping my bag on the floor.

'Ew.' Sam places the cocktail on the hall table and gives me a hug. 'Well, you're here now. Come in and say hello to Dad, he's just leaving.'

Alfie appears, wearing a soft grey cashmere V-neck over a pale pink shirt. He smells of his usual Aramis and has the same blond hair and twinkly blue eyes as Sam.

'Georgie! How are you, sweetheart?' he says, stepping forward and enveloping me in a huge bear hug.

'Dad, be careful,' Sam yells. 'You're practically crushing her.'

'Don't be silly. Everyone loves a big hug now and again.' Alfie releases me and takes a step back.

'I'm good thanks,' I say, not wanting to get into what's happening at work and spoil the evening before it's even started.

'I'm pleased to hear it, and I have to say you're looking mighty fine these days, young lady.' Alfie looks me up and down before smiling appreciatively.

'*Daaad*, stop flirting.' Sam gives Alfie a gentle nudge and we all laugh.

'Well, I better be off. Leave you two girls to it. Samantha's such a bore when she gets going,' he winks at me.

'Love you too, Daddy,' Sam teases.

'Here, have a good night.' Alfie pulls a roll of £20 notes from his pocket. 'And make sure you take taxis. No walking the streets.'

'Oh Dad, put it away,' Sam says, waving a hand.

'I insist.' He splits the notes in two. 'Here.' He hands half to me and half to Sam. 'And no arguments. From either of you,' he says, pretending to be stern as he wags his index finger between us both. I glance at Sam, feeling a bit awkward and waiting for her cue as Alfie presses the notes into my hand.

'OK. If you insist.' Sam grins at me as she reaches up to give Alfie a kiss.

'Thank you,' I say, knowing from previous experience there's absolutely no point in arguing with Alfie. I was sixteen when he first tried to give me money one Christmas. I refused, of course, only to find it inside my coat pocket when it was time to return to Nanny Jean's. I hid it inside a book in my locker at school, and later used it to buy a duvet when I moved to the bedsit.

'My pleasure. Have fun girls,' Alfie says, pulling the door open.

Once we've finished waving goodbye and Alfie's roared off in his Aston Martin, I reach inside my handbag, pull out a little gift bag and swing it in front of Sam. Her eyes light up like a child's. I'm so pleased I could get it for her.

'Happy Birthday lovely.' I lean forward, and give her a big birthday kiss on each cheek. She peers into the bag.

'Thank you honey.' She lifts out the box. As she opens it she lets out a little squeal.

'It's gorgeous, how did you know that I've always wanted one of these?' she says, holding the rainbow crystal Shamballa bracelet against her wrist.

'Lucky guess. Or maybe it was the trillion hints you've been dropping.' I can't help teasing her. She's like a big kid when it comes to birthdays, and not just her own. On my last birthday, she thoroughly spoilt me with a weekend in Barcelona that she had meant to be a surprise, but that she just couldn't resist telling me about beforehand.

'Was it really that many times? I'm so sorry, how

boring,' she says, handing me the cocktail. I take the mini rose-pink macaroon from the side of the glass and take a bite before quickly slurping a big mouthful of liquid through the silver bendy straw as we walk along the hallway and into the kitchen.

'Mmm, what's in this? It's heavenly,' I say, my mouth full of the luscious concoction.

'It's a secret recipe. Do you like it?'

'Like it? I love it.' I laugh, letting the liquid linger in my mouth. 'I'm ravenous. I've only had a Wispa since breakfast time.'

'There's a lasagne in the oven if you want some, with no garlic in it of course. Just in case you pull. I'm determined to find you a Valentine's date,' Sam says, with a cheeky grin as I swing myself up onto the granite-topped breakfast bar and kick off my wedges.

'Oh go on then, just a little bit though, not one of your monster helpings,' I reply, hoping she ignores my half-hearted instruction. Sam is a fantastic cook. The year she spent at the culinary school in Paris was definitely worth it, even if she didn't think so at the time. She spent months begging Alfie to let her go on a round-the-world cruise instead, but he was having none of it; said if she was serious about cooking then she needed to learn properly, luckily for me and my rumbling tummy.

'Don't tell me, another diet. Georgie, why do you bother? You know they don't work. *And* I bet Wispas aren't allowed.' She snorts at me with disapproval. It's OK for her, she's one of those lucky people who really can eat whatever they want and stay slim.

'Well, I lost six pounds doing *No Carbs Before Marbs*,' I say, swinging my legs and flexing my crumpled toes.

'So why are you doing another diet then? It's not like you even need to lose weight. I'd love to have your gorgeous hourglass figure. Very Marilyn Monroe. Oooh, it's the bombshell, isn't it?'

'Maybe,' I smile coyly.

'Well I hope so. And are you are all set for tonight? Nathan said he'll see us there . . . with a few friends,' Sam says, quickly changing the subject.

'What did I say about trying to fix me up?' I ask, pretending to be cross.

'I don't know, couldn't hear . . . remember?' Sam replies, flippantly.

'Well I hope his friends are an improvement on the last batch of that – whatever his name was – guy you were seeing before Nathan.'

'Trust me, if they have a fraction of the hotness that Nathan exudes, then you'll have no complaint, that's for sure.'

'Cor, I'm not sure I can wait.' We both laugh. I already feel more cheerful, looking forward to a good evening out. 'And thanks for picking up my dress for tonight. I can't believe I forgot to bring it with me this morning.'

I'd been in such a mad rush when I got up that I dashed out with only my shoes, make-up and Velcro rollers, so I had to make a mercy call to Sam and plead with her to bomb over to my flat on the other side of town.

'No problem. That's what BFFs are for. Follow me.' I grab the bowl of lasagne from the worktop and take a forkful – it tastes divine. I then follow Sam as she runs off into her baby-blue-coloured dressing room with Sylvester, her chubby cat named after his striking resemblance to the cartoon version, springing along behind her.

As I enter the room I see Sam standing by one of her wardrobes. She's beaming.

'This is your gown for this evening, madam,' she says, sounding like a camp fashion stylist. My gaze follows her outstretched arm towards the wardrobe door as she flings it open to reveal a vintage halter-neck investment dress hanging on the inside of the door.

'Where did you find this?' I ask, running my hand down the silky material.

'In the back of your wardrobe, screwed up in a ball. It still had the price tag on it. Honestly, this dress is gorgeous,' Sam says, indignantly.

'Oh Sam, you shouldn't have. I can't wear it, I'll never get into it,' I whine, with trepidation, as the memory of trying to squeeze into it comes flooding back. 'Besides, it'll smell all musty, won't it, having been scrunched up in the wardrobe for years,' I add, panic mounting at the thought of wedging my curvy bits into the ultra-clingy dress.

'I got it cleaned for you. So don't worry about that.' Sam waves her hand dismissively.

'But where's my dress? The one I planned to wear tonight? It was hanging on the back of the bathroom door,' I say. 'So I wouldn't forget it,' I then add, lamely.

'Oh, that old rag. Trust me, this dress is *reeeem*,' she says, in her best *TOWIE* voice, as she gestures her hand in a circular movement over the front of the dress. 'Just try it . . . with this miracle suit thing.' And she pulls a surgical-looking square of Lycra from behind her back and dangles it in front of me. Grabbing the pork-chop-coloured monstrosity from her, I scrutinise it. I think it is what is laughably called a 'body-shaper'. It's minuscule but I decide to give it a go. I don't have much choice, unless I want to go clubbing in my black top and trouser work combo, complete with Carrington's name badge, the pin of which has bent somehow, making it impossible to remove.

'Right, out of the room, I want to see if I can wedge myself into this. Which I imagine is going to be some feat, which I'd rather not attempt with you standing there.'

'Fantastic,' Sam shrieks, and claps her hands together. 'Just shout if you need a hand,' she adds.

'No thank you, now shoo,' I say, flapping my hand at her.

'OK, OK, I'm going.' Sam backs out of the room and closes the dressing room door behind her.

After managing to shoehorn myself into the dress, I call Sam back into the room.

'Bloody hell Georgie! You look fantastic, very curvaceous and sexy. And that dress really brings out your blue eyes and glowing complexion,' she shrieks. I feel a bit constricted, though, as the suit is an underwired all-in-one corset that vacuums everything in.

'Do you really think so?'

'Absolutely.' Sam grins.

'Thanks, honey. Just need to get my shoes now.' I head off to the hallway.

'Hang on. Try these. They'll be perfect with that dress.' From underneath the scarlet chaise longue, Sam brings out her new Gina sandals. They are absolutely exquisite, with little diamanté stones running across the strappy ankle and toe parts of the delicate shoes.

'Oh Sam I can't. They're your new ones, you haven't even worn them yet,' I say, instantly touched by her generosity.

'Please, have them, I've got loads . . . and besides, I'm not really sure they're me,' she says, crossing her slim legs and leaning back on the chaise longue.

'But I can't,' I say, desperately trying not to eye up the sandals.

'I insist.'

'Sam, I can't. Really. You could always take them

back if you don't like them.' They must have cost a fortune.

'Oh, it's not that I don't like them. I just think they'd suit you better. And I'll be offended if you don't take them,' she laughs. I look again.

'Are you definitely sure? They really are beautiful,' I say, not wanting to offend her but secretly wondering if she ever had any intention of keeping them for herself.

'Yes.'

I give her a huge hug.

'In that case, thank you my GBF.' Sam raises an eyebrow.

'Gorgeous best friend of course,' I explain, smiling and making a mental note to send her a proper thank-you card. I slip my foot into the right sandal. Twiddling my ankle in the mirror I feel a little shiver of excitement. Not bad at all – my stomach is almost flat and my best feature, my arms with their light sprinkling of freckles on the shoulders, can be seen quite nicely. Always high-light your best asset, isn't that what Gok says? Sam has certainly come up trumps this time.

'Right, so are we ready then?' I grab my clutch bag and Sam stands up and smooths down her Hervé Léger bandage dress in nude. She's teamed it with a pair of blush patent Kate Kuba wedges and fuchsia-framed geek glasses that almost cover her tiny elfin face. Her curly hair is bobbing around her shoulders and the Shamballa bracelet is sparkling on her wrist. She looks stunning.

'Come on, we'd better go before we spontaneously combust with the glamour of it all.' I slip my arm through hers. We're both chatting and giggling as we head off into the night.

8

After paying the taxi driver, we pass through a red rope that's unclipped by a doorman who looks as if he's just stepped out of a Calvin Klein photo shoot, and emerge into the club. I feel as though I've walked into a Moroccan wonderland – there are orange and gold glittery soft furnishings draped between mosaic fountains. There are even olive trees dotted in amongst the leather ottomans. We're both handed one of those cute mini Moët bottles with the drinking spouts. Complimentary to the first fifty clubbers as it's opening night.

'Mmm, I must say the view is scorching in here,' Sam says, lifting my hair to talk straight into my ear. The pulse of the uplifting Happy House beat thuds against my chest. Everywhere I look there are male models, smiling when they catch my eye, as if telepathically telling me I'm their dream woman. Whoever's come up with this marketing idea must be a genius, because it's working. Oh yes, it's working all right. I can almost feel a physical tingle of hedonism on my bare shoulders.

Scrutinising the drinking spout more closely, I see that it has *Bushka Launch Party* inscribed in rose-gold lettering on the side. Nudging Sam, I raise an eyebrow and she nods back. Simultaneously we both whip the little spouts off and stash them in our bags.

Sam yells, 'Over here,' before waving wildly. With her left hand above her head, her dress rides up and briefly flashes the side of her diamanté-topped stocking. A group of guys standing nearby nudge each other with appreciation. I glance in the direction of her yell, and striding towards us is a group of men. All of them are stunning, and a tall, athletic and seriously handsome blond one, who I guess must be Nathan, is carrying a giant heart-shaped helium balloon. He steps towards Sam, grabs her up in the air and spins her around.

'So how is the sexy birthday girl?'

Sam screams with delight, trying to keep the back of her dress from riding up too high. The pair of them lock lips. 'Ahh, and here are the others,' Nathan says, prising himself away from Sam. 'You don't mind, do you, only I invited some guys from the squash club.'

Looking to where Nathan's waving, I see a couple of tall men coming towards us. For a moment I don't believe it. I blink again to be sure, and yes, it's definitely him. Tom is heading straight towards us. My heart races. He looks even more incredible than he did in the staff canteen. I see a couple of girls eyeing him up and down as he strides past, but before I can get myself together he's standing right in front of me.

'Don't I know you from somewhere?' Tom says, fixing his chocolate-brown eyes on mine as I fidget nervously from one foot to the other.

'Oh I'm not sure,' I reply in a breezy voice, wondering if he can tell that the memory of him appearing through the canteen doors has made its way into my dreams several times already this week. Only in the dream he's naked, drenched in massage oil accentuating a rock-hard muscular chest, and begging to take me there and then across the help-yourself salad bar. Naturally the canteen of my dreams is festooned with tea lights creating a sexy shimmery glow. And I look like a siren with really big hair.

'Yes, I'm definitely sure. I know I've seen you somewhere before. Where do you work?' he says, seemingly oblivious to the effect he's having on me.

'At Carrington's. And you?' I reply, trying to sound nonchalant.

'*That's it.*' He looks pleased with himself at having worked it out. 'I was there for the announcement. Must have seen you then.' He beams a beautiful smile and my heart immediately melts. The feeling is incredible.

'Of course. Silly me, I didn't recognise you,' I say nervously, twiddling the silver stud in my right earlobe and feeling my neck tingling with the first creep of a flush from the blatant lie.

'Nice to meet you, *again*.' Still smiling, he puts his hand out to mine and the sensation is like an electric charge as his warm fingers touch mine. He leans down to my hot cheek and plants a kiss. Momentarily distracted by the faint but delicious chocolatey scent of his after-shave, I giggle in a way that I haven't since I was about five years old and instantly regret it. I'm conscious that Sam and Nathan are looking at us.

'Do you two know each other?' Sam asks, but before either of us can answer, Nathan butts in.

'See you in a sec, honey.' He makes off in search of the loo, accidentally bumping into Tom who quickly sidesteps and ends up standing adjacent to me.

'Err, no not really. Sam, this is Tom,' I say. Sam's face goes all airy as she cottons on immediately. I make big warning eyes at her not to let on that I've mentioned him and luckily our telepathic powers connect in an instant.

'Oh, how lovely to meet you.' She extends her hand without so much as a glimmer of knowing.

'Shall I get some drinks while you two find seats?' Tom offers, sounding like the perfect gentleman.

'Thank you,' I say. And without hesitation, Sam and I nod at each other before heading off.

'Ohmigod Georgie, he's hot, hot and more hot.' Sam clutches my arm. 'Bloody hell, I can see what you mean,' she squeals, performing a little skip the minute Tom is out of earshot. 'He looks like he's just stepped out of a Hollywood movie.'

'I know, but I can't believe it. Why didn't you tell me Nathan knew him?'

'I didn't know. I've not heard him mention him before, but I can get the lowdown on him now,' Sam says, triumphantly.

'No! Yes! Oh I don't know. He's way out of my league.'

'No he's not. Yes he's bloody gorgeous, but no man is out of your league, do you hear me?' Sam hisses, pretending to be cross.

'I hear you. But be discreet. Just find out if he's attached . . . a girl can dream after all, can't she?'

Finding a Moroccan mini-sofa thing, Sam sits and I carefully perform a small Houdini contortion act to get down low enough to sit next to her. As I wriggle around trying to get comfortable, the miracle suit presses on my bladder, so I have no option but to haul myself into a standing position to go in search of the Ladies.

'Where are you off to? They're going to be back soon.' Sam clutches my arm.

'Sam, it's no good, I'm busting for the loo,' I groan.

'I'll come with you, I could do with a lippy touch-up,' she replies, even though her cerise gloss is still immaculate. 'Let's wait for them and then we'll go.' She smiles.

'I'm not sure I can.' Wincing, I lean forward and put the bottle down on a low table. Sam has the same idea and leans over too. The sudden shift in the weight on the cushion propels me forward and I'm launched mercilessly onto the little dance floor. The drink flies out of my hand, shoots up and splatters all over my face. I attempt to get up but just can't bend enough. The floor is really slippery so I end up writhing around like an amateur contortionist. I try again to scrabble up onto my feet.

Sam meanwhile has managed to get up and is now bent over in hysterics as she tries to pull me up. Her laughter is infectious, which just makes it worse as I beg her to stop. Within seconds, one of the models appears. He's towering over me with a look of utter disgust on his pinched face.

'Would you like some assistance?' he drawls in an effeminate Aussie voice that completely belies his physical appearance. Feeling mortified, I shoo him away and manage to control myself a bit, but then start panicking. Tom is going to come back any second.

'This is all your fault, plying me with cocktails. Get me up before I pee all over the place,' I bellow over the music in Sam's direction. I reach up to grab Sam's hand and instantly feel like dying. Tom is standing right behind her. A quizzical grin smoulders across his chiselled face, and tucked in the crook of his beautiful elbow is an ice bucket. Four glasses are clutched in his left hand, and I wish I could just crawl away and evaporate somewhere quietly. It's Nathan who moves forward from behind Tom, Sam, and the small crowd that's now gathered around me. Bending down he scoops me up into a fireman's lift over his shoulder and carries me over to the Ladies. I can see everybody staring and I feel hot with embarrassment.

'There you go.' Nathan lets me down.

'Oh my God. Are you OK?' Sam says. Her face is covered in concern as she elbows her way through from behind Nathan's broad back. We push through the chrome door into the Ladies. 'What's that on your back?' Sam asks worriedly, as she spins me around to inspect the bulge.

'The bloody suit; the poppers have ripped off.'

'Thank God it's only that,' she breathes. 'For a moment I thought you'd broken something or an organ had popped out even,' she says, dramatically. 'Here.' She rifles in her gold clutch and pulls out a massive safety pin. 'For emergency purposes. It'll have to do,' she adds, after I look back at her with horror. Quickly realising that she's right, I rush into a cubicle and sort myself out.

Back out by the washbasins, I survey the damage. Mostly superficial, fortunately, despite my impromptu shimmy across the dance floor. With a wet hand towel, I dab the mascara lines away and then reapply some face powder, carefully blending as I go. Another coat of mascara and fresh lipstick and I'm ready. I take a deep breath, push my hair behind my ears and turn to Sam.

'Come here,' she says kindly, and I step forward. She puts her arms around me. 'Will you be OK?'

'I think so. Did you see the look on his face?' I reply, cringing at the memory.

'Yes, but you just hold your head up high and work it, baby. He's *reeeem*,' she says in her *TOWIE* accent to make me smile. 'Go grab him.'

'Hardly, after that pantomime performance.'

'Oh so what.' Sam shakes her hair back. 'Men love a girl with a sense of humour, so just laugh it off. You look a billion dollars.'

'Thanks, Sam. You're a true friend, do you know that?' I say, perking up and giving her a quick hug.

'Well, I do my best. When I haven't got my foot in my mouth of course,' she grins, and then adds, 'Georgie, look I'm really sorry about the other day, your dad and all. I didn't mean to hurt you.'

'I know you didn't,' I say, patting her arm. 'It's forgotten,' I finish, magnanimously, glad that we've cleared the air.

'Actually, I was wondering . . .' She peers at me.

'What is it?'

'Err, I just wondered whether you'd spoken to him recently?' she adds, nervously. I hesitate for a second.

'Strange you should ask, because I slipped up and answered the phone . . .' I reply, feeling uncomfortable. Sam gives me a look as though she's unsure whether to say anything else. 'Tell me?' I prompt.

'Oh nothing, I . . .'

'Come on, please just say it.'

'If you're sure?' she says warily.

'Yes I'm sure. Now will you please just get on with it?' I smile encouragingly.

'Well, I was just thinking that it's such a shame that you two can't sort things out. Alfie means the world to me, he's all I have, and I couldn't bear it if he and I fell out,' she says, sounding panicky. She looks away.

'It's OK, you've got me too, and Nathan . . . he seems really smitten, maybe he really is your "one",' I say, gently touching her arm, knowing how upset she gets about the prospect of being all alone. She looks back and manages a little smile.

'But what if something happened to your dad? And you hadn't resolved this? He made mistakes, I know, and you helped him out, there's no denying that, but do you really want to punish him forever?' I ponder on what she's said, and for a moment I waver – maybe she has a point.

'But it's not that simple,' I tell her.

'What do you mean?' Sam's eyes widen.

'What do you think it did to Mum? She was devastated. It was the stress of it all that made the multiple sclerosis develop so rapidly and cause complications. That's why she died prematurely and I ended up in care . . .' I say, in a wobbly voice, an image of Mum in the hospital bed flashing inside my head. Sam steps forward and gives me another hug.

'Georgie I'm sorry. I didn't realise that you still felt that way.' She gives me a weak smile.

'It's OK. That's just the way it is,' I say, putting on a brave face to cover the hollow feeling inside.

'But it doesn't have to be. You could forgive him and set yourself free from hating him. It wasn't your dad's fault she died.'

'Maybe.' Silence follows. 'Anyway, let's go and enjoy ourselves,' I say quickly, with a half-smile, desperate to shift the conversational focus.

'OK, but if you want to talk about it, I'm here.' Sam gives my arm a little squeeze and turns to leave. I take a big deep breath, bracing myself to face Tom again.

Nathan and Tom are sitting at the bar. They've already polished off half the bottle of wine. Nathan leaps down from his stool.

'Here you are, lovely lady. Saving it especially for you,' he says to Sam, and she bounces up, grinning like a Cheshire cat. Tom pulls out another stool for me. My tummy flips. I sit down and cross my legs and promptly let out a little yelp. The safety pin must have popped open.

'Hey, are you OK?' Tom leaps off his stool and places a hand on my arm. His face is full of concern.

'Yes, yes I'm fine,' I manage to squeak, wincing with agony. I quickly uncross my legs and let out a discreet sigh of relief.

'That was quite some floor show,' he says, sitting back down and leaning towards me. I grin in an attempt to hide my embarrassment.

'Well, I aim to please,' I say, remembering Sam's advice to laugh it off. His presence, so close to me, is totally intoxicating, and I'm aware that I feel tingly all over.

'So how long have you been working at Carrington's?' he asks, thoughtfully changing the subject. I take a sip of the cold wine and let the taste linger in my mouth. Waiting for me to answer, he smiles attentively – his impeccable manners are very appealing, I must say.

'Since school.' I swallow, relieved that we're talking about something else now. 'I started doing Saturdays and now I work full time in Women's Accessories and sometimes deputise for James. He's the floor supervisor and is also in charge of Men's Accessories and Sportswear.'

'For now.' Tom says the words quietly, but I know I'm not mistaken. He takes a large swig of his drink and looks away.

'What do you mean?' I say, a little too quickly.

'Nothing. Look, I'm so sorry. I shouldn't have said anything.' He looks a bit panicky as his eyes drop downwards.

'No, come on. You can't say something like that and then not expand,' I say, wanting to know what he knows. I shove my bag down on the bar, cringing at the slapping noise it makes. I don't want him thinking I'm hysterical.

'It's nothing, honestly,' he replies, not giving anything away. His mobile flashes on the bar, signifying the arrival of a text. 'Sorry,' he says, tapping out a reply. Irritated by the break in conversation I fiddle with the sequins on my bag, wanting to get back to his comment. If it meant what I think it does, then I have to warn James – at least then he can find another job before he's pushed out. He places the phone back on the bar.

'Anyway, no wriggling out of it,' I say, trying to sound light-hearted. 'Come on. Tell me what you meant by that comment. What do you know?' Tom scans my face, and for a second his overwhelming beauty distracts me, but I manage to hold the stare, trying not to let his charm get the better of me.

'You're not going to let it go, are you?' he says, a flash of concern on his face.

'No. Not when it comes to my friends.'

'OK. I'm sorry, it was insensitive of me, but seeing as it's you,' he starts, momentarily making me feel like I'm the only woman in the world, but then I spot a glimmer of something in his eyes before he looks away . . . like embarrassment, or shame almost, that he's resorted to schmooze. He clears his throat before continuing. 'What I meant was that we don't know what's going to happen now that Maxine's arrived. Obviously there're going to be changes and people might move around. That's all I meant.'

'So how come you just started working at Carrington's then? I mean, it seems odd to have someone joining on the same day a consultant is brought in to help us fend off a terminal decline?' I say, almost thinking aloud – surely he must have done some homework before his interview. Anyone could find out that Carrington's is struggling.

'Fair point.' He nods. 'I was headhunted,' he says, slowly.

'What for exactly?' I'm conscious that I'm now practically interrogating him, but I have to find out more.

'*Weell*,' he starts slowly, as though he's buying time to make it up as he goes along. 'Look, please don't take this the wrong way,' he eventually adds, tracing his finger around the rim of a glass. 'I was recruited a month ago by Walter to sell jewellery.' His mobile flashes again and he's saved from saying any more.

'Sorry,' he mouths, taking the call and heading towards the Gents, leaving me puzzled. My mind races through the options. Why would Walter have brought Tom in? And why did Tom imply that James's job isn't safe? What does he know?

I decide to call it a night and grab my bag from the bar. I don't fancy sitting here while Tom shows more interest in his phone than talking to me. After making my excuses to Sam, I go in search of a taxi to take me home. I need some time alone to think this all through.

9

I'm at the counter of Sam's café when I feel an arm around my shoulders.

'Mine's a black coffee and one of those Valentine cakes.' It's Eddie, and he's pointing to a luscious lemon cupcake with an enormous sparkly silver meringue peak on top, and he looks exactly how I feel.

'God, I feel terrible,' he moans as I add his order to mine (tea and my fave, the delicious red velvet) before handing over my staff discount card. 'And so would you if you'd been beavering away for that old hag, Maxine,' Eddie snorts. 'I reckon she must be at least forty.' He pulls a face and I laugh.

'Slight exaggeration. I'd put her at thirty tops.'

'Oh, don't be fooled by all that work,' he says, circling an index finger around his face. 'Bucket loads of filler. And she's a total femme fatale too, heard her purring like a phone sex worker into her BlackBerry the other day. Vom! And this morning she turned up in a fur coat and a skimpy playsuit . . . that's all she had on underneath.' He flares his nostrils. 'And I swear she smelt of SEX!'

'*Eddie! Do you mind?* I haven't even had breakfast yet.' He purses his lips and runs a finger over his hair.

'*Weell*, I pity the poor man she bedded last night, I imagine he's lying exhausted somewhere, covered in talon tracks and whimpering for mercy.' We both laugh.

'Come on. Let's get a booth before they all go,' he sniffs, nudging me with his elbow.

Taking his coffee and cake, Eddie flounces over to the far corner of the café. It's the best spot for chatting and keeping an eye on the door. He flings his jacket down.

I follow Eddie's lead and sit down next to him.

'You've got your meeting with the stick insect at eleven, haven't you?' Eddie says, tipping a sachet of sugar into his coffee and stirring it vigorously.

'Yep, can't wait.' I pull a face and for a moment I contemplate telling him about the conversation with Tom in the club, but decide not to. I want to see what Maxine has to say first.

'Oh, it'll be fine. Bound to be. I've not seen or heard anything about redundancies. Besides, there's no way The Heff will let her get rid of our best sales assistant,' he says, echoing Sam's words. He nudges me playfully across the table.

'But what if it comes out about Dad?' I ask, dropping my voice.

'But why would it? You don't even use the same

surname as him. Don't worry so much, sugar plum.'

'Well, you know how it is, especially in this new security-obsessed climate. It's not like it was when I was starting out. What if Maxine decides to drag Carrington's into the modern age and we have to go through stringent checks? You know Polly who used to work here in Celebrity Fragrances?' Eddie nods. 'I bumped into her the other day in Tesco on the industrial estate and she works in one of the big department stores up in London now. They did all sorts of security checks on her before they let her anywhere near the high-value goods. Even then they wanted to know about her immediate family too and I couldn't bear everyone knowing about Dad's mistakes and judging me with a suspicious eye. The shame of it.' I shudder.

'Honestly, you'll be fine. I'm sure as hell not going to tell anyone.'

It's nearly nine and I want to sort out the new Marc Jacobs display before we open.

'I have to go, see you later,' I say, giving Eddie a hug.

'OK, sweetness. And good luck with the meeting.'

'Thanks,' I say, waving at Sam as she ducks her head out of the kitchen on my way past.

*

Later on, I'm serving a pretty, red-haired woman with twin baby girls asleep in a fuchsia-pink double pram.

'Thank you. How would you like to pay?' I say.

'Card please.' I tap out the price, £59.99, for a gorgeous, sparkly Biba purse, and she enters her pin number. 'My treat for three months of sleepless nights,' she says, smiling and glancing at the twins.

'Ahh, they're adorable,' I say, handing her the carrier bag and sneaking a peek at the snuggly bundles with their fuzzy strawberry blonde hair and tiny rosebud lips.

'You wouldn't think so at three in the morning when one of them starts howling and sets the other one off.'

'Oh dear,' I smile diplomatically, handing her the receipt and card.

'Thanks, love. I'm off to the café upstairs now for a nice cup of coffee and a cake while these two are still snoozing.' She grins and loops the bag over the handle of the pram.

'Well, you enjoy and I highly recommend the new pinkberry Valentine cake. Divine.'

'Sounds like just the thing. See you next time.' And she wheels the pram off towards the lift.

Out of the corner of my eye, I spot Walter's wife, Camille, coming through the revolving door. Instinctively, I straighten the ring tray and busy myself with plumping a couple of bags. I catch Annie's eye and nod in Camille's direction. A breathtakingly beautiful older woman; she glides elegantly across the floor, patting her ice-blonde chignon as she heads towards my section.

'My dear, how are you today?' Camille arrives at my counter.

'Very well, thank you,' I say, politely. Camille shakes my hand and I have to mentally resist the urge to curtsey. A puff of Hermès floats around her; clad head-to-toe in Chanel, she really is something.

'Splendid. I'm off to New York for Fashion Week and wondered if you'd be kind enough to select some luggage for me.' She whips off her gloves and slips them into a vintage black Chanel bag.

'Of course, we'd be delighted to,' I say, beckoning Annie over.

'Something understated dear, not those gaudy bright colours.' Camille glances at a wheelie case in fluorescent lime green with a white splash print pattern.

'Leave it to me. I think we have just the right collection for you,' I say, swiftly retrieving a gorgeous, buttery, red leather vanity case from behind the counter. I flip open the lid to reveal the exquisite delicate pink silk interior and Camille twitches an immaculately groomed eyebrow in approval. 'It arrived just this morning from Paris.' Camille runs an expensively manicured finger over the handle.

'Delightful. And rather appropriate in the Valentine red, wouldn't you say?'

'Absolutely. Especially with Fashion Week ending on

the fourteenth February this year,' I say, having read all about it in *Grazia* magazine.

'That's settled then. I'll need the whole set and if you could organise the monogram too.'

'It will be my pleasure.' I glow.

'Thank you. I'll call by on my way back from the salon. Knew I could count on you, my dear.' She pats my arm before gliding off towards the escalator.

After unpacking the luggage collection and calling Freddie at the engravers on Birtle Street, I go through everything with Annie, making sure she knows exactly what to say and do if I'm still in the meeting when Camille returns. I duck into the cupboard behind my counter to straighten my clothes and bouf up my hair. Grabbing my bag, I head off to the staff lift.

'Chop chop.' It's Tina, and she has her crackle-manicured fingers around the cage door and a cross look on her face. 'Where are you off to?' she demands.

'To see Maxine,' I say, though it's obviously none of her business.

'Ooh, well you don't want to be late then. Do you?' she says.

'No, of course not. Thanks for waiting for me,' I say, feeling a little uneasy as I step into the lift and wrench the cage door closed.

'I've been meaning to talk to you.'

'You have?' I say, warily.

'Yes, it's about your sales sheet. Half the time I can't

read your writing so if I'm to pay your commission correctly then you need to tidy it up,' she says, smugly, like the money comes out of her own actual purse. And she's only the blooming record keeper.

'Fine, I'll try harder,' I say, feebly masking the sarcasm from my voice.

'Good.' She pauses. 'And tell Annie too. That girl is practically illiterate, I know she's half Traveller, but honestly, who spells Juicy Couture as Juicy K-A-T-O-O-R?' I open my mouth to defend Annie, but Tina carries on. 'Look Georgie, I'm sorry about snapping at you the other day. Don't know what came over me.' She smooths an imaginary stray hair from her swishy high ponytail that's scraped back so tightly her face looks as though it might burst at any moment.

'No worries, let's just forget about it shall we? So, have you set a date for the wedding yet?' I say, swiftly moving on to a topic that I know she'll love.

'Oh yes. It's going to be on Valentine's Day. Only four weeks to go!' She claps her hands together. 'And it's just perfect that February the fourteenth falls on a Sunday this year so everyone can come, and of course it will be really romantic, with loads of balloons and hearts and swans. And there might even be a pink unicorn!' Her eyes widen and my mind boggles. 'I found a place that will spray-paint one of those dinky little horses, and then I'll get someone to strap a horn to its head, plastic of course, I don't want those animal rights freaks coming after me. It's going to be a-mazing. Just like a fairytale. Of course, you're invited, but only to the evening reception. You don't mind do you?' I shake my head as if on autopilot. 'It's just that I don't think everyone will fit in otherwise,' she adds.

'Of course, I understand,' I say, thinking how being home all alone suddenly seems so much more appealing now.

'And you'll need to bring a plus one. I'm not having any singletons, apart from Eddie, of course.' It dawns on me . . . how the hell am I going to get a plus one at such short notice? Panic surges. I'll be the only person there without a date in tow.

Tina purses her lips while I swallow hard and glare at the display that flashes a red five. Only one more floor to go, thankfully. The lift grinds to a halt, breaking the awkward silence, and I breathe a huge sigh of relief as I turn to leave. But she pipes up again.

'And you will come to my hen do, won't you?' she smiles, her finger on the door hold button. 'But don't worry about trying to find someone to bring along. I have sooo many friends coming,' she says. For a moment I'm speechless, but I don't want to give her the satisfaction of knowing that she's riled me, so I manage a grimace.

'Thanks, sounds marvellous.' I step out of the lift and, turning my back, mutter, 'Can't wait,' under my breath, just as the lift starts moving again.

I make my way along the corridor towards the offices.

'You OK? You look really stressed.' Lauren's head pops up over the enormous beechwood reception desk.

'What? Oh yes sorry. It's just other people, you know . . . annoying sometimes,' I say, feeling flustered by Tina and the ridiculous competition she seems to have pulled me into. 'How come you're up here and not in the cash office?'

I notice that her eyes are swollen as if she's been crying.

'Oh, the new big boss wants me meeting and greeting. Talking of which, Maxine has insisted that I come and sit here all day. Said it looks more professional and that she doesn't have time to keep coming to the door to get people herself. I have to run around after her constantly, meaning I can't even get on with any of my real work. And now Tina's told me that I've got to stay late to catch up,' she sniffs. I shake my head. I bet she has, she'll not want to miss an opportunity to exert her authority.

'You poor thing. How's Jack?' I ask, remembering her baby.

'He's gorgeous, and he can just about walk now,' she says, her eyes lighting up. 'Thanks for asking, Georgie.'

'Don't be silly,' I reply, thinking it must be hard for her being on her own and having to leave him with her mum all day. Then I remember the copy of *Closer* in the bottom of my bag. I quickly pull it out and hand it to Lauren. 'Here, now don't let her catch you with it though.' With a quick pincer manoeuvre Lauren reaches over the desk and snatches the magazine, secreting it underneath the large appointment book in front of her. She grins up at me.

'Down the corridor, in the room on the far right. She's waiting for you. Oh, and good luck,' she whispers in a much brighter voice, waving her flashing red heart pen after me.

'Thanks Lauren,' I call back to her, and make my way off down the corridor, hoping that I won't need any luck. *Please let me keep my job, Please let me keep my job*, I say as a mantra, over and over inside my head, as I make my way along the long wood-panelled corridor.

I push open the door expecting to see Maxine, but she's not here, and by the looks of it she's got half of Home Interiors' stock crammed inside her spacious office. There's an oval polished wood table to the right of the room, while framed paintings that look expensive hang on the two walls cornering the table. There are two very large open glass cabinets containing various Swarovski crystal figurines that were definitely part of Chinaware's display just a few weeks ago. I know, because I helped Mrs Grace dust them all. Nestled amongst the figurines are a couple of framed pictures of people that I presume are Maxine's friends or family.

Slipping my handbag from my shoulder for fear of nudging one of the paintings from the wall, or worse still, crashing into the Swarovski showcase, I shuffle like a geisha over to the two black leather sofas that are positioned in a show-home style to look like a cosy seating area. Just as I'm sinking down into the soft leather, the door flings open and Maxine sashays across the room, just like the model in the Dior J'Adore advert. She's got the leg movement down to a tee, making me wonder if she's actually done professional modelling before.

'See you've made yourself at home,' she says, in a breathy American Deep South accent. Ahh, hence the pageant smile, I knew it! I bet she's the former beauty queen of Alabama or somewhere. 'Finally we meet. The infamous Georgina. Heard so much about you.' Maxine extends her right hand towards me, not bothering to exert herself too much as I try to haul myself out of the cushions. I manage to scramble forward, jutting my hand towards her as I steady myself with the other. Her hand-shake is firm, so firm that my hand smarts from the crush. And what does she mean *infamous?* She walks over to her desk and gestures for me to follow.

I scuttle over, clutching my bag and notepad in my lap. My chair is really low so I have to peer upwards to look at her, like some obsequious minion, which I guess is the point. 'Now let's see. Georgina, bit of a mouthful isn't it?' she says, perching on the corner of her desk. She starts doing ankle circles with a black patent Loub-clad foot, and I see what Eddie means about the playsuit. 'What about Gina? Yes that's it, Gina, Gina, Gina,' she says, each time in a different tone as if limbering up for an operatic performance. 'Yes I like it,' she adds, pronouncing it '*Geee-na*', and slapping her hands together with glee. 'You don't mind do you?'

'Err, well actually I prefer . . .' I start, but her immaculately manicured hand whips up with such speed it causes her Agent Provocateur scent to catch in my throat. So I end up spluttering instead.

'Oh dear, not ill are you? It's very important to be fit in the retail industry. Very exhausting on the legs,' she says, as if I don't know that already. 'You are fit, aren't you Gina?' she adds, smoothing a hand down over her bare thigh.

'Err, yes,' I manage.

'Awesome, because we've got our work cut out over the next few months. This is going to be big. Huge,' she says, whirling an immaculately manicured finger up in the air above her head like a cowboy with a lasso.

'OK, so what does that mean?' I have to know one way or the other. Maybe then I'll be able to relax a bit, if I know what I'm dealing with. At least then I can face it head on.

'Well, what do you think it means?' she says, dazzling me with her pageant smile.

'Well, I guess I want to know if my job is safe.' There, I've said it. I sit back and listen to the blood pumping in my ears.

'I can see why you might be worried about losing

your job. Given the current financial climate and your family history . . . shall we say?' She stops looking at me, and busies herself instead by circling her other ankle now. There's an uncomfortable silence. I fidget in my chair.

'How do you know about that?' The words are barely audible and I can hear the panic rising in my voice.

'Oh, someone mentioned it,' she says, breezily. Oh my God! So who else knows? My cheeks flush and, as if reading my mind, she adds, 'That's it!' as though it's just popped into her head. 'It was in your interview notes with something about it being your own personal business and not to mention it in case it upsets you. So I Googled it.' James! Lovely kind James. I breathe a little sigh of relief, knowing I can probably trust him.

'How is your father these days?'

'Well, we don't have much contact . . .' I say slowly. 'It was a long time ago,' I add, tentatively. My mind is working overtime trying to fathom out where she is going with this.

'Must have been hard though.' I can feel my hands trembling so I push them underneath the sides of my thighs.

'Yes it was,' I mutter, looking at the floor and wishing I was anywhere but here.

'I'm sure. Dreadful business. Losing everything like that. And then you being left all alone,' she says, touching my arm briefly.

'I lived with a foster family,' I say, instantly hating myself for feeling a need to explain.

'Oh dear, no other family then?'

'Not really,' I say quietly.

My only relatives, Dad's brother and his family, were living in Dubai when Mum died, with 'no space for an extra teenager' they said. The memory is scalded onto my brain along with the clinical smell of the hospital as I cuddled and stroked Mum's hair during the goodbyes. She'd been ill for so long . . . and I'd tried to look after her, even bunking off school on occasion, but it was the pneumonia that took her in the end. Her body, so weak with MS, just couldn't fight it. A jolt of grief grabs me, and for a second tears sting in my eyes. She would have been celebrating her sixtieth birthday this year.

'Well, good thinking on your part to use your mother's maiden name,' Maxine says. 'Break from the past and all that . . .'

'Look, I don't mean to be rude, but where are you going with this?'

'Don't worry. Your secret is safe with me. I trust nobody else knows, apart from James of course,' she says, changing tack now. I shake my head, knowing Eddie would never breathe a word. 'Good, because us girls have to stick together.' She leans towards me in a conspiratorial way. 'Just make sure everything else is in order, because in addition to revitalising the store, I'm going to attempt to modernise Carrington's.'

'What do you mean?' I ask, trying to keep my voice steady.

'Well, given that an exceptionally high volume of valuable items are handled on a daily basis, I've suggested HR pull their finger out and do proper checks on everyone, like other stores do. Credit checks and so on. I can't believe they haven't even bothered before now. I've already discovered there's at least ten thousand pounds' worth of shrinkage – stock unaccounted for in the last quarter alone.'

I knew it! I gulp and vow to get hold of my credit file. I'm going to have to get it sorted out, once and for all.

'So I'm not going to lose my job then?' And no sooner are the words out of my mouth, when I want to cram them back in.

'There will be changes,' she starts, and I brace myself. 'There are way too many sections in this store that don't make enough money. Every inch of floor space must earn its keep. So, I'll be assessing the viability of each section and rationalising them into bigger, more lucrative ones. For example, those homemade silk purses you have taking up a lot of shelf space, how many do you actually sell?'

'Err, well, I'm hoping to push them as Valentine gifts.' Marigold, the designer, will be heartbroken if we stop selling her stuff. 'And the tourists love them,' I venture, thinking of her working away in the little weatherboard studio on the shingle with unbroken views of the sea. Admittedly, I don't actually sell many of the purses, but customers are always intrigued to hear about the local artist who makes them.

'They're an indulgence. And one Carrington's can't afford if it's going to be successfully rejuvenated, and that's where you come in.'

'I do?' I say, perking up. Maybe this isn't going to be so bad after all. My section does pretty well compared to the others.

'I shall be assessing the sections on the ground floor by the main entrance first for visibility and profitability. Women's Accessories, Men's Accessories and Fine Jewellery. I can't believe the cabinet is hidden away up in the personal shopping suite. No, it must be downstairs right by the door, where everyone can see it and be encouraged to buy from it before they waste their money on low-value items elsewhere in the store. I want their shopping fix satiated by high-end goods.' I nod, thinking, *so do I, means more commission for me*. 'And new brand names. Big names! I want Prada. Hermès,' she gushes, her voice getting louder and more animated, and my nodding head speeds up. 'And then I'll decide who is best to sell such exclusive brands.'

My head stops and my heart sinks. *Whaat? What does she mean?* I'm the best sales assistant. Carrington's finest . . .

'Well, if you look at my sales figures, you—'

'I like to shake things up a bit.' *Hmmm. Bully for you.* 'Show me your mettle. Let's see who is *really* the best sales assistant and then they can sell those exclusive brands,' she says, triumphantly.

'Does James know about this?' I manage to say, my mind reeling. I'm going to be in direct competition with James. And how is my section ever going to compete with Fine Jewellery? One piece alone can cost the equivalent of ten Louis bags.

'He was the first to know,' she replies, scribbling something on a page in her Filofax. The room reels as I try to take it all in. 'So it will be the three of you section heads that I'll be focusing on initially.' Maxine carries on scrawling, not even bothering to look up at me.

'Three of us?' I ask tentatively, I'm guessing this is where Tom comes in. I'm glad she can't see my face.

'Yes, but you know that already, don't you?'

'Err, yes,' I gulp. I fidget in my seat as she continues to hold my stare. So Tom must have told her about our conversation in the club; that I know how he was recruited – and what he'll be selling. I knew he couldn't be trusted.

'Look Gina, there isn't much that gets past me. Are you in or out?'

'I'm in,' I say quickly, panic mounting at the prospect of being forced to go head to head with James, but knowing I don't have any choice.

'Good, so this is all about riding the recession and

revitalising Carrington's. And trying to make money of course. You and . . .' She pauses to glance at a list on the desk. 'Annie is it?' I nod. 'Yes, you need to sell as much as you possibly can. The other sections will be doing the same, and then I can make a decision on what merch stays and who is best to sell it. I may even decide to scrap a lot of the smaller and less profitable lines to make way for just a couple of select high-end ones. In my experience, this always means less staff. But seeing as you're a very good sales assistant and we have some strong in-store Valentine's promotions going on, it shouldn't be too difficult for you, should it?' Standing up, she waves a dismissive hand in my direction. 'And besides, I like winners, not losers.' And she whips a hand up and does the actual L for loser sign against her forehead. I cringe inwardly. How embarrassing.

'Of course,' I mutter, glad to have my share of the Malikov sale. That'll get my section off to a good start.

'Oh, and you'll report directly to me from now on. What day do you have off?'

'Err, Monday,' I say, praying she's not about to make me give it up. Everyone knows it's the best day off to make a weekend when you work every Saturday.

'Then your weekly one-to-one meeting with me will be at seven sharp every Tuesday morning. I like to start bright and early.' She rubs her hands together before flicking her big hair around for a bit.

'Great,' I say with a forced smile, feeling relieved that

my day off is safe. *Good for you*. I bet she's one of those crazy types that just *lurrves* a military-style boot camp session, preferably outdoors in the lashing rain, while normal people are still snuggled up in bed because it's practically the middle of the night.

'Oh, and keep the first Sunday in February free . . . the board thought a series of "team-building jollies" might keep spirits up, so I've put you down for the first session,' she adds, pulling a face as if the whole idea is totally abhorrent to her.

10

The door at the staff exit is so heavy it seems like an eternity before I eventually step out onto the pavement. I breathe in, and the salty sea air catches in my lungs. The euphoria at not losing my job has quickly subsided, leaving an empty realisation that if my section isn't deemed the most profitable, I'll most likely be unemployed. I can't seem to quell the panic that's coursing through me at the thought of that chilling prospect. It was practically impossible to revise at Nanny Jean's with the TV blaring out and Kimberley hollering all day long, so I know damn well I'll struggle to find something else with my qualifications. It didn't matter so much at the start, but these days even graduates with a degree in retail management are finding it tough to find jobs. Not that there are any other department stores in Mulberry-On-Sea, and practically none of the smaller, boutique-style shops are taking on new staff, in fact quite a few have already closed down, there are loads of empty units in the pedestrianised bit of town. Everyone is feeling the pinch.

I guess I could commute to London, but then with the huge monthly travel costs to fork out for, I'd never earn enough to cover the rest of my overheads. And James will hate me if I stay and he has to go – he took me on in the first place. And I'll be competing against Tom and I don't know anything about him.

Then there's my guilty secret debt problem, I've got to do something about it as it's bound to come out when HR do the checks. I feel as though I'm being backed into a corner.

I need some time alone. Time to think before I face the others. I decide to head for Gino's, the little Italian deli tucked down a narrow cobbled lane behind Carrington's. I haven't been there for a while; it's got a little seating area for espresso and tapas and it's perfect for my current mood.

As I walk along, pounding the hard pavement, a woman on roller skates burns past me, her white shirt billowing around like a puff of smoke as she elbows me out of the way. The roller skates remind me of Dad, and of clinging on to his hand as I attempted to balance on the pair of rainbow-coloured roller skates I got for my tenth birthday. Thinking of Dad makes me wonder what it must have been like for him all of those years ago. I ponder for a moment, and then after remembering what Sam said in the club, I pull my mobile out from my bag and scroll through the address book to find his number.

'Hello darling, what a wonderful surprise. Is everything OK?' His voice sounds worried. 'Shouldn't you be at work?' There's an awkward silence.

'I *am* at work,' I reply, a little too sharply. 'Well, I just popped out and . . . err, I'm sorry I couldn't talk to you the other day,' I manage, trying to disguise the unease in my voice. 'So how are you?' I add, awkwardly.

'I'm fine. A bit tired. Anyway, enough about me. It's so nice to hear from you,' he says, and for a moment it's as though everything that's gone on between us before has been forgotten in an instant. But then my back constricts. I start to feel as though calling him was a bad idea, and I realise that I'm just not ready to forget what he did to us . . . especially to Mum. 'You know I was telling Uncle Geoffrey how well you've done, and he said to pass on his love.' The thought of my dad's brother conjures up images of when it all happened. I remember Uncle Geoffrey bringing over suitcases full of my cousin Olivia's old cast-offs. Olivia is a couple of years older than me and has always been much taller. But 'beggars can't be choosers', that's what Uncle Geoffrey used to say when he hauled the suitcase up onto the kitchen table. Mum would thank him profusely for his generosity while I stood there shivering in my vest and knickers waiting to try on the clothes that were always too big. And all the time I was thinking I'd make sure I had nice clothes that fitted me properly when I was grown-up.

'So how's work?' he asks, plugging the gap of silence.

'Fine.' I decide not to tell him what's happened. I don't want Uncle Geoffrey to know I might be unemployed soon with grim prospects. Gloating, just like he did all those years ago in the kitchen. The thought makes me panicky, it will be near on impossible to find another job if I'm let go. There are so many people getting laid off at the moment, I'll be on the scrapheap before I'm even thirty.

'So what's up then?' he asks, knowing me too well.

'Nothing.' I hate myself for lying.

'You can always talk to me, darling . . .' His voice trails off and I feel terrible. I shouldn't have called him. Not now. Breaking the silence I mutter, 'Dad . . . please don't.'

'I'm sorry darling. I didn't mean to upset you.'

I swallow hard and feel like a fool. I should never have burdened myself with a ridiculous 125 per cent mortgage. And for what? Just to fit in? Make myself feel better? To prove a point to the girls in the play-ground? My mind spins and for a moment I feel as though I'm suffocating.

'You enjoy it darling. You've worked extremely hard and I know it wasn't easy for you, starting out with nothing and having to cope with what I did. And all alone too. But you did it, and long may it continue. I'm very proud of you.'

'Thank you,' I mumble, just about managing to mask the well of emotion that's going to burst at any moment. I have to keep the job.

'And Mum would be too,' Dad adds, quietly. Tears start streaming down my face now, I can't hold them in, and I try and force myself to stop crying. I put my free hand over my mouth so Dad can't hear the gasps. 'Hello. Georgie are you still there? Hello, hello?' I can hear Dad's voice but I can't speak. 'Damn gadgets, useless waste of time,' Dad puffs, before hanging up.

I shove my phone into my pocket and pull out an old tissue to blow my nose on. I feel utterly crap as I carry on walking.

Gino's, as always, looks warm and inviting. Its 1950s décor of blue and white tiles above caramel-coloured painted wood panels is old-fashioned but comforting, and with a bit of luck I won't bump into anybody from work in here.

'Bella! Long time no see.' Gino looks up from a huge bowl of green pesto he's lovingly spooning into small pots, and I manage to smile back, hoping my tissue rescue job performed a few minutes ago outside has worked well enough to hide the tear stains. 'What can I get you, a milky tea?'

'Yes please. And lots of sugar,' I say, suddenly craving a sugar rush like it's the only excitement on offer these days.

'Take a seat and I'll bring it over,' he says, gesturing with his hand towards the tables.

'Thank you.' I make my way over to a corner one and busy myself with draping my coat across the back of the rickety wooden chair, when Mrs Grace, my predecessor in Women's Accessories, appears at my side.

'Mind if I join you, love?' she says, unbuttoning her wool coat before patting the back of her Garnier blonde Aunty Bessie bun. I shake my head, not wanting to be rude, and she sits down opposite me. Gino arrives with our drinks and hands us two steaming pink mugs.

'Thanks Gino,' I say, and he dashes back to the counter.

'A little treat to cheer you up.' Mrs Grace pulls a red foil-wrapped chocolate heart from her granny handbag and places it on the table in front of me. Her kindness makes me well up again. 'Oh lovey, I'm sorry. I didn't mean to upset you again. Come on now, no tears. I spotted you leaving the store when I was outside having a ciggy. I could see you were upset so I followed you. Hope you don't mind.'

'Sorry.' I dab my eyes again.

'Tell me,' she says gently, handing me a napkin. 'I'm old, but sometimes a friendly ear can help.' Mrs Grace looks across at me, her crinkly eyes full of concern. And the whole story comes tumbling out like a confessional.

'You'll be fine, sweetheart,' Mrs Grace says, when I've finished telling her everything. 'I've seen it all before. These high-flying types . . . coming in and shaking us all up with their fancy ideas.' Mrs Grace crosses her arms and purses her lips. 'And I must say that Maxine one is *very* full of herself. Nothing a decent square meal wouldn't fix, mind you.'

'What do you mean?'

'Oh, it's the hunger, dear – makes them all edgy and overzealous,' she explains, rolling her eyes.

Mrs Grace has heard everything, about today's meeting with Maxine, and how I've now got to compete with James and Tom if I'm to stand a chance of keeping my job and not lose everything. I've even confided in her about my guilty secret crush on Tom, even though he can't be trusted. And how deep down I'm fed up of spending Valentine's Day on my own. Let alone going to a wedding that will no doubt be crammed full of happy couples, while I'm being 'Bridget Jones alone', unless a miracle occurs and I manage to find an actual date to invite. I yearn to look forward to 14 February, to feel excited. And light and skippy and in love, just as I was once with Brett. She also listened patiently while I told her about my debilitating debt problem and how it could totally ruin everything if it comes out. I'll be deemed a risk.

'Oh, I wish it were that easy, Mrs Grace,' I say, trying to feel brighter.

'And you tell James that he must stop touching your fingers. He has a wife,' Mrs Grace says sternly, wagging her bony finger in the air. I manage a feeble giggle, imagining James's face if I actually said that to him. Besides, he might not even speak to me now we're going to be competing. 'Though I heard on the grapevine that he and Maxine were once an item.' She folds her arms.

114

My mouth drops open.

'*Whaat?*' I manage.

'James and Maxine. They went out together after meeting on some training course in London, before he met and married his wife.' She shakes her head. 'That Maxine is now a woman scorned, I imagine. And James's future is in her hands.'

I try to take in this piece of information. It all makes sense now, his reaction when she was introduced. And Mrs Grace could be wrong about who had dumped who: what if Maxine favours James? She could still have a thing for him. Or worse still, James might rekindle what he had with her. I know he's married, but she is supermodel-stunning after all. Then where would that leave me – she's hardly going to get rid of him if they are an item, is she?

I grab my bag. 'Oh, look at the time,' I say in a breezy voice. 'I'd better go, but thanks so much for the sympathetic ear, Mrs Grace,' I say gratefully.

'Fate will see you right, my dear,' she whispers, and suddenly my mind is crystal clear. I know what I have to do. 'And don't give up on Cupid . . . his arrow will find a way to your heart,' she smiles, and gives me a big hug, enveloping me in a comforting, nostalgic mixture of stale perfume and Revlon lipstick.

11

'There you are.' Eddie runs towards me as soon as I step out of the staff lift. He looks agitated. 'Do you know where James is?'

'Err . . . no. What's up?'

'It's the Russian – seems he's in the mood for more shopping and I've been calling your section for the last half-hour at least,' he pants.

'Sorry.'

'Well, you're here now. James has gone AWOL, can't get hold of him at all and the Russian is going to be here *like any minute now*. You better hurry, he wants you to meet him outside by the main entrance.'

'*But why?*' I ask, wondering why he can't just come in the store like all the other customers. I mean, it's not as if he's mega-famous or anything. Probably just thinks it makes him look exclusive or something.

'I don't know, something about a late lunch en route to the airport.' Eddie nudges me. 'Hubba hubba,' he laughs, and I swat him on the arm.

'Stop it, you're revolting.' A shiver of panic courses

through me at the prospect of being alone with Malikov.

'You'd better watch out.'

'What do you mean?'

'Well, before you know it he'll have you drenched in Shalimar and spread-eagled across his leatherette waterbed while he sucks on a Monte Cristo and asks you to call him Daddy.'

'Err, ran-dom! Even by your standards,' I say, stifling a giggle.

'You mark my words.' Eddie folds his arms and looks at me, meaningfully.

'Oh don't be ridiculous. He probably just wants me to escort him around the store or up to the personal shopping suite. And besides, he's not that old,' I protest, desperately clinging to my own words for reassurance.

'Oh well, why not – at least it's a bit of excitement, unlike the rest of Mulberry-On-Sea.'

'If it's so boring here, why do you stay?'

'Cos you're here. The very best friend a girl could have.' He looks serious for a brief moment. 'I can talk to you and you never judge me, that counts for a lot in my book.'

'Aw, that's so nice Ed.'

'Hmm, lap it up pussycat because it's the only time I'm saying it.' I squeeze his cheek and he shoves my hand away. 'Whatevs! Now go. You don't want to keep your sugar daddy waiting.' Eddie makes a shooing action towards me.

'Ha ha,' I say, pulling a fake smile face and slinging my bag back over my shoulder before jumping inside the lift and pulling the cage door closed.

I arrive just in time to see an ominous black Maybach with privacy windows glide to a standstill right in front of the main entrance. I dive behind the huge Clarins display board and buy myself a few seconds to call James. After what feels like an eternity, he eventually answers.

'Just go without me,' he snaps uncharacteristically, after I tell him about Malikov's impromptu lunch request. 'You can manage that, can't you?' His voice sounds brittle, and I can hear a woman yelling in the background.

'Of course . . .' I mutter, feeling taken aback. 'I just wanted to check as we don't normally go out for lunch with customers. I'd hate to jeopardise anyth—'

'Just don't upset him then, and you won't.'

'James, is everything OK?' I ask, a lump suddenly forming in my throat.

'Never better . . . look, I can't talk now. Do whatever you need to.' And the line goes dead. I stare at the phone in disbelief, wondering what's got into him, before slotting it back into my bag. But I can't think about it now, not with Malikov waiting.

A henchman in a black leather coat hauls himself out and pulls open the passenger door as I walk towards the car.

'Mr Malikov, he want you for a lunch,' the henchman

says slowly in a heavy Russian accent, as if struggling to pick the right words. My nervousness makes me want to giggle, but I stifle the urge.

Sliding into the car, I pop my bag down on the floor and find that I'm sitting right next to Malikov; the armrest has been folded back and he's sitting just off centre. He's wearing a ridiculous-looking speckled grey fur hat with a pinstripe suit, complete with waistcoat, the buttons of which are straining around his bulging midriff. There's another henchman sitting in the front passenger seat with a tattoo on the side of his neck and a transparent curly plastic lead hanging from his ear. A bodyguard! Oh my God.

Malikov slowly turns to look at me before treating me to a smile that conjures up an image of Little Red Riding Hood's wolf.

'Mr Malikov . . .' I start. He tilts his head.

'My dear, what a short memory you have . . .'

I swallow, before taking a deep breath.

'Sorry. Kon,' I quickly remember, feeling uneasy at such familiarity in the intimate surroundings of his car. 'Please accept my apologies. James can't join us today, he's . . . been held up with another customer,' I say, managing to sound convincing.

'Ha!' He waves a dismissive hand. 'This is better.' He laughs, letting his gaze linger uncomfortably long. My heart feels as if it might jump right out of my chest. The car pulls away and I sit back in an attempt to relax, when the seat suddenly starts vibrating. The shock makes me gasp.

'You like it? It's for massage,' Malikov booms, looking very pleased with himself.

'It's unusual,' I manage, instantly knowing better than to disagree with him as I reach up for the grab handle in a desperate attempt to try and control my jigging body. 'How can I help you today?' I ask, the vibration from the seat making my voice sound all wobbly and ridiculous.

He waves a dismissive hand. 'I want to give you this.' He taps his cane on the back of the seat to alert the bodyguard who, after glancing in the rear-view mirror, takes a black velvet box from the glove compartment and hands it back to Malikov. 'A small gift for you.' Malikov pushes the box towards me.

'Oh, Kon. That's very generous of you but really there's no need,' I say, immediately holding my hands up to emphasise the fact that I can't accept it.

'My wife and daughter were very pleased with the matching purses. You're a clever girl.' He goes to hand me the box again and I hesitate. 'I shall be offended if you don't take it.' His eyes narrow. I swallow, remembering the Chiavaccis and James's instruction not to upset him.

'It's not that I don't want to . . . it's just that I'm not really allowed to accept gifts from customers.' The massage action ends abruptly, making the word *customer* jump up a few octaves. Instantly, my cheeks flush. I quickly try to regain some composure. 'I'm sure you understand.' He studies me. 'Only it's not appropriate for me to do so, and in any case I didn't really do anything,' I tell him, making sure I don't imply his behaviour is in any way inappropriate.

'Nonsense, you must take it. It's just a trinket and I always reward my . . . *laydeeez*,' he says, dropping his eyelids as a sleazy smile forms across his hard face. 'But there is one condition,' he adds, covertly. 'It must be our secret.' His eyes snap open wide now. 'If you tell anyone I shall deny it, my wife insists on discretion. So you must tell nobody, most of all the tax man.' He sniggers at his own joke in an attempt to mask the threat in his voice, and then lets his leg fall against mine. I can't believe his wife condones this revolting reward system.

'Of course, but I'm sorry. Really, I can't,' I say, trying to sound more insistent. Silence follows.

'But I'm not just any old customer. I like to think of us as . . . *friends*,' he says, gesturing magnanimously with both hands and allowing the words to linger suggestively as I try and ignore the pounding sound of my own heartbeat. He's ancient. Must be at least fifty. And it was all over Google about his legion of girlfriends. I remember what Eddie said about the waterbed and feel relieved I can't take the present, not even bearing to think what sexual favours he might expect in return.

'And we are.' He glares at me.

'I would if I could,' I quickly add. And then, to my surprise, he totally changes tack.

'You have class.' Malikov shakes his head vigorously as I subtly pick at the fluff that flies from his hat onto my face. 'Silly me, you cannot accept trinkets from a man you barely know. I should have realised that.' He pats my knee, sending a shock of revulsion to circuit through me, and then slips the box into his pocket. I take a deep breath and smile broadly to cover the big sigh of relief that follows.

The car takes a sharp corner just as his phone rings so I grab the opportunity to put a smidgen of distance between us and surreptitiously slide myself towards the door. I glance out of the window, trying to work out where we are, but I don't recognise the back street we're crawling through.

'Lunch is cancelled,' Malikov announces after stabbing his phone to end the call. He taps the back of the driver's seat. 'Back to Carrington's and then take me to my lawyer's. We must finalise the details of the super-injunction,' he orders, emphasising the words 'super-injunction' and sounding very showy and impressed with himself. He turns to me. 'I'm sorry my dear, but this is the price of success. Everyone at the top has one these days.' He rolls his eyes, pretending to be put out by the trappings of his perceived status. 'Another time perhaps?' and he takes my hand and plants a bristly kiss across my knuckles. I resist the urge to throw up in his lap, thinking that'll teach me to squeeze my cleavage at dodgy old pervs.

'Oh, what a shame. Well, please let us know if we can help with anything else,' I venture, feeling relieved that I won't have to endure lunch now but disappointed that I've not had the chance to talk to him about the Chiavaccis.

'Actually there is something else . . .' His voice trails off. He looks away.

'Yes?' I reply, eagerly, pushing my personal feelings about him to one side. He turns back and studies me for a moment.

'It's an associate of mine . . . but he doesn't speak English so I will act on his behalf,' he says as a statement.

'Oh, OK. Do you know what he would like to buy?' I hold my breath, hoping he wants a designer bag or three, or a nice set of luggage perhaps. A big sale to impress Maxine would be fantastic.

'Gifts for his family in Moscow. He has seven sisters. Each with a penchant for quality goods.' Malikov locks his eyes onto mine. Silence follows. 'Chanel bags!' he exclaims suddenly. 'The most expensive ones.' His eyes light up and my heart sinks. We don't stock Chanel.

'Yes the Chanel bags are very stylish, but I wonder if your friend has considered the Bottega range? I have eight of the Venetas,' I say, knowing they're still nestling in the stock cupboard. Way too pricey for our normal customers, and who can afford to pay thousands for a bag in any case?

'Do they cost more?'

'Oh yes, they're *very* expensive, everyone wants one, but I'd be happy to reserve seven of them for your associate,' I say, hoping to appeal to his sense of entitlement.

'Let him have six,' he smiles nastily, and I immediately feel sorry for the sister who will miss out. 'I want the other two . . . for my wife and daughter.'

'Wonderful,' I say, forcing a smile.

'And you will ship them? For the sisters.'

'Yes, yes of course,' I nod eagerly. This will get my section off to a good start with Maxine, and I can't wait to tell James – hopefully his half of the sales commission will cheer him up. I know we're in competition now, but Malikov was his customer originally so it's only fair to share. 'And I believe you were interested in the limited edition Chiavacci bags,' I say, tentatively, steadying my voice from showing too much excitement as the car pulls up opposite Carrington's.

'Perhaps, but the boss would need to be here. Goodbye,' he says, adjusting his hat. I shake his hand before stepping out of the car, and then realise that I've forgotten my bag. I quickly spin around to see it dangling on the end of his extended right index finger. As I lean back inside the car to retrieve it, Malikov's eyes dart down towards my cleavage and he treats me to another leer.

I'm busy tweeting about my encounter with Malikov

when I glance up to see Maxine push through the revolving doors at the front of the store. For some reason, I hesitate and hold back. And I'm glad I have because, as Maxine walks around to the side exit, James emerges from the loading bay.

I duck into a tiny alcove next to the betting shop, just in time to see them chatting. I swear James is laughing. Although it's tricky to be sure, as Maxine is standing right in front of him, but still, he's not snapping at her like he did with me just an hour or so ago. Maxine is rubbing his arm now and they look very cosy indeed. And oh my God, she's hugging him. Her lips are pressed to his ear as if she's whispering something illicit! Bound to be. My stomach lurches. I feel like an utter fool. I take a deep breath and turn away to study the odds for the upcoming football matches. When I turn back around to walk over to Carrington's, James has gone and Maxine is sashaying towards me, her hair fanning all around her like the Greek goddess, Venus, or whatever. In my peripheral vision I spot a group of suits from a nearby estate agent's office nudging each other as they gape in her direction. One of them winks and another shouts 'oi oi', but Maxine is oblivious; she has a cigarette in one hand and her mobile in the other, and it's pressed to her ear.

'Who was that?' she asks, pulling the phone away and clutching it to her chest. She traces a question mark in the air with her cigarette.

'Mr Malikov, he's a customer,' I tell her.

'Nice car,' she says, drawing in another lungful. She exhales through her nose and shakes her hair around for a bit. 'Why doesn't he come inside like everyone else?'

'I'm not sure.'

'Well, in future you need to let me know about every private customer and their personal shopping visits . . . preferably conducted within the personal shopping suite.'

'OK, if you're sure – it's not something we normally do.' My heart sinks at the prospect of being tracked like a Saturday girl on her first job.

'I'm in charge now and I want things done properly. What if something had happened to you? Then where would we be?' she says, flashing her pageant smile.

'Quite. Point taken. I'll be sure to tell you in future,' I reply.

I push through the revolving doors and make my way to the staff lift. As the lift staggers through the floors I open my bag. And I don't believe it. There, perched on top of my purse, is Malikov's suede box. Oh my God, he must have slipped it in when I was getting out of the car. He sure as hell doesn't take no for an answer.

On leaving the lift I make my way straight into the loo, and after checking the coast is clear I pull the box from my bag. As I push open the lid I let out an involuntary gasp that's quickly followed by a hushed, 'Wow.'

It's a ruby necklace and it's absolutely exquisite. I glance at the door before carefully lifting it from the box and holding it up to my neck.

As I lean across the sink to get a better look in the mirror, the gems glisten in the light. It's irresistible, so I quickly fasten it around my neck, admiring the way the rubies skim my collarbone. I allow myself a moment of fantasy, imagining that I'm a Russian princess and that this necklace is just one of many pieces in my vast collection, when the door bursts open.

I dash into the nearest cubicle and hurriedly take the necklace off, placing it carefully back into the box before stowing it back into my handbag.

12

£7,786.91. OH MY ACTUAL GOD. The saliva drains from my mouth. It's Monday morning. My day off. Wintry fresh sun is streaming through the slats of the white Venetian blind at my bedroom window and I've just finished tallying up my debts. I scan the spreadsheet again, desperately searching for an error. Surely it can't be right. I highlight the amounts and press the Autosum button again, just in case, but it's no use. The amount doesn't change. Everything is there, even a store card I used to pay for the dress I wore to Sam's birthday do, and the balance is now almost double what the dress cost in the first place. Another wave of nausea charges through me followed by a cold shiver of sweat. I reach over to the thick envelope containing the copy of my credit file. My hand is shaking but there's no way out, I have to face it.

'Bloody hell, what's this?' Sam yells, from the lounge.

'What's what?' I yell back, my eyes scanning the report.

'This necklace here on the coffee table. It's divine.'

'Oh, a customer gave it to me. I need to get it sent

back to him,' I shout back distractedly, eager to concentrate on the details in front of me. Sam stayed last night and we're just about to head off to do some shopping. Or window shopping only, in my case.

I blink to refocus my eyes before taking another look. The paper trembles in my hands. All three of my credit cards have glaring late-payment markers against them, and one is even showing as having a missed payment. One of my store cards has an arrears marker too. I feel faint now.

I grab the phone handset from the bedside table to call the credit report company. I've got to find out what my options are in getting this mess tidied up. After tapping out the number I wait for a ring tone. Silence. I hang up and try again, and still the same thing. Damn phone, and there's no dial tone. Then a woman's voice comes onto the line and I realise I've come straight through to the phone company instead.

After taking me through security she announces, 'I'm sorry, Madam, but your line has been disconnected for non-payment.'

'Non-payment? I only switched over to you a little while ago. I haven't even had a bill yet,' I protest, wincing at the condescending 'madam' reference. I can feel the skin on my back prickling.

'Well, the bills have been sent. Three in total, and since you haven't responded to any of the requests for payment, your line has been disconnected,' she says, in a bossy matter-of-fact voice.

'But I haven't had any bills, I'm sure of it,' I plead. Surely there must be some kind of mistake. There's a pause while I listen to her tapping on a keyboard.

'Well, according to the system you're on paperless billing so you would have been sent several email billing notifications.' Well, that explains it. It had seemed like such a good idea at the time. I even set up a folder in my inbox labelled 'bills to be paid', but I must have forgotten to actually pay them. My heart sinks. I feel like such a failure.

'So how much is outstanding?' I ask, delving into my bag to retrieve my purse. I pull out a credit card in anticipation.

'Three hundred and fifty-nine pounds and sixty-eight pence.' I open my mouth but for a moment the words don't come out. My tongue feels as if it's staple-gunned to the roof of my mouth.

'*Three hundred pounds?*' I stammer, feeling like an idiot as my brain works overtime to try and remember when I last paid the phone bill.

'Three hundred and fifty-nine pounds and sixty-eight pence,' she repeats, emphasising every single word, and I'm sure I detect a hint of smugness in her voice.

'But I hardly ever use the phone at home, that can't possibly be right,' I reply.

'That includes a reconnection fee of a hundred and a one-hundred-and-fifty-pound holding deposit against the next eighteen months' billing period, on top of your bill for the previous two quarters.'

This is unbelievable.

'So I have to give you an extra two hundred and fifty just to get my phone reconnected?' My voice sounds tight and I feel like crying.

'Yes. Would you like to pay now?' she asks. I want to scream 'of course I bloody well don't', but instead I read out the details from my credit card and wait while she processes it.

'I'm sorry, Madam, but the payment has been declined. Do you have another card?' My heart sinks, my cheeks burn with shame, and I feel dizzy as I pull out another credit card. I give her the details and then wait again, willing it to be OK as I imagine somebody at the credit card office spinning a giant roulette wheel.

'Yes, that's all fine now.'

'Thank you,' I reply, my hands shaking as I hang up. Everything is far from being fine. I take a gulp of air that catches in my throat. Sam taps on the half-open bedroom door. I quickly shove the credit report into my handbag before tugging at the door handle. I'll have to call them later.

'Are we still going shopping?' she beams at me, after I pull the door wide open. 'Only I thought I could wear this,' she guffaws, holding Malikov's necklace up to her neck.

'Sure,' I say, with a half-smile, as I try and forget about the credit report and the phone bill fiasco. Sam and I have never actually discussed money. Of course she knows we're in totally different leagues, but somehow it's always seemed like a taboo subject between us.

'I think these gems are real and probably worth a bit,' she says, scrutinising the necklace. 'I know – let's get it valued.' Making big pleading eyes at me, she tries to make it sound as though the idea has just popped into her head. 'I'm dying to know how much it's worth,' she says, hopping from one foot to the other, barely able to contain her excitement.

'I can't, it was a present from a customer. And we're not allowed to accept gifts.'

'Oh how exciting. Tell me about him, is he hot?'

'Hardly, he's a middle-aged Russian, with eyes like a piranha,' I say, shuddering inwardly at the memory.

'Ew.' She wrinkles her nose, and I can't help smiling.

'Anyway, it's going back,' I say, shaking my head, and feeling like a party pooper when a crestfallen look appears across her face.

'Oh come on, who's to know? And besides, it was a present, so you can do what you like with it,' she says, skipping through to the bathroom. After flicking the light on she bounces up onto the loo seat and holds the necklace up to the light so she can scrutinise it again. 'Yes, I'm sure of it. See here . . .' She pushes the necklace towards me, pointing to the largest ruby. 'The colour is so intense,' she says, knowingly.

'I'll have to take your word for it,' I reply, not ever having owned an expensive piece of jewellery.

'Aren't you curious? Oh come on, it'll be a laugh. We could pop over to Jessop Street – there're loads of jewellers around that part of town,' she pleads, and I can't help smiling at her enthusiasm.

'Sorry, I can't. Like I said, I have to return it.'

'So how come you've got it then?'

'He put it in my bag when I wasn't looking.'

'Well there you go . . . you didn't accept it so you don't have to return it.' She laughs and lets the necklace trickle through her fingers as she drops it back into the box.

*

We've been sitting in the little office at the back of the musty old jeweller's shop for almost twenty minutes.

'I haven't seen stones like these for some time. Eastern European, are they?' The wiry old jeweller lets his loupe fall down from his eye into the palm of his hand before peering back up.

'Err, I think so.' I can't believe I'm even doing this.

'Yes, it's from Russia,' Sam says, nudging me under the table with her thigh, '. . . with love!' I pull a 'stop it' face at her. 'So what do you think then?' She fixes her baby-blue eyes on the jeweller's watery ones. He hunches his scrawny shoulders further over the table.

'Is it for insurance purposes, or resale?' Silence follows. The jeweller looks up and I glance at Sam.

133

'Nei—' I start, but Sam nudges my leg again, and with my mouth still open I turn my body towards her.

'Actually, it's for insurance,' Sam says, knowingly. 'You silly thing,' she pats my arm, trying to look authentic, 'you can't keep it uninsured.'

The jeweller pulls out a little pad and scribbles on it before turning it around to show us. I stare at the figure. Oh my God. I can't believe it. My pulse quickens.

'See, I told you didn't I?' Sam says, smugly. Then turning back to the jeweller she adds, 'A generous . . . err, friend, gave it to her.'

'Very generous indeed,' the jeweller replies, eyeing me as I peer again at the figure. Oh my God, what I could do with that money. I quickly shove the thought out of my head and reach across to the box. The jeweller drops the necklace back inside and I close the lid down on it.

'Thank you for your time, but we really need to get going,' I say, briskly, before pushing the chair back and shaking the jeweller's hand. I turn to leave, and Sam follows along behind me.

As soon as we're outside, Sam is beside herself with glee.

'Didn't I tell you? How exciting,' she says, pulling her sunglasses down over her forehead to protect her face from the dazzling wintry sun. 'Are you sure about the piranha eyes? I mean, you could always make him close them . . . if you ever wanted to get jiggy with him.' She laughs out loud.

'Yuk. Stop it.'

'Ohmigod.' She stops walking and clutches my arm. 'Imagine what else he might give you . . . for a Valentine's present,' she gushes, and I pull a face.

'Please just stop it. He's vile, not my type at all. In any case, I can look after myself,' I say, a little too abruptly as I remember the glaring total on the spreadsheet, realising the mess I've actually made of it so far. My mind is working overtime as I rummage through my shopping tote searching for my sunglasses.

'Hey, come on. I was only joking,' Sam replies, placing a hand on my back.

'I know, and I'm sorry. I'm just a bit tetchy with everything that's going on at work.'

'Oh well, plenty more piranhas in the sea . . . *boom boom*.' Sam laughs at her own joke and gently elbows me in the ribs. I slip my arm through hers, and as we head off all I can think of is the figure on the paper. And *resale*! The word goes over and over in my head like an annoying jingle I can't evict.

13

'I knew you'd be back.'

'Oh. How come?' I ask, fiddling nervously with my sunglasses as the jeweller holds the shop door open for me.

'I just know the look. The look when the client realises just how much money they can have instead of a piece of jewellery they'll probably never wear. From a gentleman friend, was it?'

'Something like that,' I mutter.

'Of course, and may I reassure you that discretion is guaranteed. It happens all the time; they think they know what you like and—'

'Indeed,' I say, not wanting to engage him further in the details. I went through the motions with Sam, but it was no use. I have to do something to get my credit file back in order, not just to give myself the best possible chance of keeping my job, but because I can't take any more sleepless nights worrying about it all. So I left Sam in a quirky boutique over near the market square in the centre of town and made my way back here.

After handing the jeweller the suede box, he quickly slots his loupe into place and gives it another once-over. Satisfied that it's the same item, he scuttles off out to the back before returning with an A4-size double cheque book.

'Oh, I, err, was thinking cash?' I ask, trying to keep my voice even. There's no way I can put a cheque for such a large amount through my bank account without questions being asked. The whole bank will probably explode in shock, especially after its computer said a massive whopping 'no' to extending my overdraft.

'OK, have to be less for cash, though. And you do realise that the resale figure will be less than the one for insurance purposes. Unless you have the provenance documentation?' he asks, raising an eager eyebrow.

I shake my head.

'How much less?' I ask, wishing I didn't sound so desperate. He scrawls on the paper again and thrusts it in front of me.

'But that's *thirty per cent* less,' I state, keeping my voice low and trying to ignore the panic that's swirling in the pit of my stomach. What the hell was I thinking, coming back here? I hesitate, and clutch the handles of my tote.

'Look, I could go to twenty-eight per cent less,' he says, scribbling on the paper before swinging it around to show me. I glance down at the revised figure.

'How would twenty be?' I ask, figuring it's worth a go but feeling ashamed that I've resorted to this. He laughs.

'Twenty-six. And that's my final offer.' He goes to scribble on the paper again but I beat him to it by placing my hand down. I swallow and think of the credit report. The sleepless nights. Maxine's modernising make-over. Keeping my job. My lack of qualifications. And how I've made fifteen online applications for other jobs so far, ranging from data entry clerk to receptionist, and I haven't even managed to get an interview. Even though I can't bear the thought of leaving Carrington's, I figured I should have a backup plan. And with Maxine's warning to have everything in order, there's no other way – even the car and the flat are worth less than their outstanding finance, so I can't just sell them and save money that way.

But Mrs Grace said that fate would see me right and it has, sort of . . . Malikov didn't have to give me the necklace and nobody at work knows about it. It's enough to pay off all three credit cards plus the store card. And Malikov is bound to be offended if I return the necklace now; he'll think I've deliberately double-crossed him. I can't risk upsetting him, not after James told me not to, and not if there's a chance of him buying the Chiavacci bags. I swallow again, and a twitch starts up at the corner of my right eyelid.

'OK.' Blood pounds in my ears.

He nods, and then instructs me to follow him through to the office. 'Take a seat.' I do as I'm told and he leaves the room. My heart is racing. Fate will see me right, I say inside my head, over and over, until I've convinced myself that it's meant to be.

The door flings open and the jeweller returns with several cloth bank bags and a paper invoice that he hands to me. I quickly shove it into my bag. My mouth feels dry as he dumps the cloth bags down on the table and starts ripping the paper bands from each of the bundles of cash. He then runs each wad through the money counter before placing them into envelopes. Once he's finished counting, he pushes the pile of envelopes towards me before offering his hand. We shake on the deal and he makes his way to the door.

Just as he reaches it, he turns back to me. 'I'll leave you for a few minutes to get organised.' *Organised?* What does he mean? I feel confused. I stare at him. 'The *money*.' He motions to the table. 'You might want to put it away,' he adds, looking at me as though I'm stupid. And maybe he has a point. Perhaps I am stupid. But I can't back out now.

'Oh, yes, of course. I was just wondering whether my bag would be big enough,' I say, nervously patting my shopper, and feeling out of my depth. I wait for the click of the door before reaching out to the money. My hands are shaking, and my blood feels as though it might pump right out through my eye sockets as I lean over the table and start thrusting the envelopes into my bag.

Back at home, I run into the kitchen and grab the scissors from the drawer. I frantically cut my store cards into tiny pieces. Then I reach for the credit cards. My right hand is trembling and I feel scared. I've never felt so alone. Not even after Mum died and the social worker collected me from the hospital to take me to Nanny Jean's house – at least the buck didn't stop with me when it came to paying for everything. What if there's an emergency? I waver and then relinquish myself to the feeling of panic at not having my safety net to fall back on. I only manage to cut up one of the credit cards.

I walk into the lounge, and stand in front of the bookcase, and after squeezing my eyes tight shut I reach out to grab a book. Then I quickly ram the other credit card in between the pages, before pushing it back onto the shelf, feeling with my fingertips until it's safely back in place. I count to ten before I let myself open my eyes. Then I gather together all of my card statements and shove them into my bag. First thing tomorrow morning I'm going to pay them off. The surge of relief is over-whelming. I'll finally be able to sleep at night. I can't wait.

But there's one card left, the gold card, and I know the perfect place for that.

14

It's seven o'clock on Thursday evening, late-night shopping, and I feel sick. I'm on a break and I've already eaten two mini-tubes of sour cream and onion Pringles, half a family bag of Haribo Favourites and, in a vain attempt to ease the guilt at having eaten so many E numbers, I polish off the last of a tub of fruit salad. The canteen is empty, but as I chase a slice of kiwi around the bottom of the plastic container, James appears.

'I thought I was the only one in here,' I say, feeling uncomfortable as we haven't actually discussed the competition yet, or how he snapped at me on the phone. But before I can ask him about it he says,

'Georgie, I want to apologise for the way I spoke to you the other day. It was totally unforgivable.' He drops his eyes.

'Oh forget it. As long as you're OK,' I smile.

He hesitates before replying.

'I'm fine, just a bit stressed. Friends again?' he grins, and I smile back.

'Friends,' I agree.

'How's it going?' He perches down on the bench seat, just a few centimetres from me.

'So-so . . .' I start, but it's no use. 'Actually, that's not true. This is awful, I feel so guilty after you employed me in the first place and now we're having to compete.' He looks at me with sparkly enquiring eyes.

'Don't be, these are tough times and we all have to do what we need to.'

I can't believe he's being so decent about it.

'Look, I'll live, let's just see what happens.' He grins at me and I grin back at him and try to shove the feeling of guilt aside. He holds his gaze on me and I shift uncomfortably.

'James, I didn't tell you what happened with Malikov. He only went an—' But he holds a hand up as a signal for me to be quiet.

'I think we should stop talking about work. And seeing as I'm not your boss any more, why don't we go and grab a bite to eat later?' he says, enthusiastically.

'I'd love to but I'm fit to burst. I've just eaten my way through enough food to feed a small principality.' I instantly wish that I hadn't given him quite so much information. But James just laughs and follows it with, 'Georgie, it doesn't have to be dinner . . . you know a drink would suffice. Anyway, you have to come out with me, if only because you feel sorry for me.' I study him carefully. Is he actually asking me out? I'm not sure. It feels like he is, but after hearing about him and

Maxine, not to mention the fact he's married, it's as if I don't know him any more – maybe I never really did. But then he didn't have to put a note on my file to make sure my personal business was never mentioned, and he's hot. It's been ages since I lived dangerously.

'Come on . . . a quick drink.' He nudges me, and a giddy excitement suddenly bubbles through me. He flashes me a grin. I tell myself one drink won't hurt.

*

As we step through the low door of the intimate candlelit bar, James heads straight over to one of the booths.

'More privacy here,' he says, gesturing for me to take a seat. 'What can I get you?'

'A rosé, please,' I say, pondering on what he means by 'more privacy' while he heads over to the bar. I can't believe I'm actually alone in a bar with him. Earlier on it seemed a daring adventure, but now it feels weird, a little sordid even. What about his wife? I glance around to check there isn't anyone from work in here and then quickly bring myself back down to earth . . . it's just a drink with a work friend, that's all. But when he reappears and his fingers brush mine as he hands me the glass of wine, I know that I'm kidding myself. Maybe I should try and probe him a little, find out what he's playing at. I try the thought on for size, wishing I could just seize the moment and enjoy being

143

alone with him. Maybe James does like me, and more than just as a colleague . . . or maybe he has a habit of having affairs with women at work. My head feels as if it might burst, it's so full of possibilities, so I take a sip of wine and ponder on what I can say to find out. I open my mouth to speak at precisely the same time as his mobile rings.

'Mind if I just get this?' he whispers, gently touching my arm, and then quickly pulling his hand away before taking the call.

'Of course,' I reply, feeling tingly from his touch. He's definitely being flirty . . . I know I'm not mistaken but I'm not sure I like it. I watch him for a moment as he wanders towards the bar, pushing his hand through his hair, his shoulders relaxed. I enjoy being with him, but not like this, not in secretive booths skulking around bars praying his wife doesn't spot us. Mulberry-On-Sea can be such a small place sometimes. I'm not sure I could do that.

I quickly finish my wine and motion to him that I have to go.

'Hold on a second,' he says into the phone, and then to me, 'Please . . . don't go, I won't be long.' He covers the phone with his free hand and pulls a disappointed face.

'Sorry James, I have to be up early,' I say with a wry grin, before glancing at my watch to emphasise how late it is.

'Sure, another time perhaps?' he asks, his face scanning mine as I pull on my coat.

'Maybe.' I head off, wishing I knew what was going on and vowing to definitely find out . . . if there is another time. And part of me can't help secretly hoping there is, even though I know I really shouldn't.

15

On turning the corner of the street on my way into work for the red-eye meeting with Maxine, I see her pulling into the car park in a brand-spanking-new Audi TT. As I'm pondering on how she affords such an expensive car, she spots me.

'Terrific timing,' she gushes, as the electric window slides down. The door flings open just as the car park security guy runs over to assist her. 'Too late,' she says, dismissively, and shoos him away. As she emerges from the low-level seat, her brown cord skirt rides up over her perfect legs, and they splay open. And as she turns to step out of the car, she inadvertently flashes me a glimpse of her knickers. With a speed that could induce whiplash, I turn my head to hide the giggle, but it's no use, so I disguise it as a cough instead.

'Not ill again, are you?' She treats me to her pageant smile.

What is it with her and illness? She's obsessed. She turns back to the car and attempts to haul a pile of folders out from the foot well, after flinging a grey silk tie out of the way. *Hmmm, I wonder who the tie belongs to? She's obviously had a man in her car and he's taken his tie off. I wonder what else he took off?*

'No, I'm fine. Here, let me give you a hand,' I say, reaching out to take the folders from her and thinking *surely it wouldn't have been James?* I forcibly shove the image from my head. I really don't want to go there.

'Oh, what a good Samaritan you are,' she says jovially, and shoves the enormous stack of manila folders at me. With my chin barely reaching the top, I struggle to keep my handbag about my person. Thinking she'll take the folders once she's locked the car, I wait by the bonnet. But instead she strides off towards the staff entrance, swinging her gold-chained mini Chanel handbag with the gaiety of a Parisian girl skipping down the Champs Elysées in springtime. Presuming that I'm to follow her, I stagger along behind and then veer off towards the lift, thinking what a bloody cheek she has. I wish I hadn't bothered to give her a hand now.

'Oh no!' she bellows, with such force, for a second I contemplate flinging the folders and body-slamming the floor in case she's spotted a suicide bomber lurking. 'The lift is for fat people,' she continues, and with a self-satisfied shake of her head she breezes off.

'Well, these weigh a ton, so I'll have to see you up there,' I quip, feeling pleased with myself for standing up to her as I stomp off.

'All right then,' she calls airily.

'What are you doing in so early?' It's Eddie and he's skulking in the corner of the lift.

'I could ask you the same thing. I have my weekly one-to-one with the stick insect, what's your excuse?' I ask, my hackles still up. Eddie looks tired and dishevelled. His tie is crooked and his hair, which is usually all gelled and immaculate, is a squashed heap.

'Been here since *hell o'clock* typing up her endless reports, that's all. I'm just on my way home to get showered and changed as that ridiculously high-maintenance *sex fiend*,' he pauses to jab an angry finger towards the doors, signifying he's referring to Maxine, 'has only insisted I come straight back.'

'Oh Ed, that's torture.'

'Exactly! Even galley slaves got a break sometimes,' he says, pulling a sucking-on-a-lemon face.

I try not to laugh at his indignation.

'Do you know she even told me to find another job, if I didn't like it? Said there are plenty of people who'd jump at the chance to work with her.' Eddie crosses his arms and rolls his bloodshot eyes up towards the ceiling in a huff.

'I'm sorry. Just try to ignore her,' I say, wishing I could take my own advice. I manage to hoist the folders up against the handrail in an attempt to get some relief from their weight when the lift shudders to a halt.

'For crying out loud, not again . . . must be the second time this week I've been stuck in this sodding lift.' Eddie uncrosses his arms and stabs at the 'call' button. 'How come you've got these?' he says, glancing at the folders. 'They're personnel records . . . Maxine made me get them from HR. Of course, I checked with Walter first because they're highly confidential, but he said to do whatever she asked. The flaming turncoat that he is,' Eddie snorts.

'Oh, like an idiot I offered to give her a hand with them. I bumped into her as she pulled up in her Audi TT,' I tut.

'Oh yeah, don't start me on that. Bending my ear for days, she was, over that car. And what I'd like to know is how come Carrington's is forking out for a company car? I thought we were on the verge of a terminal decline. Walter must be dafter than he looks. "*Make sure it's the gun-metal grey*",' he says, running a suggestive hand down his chest and mimicking her breathy voice. 'Over and over, to the point where I felt like pummelling her with some gun metal myself, and you know I'm not a violent man.' He attempts a weak smile and I give him a sympathetic look.

'So how come she's managed to wangle a sports car and not a normal car then?'

'Search me. It seems madam gets whatever she wants. And you want to see how much gear she has delivered to her office every day. All designer stuff too. But one thing is for sure, the board think she's the best thing since sliced foie gras, and as for Walter, *well*, she's got him wrapped right around her toothpick of a pinkie.' He wiggles his little finger in the air, before yelling, 'Hellooo, is anyone actually there?' into the little speaker on the wall of the lift.

There's a crackle of static before a male voice bellows, 'Sorry guys, technical hitch. You'll be on your way soon.'

'Well, that's just grrrreat,' Eddie yells back.

'You know she flashed at me when she dragged herself out of the car earlier on,' I say, lowering my voice in case the speaker is still active.

'Oh *purlease*. That's way too much information,' he says, holding his hand up.

'So, how's your love life?' I ask, changing the subject, wishing I could tell him about my drink with James.

'Oh don't. Smith deserted me . . . for somebody else. Story of my life,' Eddie says, sticking his bottom lip out.

'Oh, Ed, I'm so sorry. I'd give you a hug if I could but . . .' I nod towards the folders.

'And get this, only said we could still see each other. I ask you . . . flaming cheek,' he sniffs, haughtily.

'Damn right. Hope you told him to sod off.'

'*Weell*, let's just say I'm working on it.' Eddie purses his lips, and I roll my eyes at him.

'You're such a manwhore.'

'I know. Isn't it fabulous,' he sniggers. The lift rumbles into action again. I glance at the digital display.

'Ed, you do know this lift is going up, don't you?' I tell him, and wonder if James will be in yet.

'Well there you go, proof I'm officially mentally impaired from sleep deprivation,' he sighs, waving jazz hands in the air. Then he pushes the button for the next floor.

'I'm going to knuckle-drag my weary body out here and take the customer lift down. And you know what, I don't give a fuck if I'm caught and disciplined, they can kiss my big queen arse,' he says with a flourish.

'Well try to get some sleep in the next few days,' I call after him as he staggers out theatrically. He gives me a withering smile as he slides the cage door shut behind him.

The lift is just getting ready to move when a hand flies in between a gap in the metal. Instinctively, I lean over to press the 'lift hold' button, and momentarily forget about the folders. They crash to the floor as the cage door is slid open.

'I'm so sorry. Here, let me help you.' It's Tom. I scrabble around trying to retrieve the folders, the contents of which have cascaded everywhere. Frantically, I try and cram the papers into their rightful folders. Tom is crouched down next to me, and his face is just a few centimetres from mine. I tug at the collar of my jacket. The heat in the confined space is suffocating. He hands me a heap of papers and then suddenly loses his balance and accidentally bumps into me. He quickly springs back up.

'I'm so sorry. You're not hurt are you?' he asks,

sounding concerned. I look up at him. He's so delicious that for a moment I'm not sure I can move my legs. They feel like jelly. He offers a large hand down towards me. I shove the folders under my arm and manage to haul myself up, attempting the move as daintily as I can, conscious of his eyes scanning me.

'Think that makes us quits now. You took a tumble and now I have too,' he says, grinning, and I notice that his eyes are seeking out mine. He's irresistible, but I still don't trust him after what he said in the club and then practically ignoring me in favour of his phone. I quickly turn away and bend down to retrieve the rest of the folders.

'Indeed, and err thanks for, well . . .' My voice trails off. He hands me a few more folders.

'How come you have these?' he asks, scrutinising the last one from the floor.

'Oh, they're not mine. I bumped into Maxine on her way into work with them. I'm just taking them up for her.'

'I see. So why isn't she taking them herself?' he asks, looking puzzled.

'Well, I did offer,' I say, feebly, thinking what a creep he probably thinks I am. But secretly praying that if I'm ever going to get stuck in a lift again for any length of time, then, *please please please God* . . . could it actually be *right now*.

'But she shouldn't be taking them home. I'd better

let her know.' He flashes a look of disappointment as he shakes his head. This is strange – I'm surprised he thinks he's in a position to contemplate pulling her up about it. It seems far too assured. They must be on really good terms, as I can't imagine he'd get away with it otherwise. The thought makes me feel uneasy. 'Err, on second thoughts, probably best not to,' he says, awkwardly, as though he suddenly realises he's said something he shouldn't have.

The lift arrives on the canteen floor, and after Tom leaves, I carry on mulling things over until I reach the top floor.

I finally make it to Maxine's office and dump the folders down on her desk.

'Thought you said you were fit.' She shoos me away with an imperious hand, not even bothering to say thank you. I walk away, wanting to smack her beautiful face.

'Oh Gina, something's cropped up so we'll have to have our meeting at ten thirty instead.' For a second, I don't respond, I'm too busy feeling cheated at having hauled myself out of bed at six o'clock this morning for what now appears to be no apparent reason. 'Did you hear me? I said—'

'Yes, I heard you. See you at ten thirty,' I reply, wondering what would happen if I killed her. Throttled the life out of her Restylane-riddled body, right here in her office. In a sudden melodramatic moment, I toy with the mental image of myself in an orange jumpsuit, shuffling around like an American prisoner on death row, but then quickly shove the thought from my mind. Orange really isn't a flattering colour – it's so difficult to pull off, and she's *soo* not worth it.

Eradicating the thoughts of a prison stretch, I manage to restrain myself, and make my way back to the lift. As I'm walking, I mentally write out a really scathing resignation letter in my head, to console myself with instead.

I'm waiting for the lift when my mobile buzzes in my pocket. It's Sam.

'Can you talk?' she says, clandestinely, sounding like a phoney secret agent.

'Yes,' I reply, glancing around. Her manner makes me feel paranoid all of a sudden.

'Next Thursday at six p.m. Are you free?'

'Why are you whispering?' I ask. I can barely hear her.

'You said to be discreet.' I ponder on her bizarre logic before realising what she's talking about. 'Sorry it's taken so long.' Silence follows. 'Oh hang on a sec.' I hear the oven timer ping. 'Sorry about that, just had to rescue a batch of chocolate muffins. I've got you an interview.'

It takes a few seconds to sink in. I lean against the wall, clutching the phone to my ear. The feeling of relief, that I might actually escape Maxine's clutches after all, is overwhelming.

16

'Tell me again what happened.' Maxine's voice sounds amused, but her body language contradicts her. She's draped over the corner of her desk and I'm in the low chair again, forced to look up at her.

'I dropped them in the lift. Like I said, that's why the papers might be in the wrong folders,' I say, hesitantly. The way she's looking at me, she might as well be holding up a placard with the word 'liar' emblazoned across it and be done with it. I fidget and feel guilty, even though I haven't done anything wrong.

'Well, ten out of ten for imagination.' She throws her head back and shakes her mane around for a bit.

'Look, I was trying to do you a favour by bringing them up,' I say, feeling tired and irritated now, but remembering that she holds the cards to my future. 'If you don't believe me then ask Tom, he was in the lift as well.' I notice a flicker of something, almost like pleasure, dart across her face at the mention of his name. She licks her lips.

'Hang on a minute. I let you take the folders to see if

155

you could be trusted. My job is to revitalise the store, after all, and part of that is making sure we have a team that can be trusted going forward, so I was actually doing *you* the favour,' she says, in a breezy voice. Incredible. For a moment I wonder if we're actually having the same conversation.

'I'm not sure what you mean . . .' I resist the urge to be ruder – my fate is in her hands, after all – but I'm intrigued to hear her explanation.

'By giving you the opportunity to show you can be trusted, of course.' I feel my face creasing with confusion.

'So you're telling me you gave me the folders on purpose to see if I would look through them?' I say the words slowly, her logic still not really sinking in.

'Of course.' For a moment I'm speechless.

'But you told me not to take the lift,' I say, thinking ha! I've definitely caught her out now.

'Oh, yes. Sorry about that, it was rather mean of me.' She lets out a little chuckle and then holds my stare until I have to back down and look away. 'And as predicted you couldn't resist looking, could you? And who can blame you? If it's any consolation I would have done exactly the same thing in your shoes.' She glances down at my New Look heels before wrinkling her nose. I try to work out whether this means I've passed her stupid test or not and I'm under no illusion that this could be the first of many.

'So *Gina*,' she says, and I flinch. 'Did you stumble across anything interesting in the files?' Her eyes glint, it's almost as though she's fired up by trying to create a drama.

'What difference would it make if I had?'

'What do you mean, Gina?'

'Would you mind not calling me that? My name is Georgie,' I say abruptly, and the look on her face immediately makes me wish I hadn't, but I'm not going to let her trample all over me.

'As you wish.' She studies me for a few seconds, tilting her head slightly to one side. I squirm under her scrutiny. 'And good for you for making a stand.' She points at me with her pen. 'My kind of girl,' she says, quite unexpectedly. I sit back in my chair, feeling slightly more relaxed. So the name thing was another one of her little games then.

'Tell me what you meant about making a difference,' Maxine says. Then she peers at me again and I hesitate before answering.

'You already know James, and Tom seems to be quite confident about things –' I scrutinise her face to see if I've overstepped the mark – 'and well, I feel as though you don't like me. It's as if I've already done something wrong, when in fact I'm very good at my job.'

'Like you? What's that got to do with it?' She doesn't deny it. 'And if you think James has some kind of an advantage just because we used to –' she pauses, picking her words carefully as she plucks a long red hair from her sleeve – 'know each other, well then you're right off the mark. No, James had his chance with me and he blew it. I can't overlook that.' Her face is set like concrete – does this mean James doesn't even stand a chance of keeping his job then? The silence hangs in the air for a moment and I'm not sure what to say. Maxine breaks it. 'And as for Tom, well,' she looks away, 'he's an unknown entity. Anyway, there's so much to be done, so make this easy for me.'

I ponder on this revelation. From what she's saying, if I keep her sweet, then my job is safe. She has issues with both James and Tom, but my gut instinct is niggling away. Can I trust her word? For all I know she could be secretly backing Tom, expecting me to do all the hard work to make her look good in front of The Heff and the board when Women's Accessories sales figures rocket. And then she says something else.

'Oh, and by the way. Your interview at Palmers on Thursday . . . I've cancelled it.' She stares at me, without blinking. I feel the life force drain from my body as I try and think of a response.

'But you can't do that.' I cringe at the wobbliness in my voice.

'Well I have. So deal with it. You're a good sales assistant, so I'm not letting you go . . . yet.'

My jaw drops open. And what does she mean by 'yet'?

'But, how come you know about that?' I manage to

158

mumble, feeling hot and uncomfortable at having been caught out.

'Oh, didn't you know?' she starts, with false concern. 'My old PA now works for the HR director at Palmers.' Bloody typical, she would do, wouldn't she? 'So you see, Georgie, how powerful loyalty can be, and the people that work for me are always very loyal. Question is, are you?' I open my mouth to reply, but the words won't come out. Maxine may well think that her old PA is loyal, but I'd love to know what hold she has over her to make her so.

There's a tap on the door and, after throwing a questioning look at me as I still haven't replied, Maxine yells, 'Come,' and I'm saved for the time being from having to answer, by Tina, of all people. She flings open the door and practically canters over to us, her ponytail swinging like a pendulum on speed.

'Oh Maxine, you wanted to see me,' she pants. I glance at Maxine and see a look of irritation creep across her face. She's obviously got Tina's number then.

'Stop bobbing around. It annoys me.' Maxine slaps the desk to emphasise the fact.

'Oh, I'm sorry, shall I sit down then?' Tina treats me to one of her stares as she pulls up the Chesterfield armchair from the corner and, positioning it adjacent to Maxine, she perches on the edge.

'Have you got the latest sales figures for Women's Accessories?'

'Yes, right here. I guessed you might need them. I've put them in a nice folder for you,' Tina schmoozes, handing Maxine a girly pink plastic wallet.

'Thank you.' Maxine stares at Tina, who doesn't get the hint. 'You can go now.'

'Oh, right. See you later then Maxine,' Tina says, as if she's her new best friend forever. Maxine waits for the door to close before turning to me.

'This is a bit more like it. These figures are very healthy indeed,' she says, letting out a low whistle. 'So how are you getting on with your Valentine's promotions?'

I lean forward, feeling pleased with myself. Since The Heff's announcement, sales have really stepped up. It's a complete free-for-all now, with all the sales assistants mindful of the new scaled-down numbers that might emerge following Maxine's review. We're all grabbing whatever customers we can get our hands on. Some of the others have even taken to asking every customer, 'Can I help you?' within a second of them glancing at the merch. Something we used to avoid like the plague after things got out of hand with customers getting arsy and complaining about being harassed. Janine from the bingo hall on Cheriton Way almost walloped Darren in Pens when he badgered her a little too hard. Luckily, Mrs Grace stepped in and gave Janine a voucher for a free coffee in the café by way of an apology.

'Well the high-end bag sales are really benefiting from the complimentary his-and-her massage voucher with every purchase over two hundred and seventy-five pounds.' She nods her head. 'And I've even thought ahead, because some people get engaged on Valentine's Day,' I say wistfully, wondering if I'll ever be one of them. 'So, continuing the romance theme through to summer, weddings, and so on, and bearing in mind that old adage of "customers who try . . . buy", I've set up a mirror next to my counter so customers can see how a handbag will look on their shoulder, or nestling in the crook of an elbow, in proper Kardashiantastic style.' Silence follows. 'Kim Kardashian?' I explain, but Maxine just stares at me blankly. I plough on. 'And I'm seeing plenty of single women who want to treat themselves too – who needs a man to buy us a Valentine's present anyway?'

I attempt a little laugh, but she looks horrified, so I clear my throat instead. I imagine she wouldn't dream of actually buying her own present, and why would she when she probably has a string of men lining up to spoil her with gifts? 'Yes, I've even grouped together a selection of silk scarves and summery hats for customers when trying on the designer sunglasses.' I soldier on. 'Most of the time it works, they get caught up in feeling all wedding-y and can't resist buying the whole ensemble.'

'Impressive. James and Tom could learn a thing or two from you. But then they'll never have our female advantage, will they, when it comes to seducing customers into parting with their cash?' Maxine flashes her pageant smile. 'Talking of weddings, have you been invited?' Maxine tilts her head towards the door to indicate Tina.

'Yes. But it's couples only, so—'

'Snap!' She interrupts. 'You're single too, same as me. I'm going on my own so we can keep each other company. I love a good wedding, always plenty of men around,' she says, suggestively. Maxine slaps the folder shut and, taking it as a cue to leave, I stand up. 'That's all, and keep up the good work.'

'I will, and Maxine, I am loyal, especially to my friends, and to my job of course,' I add quickly.

'Good. So you won't be assuming the grass is greener then, will you?' The threat in her voice is there, loud and clear. With my backup plan scuppered I feel even more vulnerable. I try and concentrate my mind on the possibility that she cancelled my interview at Palmers because she really doesn't want me to leave. But the feeling of paranoia that's mounting by the minute is getting harder and harder to suppress.

'No,' I say quietly, as I head towards the door, which flings open just as I reach out to the handle.

'Ahh, Georgina.' The Heff appears, looking surprised to see me and clutching an enormous bouquet of red velvet roses. 'Err, these arrived.' He throws a look in Maxine's direction.

'You can put them over there,' she says, pointing towards a side cabinet, without even bothering to look at them properly.

'Err, right you are,' The Heff booms, striding past me to place the flowers down, before settling on a sofa and flinging his arm along the back in a very casual pose. An awkward silence follows.

'That'll be all.' Maxine looks at me.

'Of course,' I reply, quickly ducking out of the door.

As I make my way back to the lift, I can't help wondering why The Heff has been relegated to delivery boy now. I'd have thought that would be another job for Eddie.

17

'I'd just like to spend some time unwinding with you, if that's OK?' It's late and James and I are the only ones in the canteen again. He looks at me, edging his fingers along the top of the table until they're almost touching mine.

'Err, well I'm not sure.' I search his face, wondering what he's up to. He never used to be so flirty with me . . . I decide to address it once and for all. I quickly pull my hand away.

'Look James, I'm flattered, really I am, but what about your wife?' I ask, scrutinising his face.

'What about her?' he says, his face not changing. I can't believe his front. He's always seemed like such a decent guy. In fact, I've seen him coming back to the office at lunchtime with armfuls of presents for her in the run-up to the Christmas holidays. I even heard him on the phone one evening, outside the big Wetherspoon's in the centre of town, when we all went out after work to celebrate Debbie in Haberdashery's fiftieth. His voice was all soft and interested.

'Well, don't you think your wife might mind?' I reply, crossly, wondering if he was this forward with Maxine.

'Soon to be ex-wife.' There's a long silence, and then it registers. I stare at him and see a puzzled look on his face.

'What did you say?' My pulse quickens.

'Oh right. You don't know, do you?' James clutches his head in his hands.

'Know what?'

'I'm getting divorced. I just presumed you knew,' he says, peeping through his fingers. He shakes his head, his voice filled with concern. 'Georgie, I'm so sorry, what must you think of me? No wonder you couldn't wait to escape from the bar that night.' I sit in silence, trying to process this information. Poor James.

'James, I didn't know.'

'It figures,' he says, shaking his head again. 'Yes, Rebecca decided she preferred my best man to me. Apparently he's more ambitious than I am, oh and better in bed, I think she also mentioned, when I wouldn't agree to let her have the cat. So, under the circumstances, I agreed to a divorce,' he finishes, with a wry smile.

'I'm sorry. Truly I am. But why didn't you tell me before now? I thought we were friends.' I can't believe it. So he's not a two-timing flirtatious rat after all. My mind races.

'We are. But you know how it is in work. There just never seemed like an appropriate moment. I guess I just presumed you knew. Eddie knows, and I thought with you and him being such good friends, he would have told you.' I think of Eddie – lovely loyal Eddie, even if he is a massive moaner; it's not his style to break a confidence, never has been.

'James, I feel dreadful now. With the uncertainty at work and everything else going on,' I say, thinking his wife must be completely insane to let him slip through her fingers. I notice the tightness in his shoulders, and for the first time I really see him. He has the look of a man who's been through the wringer.

'Well, now we've cleared that up, will you please come out for a drink with me?' He grins.

'I'd love to,' I reply, and all of my doubts about him instantly evaporate. I can't wait to call Sam, she's going to well and truly freak out over this.

18

After several large glasses of Pinot, and lots of talking and laughing, it's nearly closing time. James, who is sitting opposite me in the red leather banquette booth, leans over the narrow table towards me.

'Shall we do this again?' he says, staring straight into my eyes.

'Depends what "this" is,' I tease.

'A date, of course, unless you're in the habit of frequenting intimate bars with all of your colleagues.' He smiles and takes my hand in his, giving it a little squeeze.

'In that case, yes, why not?' I smile, thinking it might be fun, but then wondering if it's such a good idea when we're going to be competing at work, and he has just been dumped by his wife. Hmm, guess there's no harm in seeing how it goes.

'Great. But let's just keep this to ourselves – neither of us needs the wagging tongues at the moment,' he says, stroking the back of my hand. 'And the last thing I want is for you to be cited in the divorce. No, I want it to go as smoothly as possible.'

'I agree, as long as you're not just saying so in case a particular person called Maxine finds out?' I say before I can stop myself.

His face drops and I immediately know I should have kept my mouth shut. I scan his eyes for clues as to whether he still has a thing for her.

'You know about that then?' he says, staring intently at his empty wine glass. He pulls his hand away.

'Yes, you know how news travels in Carrington's.'

'It was well and truly over years ago,' he says, taking my hand again.

'So, did you two work together or something?' I say, trying to sound uninterested. I'm curious, no more, and I don't want him thinking I'm some kind of mad bunny boiler.

'Not exactly. I met her on a training course. It didn't last long though. It was around the same time I met Rebecca.'

'So I imagine Maxine was pretty pissed off at being dumped for another woman,' I say, feeling my way for fear of probing too much.

'Just a bit, but then can you blame her? I did mess her around.' I decide not to push it any further but then he says, 'Like I told her in the meeting, it was a long time ago and we have to be professional about it, given our work situation.' So they discussed it then.

'But won't it be difficult, with her overseeing things? She is the boss now, after all.'

'Sure. But it doesn't have to affect things between us, and I promise I won't betray you. Believe me . . . I know what it feels like.'

'Of course,' I say, squeezing his hand, but wondering how Maxine really feels.

'So we're agreed then? This will be our secret? I really don't want you getting dragged into the divorce proceedings . . . Rebecca is desperate to try and pin something on me, and as she refuses to move out until the house is sold . . . well, it's complicated.' He drops his eyes.

'Oh James, of course that's fine,' I agree, thinking it's probably better this way until I see where it's going.

We leave the bar, stumbling and giggling our way up the narrow basement steps, the fresh evening air exhilarating as we reach the pavement, where James grabs hold of my hand. For a moment it feels strange as his warm fingers entwine mine. I can't believe what's happened this evening. Only a few hours ago he was off-limits.

'You OK?' he says, heading towards the taxi rank, which is deserted.

'I'm great. Never better.'

At the end of the road a taxi with its light off performs a swift U-turn and grinds to a halt alongside us.

'I'm on my way home, going east, so if you're heading in my direction?' James turns to me, and as he lives the opposite way I presume the evening is over. He puts a finger on my lips and leans down to whisper into my ear.

'I'm so glad we've finally got together,' he says, softly. I tiptoe up, intending to kiss him on the cheek, but he gently turns my face towards his and kisses me tenderly, his lips soft on mine, his hand around my waist, pulling me in close. My stomach flips and my right foot actually pops up like it always does for the heroine in those soppy films.

'Sorry to break up the party.' It's the taxi driver, and he's tapping the meter. We instantly break away. James looks into my eyes and I just know he wants to continue things. In an instant I realise that I do too. I forget all my reservations and decide to go for it.

'It's Mercer Street,' James says to the taxi driver as he pulls open the door for me. I step inside and reach my hand out to his.

'Are you sure?' he asks, and I block out the doubts, focusing on the moment instead.

'Yes,' I smile. James gets in beside me and puts his arm around my shoulders. I cuddle into him and savour the feeling of anticipation at what the rest of the evening will be like. And then I remember, I still haven't managed to tell him about the extra commission coming through from Malikov. He'll be so chuffed. Perhaps we'll even go on that holiday after all. But I don't want to talk about work and spoil our night together, so I make a mental note instead before turning towards him for another kiss.

19

'Oh my God. Tell me again. And start right from the beginning, and don't you dare leave out any details. A girl needs details. Start at the bit where he threw you on the bed and ripped your knickers off,' Sam breathes in a whispery voice right into my ear. It's the morning after and we're huddled next to each other in a booth at the far corner of the café. I just couldn't wait to tell her, so the very minute James left my flat this morning, I sent Sam a text and we agreed to meet in here right away before I start work.

'Cheeky, I didn't say he ripped my knickers off,' I say, remembering how gloriously slow and sexy he was.

'I know. But there's nothing wrong with a bit of embellishment to spice things up even more.' Sam laughs. 'And you are glowing girl. Glowing. It's like there's a sex aura all around you.' She laughs and I nudge her in the ribs.

'Shush, someone might hear you. He said to be discreet – the divorce, remember.'

'I know.' She rolls her eyes. 'And you know what this means?' Sam says, stifling a squeal of excitement.

'What?'

'*Valentine's Day!* A few more dates in the bag and you'll practically be an established couple by then. What will you get him? I'm treating Nathan to an exquisite La Perla Frou Frou ruffled tulle balcony with matching ruffleback knickers and a pair of sky-high cherry-red Choo's.'

'Wow, I didn't know Jimmy Choo made man-size heels too,' I say, my mind working overtime at the possibility of spending Valentine's Day with James. I wonder if he's been invited to Tina's wedding? Bound to be. We could go together – maybe Mrs Grace was right after all.

'Ha ha, very funny. Soo, one down. And one to go.'

'What do you mean?'

'The bombshell. Tom of course . . . keep all your options open, I say.'

'Stop it!' I smile, but the mention of Tom makes me feel uncomfortable suddenly, and I'm not sure I even want to think about why that might be.

'But he's sooo HOT he's practically on fire,' she shouts with such indignation it makes me laugh out loud. I slap a hand over my mouth when one of the waitresses, Stacey, looks up from a table she's wiping nearby.

'You know, it still hasn't quite sunk in yet, this thing with James,' I whisper, pausing to ponder for a moment. 'Maybe it was a dream,' I add . . . and maybe something inside me is beginning to wish it was.

'It was no dream, trust me. Nothing gets past me, not when it comes to men. This is real, babeee,' Sam says, her voice jumping up a couple of notes.

'Yes, you're right.' But I can't stop those doubts resurfacing. 'What if it's too soon?'

'What do you mean?'

'You know . . . sleeping with him on the first date,' I say, keeping my voice really low.

'Don't be daft. You've known each other for years. Besides, it's the second date, if you want to get really specific about it.' She laughs and nudges me gently. 'Anyway, that's what the suffragettes did for us, they gave us that choice.' I grin at her bizarre logic. Maybe she's right, lots of people have flings, why shouldn't I?

'That's better,' Sam says as she sees me smile. 'So, are you feeling better about the job thing?' She winks.

'Stop it.' I smile furtively. 'Yes, I suppose so, but knowing about him and Maxine makes me feel uncomfortable,' I add, thinking what a double whammy it would be if I were to lose my job and the pair of them got back together.

'Did you ask him about her?'

'Yes, and he seems to be OK with the situation.'

'Well, there you go. Nothing to worry about then.'

'I'm not so sure. James might be over it but I don't trust Maxine. She's up to something.'

'I don't blame you for being wary. You know she called me yesterday. Apparently she's well aware that sales assistants are covering for each other so they can "abscond" during work hours to visit the café. Said she would appreciate it if I didn't indulge them as they're putting Carrington's in jeopardy. Can you believe that? Good job I have lots of other customers, or I'd be out of business once word of that gets around,' Sam snorts.

'See what I mean. She's horrible. And I wouldn't put it past her to sack me and give James my section just to try and win him back, leaving me joining the dole queue. Or . . . she'll find out he stayed last night, get all jealous and try to ruin it some other way.' Sam shakes her head. 'And OK, I know staff shouldn't be bunking off, but we've all been coming to the café for – like – forever, and it's practically recycling – if we spend our wages in here, then it's just going back into the store.'

'Good point. Although technically it doesn't because I lease the space, so the money goes to me, but hey . . . it's a nice thought. Hold on!' Sam clutches my arm, with a worried look on her face. 'You don't think she'll suggest ending my lease and putting Carrington's staff in here instead, do you, as part of her revamp?'

'Why would you think that?'

'I don't know, but a memo came this morning, inviting a member of my staff on some team-building thing.'

'That's weird,' I say, trying to work out if Sam's fear is founded. 'Oh well, maybe it was just a mistake,' I add, erring on the side of optimism. 'My session is the first Sunday in Feb. What will you do? Can't you nominate yourself and keep me company?'

'Would do hun, but I've already promised Dad I'd accompany him to some really important polo match business function.'

'Hmm,' I groan, feeling disappointed.

'I'll make Ciaran go instead. He could do with a bit of team building. Serve him right for not telling me, his TEAM MATE, about the engagement,' she snorts. 'Besides, won't James be going?'

'Ooh, I forgot about that, I checked the list and he's down for the same session.'

'See, wouldn't you rather he keep you company?' Sam pauses for a moment, then claps a hand to her mouth. 'Oh my God, I can't believe I haven't told you yet.'

'What?' I say, suddenly desperate to hear her news.

'Nathan has invited me to his parents' holiday home in Italy. Can you believe it? Not a mini-break either, no – a *whole week*.' Sam is beside herself with glee and sounds as though she's swallowed a can of helium.

'That's fantastic!' Her excitement is infectious. 'Tell me all about it,' I demand, leaning in closer to her.

'Well, his parents live by Lake Como and he wants me to meet them. They're celebrating their golden wedding anniversary, on February the fourteenth, and, well, he's invited me to the party, and to meet them of course,' she says, sounding all bubbly and happy.

'Oh Sam, I'm so thrilled for you. I take it you two are serious then?' I ask, hoping that's the case.

'Yep, meeting the parents, it doesn't get more serious than that. And Dad is thrilled.'

'I bet he is, and I'm really pleased for you too. Just imagine . . . both of us with a man at the same time – that's a rarity.'

'Sure is.'

And then it dawns on me.

'Hang on a minute. Did you say February the four-teenth? As in Valentine's Day?'

'Yes, so romantic. Why?' she replies, slowly.

'That's the day of Tina's wedding. I was hoping you'd come with me.' My heart sinks at the thought of having to go on my own or, worse, with Maxine.

'Sorry hun, no can do, I'm not missing this for anything or anyone – not Ciaran, not even my best friend.' Sam laughs. 'James will be going, though – yet another chance to keep you company.'

'Ahh, good thinking,' I say, immediately perking up at the thought.

'Anyway, I'll be there for the hen do. You know she's asked me to provide a gourmet lunch? Money no object, apparently, as long as there's a massive maca-roon mountain and a chocolate fountain, she said. I was surprised to see your name on the catering list though.'

'I was surprised too. I think I'm only invited so she

can spend the day making out I'm jealous. She thinks I'm after Ciaran,' I say, breathing a sigh of relief that Sam will be around to ease the tension.

'Mmm, is he still hanging around you a lot?'

'Not really. We tweet, that's all.'

'Still think he fancies you,' Sam says, raising her eyebrows.

'Stop it.'

'Fine. But it could explain why she's so jealous. Besides, you don't have to go to the hen do.' My heart lifts at the prospect of snubbing Tina's half-baked invite and not going, after all.

'I know, but I should keep her sweet. She's already *had a word*,' I roll my eyes, 'about my sales sheet, making threats to withhold my commission. I can't afford for her to be awkward about it and deliberately delay the payment or something,' I say. I'm banking on it to pay towards my car tax due this month.

We say our goodbyes, and as I pull my bag onto my shoulder, my mobile buzzes. It's a text message from James and I feel a soft tingle as I tap the view button to read it.

Thank you for a wonderful night. Sorry I had to dash off x.

I hug the phone to my chest, knowing last night might have felt like a dream but the message right here on the screen proves it was definitely real. I refuse to think of the consequences for now. It's just so great feeling buzzy and desirable again, for the first time since Brett broke my heart. And maybe, just maybe, I'll have an actual bona-fide date for Valentine's Day . . .

20

The atmosphere on the shop floor is feverish. Every time a customer emerges through the revolving doors there's practically a stampede to get to them first. We're all desperate to grab the sales, although I've noticed Tom doesn't join in the melee. Instead he spends most of the time talking in a hushed voice into the phone behind his counter, schmoozing brand managers for personal shopper leads, no doubt.

It's been a while since my night with James and, although we've bumped into each other a couple of times in the staff room, he's been pretty distant with me, so I can't help wondering if it was just a one-night stand after all. Maybe it's too soon – he's not even divorced yet – or maybe he wants to get back with Maxine instead. Or perhaps he's just decided it's totally inappropriate, given the work situation. I try to put it out of my mind, but then, almost as though the universe is listening, the phone behind my counter rings.

'Georgina, we have a massive bunch of flowers here for you.' My mood lifts as Betty gives me the news.

Slamming the phone down, I rush to the switchboard room and pluck the card from the hand-tied arrangement of lipstick-pink roses. The message is cryptic.

Until next time.

Trust James to be so discreet. I hug the flowers to me, revelling in our secret, and the doubt in my mind instantly disappears.

'So, who's the admirer then?' one of the guys from Menswear bellows the minute I arrive in the staff room. I ignore him and place the flowers in the sink.

Eddie saunters over to me.

'About time you got yourself a decent man,' he sniffs, then leans into me and whispers, 'Who is he?' For a brief second I contemplate telling him. I know I can trust him, but I decide not to, wanting to keep it quiet for a while longer.

'Oh, just some guy I met a few weeks ago.' I try to sound laid back, hoping the uncertainty in my voice doesn't let me down.

'Well, he must be keen. Flowers like that don't come cheap.' Eddie shakes his head knowingly.

'I know,' I say, mulling the implications over.

'God, is that the time?' he puffs dramatically, looking up at the wall clock. 'Catch you later, doll face. Madam has me running errands, got to collect something from HR.' He pushes his bottom lip out and is just about to leave when he turns back. 'Ooh, almost forgot, been meaning to tell you,' he says, lowering his voice.

'What is it?'

'Guess who I saw getting very intimate yesterday?' He steals a furtive look around the room.

'Who?' I say, immediately desperate to know.

'Only our resident supermodels, Tom and the tapeworm host,' he whispers, and I raise an eyebrow. 'The beautiful people – actually snogging they were.'

'*Really?*' I ask, trying to sound indifferent, but I can't help leaning in, ready for his response. It shouldn't matter to me, but suddenly I find it does.

'Yep, down the side of the store by the car park. I only got a glimpse as I was going past on the bus, but it looked very passionate; he had his back against a wall and she was practically licking his colon. Lucky cow, what I wouldn't do for a bit of him.' I ponder on the information for a moment. So, Maxine *is* playing me then. She must be backing Tom. 'And that's not all. I overheard her doing the phone sex thing on the BlackBerry again. All panty and flirty she was before realising her door was ajar. Never seen her move so fast when I popped my head around the door on purpose just to wind her up. Anyway, watch your back with them.'

'Mmm. Will do, and thanks for the tip-off.' I wonder if James knows about it. I make a mental note to ask him next time we're alone. 'Thanks for letting me know,' I finish.

I decide to try and avoid Tom from now on. I don't see why I should put in all the hard work while he sits around whispering into the phone waiting for Maxine to sack me. It's obviously her he's chatting to. He may be drop-dead gorgeous with impeccable manners, but it's not enough to overlook the fact he can't be trusted. I feel disproportionately upset by how this makes me feel, but quickly push the thoughts away and try to concentrate on what Eddie is saying instead.

'No problem, that's what friends are for.'

Eddie leaves and my mobile vibrates inside my pocket. Seeing it's James, I duck out into the corridor for some privacy.

'Just a quick call.' His voice sounds distant, as if he's in a tunnel.

'You OK, you sound like you've fallen down a drain?' I say, instantly wishing I'd thought of something slightly less prosaic to say.

'Yes, I'm fine. I'm in the Gents upstairs – only place I could think of for some privacy. Just about to go in to my weekly meeting with Maxine.' His voice sounds rushed.

'Oh, good luck.'

'Thanks. How are you getting on with her?' he asks, sounding genuinely interested, as though he has all the time in the world for me.

'Honestly. I'm not sure,' I say, wondering whether I should elaborate, but probably best to wait until he isn't in such a rush.

'Yeah, she can be a bit like that.' I smart momentarily

at the familiarity in his voice. 'Anyway, I was just calling to see if you fancy dinner on Saturday. I could pick you up around eightish?'

'Yes, I'd love to.'

'Great. Let's catch up properly then.' And before I have a chance to thank him for the flowers, there's a click and I realise he's ended the call.

*

Lunchtime in the canteen, and everyone's talking about the team-building event. It's in Brighton and we have to arrive the night before to be certain of an early start, which makes it a whole lot more exciting seeing as James will be there too. And we're staying overnight in a hotel. It was going to be a B&B but Sam said Caroline from the salon told her she'd overheard Camille on the phone putting her Gucci-clad foot down and insisting on doing things properly, and that Carrington's may be facing a decline but a reputation for providing quality must still be maintained.

Melissa, our sturdy plain-clothes store detective, appears to have taken on the role of events organiser and is asking everyone for a bust size. She's come up with some whacky idea of renting a room at Lucky Voice for a karaoke session on the Saturday night and making it into a bit of a stag do for Ciaran. Any excuse for a bit of debauchery, especially since she found out Tina won't be there to spoil the fun for everyone. Melissa's cousin owns a printing shop and has even offered to make up special T-shirts for us all.

'Georgie . . . just in time. What bust size shall I get you. Extra tight?' She casts a roving eye at my chest. Instinctively I cross my arms.

'In your dreams. I'll be wearing my own clothes,' I retaliate, and the others all laugh. Melissa then turns her attentions on Arnie, a warehouse guy from Sweden.

'Arnie,' Melissa starts, full of exaggerated bonhomie, 'let me guess . . . 6XL for you?'

'Aren't you getting me confused with the size of your head?' he retorts.

I relax into the atmosphere, which feels just like it used to be before Maxine turned up. We're all laughing – everybody that is, except Tom. He's still whispering into his phone. He looks up and around at us all and then carries on talking. I feel uncomfortable. Maybe he's spying for Maxine.

I glance up just in time to see Tina standing by the soup urn. She has a strange expression on her face and is busy scribbling something down in a red notebook. I wonder how long she's been standing there, and my paranoia increases. She might also be spying for Maxine! Nothing would surprise me any more. I shiver with unease.

21

After trawling through my wardrobe several times over I've decided on a butterfly print Zara maxi dress that I bought in last summer's sale, together with the Gina sandals from Sam. Glancing at the clock on the shelf, I see that I've got plenty of time to finish getting ready before James arrives.

My stomach growls, but I try and ignore it. I haven't eaten anything since breakfast – well, apart from some sushi and a KitKat, in an attempt to look as slim as possible for this evening. Just as I contemplate foraging in the kitchen for a small snack, the phone rings.

'Only me.' Sam's voice sounds full of happiness. 'All set for this evening?' she asks, brightly.

'Think so, just make-up to do, and then I'll be ready,' I say. I walk out onto the balcony and settle down on my comfy sun lounger. I've got plenty of time for a chat.

'What underwear have you got on?' she demands, and I burst into laughter at her directness.

'Well, if you must know, Sam, I'm not wearing any

yet. I'm still in my dressing gown,' I say, keeping my voice down so the neighbours don't hear.

'It's important to have good underwear on tonight,' she says, sounding all serious and mumsy.

'Yes, yes I know.'

'Why don't you wear that gorgeous black lace set?' I don't reply straight away, I'm too busy mulling over the implication and, amid the still-lingering doubts, I feel a tingle of anticipation about a repeat performance with James.

'Mmm . . . maybe. How's Nathan?' I ask, changing the subject and crossing my fingers that it's still going well. You never know with Sam.

'Oh Georgie, he's such a treat. And I think I actually might be in love with him. For real.' Her voice soars as she tells me.

'Sam that's fantastic. What about him, has he said anything?' I tread carefully, wary of putting my foot in it. Sam isn't suspicious of men like I've been since the break-up with Brett, but then Alfie has never let her down. And Sam always falls head over heels in love very quickly, although she's been caught out a few times over the years because of it.

'Oh, he's already told me he loves me,' she replies, airily, and then adds, 'which is why I'm making him wait. I'm not taking any chances this time around.'

'So you managed to offload that other guy then. Justin, wasn't it?' I say, casting my mind back.

'Oh yes, he was actually quite sweet about it when I eventually told him I wasn't interested. God, that seems like ages ago now.'

'Well that's fantastic. I'm so pleased for you. You deserve to find your *one*, your *real one*.'

'Maybe I'll tell him while we're away. I can't wait,' she exclaims. I think of the team-building do, and the heady feeling I had when James told me he'd called the hotel and asked them to put us in adjoining rooms.

'Changing the topic completely, Nathan bumped into Tom a few evenings ago at the squash club. Anyway, Nathan asked him how the new job was going but he didn't say much about it. Only that there's a woman he likes.'

I knew it.

'So that confirms it then.' I was right all along.

'What do you mean?'

'It's Maxine. They've got some ruse going on,' I say, neatly fitting the jigsaw together.

'Are you sure?'

'Eddie even saw them together. Actually snogging!' I feel slightly sick as I tell her this. Maybe I should have eaten more today; it's no wonder I feel weird.

'*Nooo,*' she replies, dramatically.

'Yep. But then when his name came up during my one-to-one with her, she commented that he's an "unknown entity". Made out like she didn't even know him. To cover her tracks, I guess.'

'How sneaky is that?' Sam says, indignantly.

'Totally,' I reply, craning my neck to keep an eye on the clock in the lounge. An hour has rushed by. 'Anyway, Sam, I must finish getting ready. He'll be here soon.'

'Oh yes, off you go. Call me as soon as you can. And remember, the black lace. He won't be able to keep his hands off you,' Sam advises before hanging up.

*

I'm checking myself again in the full-length mirror on the back of my bedroom door. The dress accentuates my curvy figure nicely and the new eyeliner in plum really brings out the turquoise of my eyes. I've even managed to get my hair looking really big. I check my false eyelashes again. Perfect! They're all velvety and fluttery. I add another slick of Benefit minty fresh California Kissin' lip gloss, which on inspection of my teeth, really does make them look extra white. A spritz of Cavalli from a tester bottle that Scarlett in Celebrity Perfumes gave me, and I'm ready and waiting for him. I lean into the mirror and, pursing my lips, I close my eyes just enough so I can peek through the lashes to see what James will see when he kisses me. I feel like a teenager again.

The sudden chime of the doorbell makes me jump and I shoot back from the mirror as though I've been caught out. He's here, and he's early. I rush to the hallway, and then pause beside the hall table. Taking a deep breath, I wait a second until my heart slows down.

I open the door and instantly the welcoming smile slips from my face. James is standing in front of me wearing scruffy old jeans and a washed-out old sweatshirt.

'I'm not stopping,' he barks. His eyes are flashing.

'James, what is it?' Something terrible has happened. God, I hope nobody has died.

'Dinner is cancelled.' He glowers at me and I instantly realise that no one is dead. He's raging angry . . . and it's with me.

'What do you mean? Look, why don't you come in?' I stand aside. He barges past me and strides off into the lounge. I hurry after him. When I get into the room, he's standing beside the fireplace, his fists clenching and unclenching. 'James, please tell me what's going on.'

'Why don't you tell *me*?' His voice is tight. He rakes a hand through his dishevelled hair and I bite down hard on my bottom lip. Swallowing, I taste blood, metallic against the mint of the lip gloss.

'James, I don't know what you're talking about.' For a brief moment, his face softens, but then quickly clouds over again.

'I'll spell it out for you, shall I?' he says, sarcastically. Then he moves away from the fireplace and, standing opposite me, I see his eyes are glimmering with rage. 'I thought I could trust you,' he shouts, his face glowering down at mine.

'You can.' I try to sound calm as I rack my brain searching for a clue as to what's happened.

'Well, I used to think so, but it turns out that you're just like the rest of them.' The insinuation is sickening.

'What do mean? I hope you're not suggesting that I'm like Rebecca.'

'Don't bring her into it,' he says, defensively, and far too quickly. So, he still holds a candle for her then. So, I was right . . . he does need more time.

'Please, just tell me what's happened.' I can hear my own heart beating.

'Like you don't know. You've been playing me all along, probably thinking that you'll just reel me in and steal my job from under me . . . and grab yourself a nice Valentine's Day present too, while you're at it. Was that your little plan?' he says, sarcastically. I've never seen him like this before. The silence that follows is excruciating.

'James, that's not true. You were the one who asked *me* out, remember?' I say, softly, in a vain attempt to try and unravel what's happened.

'Yeah, like a fool, don't remind me.'

I feel the anger rising inside me now, and I can't help retaliating. 'Well I'm sorry if the memory is so ghastly for you,' I reply, my voice trembling. Then I notice his shoulders drop and his face changes.

'Look, I'm sorry. I shouldn't have come here. Georgie, I can't do this. Us. I'm sorry . . . it's just too soon,' he says, calming down. He shoves his hands in his pockets and turns to leave.

A sudden inexplicable sense of relief rushes through me, but I still want to know what I'm supposed to have done wrong.

'James, you can't just storm in here making accusations and then waltz right out again. I know it must be hard getting divorced but . . .' I reach out to grab his arm and catch the back of his sweatshirt instead. He stops and turns towards me, a look of utter contempt on his face.

'You have no idea! Now get your thieving hands off me.' I stare at him, the tears stinging my cheeks. *Thieving!* The word is like a knife stabbing into my stomach. 'Just like your father.' I reel backwards in shock. I grab hold of the hall table as if it's an emergency buoy. James reaches out and touches my arm and I'm sure I spot a brief flicker of concern dart through his eyes, but it evaporates before I can be sure.

'But I thought you understood . . .' My voice is low, a whisper almost.

'Why, because I kept your little secret? Like a fool.' He looks away, snatching his hand back.

'So what is it exactly that I'm supposed to have stolen, James?' My voice sounds cold now, masking the churn of emotions that are swirling around inside me. He

191

reaches for the lock on the front door and pulls it open. He turns to face me.

'Malikov. Ring any bells?' My hand flies to my throat. Oh God. The necklace. He knows. Malikov must have gone back on his request for privacy and told him.

'James, please. I can explain,' I say, the words barely audible.

'Georgie, you know the rules,' he adds, suddenly sounding all businesslike and distant. My body is trembling, with fear of his anger and of losing everything I've worked so hard for.

'I know,' I murmur, hanging my head in shame.

'*Whaat?* Did you think you'd just keep all of the commission for yourself and I wouldn't find out?' There's a silence as I drag myself up to speed. So this isn't about the necklace, after all.

'God, is that what this is all about? James, I'm sorry, I meant to tell you that Malikov had bought more bags,' I say, desperate for him to see that he's got it all wrong. Hoping I can salvage something. Make it good between us again.

'So why didn't you then? He was my customer originally, what happened to us sharing the sales commission?' Silence follows.

'I tried to . . .' I pause, suddenly feeling hot and uncomfortable. I contemplate telling him everything. I search his eyes. They're full of rage, mixed with disgust, and I have my answer. I know that I can't risk it. 'Before we went for that drink, remember? And you said you didn't want to talk about work and with everything going on . . .' As the words come out I know they sound lame and I feel like a pathetic idiot. I should have made damn sure I remembered so he could have claimed his half of the commission. I hate myself.

'Don't make me laugh. Malikov won't even take my calls any more,' he says, sounding sarcastic again. He shakes his head at me and a wave of nausea washes through me.

'But I can fix it. All you need to do is add half to your sales sheet,' I plead. It's not worth falling out with him over it, but he interrupts.

'God, you are so clueless. Maxine has already made me aware of what a *fantastic* customer experience you're giving Malikov. No, it's too late for that. We're finished.'

Something inside me snaps.

'But it's OK for you to gossip behind my back with your ex-girlfriend, Maxine,' I snipe, not really thinking or caring what I say. 'Don't tell me that you didn't know she'd bring up my personal business and quite possibly use it to get rid of me?'

'Is that what you *really* think?' shaking his head at me in disbelief. But before I can answer, he's gone.

The door bounces back against the frame before slamming shut and I sink down into a heap behind it. I feel wretched. I just wish everything could go back to how it was pre-Maxine. I haven't slept properly for ages, and the constant feeling of paranoia is like a cancer spreading through every part of me. I was so stupid to think that selling the necklace to clear my debts would mean getting a proper night's sleep. The insomnia is worse now than ever.

I manage to drag myself up and into the bedroom. My nails catch as I pull at the dress, and a ripping sound resonates around the room. I hurl the dress across the floor and kick off the Gina shoes, which slam against the mirror. I tear at my underwear; the giggly phone call with Sam seems an age ago. I feel numb. So much for letting myself dream of actually having a date for the wedding. At this rate, I'm going to end up a lonely old bag with just cats for company.

22

I arrive at work and manage to dump my coat in the staff room and make it into the lift unnoticed. I've only travelled two floors before it shudders to a halt and The Heff steps in. He takes one look at my blotchy, tear-stained face before turning to face the doors. Probably petrified that I'm going to break down and get all emotional on him if he talks to me. As soon as the lift reaches the shop floor, he steps aside and feigns fascination with his mobile to avoid saying goodbye.

I make a beeline to my counter. My eyes feel raw. I peer at my reflection in the black screen of the PC and can just make out my eyes. They look like small stones peeping out from a pair of overly engorged mushrooms. No wonder Walter was scared to be alone with me.

After James's horrible exit on Saturday evening, I spent the rest of Sunday and Monday alone with two bottles of rosé to keep me company whilst I wallowed in tears. But there is one tiny consolation: I've lost five pounds in two days. So, after a pep talk from Sam, I tried to disguise my eyes, firstly with a peppermint gel eye mask that's been nestling in amongst the peas at the back of my freezer compartment, before resorting to concealer, followed by practically a whole tube of BB cream. But there's no escaping the fact that I look horrendous and it's no more than I deserve.

Stealing a look around the screen, I see that James isn't here and I puff out a little sigh of relief. I turn my phone over inside my pocket and, like I have a million times already, I contemplate calling him. All of a sudden the phone vibrates, signifying the arrival of a text message, and it startles me. My shaking hands lose their grip and the phone tumbles down onto the carpet. I hesitate for a second before reaching down to retrieve it, praying the message is from James. But it's not, it's from Eddie.

You ok flower? x

My heart drops with disappointment, but I could do with another perspective so, after squaring it with Annie, I quickly reply.

Chat? x

When I arrive at the door to the staff corridor, Eddie is hovering next to it, his face looking anxious with concern.

'What's up, sweet cheeks?' he whispers, glancing over

at the staff lift where a couple of Jo Malone concession girls are within earshot of us.

'Not here, let's go for a walk.' I motion down the corridor and he follows me. I wait until we're alone.

'Oh Ed, I've ruined everything,' I sniff, tears threatening again.

'What do you mean?' His voice is full of concern.

'Promise you won't tell a soul?'

'You know I won't, but if it makes you feel any better, then I promise. Cross my heart and hope to die a grisly, gory death,' he says, before poking his tongue out.

'I'm serious, not anyone,' I say, searching his eyes for reassurance.

'Georgie please, you're scaring me now. What is it? I give you my word that I won't breathe a word to another living soul. Not ever! Now please tell me, if you think it will help. But you don't have to . . . you know that, don't you? I'm happy to fuss you and remain oblivious of whatever dastardly deed it is you've committed.'

'I know. And thank you.' My eyes well up at his kindness.

'I've been seeing someone.'

'OK,' he starts, slowly. 'Do you want to tell me who? Although I'm pretty sure I can guess.' I blink at him. Silence follows. 'It's James, isn't it?'

I bite my lip and nod.

'How do you know?' I ask, suddenly worried

that everyone in the store will have noticed what was going on.

'Honey pie, I know you and, well, I've seen the way you two are with each other. Surely it's a good thing you finally managed to get it together,' he says, gently.

'Well yes, it was fun. At least it was until I managed to completely blow it. He thinks I deliberately stole sales commission from Malikov, instead of sharing it like we normally do. You know, as part of this horrendous recession-busting revamp thing.' Eddie raises an enquiring eyebrow. 'I meant to tell him, but with Malikov not taking his calls . . .' My voice trails off. I know it's a poor excuse. But I can't say anything about the necklace and how distracted I was – no matter how strong our friendship is, I just can't put Eddie in that position, not when he's The Heff's BA. He'd be in trouble too . . . if it ever came out that he knew and didn't report me. 'This damn revamp is ruining everything,' I add, quickly. 'He was so furious and then I lost it and accused him of bitching to Maxine about me. He knows about Dad too . . . and well, it's over.'

'Well, that explains it, sugar.' I turn to look at him.

'What do you mean?' I could hug him for not judging me.

'James has pulled out of the team-building weekend. Personal reasons apparently.' I feel crushed. I'd been clinging on to the thought that I might just be able to salvage something of our relationship over the weekend away, explain properly that I really had meant to share the commission.

'Oh, sweetheart,' Eddie puts an arm around my shoulders and I lean into him, grateful for a moment of comfort, 'I'm sure he'll come around. He's a nice guy, probably just overreacting after the way Rebecca did the dirty on him. He's bound to be a bit sensitive for a while.'

'I don't know. Maybe I should try and talk to him. You know, apologise or something.'

'Could do. But wait until after the weekend and see how you feel then.'

We turn the corner and I open my mouth to reply, but instead we both stop short. Eddie drops his arm from my shoulders. Maxine and Tom are just up ahead of us at the end of the long corridor, and she has her right arm linked through his and her body practically wrapped around his. Her left hand is stroking his chest. The pair of them look very cosy indeed. Rooted to the spot, neither of us moves. Eddie clutches my arm. We wait until they disappear inside one of the stock rooms, the door of which Maxine kicks shut behind them with the spike of her Loub.

'Did you see that?' I feel strangely satisfied that I've actually witnessed it now with my own eyes, although it doesn't quite account for the horrible sinking sensation that follows.

'Yes, very clandestine,' Eddie sniffs. I feel totally played.

I don't stand a chance of keeping my job when Maxine is in bed with Tom. And most likely James too, for all I know.

*

When I get back to the shop floor, James is back. He looks straight through me as I walk past and I feel like such a fool as the weak smile that I managed to coax onto my face in preparation for seeing him withers away. I make it to my counter and Annie gives me a memo from upstairs, saying Malikov's associate still hasn't produced photo ID and address verification so, unless he does, he can't buy the Bottega bags . . . the sale is way over the £9,000 limit for one customer transaction. I pick up the phone to call him.

'Mr Malikov is unavailable,' a growly voice says. 'I am his –' there's a pause – 'personal assistant.'

'OK, this is Georgie Hart calling from Carr—'

'He is not available,' the growly voice interrupts.

'Yes, you said,' I reply, tightly. I'm not in the mood for this.

'I will take a message.'

I hesitate, quickly weighing up what to say.

'Please tell him that it won't be possible to accommodate the request discussed at our last meeting, and would he kindly let his associate know. It's just that his associate doesn't spea—'

'Yes, he will tell him. Goodbye.' The line goes dead. I mutter 'English' to myself, before hanging up.

After flogging some Cath Kidston gear to a group of Chinese tourists, it's my lunch break. Deciding on some comfort food to cheer myself up, I make my way to the café. I'm in the queue with a large mug of squirty-cream-topped hot chocolate and two red velvet cupcakes on my tray, when I spot Tom and Maxine further up ahead at the till. Maxine grabs a carton of coconut juice from their shared tray and breezes back past the queue towards the exit. As she passes me she stops short and suddenly turns around to face me. After casting a disparaging glance at my tray, she treats me to her pageant smile and does a big hair shake before breezing off.

Tears threaten again, but I quickly start counting backwards from twenty in my head, an old trick Mum told me about when the school bullies were at their worst. I reach the till and forage in my bag for my purse, wishing again that everything could just go back to how it used to be.

'I've changed my mind on these,' I mumble to Stacey, pointing to the cakes.

'Sure.' She's just about to take the plate away when Sam appears.

'It's OK Stace. You can go on your break now. I'll take over.'

'Thanks Sam.' Stacey disappears and Sam leans around the till with a concerned look on her face.

'You OK?' she whispers.

'I'm fine.'

'No you're not. Now get off your proverbial spike and tell me what's up?' Sam smiles kindly.

'I've just lost a really big sale, James is still ignoring me and Maxine is playing me for a mug . . . so, all in all . . .' I say, keeping my voice low as I desperately try to stop my bottom lip from trembling. I fiddle with my purse.

'Shush,' Sam puts her hand over mine. 'My treat, sounds like you need them, put your purse away,' she says in a way that makes me feel as if I might cry again.

'Thank you,' I mouth.

I've just sat down at the only free table in the far corner of the packed café when Tom appears.

'Mind if I join you?' he says, tilting his head and, in spite of myself, and what I saw earlier in the corridor, and everything else that's going on, my tummy actually flips as I look up at him towering over me, his eyes sparkling and messy dark curls falling into chocolate-brown eyes. He's so incredibly hot and smells amazing. I have to force myself to get a grip.

'If you must,' I say, too sharply, and he hesitates. 'Look sorry, of course you can,' I mutter quickly, feeling ashamed that I'm adding rudeness to my list of un-attractive traits these days.

'Bad day?' Tom says, sitting down opposite me and pushing his hair away from his face. Then, stirring his espresso, he looks directly at me, waiting for my answer.

'Bad life more like,' I say dramatically, ripping a chunk of cupcake and shoving it into my mouth.

'What's happened?' he asks gently, leaning across the table and creasing his forehead in concern. I swallow and slurp at a teaspoonful of hot chocolate.

'I don't really want to talk about it,' I reply, averting my eyes from his. I bet he already knows about the Malikov bags and Maxine's bound to have told him that I 'stole' the sales commission from James. That's what lovers do – tell each other stuff. No wonder James is so furious with me.

'Well, if you change your mind, please just let me know . . . I'm a good listener,' he says in a low voice. He smiles again and for a moment I waver. I must say he's very good. He really does seem genuinely interested and caring. Maybe I've got it wrong. I don't know, my judgement is all over the place at the moment. I quickly pull myself together and look away. All part of their ruse, no doubt. Maxine's probably told him to work his charm on me in an attempt to wheedle out some misdemeanour she can use against me to cover her tracks when she lets him stay and sacks me. She'll have to find some excuse, because my section is still the most profitable. Maybe Tom will even end up running that too; she did say she would be seeing what merch stays and who was best to sell it, and from what I've seen, it's blooming obvious he's the favourite. I grab the mug of hot chocolate and stand up.

'Bye,' I say abruptly, before heading off. Tom looks up at me and there's a shadow of dismay in his eyes, but I force myself to ignore it.

23

Back on the shop floor and I've barely made it to my counter when the wall phone rings. I grab the receiver before glancing at the clock. Roll on home time – today feels like the longest day ever.

'Women's Accessories. Georgie Hart speaking,' I say, trying to sound enthusiastic. I glance over at James's section but he's busy with a customer. Then he looks over, catches me watching and quickly flicks his eyes away. My cheeks burn as I study the wall instead.

'This is Borek . . . Mr Malikov's personal assistant. He requests your company this evening at a pre-opera soirée in his suite at the Mulberry Grand Hotel.'

Silence follows.

The Grand. That's where Nathan took Sam for her birthday, and it's the best hotel for miles around. But I can't go and meet Malikov in a hotel suite. It's crazy. His car is one thing, but a hotel room? No way. And then I realise that Borek is accustomed to people automatically accepting his master's requests without question.

'Err, *weell*,' I say, hesitantly.

'You must. Mr Malikov insists you come.'

Oh God, I was hoping to slope off home and comfort-eat my way through a massive pizza polished off with a red velvet or two. Then I remember Maxine's request that she be informed – maybe she'll even come with me. It'll mean having to put up with her pageant smile and bouncy big hair for an evening, but at least I won't have to go alone. 'Actually, the last time I met with Mr Malikov he told me my boss would need to be present fo—' I say, hopefully.

'Ah,' he interjects, and then keeps me waiting. I'm sure I can hear Malikov's voice in the background.

'Yes, Mr Malikov insists your boss comes too.' My heart races . . . the Chiavacci bags, it must be. He's going to buy them. If I can secure the sale and credit the commission to James, then maybe he'll forgive me. My mood is instantly lifted.

'Wonderful, what time should we arrive?'

'Seven o'clock and the dress is –' there's a short pause – 'cocktail attire,' he finishes, as if he's just spotted the dress code description in a book about high-society etiquette.

'Of course, and thank you,' I say, before pressing to end the call. I quickly dial Maxine's extension, praying she can make it at such short notice.

'Yes?' she answers, sounding all breathy and seductive, before I've barely finished dialling her extension.

'Maxine, it's Georgie here.'

'Oh, I, err, didn't realise,' she says, quite obviously hoping it was someone else. Tom, I bet! I clear my throat.

'You wanted to know about meetings with private customers. Well, I've been invited to a drinks soirée this evening,' I say, wishing he'd given me more notice. There's a sharp intake of breath followed by a huff that sounds very much like disappointment. So she's already had enough of being kept informed of everything. Knew she would.

'Where is it?' she asks.

'Err . . . The Mulberry Grand. In his suite.' She doesn't bother to ask who the customer is.

'Oooh,' she says, sounding interested now.

'Yes, he specifically asked for you to come too,' I say, appealing to her vanity. I can't afford for her to be awkward about it. This might be my only chance to sell him the Chiavaccis. And at £4,975 each, I need to pull out all the stops.

'Well, in that case we shall go together,' she says, sounding excited, while I contemplate how long it will take me to bus it home and grab a suitable outfit.

'And it's cocktail dress,' I quickly tell her.

'Marvellous, sure I can squeeze in a quick trip out for a new Prada frock this afternoon,' she says. I hang up, thinking: good luck with that . . . I know for a fact there aren't any shops in the whole of Mulberry-On-Sea that stock Prada. This is a quintessential English seaside town, not Beverly Hills, where you can pop to Rodeo Drive whenever you feel like it.

On arrival at the Mulberry Grand we're met by a Malikov minion and ushered up and into a buttercup-yellow panelled drawing room, bursting with red heart-shaped balloons. The Valentine's theme is continued through to the main room with cardboard Cupids suspended from the chandeliers and dusty pink rose petals scattered all over the sumptuous red carpet. There must be around fifty people milling around. The women are all dressed in Versace or Gucci and sporting overbleached WAG-style hairdos and lots of gold. And the men all look like extras from a Cold War spy thriller. Stuffed into black tuxedos and knocking back spirits from crystal shot glasses, before reaching for a canapé from the trays carried by milling waitresses.

Batting a balloon away from my face, I scan the room but can't see Malikov. A waitress thrusts a tray at us and I opt for an orange juice, figuring it is best to keep a clear head. Maxine jabs a bony finger at a large bottle of Stoli Gold, hesitates and then wavers over the Cristall before finally settling on the Zyr. The waitress pours her a generous measure into a frosted shot glass complete with strawberry accompaniment nestling on the side, which Maxine necks in one before tossing the strawberry into her mouth too.

'Zakuska?' Another waitress appears in front of us, bearing a tray with a selection of bite-sized pickles and rolled-up fish on miniature slices of black bread. But Maxine bats the girl away before I get a chance to decide what to try and then turns her back to me while she hunts for another vodka waitress. She's wearing a back-plunging Prada dress that clings to her frame as if she were sewn into it. So she managed to find a stockist then.

'I thought you'd be wearing the necklace.' Malikov makes me jump as he booms the words out over my shoulder. Turning to face him, his eyes fix on mine before flickering over towards Maxine's back. It's as though he's telepathically telling me that he intended on her hearing him. Then his mouth curls up at one side until it resembles a nasty sneer. An icy hand clutches at my heart. What the hell is he playing at? I thought it was to be our secret. Maxine turns back to join us.

'I'm off for a cigarette,' she says, her face giving nothing away as she sashays off. Maybe she didn't hear him. And she obviously doesn't realise Malikov is standing next to us, because if she did then surely the cigarette could have waited. I let out a tiny sigh of relief and wait for Malikov to stop ogling Maxine's pert bottom.

'Well, I err, didn't think it really matched this dress.'

He glances down at my body before bringing his eyes back to mine.

'My associate is very disappointed.' So that's his game. The short-notice invite . . . he's annoyed after the message I left for him earlier on, saying that we couldn't

209

supply the bags without ID verification. 'I thought we were friends.' He stares at me. My stomach tightens.

'Of course,' I smile. 'I'm sorry, it's just that we have to have his ID an—'

'But you said you would ship the goods to Russia. For the sisters.'

'And I will, just as soon as the paperwork is in place. It's a legal thing. Perhaps I should talk to him and explain,' I say, seeing the Chiavacci sale and my chance to appease James floating away right before my eyes.

'You already are.' *Whaat?* What's he going on about? So there is no associate. The bags were for him all along . . . but why didn't he just say? And then I get it. He couldn't, that's the whole point. He wants the high-value goods but doesn't want to be associated with them. No wonder his 'people' made all those calls asking about CCTV, on the pretext of protecting Malikov's security. He didn't want his ugly mug caught on camera. No wonder he wanted the most expensive items and paid in cash. Dirty cash. It has to be. Probably from the sale of his guns . . . and God knows what else.

The room sways. I'm in way too deep. His disgusting flirting, planting the necklace. Why the hell didn't I just return it? I must be going mad not to have realised.

'I don't understand,' I say, desperately trying to buy some time to get my head together. He leans in towards me and, with a voice as cold as ice, he whispers,

'I know all about you.' My thighs tremble. I remember

the gun. For a moment I'm scared I might actually pass out. 'Why else would I bother with you and your provincial little store when I can buy whatever I want, wherever I want?'

I place my hand on the table to steady myself. Of course, right at the start he said he'd carried out checks. God knows what he found out about me, but he's obviously targeted me as a weak link – up to her eyes in debt so might just go for it. Ship stuff to Russia. No questions asked. Certainly no requirement for him to be bothered by mere 'paperwork'. I hate myself. What an utterly stupid fool I am.

'Perhaps I should tell your boss you accepted the necklace as a gift. Or maybe you stole it when you were in my car. Wanted to treat yourself ahead of Valentine's Day . . . because I doubt very much anyone else will be bothering,' he says, tossing me a nasty up-and-down look. I bite down hard on the inside of my bottom lip.

Malikov surveys me, scanning my face as he waits for my next move, taunting me like a cat with an injured mouse. Then something comes over me – it's like an animalistic instinct.

'What do you want?' My voice trembles, the words barely audible, but I manage to keep my eyes fixed on his. I pray to myself that the jeweller still has the necklace. And then a chilling thought seeps into my head. Something that could ruin me forever . . . if I get found out. What if he still wants me to ship stuff to Russia?

What if there's drug money too? I'll be implicated. I could go to prison and end up in some tiny cell no bigger than my bathroom with bunk beds chained to the floor and a geezer bird who stashes mobile phones up her Aunty Mary. Oh yes, I've watched the Channel Five documentaries. This is bad. Really really bad. He hesitates briefly before delivering his verdict.

'Nothing,' he spits.

'I'll return the neck—' I start, but he cuts me short.

'What are you talking about? I said nothing.' And he turns his back on me and limps away.

My head is spinning. I quickly drain the orange juice, wishing that I'd opted for one of the vodka shots now, and then manage to force my legs to carry me into the corridor. I find the bathroom and, after locking the door behind me, I crumple to the floor. My whole body is trembling. Tears fly uncontrollably down my cheeks. I feel like such a disaster – he played me right from the start in the personal shopping suite. Banking on my stupidity and desperation. The feeling of self-loathing is unbearable. I've ruined everything.

After what feels like an eternity I manage to haul myself back up onto a chair. I sit and stare at myself in the mirror, trying to unravel what just happened. And I get it. Of course. He was lying. I let out a laugh. A horrible, hysterical laugh. There is something he wants, something money can't buy, not even his vast fortune. He wants respectability. And respectable people don't resort to underhand tricks to get what they want. No wonder he was so happy to develop sudden memory loss over having given me the necklace. Thank God he didn't want it back. It's a small comfort, though, seeing as I'm now going to be looking over my shoulder, forever wondering what his next move might be.

When I return to his suite the drinking is in full swing, but I can't see Maxine or Malikov. Oh Jesus. What if he's busy stitching me up right now? As I'm working myself up into another state of frenzy, a door at the far end of the room opens and Maxine appears. She does her model walk towards me, closely followed by Malikov, but I can't quite see her face through the thick of the crowd mingled together with the Valentine's balloons. I pray my hunch is right and he's kept his mouth shut.

'Time to go,' she says, without a trace of knowing. I smile, and quickly glance at Malikov, who ignores me and turns his attentions on Maxine. 'One of my assistants will be in touch,' she says, sounding showy. 'I do hope you enjoy your opera this evening.' She treats him to her pageant smile and a big hair toss. He kisses the back of her hand, lingeringly, gazing up at her face from under his fleshy eyelids.

'Enchanted,' he says to Maxine, before throwing me a quick look of disgust. He turns back to join his friends.

'I'm going to be managing his shopping requirements from now on. Seeing as he's such a big customer,' Maxine says, tossing her hair around again as we leave the room and make our way towards the foyer.

'Oh, OK,' I say, tentatively.

'It's not a problem, is it?' she says, breezily.

'Err, no, should it be?' I ask, wondering where she's going with this.

'I don't think so.' And then she hits me with it. 'But of course the necklace will need to be returned. You know the rules.' My blood runs cold, the acid taste of bile swirls into the back of my throat. So she did hear him after all. But I can't return it, Malikov will go mental, especially after his 'nothing' comment. And I can't afford to buy it back in any case, even if the jeweller hasn't sold it on. My head spins, and the saliva drains from my mouth.

'But I didn't accept it . . . he, err . . .' She whips her hand up and I immediately stop talking. Fear fills every single pore on my body. *Please don't let her sack me. Please don't let her sack me.* I say it over and over, in synch with my hammering heart. Then I hold my breath, waiting for her to say the words, that she'll be informing security or, God forbid . . . the actual police!

'Whatever. Give it to me and I'll make sure he gets it back.' My heart skips a beat, forcing an involuntary cough to escape. 'We've all done it. In fact, you remind me so much of myself at your age. The secret is to not get caught.' She turns her face towards mine and does a little Joan Holloway pout. 'Oh, don't look so worried.

214

Your secret is safe with me. You scratch my back, and I'll scratch yours.' My heart nose-dives. I can't bear it. Maxine's hold grips even tighter now, like a hangman's noose. And I don't want to be like her. Participating in mutual back-scratching sessions. Game-playing and manipulating. I feel as though I'm suffocating and there's no way out of this nightmare that I've got myself into.

'Thank you,' I say, silently praying the jeweller still has the necklace. I can't even imagine what she'll do to me if I fail to produce it.

'Good, then we'll say no more about it,' she says, and I'm sure I detect a hint of satisfaction in her voice. Something else she has over me, and I swear I can feel the pressure of the thumbscrews as she tightens them just a little bit more.

*

The very minute my toe is over the threshold of my doorway I race down the hallway and into the lounge. Panic-stricken, I glance around and catch my reflection in the window. I quickly race over and activate the blind to shield my shame from the lights twinkling outside in the dark. Then, tearing at the bookcase, I manage to retrieve the first card I hid after grabbing and shaking out several books. I'm drenched in sweat, fear gripping my stomach as I run into the kitchen and fling open the freezer door. I grab the tub of ice cream and, after ripping the black masking tape from the lid, I claw at the rock-hard yellow mixture. My fingertips sting as I try and push down further. But it's no use. I run over to the sink and shove the tub under the hot tap. Eventually the ice cream starts to thaw, and there it is, dazzling like a proud Arabian palace in the desert. The second one that I hid: my gold credit card.

24

I've been standing outside the jeweller's shop since eight a.m. Pressing my nose up to the window, like I have a million times in the last hour as I check for signs of activity, when I suddenly hear the sound of a key. The jeweller comes into view as he ambles through the shadowy shop towards me. As soon as he unbolts the door and flicks on the lights, I tear through into the shop.

'Whoah! Where's the fire?'

'I need the necklace back. Have you still got it?' I pant, pleading with my eyes for it to be here.

'Yes, but—'

'Oh, thank God. Here, you'll have to spread the cost over these credit cards,' I puff, shoving them at him. 'Please, I have to have it straight away,' I beg, as if getting it back absolves me of ever having sold it in the first place.

'But I thought you preferred the money?' he says.

'I did, but that was then, and things have changed,' I say, not daring to look him in the eye. I wish he would just get on with it. I didn't sleep at all last night and my body is trembling with exhaustion. He scribbles on the pad and thrusts it towards me. 'Hang on. But that's more than you paid me for it,' I say, willing the panic to subside.

'That's what it's worth. If you remember, you gave me a discount because I paid you in cash,' he says, sounding indifferent. I stare at him, unable to get my head around his logic.

'Yes, but I didn't *give* you a discount as such. You told me . . .' I attempt to argue my case, but a slow cold trickle of realisation washes over me.

'Now, if you want to buy it back for cash, then that's different of course.' He looks blankly, waiting for my response. I shake my head. This can't be happening.

'But I'm not sure the cards will cover that amount though,' I say, in a hollow voice. I feel so foolish. The money I originally sold the necklace for just about managed to clear the store card and to take my credit cards back to zero.

'You could finance the shortfall,' he says, making it sound as though he's doing me an enormous favour in ripping me off. Tears threaten, and my heart plummets. Not only am I back to square one, but I'm now worse off than I was in the first place and I'm beginning to wonder whether it's worth it any more. I feel as if I'm drowning. I have to keep my job now, if only to stay afloat, so I nod my head. He scribbles on his pad again and pushes it towards me.

'That'll be twelve monthly payments.'

I brace myself before glancing down at the page. Jesus. It's almost as much as my car loan payments. The floor sways beneath me. I steady myself against the counter.

'Looks like I don't have a choice,' I say, feeling sick and momentarily wondering what would happen if I reached across, grabbed the necklace and legged it as fast as I could. But it's a ridiculous thought; I'm simply too exhausted even to reach across the desk, let alone run at any kind of speed.

'Maybe you could get a bank loan,' he offers, pretending to be helpful.

'No, I have to have the necklace back today,' I say, sharply, shuddering at the thought of what will happen to me if I don't hand it over. So instead I grimace and bear it while he busies himself with the paperwork for the ludicrously extortionate loan, which is probably illegal anyway, but I just don't have the time to argue with him.

*

After weaving through the traffic on my way to Brighton, I make it into the fast lane of the motorway and push down hard on the accelerator. My head flings back against the headrest, my heart is racing and I can't seem to stop panicking. The dialogue in my head is driving me mad, over and over, there's just no let-up. I might have cleared the arrears and missed-payment markers from my credit file, but my mountain of debt is even bigger now. Maybe I could sell the car, but then I remember the outstanding finance figure . . . it's at least two grand more than the car is worth, I can't even afford to do that. My hands are trembling on the steering wheel now and my chest is getting tight. I feel totally overwhelmed, as if everything is going to cave in on me. Tears sting in my eyes, I bite my bottom lip and take a deep breath, desperate for air, but it's no use, I feel consumed with panic and I don't feel safe.

The ghastly image of my car careering into the crash barrier flashes before me, so I quickly indicate left and get myself over into the slow lane, before flicking the air con onto maximum. The icy cold breeze fans me, but my skin is still burning with trepidation. And Malikov must have got the necklace back by now. I can barely bring myself to contemplate what he will do to me. He's bound to think I've double-crossed him. See it as a sign of indifference. I just don't know any more, I can't get a grip on reality.

I pull over into a lay-by and, after switching off the engine, I glance around the car's interior. Creamy-coloured soft leather with tan piping. The dashboard with chrome detailing, complete with matching steering wheel, just as I specified. At the time I thought it would make me feel happy, plug the gap left by losing Mum, and then Dad disappearing . . . but what use is it to me now? I feel trapped. Hot angry tears trickle down my face, slow at first, but fast now, and they won't stop. My chest heaves, up and down, until I'm sobbing hysterically. I think of Dad and what he did to us, the similarities between his behaviour and mine recently. I should talk to him. Desperation changes people; I can see that now – maybe that's why he did it. He never really explained, but then I never asked. I vow to call him at the first opportunity.

Eventually, I manage to calm down, and after touching up my make-up, I force myself to get a grip. I make my way off the motorway and out into the countryside, and as green fields replace the hard urban concrete, the tension starts to ease slightly.

*

As I drag my wheelie suitcase across the car park towards the magnificent Regency-style beachfront hotel, I realise there's nothing I can do right now to change anything, so I might as well try to enjoy the team-building event and put all my worries out of my head, if only for a little while. I'm in danger of driving myself insane otherwise.

I walk through the grand entrance door and take a look around the hotel reception area. On every one of the surrounding armchairs and sofas there's a Carrington's employee. There must be about thirty people crammed into the room, some standing, the others elbow-to-elbow on the three padded window seats. Mrs Grace is sitting in a wing chair next to the real log fire, her knitting needles click-clacking away. Lauren is hovering by the bay window saying, 'Mummy will see you tomorrow, now be a good boy for grandma' into her mobile, and Betty is fanning herself with a drinks menu and mumbling something about 'flaming hot flushes'. A couple of girls from Bedding turn up, closely followed by Suzanne from the cash office, looking fabulous in a midnight-blue maxi dress and chunky silver lace-up flatforms, with pregnant Emma from Stationery sipping from an Evian bottle while being all glowy and radiant.

I spot Eddie perched on the edge of a corner unit sipping a can of Red Bull, and let out a small sigh of relief. I make my way over. He looks wired and his eyes are like saucers, flitting around the room.

'Good to see you, Georgie Girl.' It's Ciaran, and he's standing in the centre of the room, simulating a 'lock and load' action with an imaginary machine gun. A passing waitress throws him a look of disgust, so he drops to one knee to apologise profusely to her. I've not seen Ciaran as gregarious as this before. Eddie rolls his eyes, before moving along to let me sit down.

'I'm so glad you're here,' I say, turning towards him.

'Wouldn't miss it for the world,' he replies sarcastically, before looking away.

'Eddie, what is it?' I ask, wondering why he's acting strangely. It's unlike him to be so cold. He turns his face

222

to mine and studies me for a moment, as if he can't make his mind up whether to say anything. I wait for him to tell me, but he just shrugs instead.

'Oh, it's nothing.'

'There is something, isn't there?' I ask, feeling uneasy.

'No, honestly . . . I'm just thinking this is going to be a long weekend.' He glares in Ciaran's direction, but I'm not convinced. Oh God, maybe he knows something. Of course. He's working for The Heff *and* Maxine now. He's bound to know what she has in store for the ground floor.

'Eddie, if you know anything, you would tell me, wouldn't you . . . even if it was bad news?' I ask, in a low voice.

'Sure . . . but I don't – stop being so paranoid.' I manage a smile, but inside the feeling of unease is picking up speed again. I try to shove the worry from my head, but instead it just sits there gnawing away.

I can feel Eddie's thigh twitching against mine.

'Are you sure everything's OK?' I turn to face Eddie, and he bites his lip.

'Yes, fine,' he snaps. 'I need another drink.' He jumps up and stalks off towards the bar. My heart sinks.

'What's going on with him?' Ciaran throws himself down next to me.

'I don't know, but Eddie is really uptight, and it's not like him,' I reply. He must know something, I feel sure. The uneasy feeling threatens again.

'Maybe the stress of working for that ballbuster Maxine is really getting to him,' Ciaran says, sounding concerned.

'Maybe,' I reply, distractedly. I think about work . . . and James. God, I wish he was here, and then I feel an overwhelming sense of sadness that our friendship has been ruined by a romance that barely got off the starting blocks. Maybe there's a chance to fix it when I get back. I cling on to this thought as Melissa the self-appointed organiser takes to the floor.

'Now, if you could all be quiet for a second, you'll see that on the front of the T-shirt is your name, but the important bit is on the back, that old adage that we all know and *lurrrrrve* . . .' She pauses for a second and sticks her arms out, as if she's about to start conducting an orchestra.

We all shout back in unison with her, 'What happens in Vegas stays in Vegas.' Melissa is standing in the middle of the lounge clutching her T-shirt with both hands so we can see the slogan. She starts throwing the shirts out one by one. Mrs Grace stuffs hers into her shopper, not even bothering to look at it, and mine is the tiniest scrap of cotton Lycra mix I think I've ever seen.

'Where did you find this one, Melissa, in Childrenswear?' I yell, but she's distracted by the door opening. 'Ahh, nice of you to join us, lads. Only an hour late,' Melissa says as two guys from Menswear saunter in, followed by a bloke from Home Electricals, two security guards and Charles, looking cool in a big woolly Rasta hat and leather jacket. They do lots of high fives and fist thumps before stacking their holdalls up in a mountain by the door. She hands them their T-shirts.

Melissa and one of the security guards are having a pretend boxing match when Amy, Carrington's HR manager, walks in wearing an orange tabard and holding a clipboard.

'OK, is everyone here now?' She calls our names out, ticking them off as we answer. My heart sinks when she inadvertently calls James's name and there's a short silence followed by a monotone, 'He changed sessions. My mistake' from Eddie, who has just returned from the bar with another Red Bull. Turns out Maxine delegated the task of divvying up the names for each session to him and he forgot to scrub James off the list. 'Great. Here's a schedule for each of you. Early start tomorrow morning, nine sharp, here in reception. Tonight you can do your own thing . . . all part of the board's aim for you to have some downtime and build teams.' She grins. 'Studies have shown that employees who play together, work hard together . . . so play nicely! I'm in room 109 should you need anything. I'll hand you over now to DeWayne and Vince from "Train to Gain". They'll be co-ordinating the event for us.'

A couple of overly enthusiastic guys, wearing camouflage trousers and extra-tight muscle tops with whistles on ropes around their necks, and an assortment of camping-type paraphernalia slung about their bodies, bounce into the centre of the room.

'What's that whistle for?' Mrs Grace pipes up, pointing at Vince with one of her knitting needles.

'Oh, err . . . just in case we need to get everyone's attention,' he replies, looking a bit fazed.

'Hmmm. I'm here to have a nice rest, not wriggle commando-style under one of those filthy nets you boot-camp boys are so fond of. Not with my hip playing up the way it is,' she huffs. I catch her eye and she gives me a wink before getting back to her knitting.

'Don't worry, err . . .' Vince pauses.

'Mrs Grace to you,' she sniffs.

'Yes, Mrs Grace, we won't be doing anything too arduous. We'll be spending most of the time in the hotel conference room . . . with the occasional break-out session in the hotel garden.' There's a collective groan from the Bedding girls. 'But we'll fill you in tomorrow morning. See you all then.' They both wave before throwing their hands up in the air and clapping furiously above their heads as they practically march off towards the door.

'Crap! I thought it would be tug-of-war and sudden death games. You know, like proper team building . . . where one team wins and the other one is *destroyed*!' Melissa says, before making a wanker sign towards the door. 'Nobbers!' she heckles. 'Looks like we'll just have to make the best of it. But in the meantime you heard what Amy said – teams that play hard and all that . . . sooo, it's off to the dance floor.' She makes a big Elvis-style circle with her right arm. 'Let's check out the rooms and meet back here later. We can go to the pier. Something for everyone on there,' she bellows.

'Oh, not for me dear. I'm not missing *Strictly*. And I'm looking forward to an early night with my dinner cooked for me, for a change,' Mrs Grace says.

'I'll join you,' Betty puffs, wiping her top lip with a tissue.

'But I've booked us a room in the karaoke bar at the end of the pier. It's going to be a scream.' Melissa rubs her hands together as if she can't wait to get started.

'You youngsters will have much more fun without us old biddies holding you up.' Mrs Grace is already stowing her knitting inside her shopper and reaching for the room service menu.

'OK. Well everyone else has to come then. Be there or be square, as they say.'

*

My room is in a converted old carriage block through a walkway at the back of the main hotel, so after dropping my room card into the slot of the lock, I push the door open and make my way into the bedroom with its beautifully designed array of chocolate, baby blue and caramel-coloured soft furniture. Kicking my ballet pumps, top and skinny jeans off, I lie back on the bed and my mind starts wandering. I feel sad. This damn revamp. And damn Maxine, stirring things up and distorting the facts. She probably did it on purpose, delighting in telling James how well I've been cultivating Malikov's business.

Thinking of Malikov makes me cringe. Well, Maxine is welcome to him. I just hate it that she has another secret on me. I vow to talk to James as soon as I get back. I have to try again to make him see that I didn't do it on purpose. That he can trust me. I have to at least try.

Swinging my legs down onto the floor, I get up and go over to my suitcase and grab my toiletry bag. I push the bathroom door open and the lights come on automatically. I spot the hospitality box hidden behind a brochure advertising a variety of special Valentine-themed getaways. It's black lacquered wood and crammed full of goodies. The special monogrammed toiletries smell divine, fruity like peaches and cream with a twist of citrus. There's even a plastic case of assorted nail enamels that would look great on my dressing table at home. I wonder if anyone would notice if they disappeared into my suitcase. At the very bottom, discreetly placed under a packet of strong mints, is a box of extra-pleasure condoms. Hmm, I won't be needing those. My throat tightens and the sadness over James returns.

I wander back out of the bathroom and scan the room. There's an impressive minibar stocked with chocolate, various different nut selections and every alcoholic beverage one could desire. The sight of three red mini-tubes of Pringles makes me weaken and I lift out a tub and peel back the silver foil. Savouring the taste, I walk over to the other side of the room. There's a huge wardrobe almost covering the length of one wall. I pull open the doors with my free hand, one, two, three . . . they're all the same. Rows of wooden hangers mingled in with a few pastel-pink satin-covered soft ones. There's an ironing board and a few spare blankets. I grab at the fourth door. It's another bedroom. Of course, the adjoining room. James must have forgotten to cancel it.

I can't resist having a peek inside and, seeing as the others are all over in the main part of the hotel, I decide to risk it. The room is a mirror image of mine, only with a different colour scheme, emerald green and chocolate brown. I tiptoe over to the bed and gaze down at it, thinking of what might have been if James was here. After peeping over my shoulder towards the door to check nobody is coming, I sit down. I pop another Pringle into my mouth and swing my legs over until I'm lying down. I gaze up at the ceiling; the crunching noise in my ears is deafening against the silence of the room. I close my eyes and let my mind drift off for a second, wishing our friendship wasn't ruined.

'What are you doing?' My eyes snap open with panic, and the Pringles cascade down onto the floor as I throw myself up into a standing position.

'Jesus, you scared the living daylights out of me,' I screech.

I'm standing by the side of the bed in my oldest, greyest bra, which many years ago used to be white, and my extra-comfortable-for-travelling, big red-and-white cow-print knickers that have the words '*Cheeky Cow*' emblazoned across the back. Tom is standing right in front of me.

I clutch the Pringles tube to my chest like a miniature comfort blanket. My heart is pounding and panic is swirling through me like a baby tsunami.

'I didn't mean to startle you,' he replies, managing to look amused and concerned all at the same time. I open my mouth but the words won't come out. I have to get back to my room. I drop the Pringles tube and leg it as fast as I can, slamming the adjoining door behind me.

Back in my room, and I'm trembling all over with the shock and shame of the too-close encounter. I pull off the manky underwear and ram it into the rubbish bin before flinging open the door to the minibar and grabbing two Jack Daniel's miniatures. I run into the bathroom, locking the door behind me. Feeling mortified, I guzzle one whiskey after the other, fling an enormous white fluffy towel around my body and punch out Sam's number.

'What's the matter?' In between hiccups I describe the moment of horror to her. 'OH MY GOD. OH MY ACTUAL GOD . . .' She keeps shrieking it over and over. 'He's there. How exciting . . . well, he'll certainly take your mind off James,' she giggles. 'Sorry, I don't mean to laugh, but look, keep calm, it's not that bad.'

Not that bad? It's a total embarrassment, off the scale even by my standards.

'It's horrendous,' I manage to say, dramatically, before letting out another ricochet of hiccups. I put my phone down beside the bath and, pinching my nose, I hold my breath for a count of five in a desperate attempt to steady my breathing.

'Are you still there?' Sam's voice trills out from the phone. I pick it back up.

'Yes, just trying to clear these bloody hiccups.' I hiccup again.

'Oh dear, it must be bad,' Sam giggles, remembering how this happened at school whenever I got totally overwhelmed.

'Bloody right it is. I have to spend the whole night here with him in the next room thinking I'm some kind of lunatic stalker woman with a fetish for themed knickers,' I say, and burst into a fit of nervous laughter, punctuated by more hiccups. Sam is laughing too, and for a moment neither of us can talk. I can't believe I've made such a show of myself in front of him – yet again. 'Oh God,' I groan, as fresh waves of mortification wash over me.

Sam is the first to recover.

'Right! Fetish woman, get yourself together, and if Tom says anything about, the . . . err, encounter,' she pauses momentarily to have another chuckle, 'then, like I always tell you, just laugh it off.'

'Laugh it off?' I say, incredulously. 'Oh Tom, I just love prancing around in other people's bedrooms in my manky underwear, it's such a hoot.' We both chortle again, with me venturing into hysteria territory.

'Well, you could always pretend you don't know anything about it. Like you were sleepwalking or something.' There's a short silence. 'I know! Tell him you have narcolepsy.' We both crack up laughing again.

'But I was still in his bloody bedroom and I shouted at him for startling me, so that's not going to work, is it?'

'Well, just brave it out. But don't – whatever you do – apologise. He probably couldn't believe his luck in any case.'

'Now you're being ridiculous. He's probably on the phone to Maxine right now, telling her what an idiot I am, and to bin me as soon as she's got enough sales commission out of me.'

'Hardly. Stop being so paranoid.'

'I can't. Ever since she turned up, my nerves have been all over the place.' I let out a feeble laugh.

'Well, you deserve a bit of fun then . . . and it was only a couple of dates with James. And I have to say that he wasn't exactly slow in condemning you, was he?'

I mull over what she's said, and I know that she has a point. I'm just not sure I'm quite ready to hear it.

'Oh, I don't know, part of me thinks that James just needs more time, he's bound to be suspicious and unwilling to trust after what he's been through with his wife cheating, but Tom . . . well, he's sooo hot, but he's shagging Maxine.' I pause to fantasise about him for a bit, he really is gorgeous. 'But whenever he and I are alone there's a spark . . . something. I don't know what the game is.' There's a silence while I try and work it out. 'Listen to me, like I even stand a chance with him,' I say, rapidly coming to my senses. 'Anyway, it doesn't say much about my loyalty if I just turn my attentions to Tom now.'

'But you don't owe James anything, and so what if Maxine and Tom have got some stupid game going on? Personally I don't think so. No, I think you're letting your paranoia get the better of you. You fancy the pants off him, so just go for it. Grab him with both hands . . . one on each bum cheek,' she urges. 'You never know, he could be your Valentine date, imagine that?' And for a brief moment I try, but the thought is just so ridiculous I can't even seem to get an image of it in my head.

'Have you finally gone mad?' I laugh, trying to change the subject.

'Well, think about it at least. Anyway, how do you know he's shagging Maxine? I'll ask Nathan.' And before

I can shout 'NOOO!' I hear her muffled voice quizzing him. My insides churn – what if it gets back to Tom that I've been asking about him? The shame of it. 'Right, Nathan says that as far as he knows he's not a player. A true gentleman, apparently. But then he only knows him from the club . . . but he agrees with me, and I say just go for it.'

'Stop it. I can't believe we're even having this conversation,' I say, wishing I'd never mentioned it.

'Remember what I said about James, and I was right then, wasn't I?'

'Yes. But that was totally different. He was happily married, or so I thought, and besides he asked me out. *And* we've been friends for ages.'

'OK. So next time you're alone with Tom . . . well, just try flirting a bit.' There's a scratchy sound, as if Sam has dropped the phone, but then I hear her telling Nathan that it's 'girls' talk'. 'Sorry about that, I don't want him hearing my seduction secrets,' she laughs.

'So are you having a good weekend?' I ask, keen to change the subject.

'Faab-u-lous.' I hear Sam squealing, followed by a squelchy sound that I guess to be Nathan's lips. 'Georgie, I have to go. But try to have fun. And remember . . . one on each cheek!'

The line goes dead. For a few minutes I ponder on everything Sam said. The idea is ludicrous. But perhaps I am just being paranoid – even Eddie seems to think so. I allow myself a moment to indulge in fantasising about Tom, before dragging myself back to reality. He's probably in his room right now, laughing his head off.

25

The hotel lounge is deserted when I eventually make it back down, but then I am half an hour late.

'Can you tell me which way the pier is, please?' I ask a passing uniformed girl, figuring it won't be too hard to catch up with the others, given the size of the group.

'Sure, I'll show you on a tourist map. We have some behind the reception desk.'

'Thanks,' I say, wondering if anyone would notice if I sloped off home instead. It's a miserable day outside. All grey sky with bruised-looking clouds.

'It's OK. I know the way.' It's Tom, and he must be standing right behind me. My face freezes, and then panic swirls through me. Blooming typical. I brace myself, waiting for him to say something about earlier, desperately willing my cheeks to stop burning. I swallow hard and remember Sam's advice to brave it out before turning around. But it's no use . . . the minute I see his gorgeous smiling face, I crumble.

'What are you doing here?' I ask, nerves making me sound ridiculously shrill. I cringe. His name definitely wasn't down on the list. Looking taken aback, he hesitates before answering.

'I thought I'd wait for you. You don't mind do you?'

'No, no, I . . . I guess not.'

'Great.' He smiles. 'Let's make our way over to the crazy golf then. The others were heading there first,' he says, cheerfully, gesturing for me to lead the way. I force my legs into action and head over towards the exit, willing my cheeks to stop burning. I'm speechless, and his coolness throws me. It's as if my utterly embarrassing performance in his bedroom never happened.

We make it to the promenade and manage to find the crazy golf, but the others aren't there.

'You OK?' Tom asks.

'Sure, why wouldn't I be?'

'No reason. You're very quiet, that's all. You barely said a word on the way here.'

'Well, you walk very fast,' I say, trying not to gasp as I rest my elbow on a nearby wall. It was all I could do to keep up with him, let alone hold a coherent conversation too. Besides, I'm not entirely convinced I want to talk to him, if he's in cahoots with Maxine.

'Oh, you should have said. Sorry,' he says, obliviously.

'Never mind. Look, they're obviously not here, let's go,' I say, turning to leave.

'Ahh. But it would be a shame not to have a game at least,' he says, smiling and making a pleading face.

'Are you kidding? It looks like it's about to pour down,'

I say, peering up at the thunderous black clouds.

'No. Come on, it'll be a laugh,' he gestures with his head towards the ticket booth. I hesitate. 'I love crazy golf,' he grins again and my guard subsides.

'Take one of the buggies love . . . if you're worried about getting wet,' the tattooed guy on the booth hollers out to us, pointing to a queue of miniature buggies. I frown, seriously wondering if we'll both actually fit on the minuscule seat. It would be just my luck to get wedged in and end up making an idiot of myself in front of Tom again.

'Go on! Live a little. My treat. I'll sort out the clubs and balls,' Tom adds, eagerly, already walking towards the ticket booth. I nod. So Nathan was right, he *is* the perfect gentleman. But then I remember how cosy he was with Maxine in the corridor that time. This is probably all part of their game. Well, they're not going to catch me out. Oh no no no.

*

'So, have you played golf before?' Tom asks. He locks his dark brown eyes onto mine as I turn to face him. My resolve from earlier floats away. He looks incredible. He smells incredible. Vanilla and chocolate. And no matter how hard I try, I can't seem to stop my body from tingling all over with desire for him.

'Well, a little. My dad used to show me,' I say, trying

to sound normal in spite of my pounding heart. 'He was a great player,' I then add, biting my lip at the sudden bittersweet memory.

'Sorry, I didn't mean to upset you. Has he passed away?' he asks, gently.

'Oh no, nothing like that.' I shake my head. 'We, err . . . just don't see much of each other any more,' I finish, wishing there was more room in the buggy. His thigh is pressed against mine, and the intensity of his touch feels like a furnace scalding through the fabric of my trousers.

'I'm sorry,' he says, looking as though he genuinely cares as I remember the happy times with Dad. Once again I reflect that, with everything that's happened recently, I've seen a glimpse of what it might have really been like for him all those years ago. I reiterate my promise to myself to call him when I get back.

We arrive at the first tee, and Tom leaps out of the buggy and hands me a club.

'Thanks, but I'm left-handed, so this won't be any good. I'll just watch.' Ha! I feel pleased with myself for managing to call his bluff.

'I know you are,' Tom says smoothly. 'But it's a double-sided club. I checked with the guy on the ticket booth.' *Hmmm.* He looks taken aback, and I instantly feel embarrassed by how curt I'm being with him, and secretly flattered that he noticed I was left-handed. He hands me the club, followed by a bag of balls, before heading off. I follow along behind him, studying how his perfectly cut jeans fit nicely around his impressively taut bottom. I remember Sam's bum-cheek comment, and grin.

'Are you sure you're OK?' Tom asks as I arrive next to him.

'Yes, yes I'm fine,' I reply, trying to get my lust under control and keeping my head down as I pretend to be engrossed in the red, white and blue painted wooden windmill at the first hole.

'After you,' he says, placing the ball down at my feet. I take a few steps back and get myself into position, even indulging in a few practice swings. He's standing right next to me now, distracting me with his delicious scent. I take a moment to try and garner some concentration before swinging the club, but I lose my grip and end up narrowly missing his groin when the club flies out of my hands.

'Whoa! Easy tiger.' Tom laughs.

'Oh my God, I'm so sorry,' I say, trying to keep a straight face as he cowers down pretending to be petrified. And for a moment I see the face of a much younger man. It's as if his cool exterior has thawed to reveal a very sweet boy, and it's so appealing. He picks up the club and, handing it to me, he says, 'I could give you a quick lesson before we start.' He looks so eager and enthusiastic.

'Um,' is all I can manage as he dashes around behind

me and, with his arms either side of my body, he gently, but very firmly, positions my hands into place around the club.

'OK. Now align your thumbs gently down the shaft,' he instructs, completely oblivious to the effect he's having on me. I can feel his warm body pressed against me and then he bends his knees into the back of mine and carefully thrusts them forward a few times to simulate a relaxed pose for the perfect swing. My heart is racing and an exquisite sensation between my thighs makes them tingle with longing. 'There, that should work better . . . remember to keep your body relaxed.' Oh sweet Jesus! I just about manage to nod my head. The silence lingers, apart from the sound of my pounding heart and his breath against the back of my neck. And then a buggy comes into view and the moment vanishes.

'Thought I might find you here. Not interrupting anything, am I?' It's Eddie, and he has a wicked glint in his eye as his buggy performs a spectacular swerve before stopping alongside us. He flashes me a naughty look and Tom springs away from me. I quickly turn and glance at his face. He looks nervous, bashful even. Eddie lets out a stagey cough, winks and smiles at me before mouthing 'lucky cow' when Tom isn't looking.

'Catch you later. Just came to see if you were OK, but I can see you're doing fine. The others are in the karaoke bar when you're ready.' And he whizzes away on his buggy. I smile at Tom and he smiles back, looking more assured now.

'I'm ready when you are,' he says, staring straight into my eyes as if he's trying to tell me something more. Pondering on the innuendo, I open my mouth to respond, but an ear-splitting clap of thunder beats me to it and rain lashes down upon us. We fling ourselves inside the buggy and Tom speeds off, yanking the plastic weather shields down around us.

'That was close – you're not too wet, are you?' he asks, turning his drenched face towards mine. Blimey, if only he knew. His shirt is clinging to his hard body, making him look even more spectacular. But before I can answer, the buggy hits a rock on the pathway and throws us sideways. Tom quickly leans into me, deftly manoeuvring the steering wheel to keep us from toppling over. 'Oops, I'm so sorry, I didn't hurt you, did I?'

'No, I'm fine,' I tell him, but I can feel something poking into my thigh. I look down. It's a striped notebook.

'Oh, it must have fallen out of my pocket,' he says, tentatively. I hand it to him. 'Thanks, it . . . helps me to relax,' he explains.

'What is it?' I ask without thinking, and my cheeks blush. 'I'm sorry . . . I didn't mean to pry,' I add, quickly.

'Just a few sketches,' he says, glancing away.

'Sketches? As in drawing?' I say, before mentally kicking myself for stating the obvious and sounding like an utter plum.

'Yes,' he laughs, looking more relaxed now, 'as in drawing.'

'Cool,' I say, thinking what a sexy hobby, and what a dark horse he is. 'Do you mind if I take a look?' I ask, holding the notebook up.

'OK . . . but don't tell anyone, it can be our secret,' he jokes, and then grins at me. His shoulders are relaxed and he looks different somehow – younger, and less 'work like'.

'I promise. Cross my heart and hope to die.' I give him an exaggerated wink before pulling a very serious face. He shakes his head with laughter.

'You're so funny,' he says. I frown. 'In a lovely way,' he quickly adds, making my tummy flip over and over. I flick through the pages. They're filled with pencil line drawings of animals and various European city land-marks. I pause on a magnificent one of a Venice waterway.

'Wow, these are really good.' I turn to look at him. He looks uncertain, his eyes seeking out my approval almost, and seeing this side of him feels so nice, as though I've been let in on a secret. My tummy performs a big somersault. Our eyes lock, the rain beats against the buggy, making the moment feel really intimate. But then I remember James, and Maxine, and that I need to keep my wits about me. I quickly pull myself back to reality.

'Thank you,' Tom says, and carries on driving.

*

We make it to the karaoke bar and Melissa comes dashing towards us.

'Where have you two been?' she shouts over the music, looking at me with a smirk on her face, and then at Tom.

'Playing crazy golf,' I yell defensively and far too quickly, as I scan the bar looking to see if Eddie is here.

'Well, you're just in time, get your laughing gear around these.' She hands us each a shot glass full of fluorescent green liquid. 'When Bonnie Tyler up there has finished banging on about needing a hero, there's a treat for Ciaran.' She rolls her eyes towards the little stage at the end of the room where Suzanne is revving up for the last chorus – she's got a pink crystal-encrusted microphone in one hand and a large cocktail with about three paper umbrellas, a plastic giraffe and a bunch of cherries on the side of the massive glass in the other. She sniggers.

'What are you up to?' I ask.

'Oh, you'll see, but it probably won't be your thing. Although you never know, depends which way you sway,' she winks, and a smutty leer spreads across her now drunken face. 'Jesus, I can't wait.' I let out a groan. 'Any minute now,' she finishes just as one of the security blokes bombs over.

The guys are all nudging each other, and Ciaran, having realised they're up to something, is looking panicky. The music stops and the guys from Menswear and Home Electricals start clapping and cheering.

'No waaay,' Ciaran shouts, 'you bastards. I said no dodgy stuff.' He leaps up. But before he can protest further, stripper music is playing and two girls dressed in hot pink Burlesque basques, with choppy fringes and cherry-red lips, appear in a puff of marabou and ostrich feathers. They dance through the crowd, teasing the boys as they peel off their long gloves.

After flinging off their basques, the girls start jigging up and down on the backs of their heels, making their matching hot pink nipple tassels whizz around in circles. I watch, fascinated at how they manage it, and secretly wondering whether with a bit of practice I could perform the same trick, when Eddie appears by my side.

'Pour. It's time to make mama look pretty,' he gasps in a phoney hillbilly accent, clutching a hand to his chest while simultaneously shoving a glass down and gesturing to a nearby bottle. 'On second thoughts, cut out the middle man.' He rolls his eyes to accentuate his foul mood, grabs the bottle and, after jamming it into his mouth, he tips it up and takes an enormous glug.

'Ahh, that's better,' he says, slamming the bottle back down on the table and grabbing the shot glass from my hand and necking that too.

'Well, I think they're fantastic. And I'd kill to have a body like that, and look at the power they have over all the slobbering blokes,' I say, waving a hand around the room.

The girls have finished their routine now and are weaving back through the guys who are waving notes in the air. One of the girls catches my eye and gives me a friendly wink before stuffing a tenner inside her garter.

'Well, I'm bored,' Eddie huffs. 'I'll make my own fun,' he continues, before heading off to the door at the far end of the room. I chase after him, desperate to find out what has got into him.

'Eddie, come on, tell me what's wro—' I stop mid-sentence and almost run into Eddie's back as he halts in the doorway that leads out onto a little wooden balcony area overlooking the sea. Tom is sitting on a bench, with just the moonlight to see by as he taps into his iPhone. Eddie swiftly turns around.

'Oops! Three's a crowd,' he snorts, before barging back past me, giving me a little shove out and slamming the door behind him.

'Sorry about that, don't know what his problem is,' I say, feeling put on the spot.

'Well, he has a point,' Tom replies, his messy hair making him look all windswept and utterly gorgeous, and I'm sure I detect a hint of flirtatiousness in his voice – or maybe it's just wishful thinking. 'Why don't you take a seat and keep me company for a bit?' He gestures to the space next to him.

'What are you doing out here?' I ask as the crisp night air hits my face. I perch alongside him.

'Hiding,' he replies, furtively. He turns to face me and his eyes shoot from side to side and I can't help gawping openly at him. He manages to look both petrified and damn sexy all at the same time. My guard falls away as I listen to the waves below us and glance at the twinkling shoreline in the distance. The tingle intensifies and I wonder what might happen if he actually touched me, or kissed me even. I allow myself to daydream for a flash of a moment, but then rapidly shake the thought from my mind.

'This isn't really my scene,' he whispers, leaning closer, and treating me to a quick burst of his intoxicating scent.

'Oh, it's just a surprise for Ciaran and it was bound to be sexual with Melissa in charge,' I say, and like a pubescent teenager I feel my cheeks blush at saying the word 'sexual' in front of him. I immediately feel foolish. He must think I'm ridiculously immature, especially after what he must be used to with the prom queen and supermodel . . . Maxine.

'Was it?' He stares into my eyes. The innuendo hangs in the air like a neon sign outside a cheap motel offering rooms by the hour. Blood rushes to my cheeks again.

Neither of us speaks, and then he playfully nudges me with his shoulder and whispers, 'Can I ask you a personal question?' I lean into him. His face is almost touching mine. He grins, and right now I want him to ask the question. I nod, and grin back.

'Are you really a cheeky cow?'

My mouth opens.

It closes.

I swallow and then open my mouth to reply, but his lips are on mine. It's as if a bumper pack of fireworks have all ignited, one after the other, deep inside me. And right now I don't care if games are being played. I don't care if I'm being used to sell more handbags, purses or whatever before Maxine shafts me. I don't care if James hates me. I don't care if Malikov wants to shoot me. All I care about is having Tom. It's primal, and I've never felt like this before. Not ever. I feel his hand link with mine, and in the glow of the moonlight and over the gentle sway of the sea he moves his mouth to my ear.

'I take it you like pink roses then?' For a moment I'm not sure what he means, and then I remember. The gorgeous flowers delivered to the switchboard room. So they weren't from James after all. They were a bona-fide secret-admirer bouquet. My heart skips a beat.

I lift my eyes to meet Tom's, but his face changes. He looks really worried.

'Georgie, I'm so sorry. I err . . .' he starts, lifting his

hands out slightly, and away from me. He looks terrified now. 'I'll go. Please forgive me.' He's standing now, his hand reaching out for the door. But before I can reassure him, he pulls the door open and, after hesitating momentarily to glance back at me, he's gone.

26

The low, quiet muffle of Tom's voice stirs me, and I open my eyes. I stretch my arms and legs out like a starfish. Tom is in his room, but the adjoining door to the side of my bed is slightly ajar. He disappeared after leaving the karaoke bar last night, and I must have forgotten to close the door properly.

I pull myself up and peer through the crack. He's sitting sideways on the chair at the desk wearing a grey T-shirt and jeans. He's talking softly into a black retro-style desk phone.

'Yes. Just as we said it would.' I strain to hear, wondering who he's talking to. 'We're nearly there now.' Then he clicks the handset down and I hear footsteps moving towards the hallway, followed by his door slamming shut.

I jump out of bed with a vigorous burst of energy that I'm not used to, and promptly trip over the left Gina sandal. I bend down to retrieve it, smiling at the memory of the kiss from last night but wondering why he rushed off like that. As I hunt around for the other sandal, I spot my clothes dumped in a heap by my bed. I scoop them up and my stomach rumbles. I'm starving. I ponder on room service, but *who was he talking to* pops into my head. An unnerving thread of doubt worms its way into my thoughts, and I move towards the adjoining door. It's still ajar, and a horrible sense of mistrust festers in the pit of my stomach as I tiptoe through it.

He only left a few minutes ago. My brain races, quickly calculating a feasible time span before he might return, then telling myself he's gone downstairs to have breakfast before heading straight to the conference room. My heart pounds as I rush over to the desk. But what if he forgot something and comes back? I have to be quick.

I lift the handset, and my hand trembles as I press the redial button. After the longest few seconds ever, the number he called appears on the display. It's a London number. It starts ringing. The feeling of hunger is replaced with a rush of nausea. I wish I hadn't done this now. I pull the handset away from my ear, desperate to ignore the knot of doubt, and I'm just about to disconnect the call when a voice breathes into the charged air.

'Yes?'

I drop the handset down as if it's a scalding hot iron singeing the palm of my hand and fly from the room, slamming the adjoining door behind me.

Maxine's voice.

It was Maxine.

I'd know her breathy voice anywhere. I hate her a

million times over, but not as much as I hate myself. What the hell was I thinking? I feel like a complete sucker. The flowers, his gentlemanly charm, showing me his etchings . . . I mean, come on, how clichéd is that? And I still fell for it. It was all a ruse after all. And what about James? I feel like a slapper. A horrible, guilty slapper. I barely know Tom, and it was only a kiss – admittedly a very long delicious smoochy one – but who knows what could have happened if he hadn't left so abruptly. I'm not sure I could have resisted him if we'd come back here to carry on. Tears stab my eyes.

After a quick, punishingly hot shower, I decide to go and find the others. I couldn't bear to still be here in the adjoining bedroom when Tom returns. I pull open the door and instantly grind to a standstill.

'Oh my God. What happened to you?' I ask, quickly taking in the scene. Ciaran is standing right in front of me with his fist in mid-air, as if he was just about to knock. And he's totally naked and soaking wet.

'I was minding my own business having an early morning dip in the hot tub when I'm hauled out and my shorts whipped from my body,' he says, through chattering teeth. 'And they nicked my robe. Any chance of a towel?' he pleads, clutching his manhood.

'Err, yes. Of course. Sorry, I should have offered. Help yourself,' I say, feeling flustered at this sudden interruption. Averting my eyes, I step aside and motion him towards the bathroom. 'So who was it? Actually, no, let me guess, I bet it was Melissa?' I yell through the crack of the bathroom door as I start to calm down.

'Well, get this. They only had Kate and Wills masks on, and it all happened so quickly. They obviously planned it – pathetic really.'

'It could have been worse, at least you're still inside the hotel,' I tell him, as he emerges from the bathroom, having dried off and wrapped himself in a fluffy white robe.

'Hmmm, suppose so. I had to run naked from the hot tub to the nearest indoor place, which was here. I'll throttle Melissa when I get my hands on her.'

'Do you think it was definitely her?' I ask, stupidly, before realising she's bound to have orchestrated it. I chew nervously at the side of my thumbnail; my head is still reeling.

'Of course.'

'Well, do you fancy a drink?' I head over to the mini-bar, thinking I could certainly do with one. And then blush when I remember that it's barely breakfast time.

'God no, bit early for me – my liver feels as though it might pack up at any moment. The shots in that karaoke bar were lethal,' he groans. 'A glass of water would be good though.' I nod and pour him a generous glassful, my hands still trembling slightly.

'Can I use your phone to call Melissa?'

'Sure.' I hand him my mobile, and a few seconds later he tells Melissa to get herself along to my room immediately. I make my way over to one of the armchairs and Ciaran follows.

'You OK? You look really rattled,' he says, flopping down in the seat beside me.

'Me? Yes, yes, I'm fine thanks,' I say, airily.

'You sure? Only you look kind of distracted.' He frowns. I nod, pulling my thumb away from my clenched teeth and force a smile onto my face. 'So how's it going with the revamp?' he asks, tactfully changing the subject.

'Oh, don't remind me,' I reply, glancing at the adjoining door to make sure it's definitely closed.

'That bad eh?' Before I can answer, there's a timid tap at the door. Lauren is standing in the corridor looking very nervous when I answer it.

'I've got Ciaran's stuff,' she says, tentatively, clutching a bundle of clothes.

'Well, you'd better come in then.'

'I'm really sorry, Ciaran, it was just meant as a joke,' Lauren pleads, as he makes his way over towards her.

'Who put you up to it?' Ciaran asks, trying to sound serious.

'Um,' she replies, but hesitates for too long, and then the flicker of her eyes indicates she's not alone. I pop my head out through the doorway and see Melissa and various other male colleagues skulking halfway down the corridor.

'You're for it now.' I wag a finger at Melissa, as Ciaran pushes past me to get to her.

'Oh, come on, it was only a laugh. A leg-pull for the wedding boy, that's all,' she says, adopting a pretend Kung Fu stance, but Ciaran is too quick and tips the glass of water over her head. Melissa shakes herself down like a wet dog.

'We need a picture, where's your phone?' Ciaran yells at me, and I race back into the room to retrieve it.

'Let me take one of you all,' Lauren offers. So I jump over next to Melissa, Ciaran quickly follows, and we both stick up V signs above her head.

'Thanks.' I take my phone back and scan the crowd. 'Where's Eddie?' I ask Lauren.

'Oh, he went home. Said he didn't feel well. Tom went with him.' My heart sinks at this revelation. So Tom has gone then. Talk about love them and leave them – he obviously couldn't get away from me fast enough.

27

There's a 'morning after the weekend before' silence when I arrive at work. Somebody has cranked the music up and 'Love Is All Around' is playing on a continuous loop, driving me round the twist, as Mrs Grace would say. And there's still half an hour to go until opening time.

I do a quick scan towards Tom's Fine Jewellery counter and feel relieved on seeing it's empty, but then irritated by the sight of the limited edition Valentine bottles of pink champagne he's got piled up to flog too. *Since when did Carrington's sell alcohol?* And I bet he's got a bottle or two stashed away to share with Maxine on Valentine's Day. She was obviously lying about being single.

I reach my counter, tweak the Valentine promotion board into place, just about manage to fling my bag in the locker when Tina appears. She's wearing a headband with a pair of flashing red hearts bouncing around on springs above her head, and clutching a batch of white forms that she starts dishing out.

'Thanks, what is it?' I ask, when she tosses one down

on top of the cocktail rings, narrowly missing Annie's strategically arranged miniature Cupid soft toy display. A fiver with every purchase, and they say, 'I love you' when you press the left paw, although Annie found one the other day that sounded more like 'I loathe you'. We think the battery must be dying . . . and I know the feeling. With her free arm on her hip and a bored look on her face, Tina eyes me up and down.

'Take a look and see,' she says with a curt smile. Then she flicks out her ponytail, and grins as if we're actually real friends. 'Can't wait until Sunday,' she quickly adds, in an extra loud voice. I stare at her blankly, wondering what she's going on about. 'My hen party. Oh, don't tell me you'd forgotten?' She treats me to her crazy cow smile. I groan inwardly, thinking: *don't remind me*. 'Can't wait to catch up,' she trills, as she stalks off to hand out the rest of the forms. I grab the form and see that it says 'Diversity Awareness Survey' across the top.

'Can I have everyone's attention please? If you could huddle around me. Chop chop.' She claps her hands. 'Come on, nearly opening time.' Tina's voice is bristling with efficiency. We all look up. 'Recently I've witnessed some very disappointing behaviour towards our customers from overseas that quite frankly could land us in very hot water indeed. As a responsible employee –' a little round of sniggers circulates – 'I took my concerns to Amy, the HR manager, and let me tell you . . . she was horrified! So, she asked me to make sure these forms are completed straight away.' She waves the pile of leftover documents in the air. So that's what she was busy scribbling about in her notebook. I smile inwardly, wondering when she's going to start heeding her own warning about tolerance towards others, as she sure as hell won't even tolerate me talking to or tweeting Ciaran.

There's a groan from the guys in Menswear as they flip open the forms marked 'Strictly Confidential' at the bottom of each page.

'And the document can also be found on the Carrington's web page on the HR shared drive if any of you wants to complete it online and do your bit for the environment.' She smiles, looking very pleased with herself for being so forward-thinking.

'Wouldn't it have been better not to have printed any at all in that case?' Melissa points out. 'And it says to insert a cross if completing the form electronically and use a black pen if writing the answers,' Melissa adds with a wicked glint in her eyes. 'So what do I do with the pen then?' There's silence as we all wait for the punch line. 'Whatever you want,' Tina steps in. 'Even you can work that one out.' She looks as though she might be regretting her overzealousness now.

I busy myself with completing the form. I don't like Tina but I don't want to upset her either, not when she holds the key to my commission payments. Everyone flicks through the form, a couple of Home Electrical guys pause on the section about criminal convictions, and after debating whether a caution for a drive-by gobbing incident counts, they move on to the sexual orientation section.

Having delivered the forms, Tina stalks off, the flashing red hearts bouncing wildly and her denim wedge slingbacks slapping furiously as she gathers speed. With almost comedic timing, she catches her pocket on the outstretched hand of the Missoni mannequin, yanking it free as she flounces from the floor.

Show over, I'm crouching down to retrieve my phone when Maxine suddenly appears from behind me. 'Hi there.'

The smile immediately slips from my face and, after flinging the phone back into my bag, I jump up so that for once I'm operating from the same level as her.

'Oh Maxine, I didn't see you there. How are you?'

Ignoring my question she says, 'How was the team-building event?' and then stares at me blankly while waiting for my answer.

'Err, yes, you know how these things are,' I say, smarting from her directness and conscious that my cheeks are threatening a blush. Out of the corner of my eye I can see the others all pretending to be busy, but I know they're listening intently.

'No. Not really. I heard that it was, let me see, what was it that Tom said? Oh, predictable, yes that's it.' *Predictable?* What's that supposed to mean? God, I hope he's not referring to me. 'Anyway, I won't keep you, I have some visual merchandising to attend to.' She does her pageant smile before breezing off towards Tom's Fine Jewellery section.

'Of course, and I'm straight on it,' I mutter, grabbing the earring display and straightening the price tags. I gulp, wondering what else Tom told her. Surely he wouldn't have said anything about the kiss. And then it dawns on me – *predictable*. Of course, he's used to getting any girl he wants and I was no different.

My face flushes hot at the possibilities of his implication. He reeled me in just like some grateful groupie.

Mortified, I make my way over to the DKNY display. On my way back I spot James coming through the fire door. I feel a pang of guilt. I waver for a moment, but then decide I have to put this right.

'James, please can I talk to you?' He looks at me, but doesn't reply for a few seconds, as if hesitating over his decision. I look back at him, pleading with my eyes.

'OK, but let's make it quick,' he eventually agrees, and I sense the prompt for speed is his way of staying in charge. We dip into the corridor.

'James, I'm truly sorry for what I did.' He stares at me, studying my face as if he's trying to work out if I mean it.

'Look, like I said, I'm just not ready,' he says, putting his palms up in protest. He turns to leave.

'James, please. I've been a rotten friend, I know. But

please, hear me out, let me try and make it up to you.'
He stops and I notice his shoulders soften, and then to
my surprise he turns around and smiles at me.

'Sure. No harm in talking. But not here, what time's
your break?'

'Ten thirty.'

'Fine, I'll meet you in the café upstairs.'

*

When I arrive in the café, Sam nods towards the booth
in the far corner before holding up crossed fingers and
mouthing 'good luck'. James is sitting with his back to
the café. He motions for me to sit opposite him,
presumably so there's less chance of us being spotted
together.

'James, I know I ruined things between us, but I hate
it that we're not even talking. Before –' I hesitate, picking
my words carefully – 'everything changed, we were good
friends, weren't we?' He looks at me; his face gives
nothing away. Mentally, I will him to go with me.

'I know. And I'm sorry how things have turned out
between us.' My heart lifts. At last! We're talking, and
on the same wavelength.

'Me too. But I was hoping that we might at least be
friends again. Maybe even work together to scupper
Maxine and Tom,' I say, optimistically, thinking how
lovely it would be if I was back in favour with him.

'What do you mean?' he asks, his forehead crinkling into a frown.

'Well, I don't think Maxine's makeover is being conducted fairly.' I stare at him, trying to gauge his thoughts.

'But what makes you think that?' He looks at me intently.

'Because they're having an affair. I've seen them together, arm in arm. And Eddie spotted them too, actually snogging.'

He ponders this for a while and then lets out a long whistle.

'So that's her game then.' His jaw tightens.

'You think so too, that they're up to something then?' I feel relieved I'm not the only one who believes something dodgy is going on. It's hard to think straight these days. James nods and reaches for his coffee.

'I knew it. I just knew it. What an idiot I've been.' He shoves a hand through his hair.

'What do you mean?'

'She's been playing us both.' Ha! A little feeling of satisfaction waves through me. I was right about her and Tom all along. I can't believe I ruined everything with James. Kind, decent James. What was I thinking? Men like Tom don't go for women like me. I should have known I'd be just a conquest, at best.

'Georgie, I'm so sorry.' James looks over at me, his eyes full of concern now. My heart drops.

'What for?' The feeling of satisfaction withers and I feel uneasy now. I'm not sure I want to hear his apology if it's something to do with him and Maxine.

'Malikov.'

'Oh, don't remind me, please. And you don't need to apologise, I was the one in the wrong. I should have made sure I updated you straight away,' I say, grateful Maxine hasn't lured him into bed again.

'But I overreacted. And I said some unforgivable things to you.' He pulls his eyes away from mine.

'It's understandable. After everything you've been through,' I say, concerned that he seems to be blaming himself, when it was all my fault.

'No, please hear me out. When Maxine went through my sales sheet she accused me of stealing Malikov from you. Wouldn't have it that I organised his original visit and we had shared the commission. And then when she accused me of dirty tricks, I guess I just saw red.'

'Oh James, I'm so sorry.'

'I know you are, Georgie, but there's something else I want you to know.' My heart starts beating harder and my palms feel hot. I brace myself for what he's going to say next. 'I'm really sorry for what I said . . . the stupid Valentine's present thing and comparing you to your dad.'

'But how did you know in the first place?' I ask, bracing myself for his answer.

'Oh, I've always known,' he says, casually. 'Can't

remember how. It was in all the papers years ago, wasn't it, and I think I just twigged, but it's no reflection on you. I like to take people as I find them – it was just an easy insult to hurl. I'm sorry, really, I am.'

Relief floods through me, quickly followed by sadness that I ever doubted him. He knew all along and never judged me. That's pretty amazing.

'James, I overreacted too.' His eyes lock onto mine. For a moment neither of us says anything.

'You know, she's been at me ever since she came here,' James says, wearily. 'Even implied that I can keep my job . . . if I sleep with her.'

I'm stunned.

I don't want to hear any more about him and her, and then I remember Tom and what happened between us and I feel like such a hypocrite. So she's been manipulating James all along. And so much for her female solidarity then, telling me 'us girls need to stick together'.

'What shall we do?' he asks, his voice sounding hollow. I ponder on the situation before replying.

'Well, we'll both work hard on selling as much as we can, and may the best man, or indeed woman, win.' I grin. 'If our sales figures are higher than Tom's – well, then she just can't sack us and keep him on, can she? That would be so obvious; the board would never let her do that, would they?' I feel triumphant, and pleased that James and I seem to be friends again. But then I suddenly remember what Maxine told me in my first

264

meeting with her, and my heart plummets. 'Hang on a minute. That's not going to work, unless our sections make exactly the same amount of money, which is pretty impossible to guarantee. One of us will be deemed a loser and she's already told me she doesn't do "losers",' I say, despondently, making a feeble 'L for loser' sign like she did. 'No, we need to get more information on what's really going on, get some proof,' I add, sounding conspiratorial. We both look at each other for inspiration, and then a few seconds later we come to the same conclusion, at precisely the same moment.

'Eddie!'

James pulls out his mobile. There's a brief silence before Eddie answers.

'Ed. James here. Can you talk?' James pulls his mobile back from his ear and leans into me so I can hear too.

'Briefly. Maxine, or "Cruella De V-i-l-e", as I've renamed her, is in the kitchenette . . . purring to a phone sex client, no doubt,' Eddie hisses, and I giggle.

'Well, how would you like to get your own back on her?' James glances at me, a grin forming on his face. My heart pounds; it's fantastic that he doesn't think badly of me any more.

'I'm listening . . .' Eddie says slowly, his voice perking up.

'I've got Georgie here with me.' James smiles at me, and I instantly feel happier, glad I made the effort to make things right between us.

'Hello,' I say, into the phone.

'Hi *girlfrieeend*.' I laugh.

'We're in the café,' James tells him.

'I'm there.' And before James can say any more, the line goes dead.

A few minutes later, Eddie appears. He throws himself into the booth next to me.

'Got here as fast as my little trotters could carry me,' he pants. James and I laugh at the state of him. Eddie looks as though he's practically launched himself down from upstairs. His face is flushed and he can hardly breathe, he's that eager to get one over Maxine. We quickly bring him up to speed, telling him about the mind games she's been playing with each of us.

'And she's having an affair with Tom,' I end. Eddie throws me a confused look, but I know my secret is safe. Then he flings his hand up theatrically and quickly gasps in horror.

'*Weell*. Calm now, children. I can raise you on that one.' A cheeky smile unfolds across Eddie's lips. He flings one leg over the other and, after leaning forward, he rubs his hands together, savouring the anticipation. James and I stare at him. 'Oh yes, Madam Fifi is having an affair all right.' He pauses to look at each of us in turn. I can feel my cheeks burning – so Tom was just playing with me after all. This confirms it. I allow the last little drop of hope, that our moment of intimacy was something more, to trickle away. '. . . But it's not with Tom.'

Whaat! My heart feels as though it's going to burst right out of my chest.

'But you saw them snogging,' I gasp, 'and I saw them with my own eyes, in the corridor. And he phoned her. On a Sunday. Why would he do that?'

'Who with, then?' It's James who asks.

After a furtive look around the café, Eddie whispers, 'Only . . .' His eyes dart from side to side. '. . . The Heff.'

'Walter?' James and I say together in disbelief. There's a stunned silence. I can't believe it.

'Hush now, we don't want all and sundry to know . . . at this stage,' Eddie sniggers, with an evil glint in his eye.

'So that's how she wangled the job here then,' I say, mulling it all over.

'Of course. Oh, and that's not all. We're talking the Audi, the stratospheric salary. I mean, I know she's a retail consultant, but come on,' Eddie sniffs, before pulling a haughty face. 'Anyway, she's working *me* like some Vaudeville circus act and coming and going as she pleases, and wearing that slutty perfume and flinging her fur coat around and practically running her phone sex line out of her office,' Eddie continues, counting out the misdemeanours on his hand as he reels them off one by one. 'Yes, she's so smug she's practically licking her own arse.' He crosses his arms with indignation. I stifle a snigger and James shakes his head at Eddie. 'Oh, and not forgetting the pied-à-terre secret mews house in London.' Eddie's eyes dart around the café. 'They spend practically every weekend there, you know,' he mouths, with a look of disgust on his face.

'Really,' I snort.

'You know, I even overheard Walter lying to Camille, telling her he was attending the team-building event just so he could stay at the house last weekend.'

My brain instantly goes into overdrive. So Tom must be in on the secret then. I wonder whether Walter knows about her and Tom – maybe it's a love triangle. My head is spinning. And, come to think of it, I wonder if Walter knows about her trying it on with James as well.

'How do you know she isn't sleeping with Tom too?' I ask, trying not to sound too bothered about it. Eddie flashes me another look.

'Well, she may well be . . . but if she is, then Walter won't be happy. No, he likes his affairs to be exclusive,' Eddie says, nonchalantly, before inspecting his nails.

'Maybe we should tell him,' I offer, eager for the pair of them to get their comeuppance.

'Tell Camille, more like. She's the one with the money, after all. Serve the old bastard right for shafting me into a life of slavery,' Eddie snorts.

James shakes his head.

'No, we need to come up with something more

concrete. We don't even know for sure she's sleeping with them both,' James says, distractedly. His forehead creases as he tries to formulate a plan.

'Leave it to me,' Eddie says, leaning back and spreading his arms along the back of the train seat like some Mafia mogul planning a hit. 'Madam deserves everything she gets. You know, she told me to go and find a job in Poundland if I didn't like it, when I dared to voice an opinion about my disgusting workload the other day. No, by the time I've finished with her she'll be spending the next ten years to her retirement date examining her own backside and wondering where her career went. I'd love to see her face when I tell *her* to go and get a job in Poundland.'

I laugh out loud, imagining Maxine stacking the shelves and scaring the customers away.

'Whaat?' Eddie says, trying to look all innocent.

'You are so outrageous,' I say.

'*Weell* . . . she must be pushing fifty-odd at least,' he snorts. James and I laugh as Eddie frivolously adds at least fifteen years on to her.

'But what are you going to do?' I ask, desperate to know what Eddie has in mind.

'I'm not sure yet, but I'll think of something. I've already been fantasising over a few options during the darker moments of the last few weeks, and now I know that I'll be shoving her comeuppance down her throat for all three of us . . . well, it'll be all the sweeter.'

'Just be careful,' I reply, getting up to give Eddie a hug, and James shakes his hand.

'Oh I will. And believe me, the pleasure is going to be all mine,' he says slowly, winking at us both.

28

Sam glances over in my direction and, catching my eye, we share a knowing look. The hen party has only been going for an hour or so and already I just want it to be over. Tina hasn't stopped telling us how much Ciaran loves her and how he's proved it by spending so much money on the wedding and how romantic it's going to be blah-blah-blah. And she must have already reminded us, a trillion times at least, that she's getting married on Valentine's Day. It's not even ten o'clock. This is going to be a long day. I just hope she doesn't ask if I've found a date yet, which I haven't, of course, so I'm trying not to think about it.

We're all in the chill-out room and Tina is sitting on a big taupe-coloured leather beanbag in the middle, surrounded by the girls from Lingerie. Lauren is here, Tina's carbon-copy-looking friend Karen, and a couple of girls from the hairdresser's next door are milling around the heaving buffet table looking uncomfortable and muttering about why they've been invited.

'So, Georgie, tell us all about the team-building event.

It must have been so much fun,' Tina prompts, her jaw muscle flexing. My heart sinks.

'Not really; in fact it was pretty dull,' I mutter, leaning forward to take a handful of kettle crisps, hoping she'll get the hint.

'Oh, I bet it wasn't. Ladies, who wants to hear all the gossip?' Tina flashes a look around the room, hoping to drum up some support for her request. Sam, who's now hovering nearby, and out of sight of Tina, makes big warning eyes at me.

'Really, it was actually quite boring. You know, the usual thing.' I grin and push a few more crisps into my mouth. I wish she'd drop it.

'Oh, something must have happened. Come on, we all want to know.' Tina's eyes dart around the room again, provoking a half-hearted mumble of encouragement from the Lingerie girls. My face flushes. I've been dreading this moment. Ever since she squeezed out the reluctant invite in the lift, I've been intrigued to know the reason behind it, and now I know. She's obviously decided on the 'keep your enemies closer' approach, thinking we're friends somehow because I'm at her hen do, and I'll spill the beans about Ciaran's night away from her. Not that he got up to anything that I know of, but I don't know what he's told her, or – more importantly – what he hasn't.

'Tina, I'd much sooner hear about the wedding. Have you got a picture of your dress?' It's Lauren who rescues me. Tina, taken aback by the normally unassertive Lauren's request, stares at her for a second. I want to hug her for taking the heat off me.

'Of course not, it's a surprise. But I can tell you that it cost almost two thousand pounds. Can you imagine that, Lauren?' The girls all stare at Lauren, who's fidgeting uncomfortably. Tina is glaring at her and I can't help thinking what a pity it is she can't even enjoy her own hen party.

'Wow, it must be fantastic, is it a designer dress?' I ask, eager to ease Lauren's embarrassment and steer the conversation away from the weekend.

'Of course,' she snorts.

Caroline, the salon owner, closes her eyes for a second, and then, drawing in a deep breath, she marches into the middle of the floor and smooths down her black tunic top.

'OK ladies, if you could finish up now, we need to get started on the treatments,' she says, brightly, rubbing her hands together in an attempt to chivvy everyone along and bring a halt to Tina's incessant drilling for information.

Tina grabs the treatment schedule handed to her by one of the therapists, and I let out a little sigh of relief as she scrutinises it, appearing to have forgotten about interrogating me.

'Only a few more hours to go,' Sam mouths from behind the multicoloured macaroon mountain, as I glance over, roll my eyes and bite down hard into a stuffed olive.

The therapists are handing out thick white towelling robes for each of us to wear. The Lingerie girls jump up and rush towards the changing rooms. I glance at my schedule and see I'm having a pedicure at four thirty, but Tina and the Lingerie girls are having the works – full body massages, facials, gel nails and vajazzles.

'Ladies, before you all go and get changed, I've bought a little present for each of you.' The girls hurtle back to their seats. Tina is standing up now and motioning over to a huge cardboard box that's sitting in the corner underneath the window. Then she skips over to it and flings open the lid.

'Da-daaa,' she squeals, like a magician's assistant, before pulling out the handbags, each one in its own black-and-white striped Anya Hindmarch dust bag. My pulse quickens. I've wanted one for ages, but they're way out of my price bracket, even with my staff discount card. Tina starts taking a bag to each girl.

'Oh my God. Tina, you're so generous,' coos Karen, as she reaches inside the dust bag. Karen leans forward and plants a little kiss on Tina's smug-looking face.

'It's nothing,' Tina smirks, shaking her ponytail and basking in the misplaced glory Ciaran's money has bought her. The Lingerie girls are all ripping open the dust bags and Tina is back over by the box now. 'Oh dear,' Tina shouts over from the other side of the room, and the commotion halts. 'It looks like I may have tallied up the numbers incorrectly. Has everybody got a bag?' she asks, mock concern spread all over her face. I gingerly shake my head, not wanting to look greedy, and then so does Lauren. She doesn't have one either. Karen and the Lingerie girls start wandering off to get changed, taking their bags with them but not bothering to reply to Tina's question. For a glimmer of a moment I feel sorry for her, trying to buy friendship from workmates that clearly don't really like her.

'Oops, there's only one left.' Tina reaches into the bottom of the box and Lauren's face drops; she's practically on the verge of tears.

'It's fine, Tina, let Lauren have it,' I say. Lauren darts a hesitant look in my direction. I smile and nod at her, and then catch Sam discreetly making big eyes at me again. I should have guessed. Lauren steps forward and, clutching the package to her chest, she turns around to face me.

'Thank you, Georgie. Thank you so much.'

Tina's face is a mixture of anger and dismay.

'Well actually, Lauren, it's me you have to thank,' she says, poking Lauren in the back. Lauren spins around and mumbles an apology, her face turning crimson with embarrassment, and I don't feel sorry for Tina any more.

'OK ladies, shall we get going?' Caroline says, brightly, and starts herding the girls towards the door. Sam winks at me as I walk past the buffet table and I just about manage to force a grimace.

On a small clear Perspex table that's been placed just outside the entrance, there are crystal glasses brimming with white wine spritzer. Sam has thought of everything. I help myself to one and take a huge gulp of the fruity, fresh liquid, almost downing the whole glass in one.

I make my way into the changing room. The girls are all milling around. Some are already wearing their robes, whilst the others are standing around in their underwear, quaffing as much wine as they can. I dump my bag in a locker and start getting undressed. The girls soon finish up and start filtering back to the waiting area, eager for their treatments. I toss my clothes in the locker too, pull on the robe and count to ten. I'm glad to be alone for a moment.

*

While the others are having their treatments, I persuade Sam to abandon the buffet table so we can catch up before my pedicure. The waiting area is empty when we get there, so we flop down into the candy-striped cushioned steamer chairs. The manicure tables are to our left and directly in front of us are a couple of treatment rooms.

'Fancy another drink?' Sam raises her eyebrows at me.

'Oh go on then, I think I need it.' Sam pads over to another small table bearing an enormous jug with what looks like Sangria inside. She brings the whole jug back with two tumblers.

'We might as well get stuck in. My pedicure isn't until four thirty,' I tell her.

Sam tips the jug and a couple of pineapple chunks plop into the tumbler, followed by a generous measure of the magenta-coloured concoction.

'Bottoms up.' I chink my glass against the side of Sam's.

'Mmmm, not bad. Needs a bit of a kick though.' Sam pulls out a small bottle of tequila from her pocket and we exchange a wicked look. 'I thought I'd better bring some emergency rations, just in case,' she explains, waving the bottle at me.

'Good thinking,' I say enthusiastically and, before I can protest, she tips a generous measure into my drink. I take a slug. The liquid, now with the added kick from the tequila, warms me as it trickles down into my stomach, and I instantly feel more relaxed.

'A few more of these, and I think I might actually enjoy today after all,' I breeze, feeling looser already.

'That's a girl. Get it down you.' She pours me another generous tot. 'It was nice of you to let Lauren have that bag, it must have been a wrench to pass it up.'

'No, not really, I spend all day with bags like that,' I smile. 'I wanted her to have it. Anyway, let's face it . . .

she did rescue me from Tina's inquisition about the team-building weekend.'

'Yes, that was sooo funny when you told me about Ciaran being starkers in your bedroom.'

My vision is a little misty as I reach over to chink Sam's glass again. She's also on her way to tipsyland as she misjudges the distance between us and ends up toasting my arm instead.

'Oops, better slow down.' We glance at each other and giggle.

Suddenly, the door to one of the treatment rooms bursts open and Tina appears, clutching a towel to her naked body. Her face is covered in a fluorescent green face mask. She's huffing like a mini Incredible Hulk revving up for a gigantic hissy fit. Caroline is standing behind her with a look of utter horror on her face. My lips freeze on the glass. Tina struts over towards us and positions herself squarely between the two steamer chairs. She throws a look of disgust at Sam before turning to me. I swallow. Tina opens her mouth, immediately closes it and then hesitates for a moment before opening it again.

'Can you *purleease* keep the noise down. Your cackling is ruining my treatments. In fact, it's probably best if you go, Georgina, you're quite clearly not taking today seriously. And you are supposed to be on duty at the buffet table – that's what I employed you to do,' she snaps at Sam.

'Sorry, we didn't mea—' But before Sam can finish her sentence, Tina turns and flounces back into the treatment room. Caroline turns to close the door behind her and mouths 'sorry' at us before shaking her head. Sam and I exchange furtive glances. 'Come on. I think we've more than outstayed our welcome,' Sam whispers, as we leg it back to the chill-out room.

29

'You OK?' Sam asks, softly. After Tina's outburst yesterday, Sam stayed behind on buffet duties, while I dashed out for a sobering chicken salad. I then headed home to catch up on my ironing and get an early night before work today. I asked Maxine if I could do some extra hours to improve my chances of being kept on, so it's Monday afternoon and I'm on the phone in the vestibule behind my counter.

'I'm fine. Relieved I managed to escape yesterday,' I reply discreetly into the mouthpiece.

'Lucky you. I was there until late, stuffing stupid vol-au-vents. I mean, who even likes those these days?' Sam tuts. 'Anyway, I have to know. What *was* Ciaran doing in your room, naked?'

'Oh don't ask, Melissa nicked his clothes while he was in the hot tub. It was a prank, that's all.' And then it dawns on me. 'Oh my God. Do you think Tina heard me?'

'It occurred to me later that she must have done – that's why she came flying out of the room, not because we were laughing.'

'So why didn't she say anything then? You know how possessive she is.' I feel uneasy. I cast a quick look around the near empty floor.

'Maybe she's over all that, now the wedding is so close,' Sam says.

'Mmmm, I'm not so sure. She hates me, always has. She's up to something.'

'Is she really that clever though?'

'Remember what she said about my sales sheet? I wouldn't put it past her to scrub stuff off so Maxine thinks I'm a crap sales assistant who can't sell anything any more, just to get rid of me,' I reply.

'Now you're just being paranoid. You know I overheard her bitching about Ciaran having to work through his lunch breaks and stay late all the time? Think she wanted me to hear. But he doesn't, I certainly don't make him.'

'Really? Maybe he's got another woman,' I say, deviously.

'If he's got any sense,' Sam replies. 'Anyway, I've got a stock order and a VAT return to catch up on, so I've let the others go home early.'

'OK. Good luck, yell if you need a hand,' I say, knowing how Sam hates form-filling and anything maths-related.

'Will do.'

'And that business with her bags, well, just so you know, they're fake. I had a peek at Lauren's. The stitching was all wonky, a dead giveaway,' I say.

'What a scheming cow. You know, Ciaran thinks he

forked out for the genuine article, so Tina has done very well out of her little scam. I've a good mind to tell him. That would shut her up,' Sam rants.

'The thing that gets me is how far she's prepared to go to ensure she doesn't lose out financially,' I say, and then suddenly feel awkward, when I contemplate my own behaviour with the necklace. 'But then I suppose I'm no better,' I add, feebly.

'What do you mean? You're nothing like her,' Sam says, indignantly.

'Well, in my desperation to keep my job . . . let's just say I've done some things I'm not proud of,' I say, feeling ashamed all over again.

'It's hardly the same thing though, it's work. A necessity. It's not like you're marrying somebody, *just for their money.*'

'True. But what about the pact I've made with James? We've even roped in Eddie to make sure Maxine and Tom don't get away with their scam.'

I used to pride myself on playing fair but that's all changed now. I want to be the one who gets to sell Prada and Hermès because I'm the best sales assistant, not because Eddie manages to discredit Maxine and Tom.

'But that's different.'

'How is it? It still all boils down to money. No, I'm no better than Tina, or Maxine and Tom come to think of it. God, I've even fallen for him knowing he was using me as part of his stupid game. So what does that make me?'

'Normal? He's drop-dead gorgeous. Your "crime", if you must label it as such, was one of passion.' Sam giggles. 'So it doesn't count anyway,' she snorts.

'Trust you to see it like that.'

'Sorry hun, I have to go, a couple of guys in suits have just turned up. Probably reps from a coffee company, they're always on at me to change brands. Let me get rid of them and we'll chat later.' Sam blows a squelchy mwah kiss down the phone before hanging up.

Plumping up a DKNY tote, I ponder on our conversation, wishing I could be as bubbly and positive about life and everything as Sam is. But I just can't seem to shift this constant feeling of dread. If I could just get some sleep.

I wander back to my counter, click on the Carrington's staff website and find what I'm looking for – a new initiative suggested by you-know-who – Tina of course! She's started posting our sales sheets up for everyone to see. I scroll down and notice I'm still in the lead, but feel uneasy, as the difference between James and me, he's next on the list, is the exact worth of the extra stuff Malikov bought. I console myself with knowing we at least seem to be friends again. But his angry outburst, comparing me to Dad, continues to niggle away inside. I think of Dad and it makes me feel ashamed that I've been so quick to judge him, not ever stopping to wonder what made him do what he did.

'Penny for your thoughts, daydreamer.' Ciaran appears

at my counter and he looks exhausted. There are dark circles under his eyes and his shoulders are hunched. 'You OK? How was the hen do?'

'Oh, err . . . it was great,' I say, vaguely. 'How are you? You look really tired,' I add, changing the subject and hoping Sam and I haven't scuppered his chances of getting married, but then wondering whether we might in fact have done him a favour anyway. He leans against my counter.

'Not too bad,' he replies, his head bent down and eyes peering up at me. He looks as though he has the weight of the whole world on his shoulders.

'Before you say anything, I'm really sorry if we landed you in it.'

'What do you mean?' he says, frowning. So Tina hasn't said anything then. Maybe she didn't hear after all.

'Oh, nothing. I just got my wires crossed, that's all.' No point in worrying him. 'So how are the wedding plans coming along?'

'I'm not really sure. Tina is in charge of it all.' His shoulders droop and he looks sad. My heart goes out to him. Surely he could just call it off, if it's this bad, I've never seen him look so miserable.

'Ciaran,' I say, hesitantly. 'You don't have to do this if you don't want to.'

'I know.' He picks at an imaginary loose thread on his trousers, his head hanging down again. 'But you'll be pleased to know that Tina has upgraded your invite to the whole do. Her way of burying the hatchet – she says you guys are getting quite friendly these days.'

'Fab,' I say, attempting to sound cheery, but remembering the handbag scam, I'm sure she fixed the numbers on purpose. I wonder what game is being played out now.

A sad smile threatens on his face. It's as if he's given up completely. My heart drops. I was hoping I'd be let off the hook or, better still, Ciaran would come to his senses and call the whole thing off. But no such luck. He looks at me as if he wants to say something else.

'What is it, Ciaran?' I say, gently touching his arm and wondering what I can do to make it better for him.

'Not here,' he says, casting a look around. He looks nervous now. 'But I do need to talk to you. Can we get together tonight after work?' He glances up at me with a strange look on his face.

'Err, sure.' I raise an eyebrow and wonder what's up, but he shoves his hands in his pockets and wanders off. I click to open the sales chart again and see I'm no longer in the lead, James is. Surprisingly, I don't feel panicky at all. Instead there's a weird feeling, sort of detached, and one I'm not used to.

The wall phone rings and, seeing it's Sam's café, I grab the phone to my ear and duck into the vestibule.

'Managed to get rid of the suits then,' I laugh. There's a silence. 'Sam, are you there, hello? *Hello hello helloooo?*'

I sing, jovially. But there's still silence. I look at the handset and, just as I'm about to hang up, a male voice comes onto the line.

'Georgie, can you come up to the café please?' A cold shiver trickles up my spine.

'Who is this?' I ask, nervously.

'If you could just come up here please.'

I try to mask a surging feeling of unease.

'Sam has just received some devastating news,' he tries again, before adding, 'Look, it might be better if you just come here.'

'Please. Just tell me,' I plead. Fear filling every part of me now.

And then he tells me.

'Her father died suddenly this afternoon.'

Tears pierce my eyes. Oh no, please God don't let this happen to Sam. My mind races to Mum and a hollow gasp squeezes from my throat. Oh Alfie. Lovely, happy, caring, kind Alfie. The perfect dad, who always made everything better.

'I'm coming now.' I slam the phone down and pull out my mobile. As if on autopilot I hastily type out a Twitter DM to Ciaran, cancelling tonight.

After telling Annie, I run to the staff lift, fling the cage door shut and jam my hand on the button. Tears pour down my face. Nathan. I have to call Nathan for her. I can't wait for the lift to galvanise into action, so I head to the stairs instead. Grabbing the handrail, I haul myself two steps at a time all the way up to the café that has a 'closed' sign on the window.

I fling open the door and see Sam crouched in a sobbing huddle on the kitchen floor. Two men in suits are standing over her. One of them bends down and attempts to touch her arm, but she shrinks away. I run to her. Both men stand aside. I throw my arms around her trembling body. She subsides into me and the noise that escapes from her tiny body is primal, like nothing I've ever heard before. I rock her in my arms until another pair of arms appears around us. I look up and see Nathan kneeling around us.

'I've got her. It's OK. I've got her.' His voice is trembling. I drag myself up and stand motionless, staring at my best friend. Knowing the agony she is feeling and wishing I could snatch it away for her. Spare her the pain. It's as if time has stood still.

'Does she have any other family that we could contact for her?' one of the men asks me. I shake my head. Tears slide down my face.

'No. He was her only family,' I say, my voice small and wobbly. The man hands me his card, and through the tears I manage to make out the Mulberry-On-Sea Police logo. I shudder, remembering the last time I saw one of these. They leave quietly and I stare at my best friend, rocking, as her world falls apart.

30

Alfie just collapsed in his office – a heart attack – and he was gone, just like that. His PA worked on him and then the ambulance crew took over, but it was no use. Sam is beside herself with grief and hates herself for not having been there with him. She didn't even get to say goodbye. It's as if her whole existence has been shattered and I can't stop thinking back to when Mum went, the feeling of sheer helplessness . . . but at least I got to say goodbye.

And it really does put things in perspective. Worrying about being on my own for Valentine's Day and not having a date to take to the wedding just seems so trivial now. When people are dying, what does it really matter if I don't have a man in tow? I've decided to flout Tina's 'no singletons' rule and go to the wedding on my own. What's the worst she can do? She probably won't even notice me anyway and it's better than having to put up with Maxine all day long.

Of course, Sam and Nathan's trip to Italy has been cancelled for now, and I've managed to take a few days off to look after Sam. We're staying in Alfie's villa on the private beach estate just along the coast from Mulberry-On-Sea. He bought the villa a few years ago to be nearer to Sam when he wasn't travelling. His apartment overlooking Regent's Park in London, and rarely used, is being looked after by Yana, Alfie's housekeeper, until Sam can bear to go there and organise things.

We've spent the last few days just sitting, with Sam crying and me fielding telephone calls, taking delivery of flowers and condolence cards, but listening mainly. One minute she's sobbing in my arms, the next she's screaming, consumed with anger and mentally searching for something or someone to blame.

'I'll make some more tea,' I say, not really knowing what else to do. Nathan nods and Sam looks up from the cashmere jumper she has entwined in her fingers. It belonged to Alfie, and the faint smell of his Aramis aftershave still lingers.

'Do you think we should call the doctor?' Nathan says, following me into the kitchen. 'I can't bear seeing her like this – she's not even eating and I have no idea when she last had a shower.' His shoulders sag and I reach a hand out to rub his arm before flicking the kettle on.

'She's grieving; there isn't anything the doctor can do to take away the pain,' I say quietly. 'It won't ever go away, but she'll learn to live with it.' I chew the inside of my mouth in an attempt to stem my own feelings of grief. I'm trying really hard not to think of Mum and how I felt when she first died – the loneliness, the fear. I need to be strong for Sam. And I'm also trying not to let her see my sorrow at losing Alfie. I know he wasn't my dad, but that never stopped me from wishing he was.

'Oh God, I hope so. For her sake, and mine.' He looks away. 'Does that make me a bad person?'

'Of course not.'

'I just want her back. The bubbly, generous, kind, outspoken Sam that I fell for. I'm scared Georgie. Really scared,' he says, pushing a hand through his dishevelled hair.

'I know. Me too,' I say, gently.

'But you seem so calm. And you've been such an amazing support for her, whereas me . . . well, I crumble when I see her in this amount of pain. I just wish I could do something to make it better.'

'Being here is exactly what she needs right now,' I say, pouring milk into the mugs. 'She'll come back to us. She may change a little, but she'll definitely be back. I promise.' I smile and pick up the mugs.

'Thanks Georgie. I . . .' He pauses. '. . . We both couldn't get through this without you.'

'She's my friend. You too. It's what we do.'

After handing Sam her tea, and giving her shoulder a little squeeze, I sit down opposite her. She's staring at the cashmere jumper.

'Sam, can I do anything? Do you want to talk?'

'No. Just sit with me,' she says, not even looking up.

I take a sip of my tea and think about work, wondering if it's still all worth it. There must be more to life than scrapping over sales in a desperate bid to keep my job and stay one step ahead of the game. And it's only going to get worse if I manage to stay on and end up slaving for Maxine. I wish I didn't have the flat, the car and my debt problem to support. Then I could just sod off on one of those volunteer charity working breaks that I've read about in magazines. The girls come back looking all refreshed and wholesome, not haggard before their time like I am.

I've not slept at all for the last few nights, tossing and turning, thinking about Alfie, worrying about Sam and everything else that's going on at work. I just wish the game could be over, but I suppose it never will be, not really. Even if I get to stay at Carrington's and spend the next forty years working my arse off, I'll never be free. There'll always be a Maxine, a revamp, or someone like Tina I have to watch my back with just to stay one step ahead.

I've reached the point now where I just want to know what's happening, what has Maxine got planned? Am I going to get to sell Prada and Hermès bags or be unemployed? The wait is excruciating. We've been told we'll know one day next week, which might as well be an eternity away. And when I was last at work, Tom was

291

avoiding me, not even bothering to hold the lift like the rest of us do when we see somebody running to catch it. Maybe Maxine has already told him his job is safe so he figures he doesn't even need to bother trying to distract me any more.

31

It's 14 February and the big day has finally arrived. I've managed to shove myself into a big puffy gold vintage gown that I hired from a dress agency to keep costs down. It didn't seem too bad in the shop, but now I just look like a giant Ferrero Rocher. The dress code is 'movie star glamour', but I can't afford anything new and I must have put on a few pounds, as everything in my wardrobe is either catching under the arms or the bulge of my stomach is slightly more prominent than it ever was before. But then the stress is like a tonne weight permanently shackled to my body, so it's been goodbye *No Carbs Before Marbs* and hello to my loyal friend . . . Red Velvet.

I spritz another generous shower of perfume onto the insides of my wrists – well, it's aftershave really. It's Tom Ford for men, another tester from Scarlett, and it's so delicious and sexy and about as close as I'm getting to having an actual man of my own these days. But at least I'm not going to be home alone for a change, small mercies and all that. And I have a Valentine's card! Found it pushed under my front door this morning in a crimson envelope:

Georgie, Thinking of you xxx

I know it's from Dad, he's been sending me one every year since I was a little girl, and even though he disguises his handwriting and tries to make it sound as if it's from somebody else, I still know it's from him.

I slip my feet into the Gina sandals before glancing in the hall mirror. The face looking back at me looks different somehow and I don't think it's just the make-up, which is more glamorous than my usual style. No, it's as if it belongs to somebody else, someone I don't recognise any more. My mobile rings and, seeing that it's Sam, I flip it open.

'Hi honey, how are you today?' I ask, tentatively, hoping she'll be able to talk to me. When I called her last night there was only silence punctuated by the odd snuffle and sniff until she managed to utter 'OK' when I said I'd call again in an hour. I had a long chat with Nathan instead and he said she'd been lying on her bed all day listening to Frank Sinatra songs and staring at the ceiling. Alfie was a big fan.

'OK. It's the wedding today, isn't it?' Her voice is flat and lacking in any emotion.

'Yes, that's right. I don't have to go though. I can spend the day with you instead.'

'Yes you do. Ciaran will feel let down if you don't turn up. And I shouldn't have declined his invitation. He works for me but that didn't even matter when Nathan invited me to Italy . . . what was I thinking?' she says, sounding like a robot.

'Oh, please don't be hard on yourself. Look, I don't have to go, I'd much sooner be taking care of you.' I pause, letting the thought sit with her for a moment. 'You're my best friend,' I add, softly, unsure of what else to say to her.

'I know. But I'm going to see the funeral people today.' Her voice wobbles on the word 'funeral' and I'm instantly transported back to Mum's one.

'Well then, let me come with you. *Please*. You don't want to go on your own.' I'm conscious of sounding as if I'm telling her what to do. And then instantly feel guilty that the chance of forgoing the wedding springs into my mind so temptingly.

'No. I'm going on my own. Nathan wanted to come too but I want to do this for Dad. He did everything for me, so it's the least I can do.' Her voice trails off. 'But there is something you can do for me.'

'Anything,' I say, quickly.

'Go to the wedding and, if you get the chance, then please apologise to Ciaran on my behalf. Say I'm sorry I let him down.'

'Oh Sam, I will, but you haven't let anyone down.'

'Yes I have. I let Dad down . . . I should have been there with him,' she says, matter-of-factly, and a short silence follows.

'That's not true.'

'Please. Just go to the wedding.'

'OK, if you're sure. But if you change your mind, at any time, then just call me or text, and I'll come.'

'I will.' There's a pause. 'And thank you,' she adds, her voice sounding a little softer now. 'Georgie, you will come to the funeral with me, won't you?'

'Yes. Yes of course, I'll be right there next to you, for the funeral and for always.' I say goodbye and take another peek in the hall mirror before leaving.

*

At the entrance to the manor house, a throng of guests are milling around. There's a long, ruby-red carpet weaving all the way up and along the gravel driveway to create the Oscar-themed wedding that Tina chose. Faux paparazzi are busy flashing their cameras at the arriving guests.

'Over here, smile. Yes, *wooork iiit*,' a pap bellows at me the minute I step out of the cab. I manage a weak smile as I remember to lift the ankle-length dress up just enough to make sure that I don't catch the toe of my sandal in it. I couldn't bear to fall flat on my face in front of all the people who are milling around up ahead of me. I feel self-conscious with them all gazing in my direction. Everywhere I look there are beautiful people I don't recognise. Couples. The women in sparkly cocktail dresses and the men in black tuxedos.

'Ignore them. They're just for show, they're not real guests. From some wannabe agency or other. "Permanently resting" actors, most likely.' Eddie appears at my side, his razor tongue sharpened to perfection as usual.

'Thank God you're here,' I say, relieved to see a familiar face. He looks me up and down and then lets out a whistle of approval.

'Baby doll, you look fierce,' he says, clicking his fingers in a Z shape around me. I laugh and hook my arm through his and we make our way up the red carpet and into the foyer that's crammed with a trillion rose-pink heart-shaped metallic balloons. Just inside the huge glass doors is a huddle of pretend fans, and they're all waving autograph books and screaming to get our attention. Eddie grabs one of the books, and milking the moment to the max he scrawls his signature before tossing the book back into the crowd. I cringe inside and bat a balloon away from my face, half wishing that I was home alone scoffing a chocolate bar, after all.

'This is so embarrassing . . . and how come she's managed to pull this off in under a couple of months? Weddings on this scale usually take a good year to organise,' I whisper in Eddie's ear.

'Yep, they totes do, but madam gets what madam wants, doesn't she? Probably had the venue on a retainer from the very first moment she clapped eyes on Ciaran. You know how showy she is, anyway. I think Ciaran's wealthy parents footed the bill and I guess you can have whatever you want whenever you want . . . if you chuck enough money at it. Wouldn't surprise me if One Direction show up and sing a special *a cappella* Valentine song especially for her,' Eddie snorts.

'Really?' I say, perking up at the prospect of getting close to Harry.

'*Weell* . . . that might be stretching the budget just a little bit, but who knows?' Eddie shrugs his shoulders. 'Ciaran didn't get much of a say, so I guess anything is possible.'

'Oh I see,' I reply, thinking how sad, and wondering whether it's too late to locate Ciaran and shake some sense into him.

'Anyway, let the show begin,' he says flamboyantly as he grabs a flute of pink champagne from one of the nearby waiters and makes off towards the glass-domed atrium. Catching my breath, I push my silver clutch bag under my arm and take two glasses of the pink champagne. I know I'm not going to enjoy today so I need all the sustenance I can garner. I take a big gulp of the bubbly liquid and immediately wince as the glands under my ears smart from the shock of the bittersweet liquid. I glance around, noting that there don't appear to be any other real guests here yet. I finish the flute, so, clutching the other one, I make my way through to the atrium.

The scent from the long-stemmed pink lilies hits my nostrils. There must be at least twenty head-height marble pillars dotted around the perimeter, each displaying a gigantic floral arrangement. To my left there's an enormous easel detailing the seating plan. I head towards it, eager to see who Tina has sat me next to. As I scan, looking for my name, I feel a hand on my back.

'Hi there. You're on the same table as me.' I spin around and James is standing right in front of me. He looks gorgeous in his creamy white tuxedo with matching bow tie. 'You look amazing,' he says, looking me up and down, and then leaning towards me he plants a soft kiss on my cheek. I catch a whiff of his spicy aftershave and wish again that things could have been different.

'And you don't look too bad yourself,' I reply, smiling warmly. There's an awkward silence and I start bobbing from one foot to the other. I quickly stop when James's gaze wanders down towards my feet.

'Nice sandals,' he says, grinning at me.

'Thanks.' I feel like a teenager on her first Valentine's date. He's being very complimentary; I feel a bit awkward.

'Georgie, I was wondering whether, now that we've cleared the air between us . . .' He looks into my eyes and then pauses momentarily. I wait for him to carry on, curious to hear what he's about to say. But before he can finish the sentence, Maxine appears unexpectedly from behind one of the flower arrangements, startling me in the process. I grasp the flute as it topples in my hand, just managing to save it from crashing to the floor.

'Not interrupting anything *priiivate*, am I?' she says

in an extra breathy voice, lingering on the word 'private', as if it's a rampant rabbit sex toy, and all for her. She slings her crimson chiffon wrap, which has slipped from her shoulder, back into place. Impulsively I spring apart from James, blushing at her innuendo.

'Georgie, I want to talk to you,' she continues. She does her pageant smile and my heart sinks. I quickly shake the spilt champagne from the back of my hand before nodding back at her. 'Away from here.' She shakes her big hair back and attempts to cock a newly Botoxed eyebrow at me.

She knows!

She knows what happened between Tom and me. And on top of the other secrets she has on me she must have decided it's tipped the scales. She's going to sack me. I just know it. It's one thing being let go as part of a recession-busting revamp, but to be sacked for snogging your boss's lover – well, it's unimaginable. And on Valentine's Day too! Talk about irony. But I can't believe she's about to do it here, at a wedding. I brace myself for the showdown that's bound to come any minute now.

'Follow me,' she orders, and I do, deftly batting the wrap from hitting my face as she swings around fast and sashays off, her Agent Provocateur scent wafting behind her like a lethal vapour trail.

'Sit down,' Maxine says, as we enter her room. An enormous bouquet of red roses is perched upside down on top of the trouser press, as if it was thrown from the bed opposite. Clothes are strewn all over the floor, so I pick my way through on tiptoe, only just managing to avoid a shocking tangerine-coloured lacy negligee and pair of purple snakeskin cowboy boots.

I wonder who the saucy cowgirl look was for. Was it Walter who kept her company, or maybe it was Tom — or, perhaps, both of them? My mind is racing. Nothing would surprise me any more. A sudden image of Maxine screaming 'giddy up' pops into my mind and instantly I cringe at the thought of her riding bareback astride Walter. I can't even bring myself to imagine the same scenario with Tom taking Walter's place.

Spotting two chairs over by the window, I reluctantly do as she's ordered. But instead of adopting her usual towering-above-me position, she sits in the adjacent chair to mine and crosses her legs. I fidget with my clutch bag, unable to make my mind up whether to place it on the table beside me or keep it in my lap. I decide on the latter, figuring it's better to have something to hold on to.

'Maxine, I'm sorry. I didn't mea—' I start, but she promptly flings up a hand. Her eyes are glinting, as if she's on some weird power trip.

'Don't be,' she says, suddenly changing tack.

'But, I . . .' My voice trembles. Her face softens a little, which only makes my anxiety surge even more. I place the champagne glass down on the floor beside the chair leg and surreptitiously wipe my sweaty palms down the back of my clutch bag. I wish she'd just get on with it.

'You're only a couple of hundred short, but no, my mind is made up.' *A couple of hundred.* My head is spinning trying to catch up. This must be about the sales figures, and not about my indiscretion with Tom. I allow myself to relax for a moment and let out a small silent sigh of relief as she looks away to slap the wrap into place again. 'Damn thing. Don't you just hate wearing these ridiculous outfits?' She looks me up and down, before wrenching the wrap from her neck and slinging it across the room.

'Err yes, I suppose so,' I venture, praying I've got it right. Her face has changed now, back to her usual aloof look, and a little shiver trickles down my spine. Maybe I've got it wrong then.

'Do you like working at Carrington's?' I swallow hard, wondering why she's talking about this today, at a wedding. Surely it could have waited until we were at work?

'Yes, yes of course I do,' I blurt, taken aback at the directness of her question at such an inappropriate time. Then she fixes her stare on me and I'm forced to look away.

'Only just recently I haven't been so convinced. You seem distracted. As if you'd rather be somewhere else.' She fixes her eyes on mine. I swallow hard.

'No, I don't think so,' I manage to reply, knowing what she's saying does have a ring of truth to it. I hadn't realised it had been quite so obvious, though. I have been preoccupied with worrying about Sam, losing Alfie, and thinking about the plan with James and Eddie – never mind fretting about my debts, the necklace, seeing if I might be able to salvage something of my relationship with Dad and everything else that has gone on. The thought of our plan makes me blush and I remember her chilling words about making it her business to know everything. Please don't let her have found out about it. I don't think I could bear the backlash.

'Hmmm, well, if you're going to be the new floor supervisor then you have to stay focused at all times.'

I snap back to attention.

'The *supervisor*?' Did I hear her right? My pulse quickens. Maybe I'm off the hook after all.

'Yes, that's right. I've made my recommendations to the board and spoken to HR. It's all been agreed. Your section is the most popular, which is really no surprise – I mean, who doesn't love a luxury handbag or three? And you just wait until those Prada and Hermès beauties arrive,' she smiles, a real smile this time, and one that meets her eyes, and then puts her hand out to me.

'Well, I . . . err . . . don't know what to say.' And I don't. I shake her hand, feeling puzzled at this sudden twist. But then a surge of adrenalin bolts through me. A floor supervisor! Me. I wonder if my salary will increase. This means security. No more worrying and sleepless nights – all of it is mine for the taking. But why do I still feel uneasy and a little deflated? I thought this was what I wanted, but now I'm not so sure.

'But, James is the floor supervisor,' I hear myself saying. 'And he made the most sales, surely the job should still be his,' I add, desperate to try and make the decision a fair one, made on merit, and then I immediately feel like a naïve idiot for thinking that it was ever about fairness at all.

'Maybe. But no, like I said, us girls need to stick together. Just tread carefully when you break it to them. You know how tetchy men can get.'

'Break it to them?' My stomach turns.

'Of course. You're in charge now so you can tell James and Tom they're no longer required. Redundant. Whatever spin you want to put on it. But it all boils down to the same thing. Just get rid of them.' She flaps a dismissive hand into the air between us.

'But, I . . .' I gulp. I can't believe this. Surely HR should deal with this kind of thing? I need to talk to Amy, but then what if Maxine finds out and thinks I'm checking up on her, that I've gone behind her back? This is a nightmare. How am I going to tell James he has to leave when I've stolen his job out from under him? The thought fills me with dread. It's like an icy hand clutching at my insides. And Tom? Oh my God, what am I going to say to him?

This is bad. Really bad. And I'm not sure I can do what's she asking. It just doesn't make sense – why would she make me a supervisor when James clearly won on the sales, which is what it was supposed to be all about?

And he has the experience. Then, for a flash of a second, I feel a stab of guilt. So she wasn't playing me after all, and I've even gone and roped in Eddie to stitch her up. But I saw her with Tom, with my very own eyes. I didn't imagine it and she definitely answered the phone on that Sunday morning.

Maybe this is her sick way of getting revenge on James for choosing another woman over her, and she's prepared to sacrifice Tom in the process. God, maybe she does know what happened with Tom and this is her punishment to him for taking their ruse too far. My head is spinning, lurching from one sickening possibility to the other. I just can't believe it. A sinking feeling cloaks itself around me. If I accept this job then I'll become a puppet, dancing to her tune forever, with the threat of the strings being cut at any moment. I just don't know if I can go that far to ensure my financial security.

'I'll need your formal acceptance by close of play on Tuesday.' She jumps up and, grabbing the wrap from the floor, she turns around, flaps her hand behind her backside to indicate that I'm to follow her, and heads towards the door. Once again I scuttle along behind, my mind working overtime.

32

After managing to escape from Maxine, I make my way back into the atrium and take another flute from a passing waitress.

'Take two,' she says. 'Looks as though you could do with it.' She grins at me.

'You're right.' I smile back gratefully. 'Thanks.'

There are more people milling around now. A quartet is playing light jazz music and there's a happy wedding atmosphere. I spot Melissa standing alone near the fire exit and wander over to join her.

'Cor, you scrub up well,' Melissa the store detective says, shimmying her ample cleavage which is tethered in, only just, by a lime-green scoop-necked Lycra dress. She's holding a pint of Guinness.

'Thanks Mel. How come you've got Guinness?' I ask, eager to engage her in conversation. I can see James standing just a few inches away, chatting to a guy who must be related to Ciaran – he's the spitting image of him. The job promotion still hasn't really sunk in, and I'm not sure I'm going to be able to keep it from James.

But I have to, at least until I've got my head around Maxine's sneaky plan.

'Just asked the waiter for it. Shampoo gives me gut-ache.' She pulls a groaning face.

'So when do you start your training course?' I ask, remembering that she handed in her notice last week and is off to become a prison warder.

'End of the month, and I can't wait. It's just not the same at Carrington's any more,' she says, downing the last of her pint. I stare at her, pondering on what she's just said.

'I know,' I reply, softly. I know. The thought lingers on.

'You'll come to my leaving do though, won't you? A ten-pint challenge in the Nag's Head. First one down buys the kebabs on the way home,' she says, like she can't wait to get started. I groan at her idea of a good evening and then, just as I open my mouth to reply, Tom, who must have been standing behind me, turns to join us. He's wearing a beautifully cut black tuxedo, white shirt and loose bow tie. His dark curls are gelled back and he looks just like a Hollywood A-lister at a film premiere. And no matter how hard I try, I just can't stop my stomach flipping, my groin tingling and my heart racing all at the same time. It's a mixture of sexual excitement and raw nerves, and there's no hiding from him.

The atrium is buzzing now with guests. Some of the

others from work are here, all necking drinks like there's no tomorrow. Mrs Grace has just arrived and is busy telling Stan to stop fiddling with his tie. He rolls his eyes and she bats his hand away from his collar before sipping the champagne and wrinkling her nose.

'Hi Georgie,' Tom says, letting his gaze linger on me. I feel awkward. It's the first time he's spoken directly to me since that moment in Brighton. 'What's this about a party?' He turns to Melissa.

'My leaving do – you'll be there, won't you?' Melissa says. The atrium is filling up so quickly there's barely room to move now, and Tom is standing right next to me, my bare arm tantalisingly close against his sleeve.

'Depends . . . will Georgie be there too?' Tom smiles, and I almost choke on my champagne. I can feel my cheeks getting hot. There's a momentary silence.

'Nice one. You two . . . right pair of bluffers. Never would have guessed you were at it,' Melissa broadcasts in a too-loud voice, and treats me to a massive wink before sauntering off in search of a waiter. I'm speechless. I just wish the ground would come back and swallow me up. My whole body is singeing with embarrassment.

'Sorry about that. It's Melissa, you know how she is . . .' I manage to mutter, not daring to look at Tom. I drain the last of my drink. I can't move. There are people crammed all around me. There's no escape.

'Why are you apologising?' He manages to turn in

the confined space so he's facing me now. I glance up. He stares straight into my eyes, holding my gaze and not faltering. I gulp, unsure of what to say. Suddenly I wonder where Maxine is – she could be watching us. Then I wonder whether he already knows about my promotion.

'Well, you know . . .' is all I can muster.

'No I don't. Please tell me,' he says, still holding eye contact. I feel sick. I don't want to have to spell it out to him.

'Well, after what happened. I mean, I know it was just a kiss and all . . . but well,' I babble, waving a hand around and cringing all over.

'Not for me it wasn't,' he interrupts, and my heart actually misses a beat.

'But you left in such a hurry,' I stutter. 'And you've been avoiding me ever since,' I add, desperately trying to regain some composure and control.

'I haven't.' He looks bemused.

'Yes you have. Just the other day you let the lift go without me. You could have easily waited but you chose not to,' I say, thinking, *there*, let's hear what you have to say about that.

'I don't remember, but I'm sorry if I did. It wasn't intentional. And if I have been avoiding you it's only because . . . well, I thought I might have overstepped the mark.' Sadness clouds his eyes. He looks away.

'But I didn't realise.'

Tom laughs and a fizzle of electricity shoots up my arm as his fingers gently stoke mine. Then a bald-headed, beer-bellied man tries to squeeze behind me to get through the crowd, and as he stumbles into my back I'm suddenly catapulted into Tom's chest. I draw in his delicious scent as he places his hands, one on each of my arms, to rescue me from being winded. The feeling is so intense it makes me gasp. But then I quickly pull away. I'm not falling for it a second time.

'But you told Maxine the weekend was "predictable". What did you mean by that?' I can't look him in the eye.

'Predictable?' He ponders for a moment. 'Oh yes, I was just making conversation. She wanted to know what happened, so I told her . . . you know, people started off not liking the idea of team activities but soon got over it and ended up enjoying themselves – a typical team-building event,' he says, casually. Then he touches my chin and gently turns my face towards his. My heart surges again as he leans down to whisper in my ear. 'Georgie, what happened to you to make you so mistrusting?' Silence follows. I pull away. 'Have a bit more faith, I wasn't talking about you. Far from it.'

'But what about Maxine?' The words are out of my mouth before I know it. His face changes, he looks at me blankly, his forehead creases. 'The phone call?' I say, trying to jog his memory. I feel more confident now. I'm not losing my job after all, and in spite of what he's just said, I still want to know if he's been sleeping with Maxine.

'What phone call?' he says, genuinely looking as if he has no idea what I'm talking about.

'You know, the one from the hotel room, I err . . . overheard you, the door was open.' I feel nervous now and immediately regret having said anything. And then, God I hope he doesn't ask me how I know. I quickly rack my brains searching for a suitable explanation, and I realise I'm bobbing again from one foot to the other. I quickly stop.

'Why would you think I was talking to Maxine?' he asks, creasing his forehead. The nerves are replaced by a panic now that's slowly building up inside me.

'*Weell*,' I start, stalling for time. 'I just presumed you were,' I finish, swallowing hard. The last thing I want is him thinking that I'm some kind of nutcase snooper, especially if there's even the slightest chance I've got it all wrong, somehow. Maybe he is for real.

'But why Maxine?' Jesus, he's not going to let this drop. I swallow again and decide to confront him.

'Because you're sleeping with her?' I say, tentatively. His face doesn't move. A wave of nausea rides up through me.

He laughs, and I feel so insecure. 'That's absurd. Why would you think that?' His eyes are still smiling and he strokes my hand again.

'I saw you with her in the corridor. She had her arm

311

in yours, she was practically pawing you.' His forehead creases again as if he's trying to remember. 'And you were seen together, actually snogging by the car park.' Ha! Try wriggling out of it now. I have to look away because the physical attraction to him is so intense that it's making me feel confused and clouding my judgement. How can I be this attracted to a man when I'm sure he's having an affair with another woman, my boss? I take a deep breath in an attempt to clear my head.

'Of course!' he says, as though he's suddenly recovered from temporary amnesia. 'The car park. Hmmm, but we weren't kissing as in *kissing* kissing.' I frown and he shakes his head and lets out a big puff of air as if he's annoyed.

'Well, what kind of kissing was it then?' I ask, confused. And he hasn't denied it.

'It's a bit awkward really.' He casts a look around before leaning in.

'Try me.'

'She grabbed me! And well . . . she's just a man-eater. I didn't stand a chance. Honest to God, she just lunged at me, and before I knew it I was body-slammed up against the wall.' He pulls a face and makes big eyes. The way he says man-eater, as though he's genuinely terrified of her, makes me giggle. And I can't stop, I feel slightly hysterical. I quickly force myself to get it together. 'And Georgie, I was talking to Walter that morning. I'm not sleeping with Maxine, or anybody else for that matter.' He stares into my eyes again. 'But I would love to continue things with you. Be my Valentine?' He looks downwards, treating me to a flash of his long velvety eyelashes. 'If you want to, that is. I'll even throw in the odd sketch and a few crazy golf lessons,' he adds, looking back up and treating me to a really cheeky, sexy grin. His eyes draw me in. My heart soars. A lovely feeling of relief washes over me. Relief from knowing he wasn't playing with me after all, and then heightened relief when it dawns on me that he hasn't twigged about the phone call. No, he's not even suspicious. In an instant I realise just how incredible he is. And . . . at last! I have my very own bona-fide Valentine. This is turning into a fantastic day. The best Valentine's Day ever.

But there's something niggling me, casting a shadow. I can't help wondering why he was talking to Walter, and will he still want me if I become the new floor supervisor and promptly sack him?

As I'm mulling this over, an amplified bell chimes, stealing my moment to respond. Then a rosy-cheeked toastmaster, standing on a podium and waving a bell in front of a microphone, announces that a buffet lunch is being served and that we're all to proceed into the Gainsborough room, where we can wait for the bride to arrive for the wedding ceremony that will be taking place on the lawn outside.

Tom leans into my neck and whispers, 'Let's continue this later.' And the pack of fireworks that exploded for me that night in Brighton is suddenly rekindled and explodes inside me all over again. Tom squeezes my hand and turns to make his way to the buffet. I follow after him, feeling as though I'm gliding along on the biggest cloud in the sky as I'm jostled through to the other room.

I see James just up ahead and a stab of guilt stings, throwing me back down to earth. I try and avoid him by pretending to fiddle with something in my clutch bag, but it's no use, he spots me and waves for me to come over.

'Wondered where you'd got to. You OK?' he says, brightly. His hair is nicely dishevelled and he looks sexy, but in a completely different way from Tom – more schoolboyish and wholesome rather than supermodel-lish and a bit naughty.

'Yes, yes I'm fine. Been mingling, you know how it is.' The words trip from my mouth and I immediately feel like a fraud. I glance at his face; he looks happy and relaxed. We've made a pact, how can I go back on that and hurt him again? He'll never forgive me a second time. A tension headache threatens around the nape of my neck. I feel as though I've been plunged into an impossible situation. Two gorgeous men and one promotion for the taking. I just wish that I could have it all, but I know I can't.

33

There must be at least a dozen circular buffet tables dotted around the Gainsborough room. Each has its own romantic pet name with details of its wares on a placard standing on a long weighted wire stem. In between the tables are life-size cardboard cutouts of a cartoon Cupid in a variety of cutesy poses. The nearest one is winking at me.

I wander over to a table called 'Valentine Foufou' and it's loaded with oysters packed into trays of crushed ice. Next to it is a table labelled 'Bobble Bunny – Royal Sevruga Caviar on buckwheat blinis'. I pop one into my mouth and instantly wish I hadn't. The salty little balls bounce around on my tongue, tasting vile as I surreptitiously wash them down with the last of my champagne. I head over to the 'Snuggles – Fifteen varieties of cheese' table and ponder on which one to try. As I decide on a creamy goat's cheese with a walnut oil drizzle, I feel a light tap on my shoulder. I turn around to see Lauren standing in front of me. She's wearing jeans and a sweatshirt and her hair is all bedraggled.

'Georgie. I'm sorry, but, err, it's Tina . . . she wants to see you,' Lauren says, not looking at me. My heart drops. I place the empty flute down on the table and wipe my lips on one of the T&C gold-embossed napkins.

'What do you mean? See me, but why?' I say, panic welling. Why does she want to see me? Today, on her wedding day? Surely I'm the last person she wants to clap eyes on.

'I don't know. She . . . she just seems really fired up. She just told me to come and get you.' Lauren looks as though she's about to burst into tears.

'It's OK, it's not your fault,' I say softly, placing my hand on her arm. 'Where is she?' I ask, praying for it to be over with quickly.

'I'll take you.' I follow Lauren as she practically runs from the room. Reaching the hallway, I have to break into a little jog to try and keep up with her.

'Lauren, wait up, what's the rush?' I pant, just managing to catch up as she dashes along.

'She told me to be fast. The wedding ceremony is due to start soon.' Lauren keeps running.

'Lauren, can I ask you something?' She stops and turns to me. Her tiny face is almost trembling. She's like a timid little puppy. 'Why do you let her push you around like this?'

'Because she's my boss, she has all the power.' As soon as the words come out of her mouth, I think of Maxine. That's what it will be like for me if I take her up on the job offer. I can just envisage it, being *her* bitch. I shudder at the thought, but what's the alternative? Up to my eyes in debt with no means of supporting myself? My flat repossessed? It doesn't bear thinking about.

'But why don't you try to find another job?' I ask, thinking, *yes*, and why don't I? But it's easier said than done in today's climate. Just last night they were saying on the news how bad the job market is, and I still haven't heard back about any of the applications I've made. And if I were lucky enough to get an interview, I'd be scrapping with fifty other people for just one job while worrying myself sick that Maxine might find out.

'Because she'll give me a rubbish reference. She's already told me so. I can't take the chance and end up being out of work. Not when I have Jack to think of.'

'But she can't do that . . . it's illegal.'

'I know, but you know what she's like, she'll find some way to jeopardise things for me.'

'I'm sorry Lauren, I wish there was something I could do.' I squeeze her arm. 'And why aren't you dressed up like everybody else?' I add, glancing again at her clothes.

'I'm not here as a guest. She's paying me to be her assistant for the day,' Lauren says breathlessly, trying to muster up a smile. Typical Tina. 'Georgie?' she says slowly, looking unsure.

'What is it?'

'Err, there is something you might be able to help me with.' She looks really anxious.

'Sure, what's up?' I ask, gently.

'Not here. Can I call you?' She bites her lip.

'Of course you can. Anytime,' I say, hoping she's not in any serious trouble. We keep jogging until we reach the bridal suite. Lauren taps on the door. There's no answer. We wait a few moments and then Karen, dressed in an unforgiving sky-blue satin bridesmaid dress, pulls the door open. A voice yells out from within the suite.

'Send her in, and then you can both leave.' It's Tina dismissing her minions, and I feel like having it out with her once and for all. Who the hell does she think she is? But it's her wedding day, so I take a deep breath and make my way in.

'What's this all about?' I ask, pushing the heavy door closed behind me. For a moment I hesitate. Tina looks beautiful: her hair is piled high up on her head, with little diamanté butterfly clips dotted in between the twines of her braids. Her dress is exquisite – a cinched-in bodice and an enormous *Big Fat Gypsy Wedding*-style meringue, with what must be a trillion Swarovski crystals glittering through the multiple layers of tulle. But her eyes are glinting with anger and there's a sinister smugness as well, almost like pleasure. Clutched in her right hand is a mobile phone.

'Georgina, I know we haven't always seen eye to eye on things, and I know it must have been hard for you . . .' she starts.

'What do you mean "hard for me"?' I interrupt, wondering where this is leading.

'Well. You know with me about to be married to . . . well, the man of your dreams, shall we say?' Her voice is loaded with pity.

'Man of my dreams? What do you mean?' I can't believe she's still harping on about this. Yes, Ciaran is a workmate, but hardly compares with Tom.

'Oh come on. Don't try and pretend any more, Georgina. You've been after Ciaran ever since you first clapped eyes on him.' Her voice escalates. She's standing squarely in front of me now, her free hand perched on her meringue-covered hip, making her look like a big fluffy teapot.

'Don't be so ridiculous.' I almost laugh out loud at the absurdity. But I manage to restrain myself when I see another flash of rage dart between her eyes. I decide to change tack. 'Tina, will you drop this crazy competition? Please. It's your wedding day, don't spoil it for yourself.'

'Crazy? I don't think so. I'd say pretty accurate actually.' She leans towards me and I can feel her breath on my face. Leaning back, I try to put some distance between us.

'Well you're wrong, and I'm sick of this, Tina. Yes he can be a bit flirty, but it's just work banter. You know what it's like in Carrington's, lots of men do it, we have a laugh at work . . . or we used to,' I say, unable to offer any more of an explanation to try and make her see sense.

'Will you listen to yourself? *Lots of men*. Just who do you think you are?' A glob of spittle threatens at the corner of her mouth.

'Tina, that's not what I meant. Why don't you just concentrate on the wedding?' I say, hoping to calm things down. 'Don't spoil it for yourself.'

'Look I'm not mad, so don't try and insult me. I know something is going on.' Her bottom lip trembles, and for a moment I feel sorry for her – she truly believes that Ciaran isn't hers, and only hers. What a hideous feeling to have on your wedding day. 'Why else was he in your hotel room? Naked!'

I knew it. She heard everything. I gasp and clutch my neck.

'Tina, it wasn't what you think.' But before I can explain, she butts in.

'And all those evenings where he doesn't answer his mobile. Supposedly working. Anyway I've got proof.' She pulls a face at me before turning away.

'What do you mean proof?' I say nervously, racking my brain to work out what she's managed to conjure up.

'Proof. See. Right here.' She shakes the phone at me.

'What is it?' I dread to think what she might have on Ciaran, or worse still what she thinks she has on me. Reason tells me there can't be anything, but she seems so convinced that now I'm beginning to doubt myself.

'I don't know. Why don't you tell me?' and after tapping a few buttons on the phone, she shoves it at me, slapping it into my chest. Instinctively, I grab it as I step back from her force. Then I push it out in front of me. My hands are trembling as I read the Twitter DM on the screen.

Sorry can't meet tonight as planned. Sam's Dad just died. Sure you'll understand. Luv Gxxx

'Where did you get this? This is a private direct message. You can't just go trawling through other people's Twitter feeds,' I exclaim, wondering what this has to do with anything. It's hardly proof.

'Oh, I didn't need to do that,' she hisses, smugly.

'So how did you get to see it then?' I swallow and feel the paranoia surging again.

'Ciaran of course. His pathetic attempt at proving he wasn't with *you* that night.' She spits the word 'you' at me and casts a look of contempt up and down my body. 'But I don't believe him. This is just a way of covering your tracks. So why don't you tell me all about it?' She flashes a sickening smile in my direction.

'Tina, this is mad,' I say, frantically jabbing at the screen with my finger.

'Oh don't give me that.' Tina grabs the phone back from me and is standing even closer now. Her face is red and her neck is developing a blotchy rash that's spreading like a wild bushfire. I can't prise my eyes away from her face. It's as if it's swelling up right in front of me. For a bizarre moment I imagine it exploding, her Restylane fillers splattering all over me. The eerie silence pulls me back into the moment. Tina is still staring at me, her face triumphant now. As though she thinks she's won.

'Tina, I'm sick of this. Do you really think there's something going on between Ciaran and me? Really, come on, he's marrying *you*, that must tell you something. Why else would he be doing that? It's not as though you've got a gun to his head. Even you must know how far-fetched this all sounds,' I say, desperately trying to make her see sense.

'What do you mean, *even me*? God you are so far up yourself, it's untrue.'

Tina marches over to the window, her dress making a furious swooshing sound as she moves.

'Sorry, I didn't mean it like that. I'm just tired of all this.'

'I bet you are. Anyone would be, given all your . . . "extra-curricular" activity, shall we say.' She gives me a smarmy smile.

'What do you mean?'

'Oh, don't come all innocent with me. Ciaran told me.'

'Told you what?'

'That he's been seeing you.'

'He actually said those specific words, did he?' My

eyelid twitches. This is insane, why on earth would he say that?

'Well, he said he's been staying late practically every night to help out with flyers and promotions and stuff. But I know that's just a cover – probably didn't want to hurt me with the actual details of your filthy little affair.' As the torrent of words comes out, a cold trickle of realisation makes me shiver. If what she says is true, then where has Ciaran really been, because I haven't seen him staying late after work. Maybe he *has* got another woman on the side, after all, and Tina is convinced it's me!

'Anyway, I want you to stop seeing him. Do you hear me? After today, he'll be a married man and I want you to keep away from him. Don't talk to him, don't tweet him, and don't even look at him. In fact, don't set foot inside the Cupcakes at Carrington's café ever again. Do you get it?' she yells, jabbing a finger in my direction.

'But that's ridiculous. We work in the same place, and we're mates. And my best friend owns the café. Anyway, what does Ciaran have to say about these rules then?' I ask, wondering if it's what he wanted to speak to me about the other evening.

'Nothing. And I don't want you discussing this with him. Do you hear me?' She glares at me.

'Oh I see. So you're expecting me to just stop talking to him, ignore him. Not visit the café? Is that it?' I say, not believing that I'm actually discussing this proposition. 'So how's that going to work then?' My blood is pumping even harder now. So Ciaran doesn't even know about Tina's demand. It's ridiculous and it's not going to happen.

'Well, you can't have it all. If you want to take Maxine up on her offer, that is.'

Whaat? How the hell does she know? Suddenly, a shot of panic billows through me. Dad! What if she knows about that as well?

'And what does that mean?' I say, barely able to bring myself to listen to the answer. She taps the mobile a bit more before shoving it at me again. Scrutinising the screen for clues, I feel dizzy and suddenly realise I've been holding my breath for a couple of seconds. I take a huge inward breath and release out all of the tension with a big puff.

'Oh you might huff, madam. But you won't get away with it.'

'What do you mean?' My voice wobbles momentarily and tears sting. I quickly blink to push them away, mentally counting backwards. She's not going to do this to me. I swallow hard and stare back at her.

'Well, you've broken the law so I'm going to report you, and then you'll be sacked when the police arrest you.'

'Oh for fuck's sake, what are you going on about now?' I demand, exasperation burning through me.

'Oh, I'd watch what I was saying if I were you, *Georgina.* Look here at your Twitter feed.'

Went in a mega-loaded Russian oligarch's car today. How starry is that? #customerwithasuper-injunction

She lets out a spiteful little giggle.

'So?' I say, desperately trying to fathom out where this is going.

'Is that all you can say? What about the super-injunction?'

'It's true. He has,' I say, feeling nervous now. Maybe I shouldn't have been quite so specific about his personal business. A momentary lapse; I'm usually so careful about other people's privacy, knowing first-hand what intrusion feels like. I mentally kick myself.

'Yes, but nobody is supposed to know. It's confidential. THAT'S. THE. WHOLE. POINT. OF. THEM,' she says, emphasising each word in a slow, deliberate voice, like I'm the village idiot. A triumphant smile spreads across her face. 'So, do you see my dilemma, Georgina?' There's a moment of silence, and I know it's a rhetorical question, but then it dawns on me. So this is why she upgraded my wedding invitation, just so she could play her trump card.

'You can't be serious? For God's sake, Tina, that's insane.'

'Is it? Only I think divulging personal information about a Carrington's private customer having a super-injunction – the simple fact that you've told the whole

325

of Twitter it exists – is actually a very serious offence indeed. And well, that's exactly what you've committed, isn't it? I wonder what Mr Malikov would have to say about this?' I can feel adrenalin pulsing around my heart. It's getting faster and faster. The room wobbles, and I clutch at a beechwood cabinet to steady myself. 'In fact, you're no better than your father. A criminal. Insider trading. Fraud. And didn't he take out loans in your name leaving you to pay them?' I swallow hard. She's obviously done her homework. I remember a particularly nasty article in a trashy newspaper mentioning this hideous reality at the time. I was nineteen and Dad was out on licence so I didn't report him, but the bank found out and told the police anyway. He ended up back inside. 'Bet you're still paying them off now. What kind of a father does that to his own daughter?' Tears sting in my eyes. 'You never know, you might even end up in prison as well.'

A hateful smile spreads across her face, but it quickly diminishes. The ring of her words throws me right back to the playground taunts, as if it happened just yesterday. The court when the guilty verdict was read out. Mum crying, gripping my hand in a desperate attempt to garner a modicum of strength to cope with it all. And that was the pivotal point. The very moment our lives changed forever. Dad went away, Mum died not long after and I was sent to Nanny Jean's, where I cried myself to sleep every night for over a year.

I step forward and as if in slow motion I reach out to slap her face, but she grabs my wrist and, after twisting it, yanks my arm backwards. The pain is excruciating. I bend over with agony and she leans down so her face is practically pressing into mine.

'Now you listen to me, you stuck-up bitch. You will keep away from Ciaran. You will not even look in his direction. You will not visit the café where he works. Ever again. You will forget he even exists. And, if you can't do that, then this phone becomes my insurance, because Ciaran is *my* insurance and I won't let you steal that away from me.' She spits every word directly into my face and I contemplate grabbing the phone and deleting the tweet but, as if reading my mind, she carries on. 'I've got a screenshot saved on a memory stick.' She shoves me away from her.

I clutch my arm, which is throbbing and raw from the embedded prints of her nails, but strangely I feel very calm. I look her up and down, and it's a look of utter pity.

'Go to hell, Tina,' I say, desperately trying to keep the rising fear from my voice. She glares at me, the phone clutched tightly in her balled fist. Her mouth drops open. She closes it and opens it again, in quick succession, like a fish gasping for air. I turn and, hoisting my dress up, I march from the room.

34

I will always hate Valentine's Day from now on. After crashing through the door to the loos, I throw myself into one of the cubicles. Pushing the toilet seat down, I perch on top of it. My hands are shaking as I pull my mobile from my bag. I need to talk to Sam. I find her number in my favourites list and my finger goes to the green call button. But I hesitate, and quickly snap the phone shut. She has enough to deal with. No, I'm doing this on my own now.

I sit for a while, drawing in the silence and running through everything that has happened. And we haven't even got to the actual wedding part yet. A plan starts to hatch in my head and for the first time since that day in the canteen when Maxine turned up, I can actually think straight. I know what I need to do, but there's something else I want to do first . . . something I should have done a long time ago. I flip open my phone to call Dad.

*

'Yo go, G. Over here.' It's Melissa, and she beckons me over. 'You're just in time.' I scan the lawn. Most of the guests are seated, but there's a small crowd standing at the back. I make my way over to stand with Melissa. Ciaran is up at the front, turned towards Tina, who is making her way very slowly down the flower-lined aisle in between the rows of chairs. A harp is playing and Tina is taking her time, ensuring everyone notices her, and oh my God . . . she's got a pink miniature Shetland pony on a lead, draped in white tulle with a wonky plastic horn perched on the side of its head.

Ciaran's face is smiling, but he doesn't look how I'd imagine a groom should look – not that I've been to many weddings, so I'm no expert. His eyes are darting through the crowd as if he's searching for something, or somebody. He looks in my direction and then quickly flicks his eyes away. Eddie is standing next to me. He sniffs loudly to get my attention.

'Could she take any longer?' Eddie is twitching all over like an overcharged electricity cable. 'Yes, yes move along . . . nothing to see here,' he says sarcastically and far too loudly.

'Eddie, what's got into you?' I ask, transfixed at the state of him.

'Nothing,' he snorts, waving his flute.

'Ed, you might want to slow down a bit,' I whisper, leaning in close to him so nobody else can hear.

'Oh no, the fun hasn't even started yet,' he says, as if

he knows something I don't. I tear my eyes away from him and see Tina has made it to the front. The service begins and I'm sure Ciaran sways ever so slightly. I blink and look again, I must be mistaken, and it's probably just the sun catching in my eyes. The registrar starts the service, and I feel like screaming out 'yes' when he gets to the 'if any person present knows of any lawful impediment' bit. But Tina being an actual hateful cow probably doesn't count. They exchange vows, and I'm definitely not mistaken this time.

'I . . . err, I . . .' Ciaran is definitely swaying, and for a sickening moment I think he actually might keel over. His best man flies up to check he's OK. I wrestle with my conscience to stifle the voice inside me that wants to scream out 'don't do it', right here in public, but it's too late. Ciaran makes it through, and now Tina has her lips shoved out for a kiss.

*

Piercing my thoughts, the toastmaster's booming voice announces the dining hall is now open for the wedding breakfast. I turn and follow the crowd inside.

My head is spinning with thoughts of the promotion now. And James and Tom, and Tina's sordid blackmail attempt. Fear swirls, but I just have to keep calm. If I think it all through I can make it work, I just know I can.

The chandeliered dining hall is filled to bursting point with circular tables. I manage to find mine, which is unsurprisingly near the fire exit door and at the very back of the room. And furthest away from the top table, which is a miniature version of all the other tables, but with two enormous carved wooden thrones behind it, and it's perched up on a white, velvet-draped platform.

I study the menu. Grilled Wagyu fillet steak with a marble score of nine, whatever that is, or pan-fried John Dory with a smoked foie-gras mousse and red cabbage. I'm not sure I like the sound of either of them, but then my eyes are drawn down to the Valrhona chocolate soufflé with clotted cream, and I definitely like the sound of that.

I can't wait for the dinner and the speeches to be over so I can make my excuses and leave. I need time to concentrate after everything that's happened today. Maxine wants her answer in less than forty-eight hours.

The band is playing again in the corner of the room, filling it with a lively version of 'My Funny Valentine', so I try to concentrate on the music instead, just to get some peace for a moment from the chatter inside my head.

Eddie arrives and plonks himself down in the seat on my right, closely followed by James, who, after checking the place cards, sits down on the other side of the table, opposite me. An elderly couple accompanied by a bustling woman, who I presume to be their carer, sits down next to Eddie. I glance to my left and see Melissa's name on the place card next to me. Then the wine waiter appears.

'Fish or steak, madam?' he asks in a bored voice. I opt for the fish and he pours me a generous measure from a bottle of white wine. I take a long mouthful and, after swallowing the fruity liquid, my mind jumps to Maxine and Tina. Once again I'm stuck in a Catch-22 situation. Either way I'm finished. James and Tom will hate me if I become Maxine's bitch and do what she's asked. But then the thought of Tina carrying out her threat fills me with a different kind of dread. It's a tentative threat, but in these privacy-obsessed times of phone hacking and injunctions galore, she could probably make the allegations stick. And if she tells Malikov, I bet he'll seize the opportunity to punish me for spoiling his scam to launder dirty money through Carrington's. It would be like a dream come true for him. He gets to 'defend' his privacy in public while at the same time milking the kudos of everyone knowing he has a super-injunction, just like all the other 'important' people he covets. At the very least that adage of 'no smoke without fire' will haunt me forever.

I spot Maxine striding through the room, closely followed by Walter. Guess Camille must still be in New York for Fashion Week. I draw a sharp breath and pray Maxine's not sitting at our table. Luckily she stops at another one. Melissa appears from behind me and takes her seat, just about managing not to slosh her Guinness over the pristine white linen tablecloth. I take another mouthful of wine and see Tom looking at the seating plan before making his way over. He's heading towards my table and that feeling I get whenever I set eyes on him surges straight through me again. Reaching the table he quickly checks the number and, after politely saying hello to each of us, he sits down.

Melissa nudges me hard, as if I haven't noticed Tom sitting opposite me. I kick her back even harder under the table. She leans into me.

'I could ride him like a stallion in the Grand National!' She elbows me and I splutter wine.

'Shush,' I say, wiping my chin.

'G, you are one lucky mare,' she says, totally ignoring my pleas. 'Tell me . . . when you were utterly spent after your first shag, were you like *fuuuck*?'

'Err, not exactly, we haven—'

'Shut uuup! I can practically touch the sexual tension between you two. Ever considered a threesome?'

The music stops and the bandmaster calls for our attention.

'Ladies and Gentlemen, may I present Mr and Mrs Murphy?' Then the whole room starts clapping and whistling. Everybody is standing up as the main doors fly open. Ciaran and Tina make their entrance. Tina's head is held high, she has a smile on her face, but I'm sure I detect an aura of smugness at the corners of her eyes as she surveys the room on her way over to the podium. Ciaran is smiling too, but it isn't his usual big grin; it's as if he's on autopilot. His body looks stiff and uncomfortable in the grey morning suit. They reach the podium and, after mounting the flight of steps, Ciaran sits down at the table. Embarrassingly, Tina stays standing, muttering something through gritted teeth as she attempts to keep the smile in place. Ciaran quickly jumps up and pulls the other chair out for her.

'That's my girl. Start as you mean to go on,' a fat middle-aged man booms up from the table nearest to them.

The band starts up again and the food starts to arrive. Tom is busy chatting to an older, sensibly dressed woman, on his right-hand side. James is sipping wine, in between glancing over at me. I smile back at him and push the lobster ravioli starter around my plate, thinking about Maxine's instruction and Tina's threat again, I can't decide what's scarier. 'I need to talk to you later,' I whisper to Eddie, but he seems preoccupied and just nods quickly in response.

*

As the waiters clear the main course plates, Tina suddenly stands up and clicks her fingers towards the band. Realising it's a cue to stop playing, the music peters out, ending with a lone cymbal crash that's followed by an awkward silence.

'Can I have everyone's attention, please?' Tina shouts, tapping the side of the microphone. 'I know this is an unusual request as we haven't actually got to the formal speeches part of this *dream* Valentine's Day yet. But, I have to introduce a very important person.' She pauses for a moment to scan the room, big smug smile still in place and head held high like she's announcing the arrival of royalty. 'Walter Davenport!' She shoves the microphone under her arm and does a little clap, followed by a simpering giggle as we all crane to stare at him.

'What's going on?' It's the old man on our table and he's practically shouting the words out.

'Nothing dear. Just another one of those famous people. They're everywhere these days,' his wife says, before patting his tweed-jacketed arm. Then the fat beer-bellied man at the front table bellows, 'Shuuushh. Our Tina is talking.'

'Thank you Daddy,' Tina continues, in a weird Baby Jane-style voice before treating her Dad to an air kiss.

I discreetly glance at my watch, wondering when the charade will be over, and notice Tom staring over in my direction. I smile at him. Tina's shrill voice punctures my thoughts.

'As I was saying. Walter has very kindly offered to say a few words, on today, the wedding day of two of his most . . . *senior* employees.' Her eyes dart around the room again, as if she's mentally challenging us to dare imply otherwise about her status within the store, especially as the boss is making a speech on her special day. She must be important. Ciaran looks up at her, his face expressionless and distant, as though he's watching by satellite. Walter stands up, looking a little awkward and unprepared, and a band member rushes another microphone over to him.

'Well, I'll start by congratulating Ciaran, and of course, err . . .' There's another awkward silence. I take Melissa's untouched wine glass and swallow a big mouthful.

'Oh get on with it,' Eddie mutters under his breath.

'The new Mrs Murphy,' Walter continues, and we all breathe a sigh of relief.

Tom catches my eye. I glance at him, wishing I could tell him what Maxine wants me to do. He smiles back, making himself look even more adorable.

'Yes, marriage is a wonderful institution,' Walter continues, amid a discreet round of sniggers from some of the Carrington's staff. I sneak a look at Maxine and catch her smirking and eyeing up a guy sitting opposite her. 'Yes, Ciaran is a fine fellow, a real man's man.'

'Sweet Jesus, could he milk the moment any more?' Eddie whispers in my ear.

Ciaran looks embarrassed and lowers his eyes downwards. He runs a finger along the inside of his collar before draining his glass and reaching out to the bottle for a refill. Tina flashes him a look just as he's about to take another mouthful, and he puts the glass back down.

Walter regales on how Ciaran did us proud last year at the retail industry rugby bonanza, before asking us all to raise our glasses again to the lovely couple. He sits down and Tina's dad hauls himself up into a standing position.

After pumping Walter's hand and slapping him too hard on the back, Tina's dad attempts a little jog up the stairs to the podium.

'Phew. Not as fit as I used to be,' he pants, clutching at his chest. 'Ladies and Gentlemen, in case you don't know, this gorgeous girl sitting here is my little princess.' He bends down and plants a big kiss on Tina's eager upturned cheek. 'Isn't she lovely?' There's a dutiful mutter of 'yes'. 'Takes after me in the looks department . . . no offence love,' he chortles, throwing a mock sorry face down at a woman I presume to be Tina's mum. 'Oops, I'm in for it now. Gonna cop a mouthful from the ex-missus,' he says, running an index finger across his neck. 'Probably bump up my maintenance payments again. *Ker-ching!*'

Furtive glances circuit the room. We're all wondering where he's going with this unconventional speech.

'Get on with it,' shouts a wiry-looking man sitting next to Tina's mum. Tina treats him to one of her death stares.

'Oops, upset her new fella as well now!' Tina's dad

takes another deep breath. 'So, Ciaran, I take it you're the happiest man alive today . . . and who can blame you? You've just married the best girl in the world.' Tina beams up at her dad and Ciaran drains his glass again. His face is flushed red and he has a distant look in his eyes. And he keeps scanning the room. He looks so uncomfortable, I feel sorry for him. He nods slowly, and pours himself some more wine. 'You wanna slow down on the old laughing juice, or you'll end up like me.' Tina's dad pats his ample belly and a roar of laughter erupts from his table. Ciaran looks oblivious as he stares intently into his wine glass. I can't believe he's drinking so much. He looks really miserable, but I don't understand why. I thought this was what he wanted.

35

The chocolate mousse was to die for, but having eaten my own, and Melissa's, after she staggered off in search of more Guinness, I feel well and truly stuffed. James is sitting next to me now.

'I'm impressed. I like a girl with a proper appetite,' he whispers.

I'm glad we're friends again, but I am acutely conscious of Tom sitting right opposite me. I suddenly realise that I definitely don't want him to get the wrong idea that there is anything more between me and James.

'James, I need to talk to you . . .' I swallow, keeping my voice low. But before I can say anything else, Ciaran's best man calls for silence.

'Thanks guys. I'll keep it brief, but I'd be failing in my best man duty if I didn't tell you a bit more about my mate here.' He grins at Ciaran, who thrusts his glass up in acknowledgement to him, narrowly missing Tina's dress as his wine sloshes around precariously. Why is he drinking so much? It's like he's given up, I just don't get it. 'Sorry Tina . . . but we couldn't let him get away with it.' He then grins apologetically at Tina, who manages a tight smile. 'Right, so moving swiftly on,' he rubs his hands together, 'I'll start by saying how lovely the bride looks.' Tina's smile broadens now. 'As do the bridesmaids.' There's a polite clapping session before he continues.

'Well, what can I tell you about Ciaran, other than that he's a ferocious fly-half and he sure kicks like a mule, and I should know, I've got the bruises to prove it.' We all laugh. 'And that's not just from the rugby field – oh no, have you seen this man wrestle? A tiger, I tell you, a tiger he is.' Ciaran is shaking his head, and his mate is feigning fear as he looks sideways at Ciaran.

There's more laughter and Ciaran mutters something to himself. What's got into him? I wonder if he's having regrets already.

'And then there are the cars, the faster the better, just like him. Yes, Tina knows what I'm talking about.' The best man winks at Tina and Ciaran busies himself with his glass before mumbling again under his breath. 'Yes, I'll echo what Walter said . . . our Ciaran is a real man's ma—' But before he can carry on, Ciaran is up on his feet now, waving his hands and shaking his head. He grabs the microphone from his mate's hand.

'Testing. One, two, three.' He blows into the microphone and then laughs to himself. He's swaying gently.

Ciaran motions for his mate to sit down.

'Ladies and Gentlemen. Can I have your attention *pleeeease?*' He tugs at his cravat and, after managing to wrestle it free from his neck, he winds it up into a ball and wings it up into the air and out towards the tables. It lands on a chandelier. There's a collective gasp. I can't believe he's this drunk at his own wedding. It's just not like him.

Ciaran's best man quickly makes his way back over to the podium. They exchange a few words before Tina shoos him away. She has the fake smile back in place and is looking up at Ciaran, waiting to bask in the praise that she's anticipating from his speech.

'I just want to say a few words.' Tina eagerly looks around the room as if she's checking to make sure we're all listening, before looking back at Ciaran.

'This isn't easy. In fact I've been dreading this moment for months.' He pauses, and takes a swig of his drink.

'That's nerves lad, nothing to be ashamed of,' Tina's dad bellows out, and Tina, oblivious to Ciaran's meltdown, pulls an 'aaahh' face before patting his arm like he's her pet poodle.

'You see . . .' We're all looking at Ciaran, waiting for him to carry on. 'Yes, I want to thank my parents, for everything they've done for me,' he continues. He bows his head in their direction. 'And of course my lovely bride. I, err especially want to say . . .' Ciaran stops again and Tina is scanning the room, making sure we're all catching her moment of glory. She's practically bobbing up and down with anticipation. The room is silent; even the waiters have stopped moving around.

'Err, shit. Look, I'm sorry but this, this, is err . . . no good.' He shakes his head. Jesus, what's he doing? My hand freezes around the wine glass. I glance across at Tom, who darts a worried look back at me, eyebrows furrowed.

'Tina, I'm so sorry. I didn't mean for it to be like this bu—' Tears glisten in his eyes, and he quickly wipes them away, using the cuff of his jacket.

'Is he OK, do you think?' I whisper to Eddie. He just shrugs his shoulders. A seed of doubt is niggling within me.

'Tina, I'm so sorry, but I can't, I, err, I can't lie any more.' Ciaran shakes his head. For a moment Tina's face is cemented into a rictus of horror that suddenly cracks. The room descends into a deathly silence.

'What do you mean?' she whispers.

'I'm sorry, but I. Um, I just can't keep it to myself any more.' Ciaran looks as though he's suddenly come alive now. His shoulders are back and he's looking straight at Tina.

'I just knew it. You bitch, you lying bitch,' Tina screams. She turns towards me, jabbing her finger in the air. Feeling horrified, I look at Tom again, hoping I'm managing to convey my total confusion at this development. Am I imagining it, or has his face changed a little?

'I'm in love with somebody else.' Ciaran stops again,

and everyone turns back to stare at him. But this time the silence hangs in the air. Tina is throwing killer looks at me, her mouth hanging open and a fury boiling up that's making her face redden. I pretend to fiddle with my bag to avoid her glare. I can feel a rivulet of sweat snaking down my spine.

Suddenly, everyone in the room cranes to stare at me. My cheeks are burning. I can feel Eddie's thigh twitching furiously up and down against my chair. What the hell is Ciaran doing? He's staring straight over here. And then I notice his eyes. The proverbial penny drops. He's not looking at me. OH MY ACTUAL GOD! How come I never realised?

'With Eddie . . .' Ciaran says, his voice barely audible, but there's no mistaking what he's just come out with. He leaps off the podium and sprints across the room towards the doors. I can't believe it. My mouth drops open. I turn to Eddie.

'Ciaran is your Smith,' I mutter in a daze, but Eddie flies up into a standing position, knocking his chair back behind him and running off after Ciaran. The silence is still hanging. Even Tina is speechless and totally motionless now. I can't move. I'm stunned as I glance across the table. Tom is looking at me, relief spread across his face. The silence is pointed.

'What did he say?' The old man's voice reverberates around the room.

Tina lets out a piercing shriek before yelling after

Ciaran, 'You won't get away with this you know.' And then she puts her hands to her face. 'I thought he loved me. He sai—' Tina is sobbing now, black streaks of mascara streaming down her face, and I feel a sudden rush of sorrow for her. She really thought she'd bagged her prince. On Valentine's Day too. Doesn't get more brutal than that.

'I've got to go to him,' I mumble to no one in particular, managing an apologetic shrug towards Tom. 'Eddie's my best friend,' I stammer, and then stumble as I try to stand up. My legs have turned to jelly, it must be the shock. I steal another glance at Tina, and she catches me looking.

'Nothing's changed,' she mouths, scrubbing furiously at her tearstained face. Her eyes are glinting with a mixture of revenge and hatred. She must think I was in on the secret. I know she'll stop at nothing to make us all pay, and the look on her face tells me I'm the first in line. If I accept the promotion then I'll have to cut Ciaran off, my best friend's boyfriend, and right when they're both going to need their friends the most. I can't do that to Eddie, especially when he's been such a loyal friend to me. And I shudder at the thought of what Tina will do to him.

I manage to stand up. Tom catches my eye and smiles as I dash from the room. I throw open the huge swing doors and run down the long corridor towards the atrium.

Where would they go? I think quickly, bending over

to recover from the run and the shock. Everything slots into place. Eddie sniping at Ciaran. Ciaran always loitering around when Eddie was chatting to me on the shop floor – he wasn't interested in me at all. I knew it was a ridiculous notion. It was Eddie he'd come to see. And, of course, Eddie's weird behaviour in Brighton; he didn't want Ciaran to go through with the wedding either. Yes, it all makes sense now, but for a second I feel a stab of hurt they didn't confide in me.

My heart is racing. Any minute now and Tina is going to be beating a warpath down to us. I want to find my friends before she lays into them. I fling open the nearest door, it's a private dining room and it's empty. I run to the next one, it's also empty.

Then I hear voices. I push open the door gingerly. Ciaran is slumped forward in an armchair by the window; he has his head in his hands and Eddie is kneeling down in front of him with his arms around Ciaran's shoulders.

'Can I come in?'

Eddie looks up at me. His eyes are watery, as though he's been crying. He nods, not looking me in the eye. Ciaran lifts his head, his eyes are red raw.

'Georgie, I'm so sorry. I-I don't know how to apologise.' Eddie bows his head. Tears prick my eyes. My heart goes out to them both.

'Why didn't you just say? It would have been OK, you know,' I say, softly. Ciaran swallows hard.

'I think I just got used to keeping the secret. Where I come from, people aren't gay. End of.'

'But you can't change who you are.'

'True, but sometimes you try to. Especially when you're brought up to believe acting on gay urges is sinful, and my mother is practically on first-name terms with the Pope, she's been to the Vatican that many times.' He attempts a wry smile. 'And now I've shamed her in the worst way possible. It was already bad enough that the wedding wasn't in a church. I hated lying, but I soon learnt . . . you know, I even told one of the teachers at school, years ago. I was about thirteen. Asked her if I really would go to hell for liking boys. The following Monday, she reassured me she'd had a mass said for me and that I must never let those words of the devil cross my lips again. For some crazy reason I thought if I got married then my secret would always be safe. I'd be "normal" and "respectable" and those things that mean everything to people like my parents.' Eddie squeezes Ciaran's hand. 'I thought it might be different when I came to England, that I'd have the courage to be myself. But well, as time went by, it became harder and harder. You know how nervy everyone gets when things aren't as they originally appear.' The words tumble from his mouth. And yes, I know exactly what he means.

'Ciaran, it makes no difference,' I say. 'You're a mate. That's all that matters.' I move closer to Ciaran and throw my arms around his stiff shoulders, knowing first-hand what it feels like to be judged by other people's perceptions of you. Eddie looks up at me.

'Thank you,' he mouths, and I notice his body is totally relaxed now. He's not twitching any more. Then something occurs to me.

'Hang on a minute – you let me take crap from Tina deliberately, didn't you? You must have heard the rumours about Ciaran fancying me. Everyone thought that was the reason he hung around the shop floor all the time.' I look over at Ciaran and Eddie.

'It's all my fault,' Ciaran starts. 'I'm so sorry, Georgie, I really am. Eddie begged me to come clean with you. And I tried, several times – that's why I was on the shop floor so much – but there just never seemed like a right moment. I hated letting you be our smokescreen, but when Tina got it into her head you were after me, well . . . I guess it just seemed easier to let you be the object of her attention. And then I worried that if you knew the truth about me and Eddie, then you might inadvertently let it slip to Tina, if she pushed you hard enough. And God knows she's enough to push anyone over the edge.' He manages a wry smile. 'I was determined to tell you that night Sam's dad died.' Ciaran looks at me, his eyes begging for forgiveness.

If only he knew. Tina's threat still rings in my ears. I pull myself back to the moment. I can't tell him yet. This isn't the time, or the place.

'I remember.' I nod. 'And I'm not being funny, but

maybe we should have guessed.' I shrug my shoulders and they frown at me.

'*Weell*, you know . . . your penchant for a nice pink fondant fancy.' I smirk to lighten the mood, and they both grin. Eddie jumps up to give me a big squeeze.

'I blooming love you,' he says, before straightening his jacket and pulling a flouncy face.

'And I'm just tired of pretending. All that finger-*pistolling* to try and prove my alpha-male status . . . OK, so I just made up a word,' Ciaran shrugs, before firing a feeble finger-pistol one last time. We all laugh. 'But you know what I mean.' And we certainly do.

36

It's Tuesday morning and from the beaming smile stretched across Eddie's face, it's obvious he's overflowing with happiness. His eyes are sparkling, a total contrast to my bloodshot turquoise ones as I peer into the lift mirror to inspect them.

'Thanks for coming in today . . . after everything that's happened over the weekend,' I say, quickly smudging on some concealer in an attempt to disguise the puffy circles that are hanging like parachutes under my eyes.

'No problem, honey pie, it's the least I could do. Are you all set for the meeting?' he smiles, encouragingly. I called Eddie yesterday, after he and Ciaran sent flowers by way of apology for letting me be their unknowing decoy. I ended up telling him about the promotion and how I'd been stewing over my options. I've not slept since the night before the wedding. I'm exhausted, but I know what I've got to do, and to lend some moral support Eddie's kindly offered to sit in on the meeting with James and Tom. I just have to convince Maxine I need him there.

'Just about,' I reply, inhaling hard through my nose and out through my mouth. I can't wait to get it over and done with. 'How's Ciaran?' I ask, tentatively. I'm keeping Tina's demand to myself for now.

'He'll be fine. His parents are still talking to him, just about . . . guess it's going to take time. He's taken this week off to try and sort things out with Tina. He still feels terrible about it all,' Eddie sighs. 'But it's not as though she was wearing wings throughout . . . but he insists on shouldering all of the blame.' He rolls his eyes, and I manage a smirk. Poor Ciaran, I dread to think what hoops she'll have him jumping through now.

'OK, see you later,' I say, as the lift pings.

'Can't wait. Just call if you need to,' he says, blowing me a kiss as I wrench the lift door closed.

I make my way straight into the staff room to call Maxine.

'Yes,' she purrs after the first ring.

'Maxine, I've made my decision, and I'd like to use your office to let James and Tom know.' I pause, letting the words sink in.

'Awesome. Be my guest,' she says, enthusiastically. 'I'll sit in . . . just in case they take it badly,' she quickly adds. Unable to resist the opportunity to gloat, more like. So predictable.

'Sure, and I was thinking it might be a good idea to have Eddie there to take notes, with it being such a sensitive meeting. I don't want to contravene any employment rules,' I say, willing her to agree. I'm not sure I can do it without him there and I tried calling Amy yesterday, but she's on a training course in London and her assistant, Zoe, said to do whatever Maxine asked as Walter would have authorised it in any case.

'Good idea. What time?'

'Is four o'clock OK?' I ask, thinking that will leave me plenty of time to get over to Hanley Cross and back. 'I've got to pop out before th—' But she cuts in.

'Yes, yes whatever,' she says, rudely, as if details are mere trivia, and she's not to be bothered with them.

'See you there then.'

'Perfect. And then we can finish up early and celebrate after you've done the deed.' She hangs up. I glance at my watch. Not long to go until I get what I want.

*

On turning into the road of the dreary sink estate on the outskirts of Mulberry-On-Sea, a rush of sadness washes over me. I glance at my watch, knowing I need to keep an eye on the time. I reach the entrance door to the block of flats and, after finding the correct number, I jam my finger on the buzzer. But before the intercom jumps into action, the door swings open and he comes out to meet me.

'Oh darling, it's so lovely to see you. I'm thrilled you

came.' It's Dad, and I'm shocked at how old he looks – properly old, like he's someone's granddad, and not the vibrant man that I remember swinging me around and around in the garden all those years ago. His hair, which used to be thick and black, is now thin and dappled with grey, and he has a hint of a stoop. I feel awkward. It's been so long. He senses it, I'm sure, and places a reassuring arm around me before giving my shoulders a gentle squeeze.

'Come in, are you hungry? I've made your favourite . . . chicken salad sandwiches with chocolate teacakes. Although, come to think of it, you've probably grown out of the teacakes by now,' he chuckles, attempting to lighten the mood and put me at ease.

'It sounds perfect, and I still love teacakes,' I say, wondering how long it's been since I last had one. Mum used to pack them for me to take to school. I'm surprised he's remembered. We turn and walk towards the block when a very shiny black Labrador comes bounding over, her whole body wriggling with excitement. 'Hey, who are you?'

'Georgie, meet Dusty,' he says, clicking his fingers at her. She sits immediately, her tail sweeping the floor expectantly.

'She's gorgeous, and so well behaved,' I say, grateful for the distraction. I stroke her under the chin and she thanks me by nuzzling her face into the palm of my hand.

'And great company too . . . aren't you girl?' he replies, and I'm sure I detect a hint of loneliness.

*

Sitting around the chipped Formica table in Dad's tired little studio flat, we've already chatted about the weather, the neighbours and the state of the economy. Dusty has licked my hand, several times, in attempt at procuring a teacake, before eventually giving up and falling asleep curled up at my feet. Now she's snoring, her paws twitching as she dreams of running free in a massive meadow, no doubt. I bend down to stroke her ear, before glancing at my watch. Only three hours to go before the meeting. A wave of anxiety pulls inside me, I hope I've made the right decision. I think of James and Tom and what their reactions will be when I break the news.

'Do you need to go? Of course you have to get back to work,' he says.

'I do, but I'm OK for a bit longer. I, err . . . I, just want to make sure we can—' I stop, and pick at the crust of a sandwich, unsure of what to say next.

'Shall I make it easy, sweetheart?' It's Dad who plucks up the courage to steer the conversation in the direction that we both know it needs to go in. I nod, before taking another sip of the milky tea. Just how I like it. He remembered that too. 'I was overjoyed when you called on Saturday, elated when you said you wanted to sort things out. I can't begin to tell you how happy,' he starts, slowly, as if he's treading carefully. Searching for the right words to say. I smile, and glance down at Dusty, before looking over in his direction. He has every right to be fed up with me. For years I've snubbed him, avoided his calls, and pretended he doesn't exist, but he's never once retaliated. He's never given up. It's strange, but in a way I have Tina to thank for helping me put things into perspective. When she stood there in that hotel room, sneering, trying to make me feel ashamed, just like Kimberley and her school friends did all those years ago, I realised I was no better. I've blamed Dad, and for what? To make him feel ashamed, just as Tina tried with me.

Sam was right. I can forgive him. And I'm tired of being angry. With him. With the multiple sclerosis. With the care system. After everything that's happened, with the necklace, the games at work, my careless tweet . . . it's made me realise that he's only human: we're all capable of doing things we wouldn't normally do when put under extreme pressure, just like me selling the necklace when I knew it was wrong, I'm sure Dad knew it was wrong when he took out the loan in my name to pay off his gambling debts. And he must have been desperate to take the chances he did at work, I know that now. That's why I called him from the wedding. That . . . and, well, what Sam said in the club that night has been playing on my mind. I couldn't bear it if something happened to him, like it did to Alfie, and things were still horrible between us. I've not even given him a chance to explain how it was for him all those years ago.

'I've missed you so much, but I completely understand why, well . . . why things have been so difficult since . . . since Mum died. You were all alone and there was nothing I could do from inside the prison to stop them taking you.' Dad pauses, and I take another sip of tea. His eyes flick to my trembling hand as I place the cup back down on the table. 'There isn't a day that goes by when I don't think of her, still, after all these years. And I know I was to blame. And for you ending up in care. I let you both down so badly.' He turns away. I bite my lip, and push my nails into the palm of my hand to stem the tears. It's the same for me, but I never stopped to think he missed her too. He looks as if he has the whole world balanced across the back of his shoulders. He lost his wife, his childhood sweetheart. Attending her funeral handcuffed to a prison warder, stripped of his dignity too. He lost everything, including me. And for all this time I've told myself he deserved it, that it was his own fault.

'Dad, please . . . pneumonia killed her, not you. The MS made her so weak. I know that now.' But it was easier, I suppose, to blame him. I couldn't bring myself to accept any part of my anger was – or could be – directed at Mum and the illness.

A silent tear trickles down his creased cheek as he draws a breath, pushing his shoulders back to open up his chest. I reach my hand over to his and it's as if he's finally been given permission to stop torturing himself with guilt. And something changes in me too. I don't feel scared any more. By forgiving him, I've thrown off the feeling of stigma that's clung to me for so long. I've taken back the power that I gave away – to the likes of Maxine, Tina, those spiteful little girls in the playground, and at the foster home where I didn't really fit in or belong – the very moment I made Dad my guilty secret and blamed him for everything that happened to me.

'Stupid old man . . .' he mutters, wiping his face with a wodge of kitchen roll. 'How about another cup of tea?'

'Yes please.' I can tell he's keen to busy himself. He pats my shoulder on his way over towards the kettle. 'I know darling. I know it was the illness, I do . . . but what I did destroyed her too. She was so proud of me, you both were. That's the irony I suppose. I used to think being a good husband and father for you was all about money.'

'You were so much more than that, Dad. Remember the fun we used to have in the park, and on holiday? You must remember the time I covered you in leaves and Mum pretended to . . .' My voice trembles before trailing off. It feels strange talking about Mum. Nobody knew her like Dad and I did, yet we've never spoken about her. Dad's tried to on the odd occasion when I've inadvertently taken his call, but it's as if I've wanted to keep her memory all to myself.

'But money gives you choice, darling. You know that. Look how well you've done for yourself.' He pauses. I glance away, if only he knew. 'And nice holidays. Cars. A decent education. I wanted you to have everything . . . everything I didn't have when I was growing up. I guess I just didn't know when to stop. I think of the promotion and the choices it could give me, Louise in HR confirmed a salary increase, and I know exactly what he means.

Silence follows.

'Do you miss those things?' I ask, as he places a steaming cup down in front of me. He shakes his head, before reaching into his pocket for a dog treat. Dusty, now wide awake, wiggles her body in anticipation. With a flick of his hand, she obeys immediately and sits, tilts her head back and catches the treat. I'm impressed, he's obviously spent hours training her and the bond between them is touching.

'No. I have everything I need right here,' he starts, looking first at me and then at Dusty. 'In many ways prison saved me. Banking isn't glamorous, you start off thinking it is, when you're young and cocky. But it soon sucks you in until you think you're invincible. You become arrogant. Convinced you're untouchable and better than everyone else,' he looks away, 'and that's when the stakes become too high. You want more and more, like a drug . . . only it's never enough. There's always a monkey further up the tree than you.'

I look away. I've taken risks, and what for? So I can swing in the trees with the monkeys? To plug the void of inadequacy that comes from being bullied? To ease the pain of being all alone? Shake off the stigma of being 'in care'?

'And the gambling?' I ask, tentatively, knowing that it was his addiction to late-night illegal poker games that pushed him to borrow money in my name and raise the stakes on the trade floor. Selling secrets to the highest bidder in order to honour his debts. He smiles softly.

'Darling, it's exactly the same thing. Only what happens on trade floors around the world isn't illegal, although . . . God knows, most of it should be,' he says, shaking his head. 'No, I kicked that demon into touch when I was inside, and I'll never, ever, let it get a hold on me again. Poison ivy, that's what it is, insidious and nasty. Chokes everything good out of life.'

'I know,' I say, quietly, thinking of the necklace and the narrow escape I had. I could so easily have found myself sucked into a world of money laundering and high stakes.

'Anyway, enough of the gloom. Tomorrow is another day as they say.' He claps his hands together. 'Are you still OK for time? I could show you my pot plants if you like.' He smiles, and I'm glad I came to see him. It's a start.

'I'm sorry, but I'm going to have to get back to work,' I reply, glancing at the kitchen clock and realising that a whole hour has passed by already. I can't afford to be late for the meeting. 'But I'll come again. I promise,' I say, pulling my handbag onto my shoulder.

'You will?' he says, his eyes lighting up.

'Yes.'

'Well that's the best news I've had, in . . . well years,' he says, cheerily, and he looks lighter, instantly younger. I make my way out, and he follows close behind me. As I stand aside to let him open the door, he places a hand on my left arm. 'Sweetheart, I know I can't change the past, or change what I did to you. But I can change what I do and I give you my absolute promise I will do everything I possibly can to make the future better. If you'll let me?' His eyes search mine. My heart softens, and I know it's time to let go. To forgive him. Mum never stopped loving him, she told me so just before she died, and I don't think I ever did, not really.

'Maybe we can work on it together,' I say, grinning, and he takes both my hands in his. He squeezes them tight and I feel happy. Optimistic. I know that we'll both give it our best shot.

'Before you go, I nearly forgot. Here,' Dad says, gently letting go of my hands and pulling a crumpled envelope from his pocket. 'Happy Valentine's Day, darling. Sorry it's a bit late. I forgot to post it in time. And then when you called I thought it would be nice to give it to you in person for a change.'

'Oh Dad, thank you,' I say, giving him a big cuddle and wondering who the other card was from then . . . how intriguing.

37

Both men are already sitting on the black sofas when I arrive in Maxine's office. Eddie is hovering next to Maxine's desk with his notepad poised, and Maxine's perched on the corner with her usual crossed-leg pose with an eager glint in her eye. It's obvious she can't wait to witness their humiliation, and I just want to get this over with. I clench my fists and then quickly release them in an attempt to dry the sweat that's accumulated in my palms. My heart is racing and I can't look either of them in the eye. But it has to be done.

Lauren pops her head around the door, just as I turn to close it.

'Shall I bring drinks?' she whispers.

'Maybe later,' I say, giving her a wink as she closes the door. I walk into the middle of the room and, after glancing at the clock, I shake my dark bob out and straighten my top. I realise my fingers are shaking. It'll soon be over with.

'James, Tom,' I start, looking at each of them in turn. I swallow. I can't believe this moment has actually arrived. 'Thank you for meeting with me . . .' I pause. Tom is smiling up at me, just like he did at the wedding. I waver. I don't know if I can do it, but I have to. I force myself to focus. I've made the decision and there's no going back now. James is looking at the floor as if he knows what's coming. 'At such short notice. I'm afraid I have some news you may not like. Maxine has offered me a promotion to floor supervisor.' I quickly glance up at the wall clock and then to Eddie, who gives me a little nod of reassurance. My stomach churns, I wish there was another way. I bite my lip, willing them to understand why I'm doing this. 'And . . .' I falter, and sneak a look at Maxine as she shakes her hair back, relishing the show she's orchestrated. She nods for me to continue. Out of the corner of my eye I see Eddie glance at the clock too.

'I'm sorry, but Maxine's decision is final, neither of you are required any more.' Eddie's eyes dart towards the door. The room is filled with a loaded silence. My heart is pounding. I think I might actually faint. James is staring at me now, confusion and hurt clouding his eyes. Maxine is practically panting with glee. I will them both to hear me out so they can understand why I'm doing this. 'Which is why I've decided not to accept her offer. I'm leaving.' I grin sheepishly at them. Their eyes are riveted on me now, and nobody says a word. 'I've had enough of this game,' I finish, and swallow hard.

I can hear blood pumping in my ears. I'm not playing

this pathetic game for a second longer. I'm choosing my friends, my family, and my sanity. No sooner are the words out of my mouth than I feel fantastic. It's like a massive cancerous growth has been excised from my body. I feel light. I feel free, and I feel giddy – giddy with the euphoria mixed with anticipation at what this means. Then a serene sense of calm descends over me. I think of Mum, and Dad, and then I know it's all going to be OK. It's as if Mum's telling me so. The happy times with her are all around me. I don't have to be inside Carrington's any more to remember them, not when they are right here in my heart forever.

Maxine's face is rigid, her eyes are almost bulging out of their sockets, and it makes every agonising second since that moment in her hotel room worth it a million times over.

'But you can't,' she breathes, before falling silent. James shakes his head and throws a look of contempt in Maxine's direction. Tom has his head bowed. I spot him flick his shirtsleeve back to see his watch, and for a moment it throws me, but before I can work out why, the door bursts open.

'Not too late, am I?' It's Camille, wearing a beautiful vintage mink Balenciaga cape with matching fascinator. She looks as if she's just stepped off the front cover of *Vogue*, circa 1950. 'Well done, my dear, I knew you could do it,' she says, gently patting my arm and enveloping me in her signature Hermès perfume. And thank

God she's here. Right on cue. The relief is over-whelming. I didn't want to hurt James and Tom for a second longer, but this was the only way Eddie and I could think of to get Maxine here for her long-overdue comeuppance.

'Who the hell are you?' Maxine demands.

'Camille Carrington-Davenport. And I take it you're Maxine,' she says, in a very breezy voice. Maxine's face freezes with horror.

'You can't just storm in here like you own the place.' Maxine is up on her feet now, with her hands on her hips. She glares at Camille and then back at me, as if she can't decide which one of us to deal with first.

'Oh, but I can,' Camille says, lighting up a More Menthol before puffing a smoke ring into Maxine's face.

'Is this some kind of joke?' Maxine butts in, her eyes scanning the room. We all stare at her. 'Because guess what . . . it's not funny,' she says, her voice sounding slightly hysterical. 'And you can't light up in here,' she adds, batting the smoke away. Her eyes are darting around the room. She knows she's cornered and that Camille is going to wipe the floor with her.

'You see, that's where you're wrong. This *place*, as you say –' Camille pauses to sweep a hand in the air – 'belongs to me. So I can do what I like.' A stunned silence envelops the room as we all watch the showdown unfolding.

'What are you going on about? Walter is the boss here . . . he owns the company,' she spits the words, her eyes darting between me and Camille.

'Oh, he obviously didn't tell you. My grandfather, Harry Carrington, founded this business and I inherited it. I'm the major shareholder. The one with the money!' She pauses to let Maxine catch up. 'My husband is just the figurehead, a front man, if you like. He doesn't own the company. No, he prefers pursuing other interests.' Camille draws on her cigarette. 'And I have to say you are a little older than his usual dalliances.' Camille casts a disparaging up-and-down look at Maxine, whose mouth falls open. I manage to stifle a snigger. Nobody says a word. The silence is broken by the door bouncing open.

'What are you doing here?' We all turn to see Walter striding into the room with a petrified look stamped on his face. 'The girl outside said you were here. But you never come up to the executive floor,' he puffs, looking first at Camille and then at Maxine, and then to the rest of us as he tries to take in what's happening. Eddie and I exchange furtive looks. Well done, Lauren, she made the call to Walter right on time, just as we planned. It's all coming together nicely.

'So glad you could join us, darling. I have something here for you.' And from her bespoke Anya Hindmarch crocodile clutch, Camille whips out a Dictaphone.

'What is that?' Walter asks, nervously, his eyes darting

towards Maxine. She throws him a warning look, as if she's telepathically telling him to 'shut the fuck up'.

'Calm down dear, and close your mouth. It's not an attractive look.' Walter's face turns scarlet and he quickly closes his mouth like an obedient child. Eddie, barely able to contain himself, lets out a little squeal of delight that he instantly attempts to cover up with a cough.

Camille places an expensively manicured fingernail over the play button and presses down on it. Eddie makes big eyes at me and grins. Maxine gasps as her voice bellows out from the tiny machine. We all stand rooted to the spot as we listen to Maxine telling James he can keep his job if he sleeps with her. I look over at James, but he doesn't see me; his head is bowed. There's a short pause before her voice pipes up again from the machine, only this time she's talking more softly, whispering almost. She's asking Tom how much he wants to keep his job. Her voice sounds all panty and flirty. I stare at Tom. He glances at me, and then at the floor. I pull my eyes away. My heart is almost pounding right out of my chest. Then Tom's voice can be heard telling Maxine 'not that much', and can she please stop throwing herself at him, it's totally inappropriate.

He turned her down. A shudder of relief washes over me. So he really was telling the truth. A 'true gentleman', that's what Nathan said. I wasn't sure, but now I have absolute proof. Tom looks up and our eyes meet. He winks at me and my stomach flips.

366

Yesterday, Eddie told me all about the Dictaphone he'd planted in Maxine's office, after I told him what happened at the wedding and my decision to leave, and how our plan to scupper Maxine was redundant now. But it was too late. Eddie had already put in a call to Camille, figuring she'd be very interested in listening to what went on in Maxine's office. And she was – Camille contacted Eddie the very minute she stepped off her private jet back from New York Fashion Week.

Maxine's face is a picture of disbelief mixed with pure white rage. Her pouty lips are pursed tight.

'Oh, and I think there might be more,' Camille says, calmly, and out of the corner of my eye I spot Eddie smirking and slowly nodding his head, relishing his moment of revenge. Camille clicks the machine again, and this time Maxine is congratulating me for stealing Malikov away from James and gushing at how pleased she is I'm in the lead and that a woman is teaching those men a thing or two. I clasp a hand to my neck. My face flushes. I look over to James, and he looks back this time, and shaking his head he smiles.

Sucking her teeth like Hannibal anticipating a nice Chianti, Maxine's raging eyes hover on each of us in turn before landing on Camille.

'How dare you illegally bug my office?' she screeches, fury pulsing through her.

'Oh it wasn't me. Didn't I say?' Camille casually glances around the room before taking another big lungful of her More Menthol and puffing it up into the air. 'It was Eddie. And, because he's so *loyal* – you know that quality I hear you're always claiming to possess and inspire in others – well, naturally he had to make me aware of your machinations.' Then Camille takes another draw before puffing a huge smoke circle into Maxine's seething face. Eddie looks as though he might burst with satisfaction as he witnesses Maxine being slapped down to size. 'Let's play the last part.' Camille presses the play button again, and this time Maxine and Walter are whispering; she's telling him he must leave Camille and what a powerful force they would be, running Carrington's together, and then a series of moans and grunts fill the air. The sound of Walter and Maxine getting it on makes me feel queasy and I have to steady myself against the corner of her desk. Camille stops the tape. Eddie lets out a muffled snigger and Walter storms out of the room, leaving Maxine to face the music alone.

I spot Lauren hovering in the doorway with a huge grin on her face. She's heard it all. I beckon for her to come in and she does. I want her to witness Maxine, her bully, being slapped into place.

'Oh and there's something else my husband didn't tell you,' Camille continues, smiling in Tom's direction. I look over at Eddie – what's going on now? But he shrugs and then shakes his head like he has no idea either. 'Walter is retiring.' There's a collective gasp.

'Yes, and I've bought the store.'

We all stare at each other in disbelief. I can feel my chest quivering as I attempt to try and cope with this rollercoaster of revelations. My mouth falls open. I quickly close it. My pulse is racing. Oh my God. OH MY ACTUAL GOD. I can't take my eyes off him. It's Tom. What is he talking about?

'Tom is the new major shareholder of Carrington's,' Camille says, smiling again at Tom. 'He's my nephew . . . My brother, Vaughan Carrington, never showed much interest in the store, which is why our late father left it to me. And Tom's mother is Isabella Rossi from the Italian Rossi dynasty. You obviously don't know the name,' she adds, casting a dismissive look in Maxine's direction. 'Well, Tom's independently and tremendously wealthy and, after seeing the potential of Carrington's from the ground floor, as it were, has made me an exceedingly generous offer that, well, I simply can't refuse.' She takes one last puff before letting the cigarette butt fall into a cup on Maxine's desk. 'Yes. It's been finalised, and the board is in agreement. Walter wanted to make the announcement himself, naturally, but after his recent disastrous decision,' she pauses to glance at Maxine again, 'I decided to take matters into my own hands and put a stop to all this silliness. What Carrington's needs is an enthusiastic, energetic leader with a team of loyal, longstanding staff, not divisive competitions to see who gets to keep their job.'

Tom turns to face me, his eyes searching mine for

forgiveness. It starts to sink in. Tom Rossi is really Tom Carrington. James and I stare at each other in disbelief. So that's why Tom called the London number from the hotel, probably updating Walter on his undercover findings . . . and Walter must have been at the mews house with Maxine. That's how she came to answer the phone. Tom was calling Walter, not Maxine!

It all makes sense now. The secret phone calls Tom used to spend all day conducting; when we all thought he was schmoozing the brand managers, he was probably chatting to his lawyers and business advisers. Then there was the secrecy shrouding his appointment in the first place. I knew it didn't stack up. And he hardly sold any of the Fine Jewellery collection, but then obviously he's not a real sales assistant at all.

Maxine is coughing now, practically choking. She's raging. She's been sleeping with the wrong man. Walter has been taking her for a ride, literally. The thought makes me laugh, and the relief of it all fitting into place gives my laugh a tinge of hysteria. Tom is up on his feet now and he glances at me again before turning to Maxine.

'And you're the one who is no longer required,' Tom says, his voice sounding sexy and very authoritative all at the same time. Maxine's jaw drops.

'*Whaat?* You can't fire me on the back of a stupid tape. I, I . . . err, was just seeing who was most committed to Carrington's,' she splutters, stalling for time as she concocts her explanation. Her lips, which are caked in scarlet lipstick, part into a hideous grimace.

'I think you'll find that blackmail constitutes an abuse of your position,' Tom says, calmly.

'What are you bleating on about? You're just a . . . secret aristocrat hiding behind your mummy's name,' she stutters. 'You won't last five minutes running this faded dump. Run it into the ground, more like.' Maxine's eyes are glinting at Camille now, as she looks her up and down, the disgust growing on her tight face, like cultured mould in a Petri dish. There's a silence as she scans the room and then she explodes.

'Well this is *very* cosy. Is this the best you could all come up with?' she hisses, switching her glare over to Eddie. 'What a pathetic bunch you are. And what about your dirty little secret?' She turns to face Eddie. 'Oh yes, I've known what you've been up to for some time now, all that *emotional wanking* down the phone to lover boy. Did you really think I wouldn't work it out?' Nobody moves and none of us dares to say anything. The atmosphere is charged with her venom. It's as if we're all frozen with shock. 'And not forgetting your fag-hag.' She throws a sarcastic-looking smile at me. 'Manage to run up any more debts recently?' She glares at me, rage seeping from every pore. I feel the creep of a flush – so she knew all along, and then I realise. Of course, she kept quiet about it on purpose – more ammunition to use against me.

'That's enough. And there's also the matter of your expense claims.' Tom steps forward and pulls a thick white envelope out from his inside breast pocket and hands it to Maxine. 'It's all inside. Details of your four-hundred-pound bottles of wine. Cashmere sweaters. Burberry handbags. A selection of Anne Summers special, err –' Tom pauses to clear his throat – 'Valentine-themed toys. And a two-thousand-pound designer cocktail dress couriered all the way from Harrods . . . if I'm not mistaken. And, of course, your formal dismissal letter for gross misconduct.' Maxine looks as if she might explode with indignation. Of course, the Prada dress, so that's how she got her immaculately manicured mitts on one. I absolutely knew none of the shops in Mulberry-On-Sea stocked Prada. And I can't believe she tried to wangle that lot through on expenses.

After the wedding, Lauren had called me at home and, during our heart to heart, she'd told me all about Maxine's expenses fiddle and how unhappy she was that Maxine was getting her to fill in her expenses spreadsheet with more and more illicit items, on top of the daily humiliation rituals. So, naturally I passed the evidence on to Eddie, who gave it to Camille to go with the tape. We knew the tape alone wouldn't be enough to bring her down. Camille must have then given the evidence to Tom and, given his secret position – well, no wonder he was sitting there looking so unfazed when I revealed Maxine's trump card to sack them both and make me her puppet.

Camille steps over to the phone on Maxine's desk and makes a quick call.

'Yes, we're ready for you now.'

Eddie smiles at me. We both know what's coming next. Then I turn to look at James and his eyes meet mine. He smiles broadly and then slowly nods his head. I knew he'd understand. There was no way I could just leave without making sure Maxine went too, and that he'd then be in with a chance of keeping his job.

The door flies open again and two sturdy-looking men in dark suits stride into the centre of the room. Security. Camille nods her head towards Maxine.

'You'll need to come with us,' the bald one says, as he steps over to where Maxine's standing.

'Get your hands off me,' she screams at the taller of the two men, when he places a hand around her elbow. She then yanks her arm away and attempts to launch herself over her desk in an attempt to get to the drawers.

'Please touch nothing. Your personal items will be packaged up for you.'

The other man turns to Lauren.

'Would you mind bagging up Maxine's personal items?' he says, handing her a roll of black sacks.

'It will be my pleasure,' she grins, ripping one of the sacks from the roll and flashing a smug smile in Maxine's direction.

'Don't you dare touch my stuff. I'll sue you for this. You won't get away with it, cretins, the lot of you. Feeble, weak-minded *cretiiins*,' Maxine screeches as the security guys each grab an arm and bundle her from the room. '*Walteeer*. Where the fuck are you? How dare you deceive me like this? You spineless bastaaard!' she shrieks as she's marched down the corridor.

I let out a massive sigh of relief and feel thankful we managed to pull it off. James and Eddie are deep in conversation now. Camille is helping Lauren in tossing Maxine's stuff into a sack. Tom moves close to me, provoking the now familiar tingle to shoot up my thighs.

'Are you sure this is what you want?' he says, managing to sound intimate, despite the others being here. I hesitate. I love working at Carrington's. And my friends are here. 'There's no need to leave now.'

'But what about James?' I ask, holding his eye contact. A fluttery feeling trickles through me.

'Don't worry, I have a new position in mind for him.' Tom turns to face James, who breaks off from his conversation. 'How do you fancy being our new customer relations manager? I hear you're very good with high-end private customers, and I seem to have gone off consultants.'

My phone vibrates inside my pocket so I leave everyone talking and step outside the room. Seeing it's Sam, and I can't ignore her, she might need me, I press to answer immediately.

'Sam, you are not going to believe what's happened today,' I gush. My heart is pounding and my hands are shaking with the sheer magnitude of it all.

'Come and tell me . . . please. I'm in the café doing some baking. I find it helps. Quite cathartic really. And I've got a giant red velvet cupcakezilla here with your name on. Still warm, and I'm just about to lash a dollop of butter cream frosting with pink glitter sprinkles all over it,' Sam says. Her voice is quiet but then she adds, 'I've really missed you,' and sounds lighter than she has for several weeks now.

'Try and stop me. I'm on my way.' I slot the phone back into my pocket and head off to Cupcakes at Carrington's. I can't wait to tell Sam all about it. And I can practically taste the gooey cakey-sweet loveliness already. Mm-mmm.

Epilogue

Italy, three months later . . .

The blistering sun dazzles my eyes as I glance up from the sun lounger. I can hear the faint sound of Adele's velvety voice floating up from the veranda beneath me. The electric blue and green hue of the lake glistens in the distance down the hillside. I shake out the day-old air-freighted copy of *The Times* and scan the pages. I'm just about to flip over another page when something catches my eye. Malikov. Pushing my sunglasses back, I sit up to read the article.

> *Russian businessman, Konstantin Malikov, was arrested yesterday as he stepped off his yacht in Cannes, amid allegations of bribery, money laundering and illegal arms supplies. Bratva connections have not been ruled out.*

I snap the paper shut and push it back under the sun lounger. Thank God that's all behind me now. I lie back down. I can hear footsteps in the distance. Lifting my sunglasses again and squinting in the sun, I look around the infinity pool. Somebody is walking along the very far side, but I can't make out who it is. As the sun shimmers against the water it blinds me, and I'm forced to look away. I trickle sun cream over my hot skin and start blending in the divine coconut and almond lotion. The figure is heading towards the little bar area now; maybe it's another guest arrived early for Sam and Nathan's wedding on Saturday, here at his parents' villa overlooking Lake Como. They opted for just family and very close friends. An intimate gathering.

After wiping my hands on a towel, I take a sip of the Parma Violet cocktail Sam created especially for the occasion. Her signature drink, as she calls it. I glance over towards her sun lounger. It's deserted.

Soon after the funeral, held in the packed Our Lady Star of the Sea Church in Mulberry-On-Sea, followed by a private scattering of Alfie's ashes on the moonlit beach, just Sam and I, as she requested, stood together on the sand listening to Alfie's favourite song, 'Moon River', on an iPod. I held her hand tightly in mine and whispered words of comfort, willing her to be brave. The following morning, Sam decided life was far too short. She had met her 'one' and promptly proposed to Nathan. He, of course, was delighted, and immediately produced an exquisite pear-shaped pink diamond ring he'd been planning to surprise her with on the evening of that horrible day of Alfie's death.

I smile at the memory of her phone call, where she shrieked with delight before sobbing her heart out on remembering that Alfie wouldn't be around to give her away. And then I promptly burst into tears when she asked if I thought my dad would mind doing the honours in his place. Dad was thrilled, and came over a little teary when Sam took him off to Alfie's favourite restaurant, The Ivy, for dinner, and told him that she'd be very proud if he would step into Alfie's shoes and escort her down the aisle.

Things are going really well between Dad and me now, and Sam asking him to give her away was a huge turning point for us both, like he finally has a real seal of approval.

My ringing mobile interrupts my thoughts. So, on seeing that it's Eddie, I press the green answer button to talk to him.

'Baby cakes! Just a quickie.' He pauses for maximum impact. 'I have delicious gossip,' he adds dramatically, to open the conversation. I laugh, typical Eddie, although I have to say he's calmed down a little since he and Ciaran moved in together.

'Oh yes?'

'You'll never guess who I spotted in Boots selling Z-list celebrity perfumes?' But before I can hazard a guess he screams in my ear. 'Only that shovel-carrying troll. Tina!' I think back to her departure. Remember those diversity awareness forms, the *highly confidential* ones? Well, Tina only went and left them out on her desk one night and didn't even realise when a kind Samaritan – rumour is it was Lauren – took them for safekeeping and later gave them to Amy with an anonymous Post-it note explanation on. Tina was disciplined over it, which she took great offence at, and ended up leaving in a huff when her demands for the 'real culprit who grassed her up' be sacked instead, fell on deaf ears.

The upside of the whole sorry affair was that Lauren passed her NVQ exams, got promoted, and now works properly alongside Doris and Suzanne in the cash office while Jack plays happily in the new Carrington's crèche. One of the first things Tom did when he took over was organise a staff questionnaire, asking what single change would make the most difference to everyone. Accessible and affordable childcare was the answer. Which is hardly surprising given that the majority of Carrington's employees are women. Mrs Grace said it was a miracle, and something she never envisaged witnessing in her lifetime, before launching into a long story about how her Terry had a wooden beer crate for a crib because everyone just had to make do back then.

'Poor Tina. Well I actually feel sorry for her,' I say. 'It's a bit of a slap down from calling yourself the accounts manager,' I remind him, before draining the last of my cocktail.

'Oh *purlease*. Cry me a fucking river. That girl is pure poison. No it serves her right.' He sniffs. 'And what about the prom queen?'

'Oh God, what about her?' I say, not wanting to be reminded of all that. Eddie draws in a big breath to create maximum impact.

'I heard she's been deported!'

'What do you mean, *deported*?' I snort.

'Back to Alabama, or wherever it is she comes from. Melissa told me.' Eddie drops his voice. 'OK, this is strictly confidential. Mel could lose her job at the prison. Swear on your life.'

'I swear.'

'Apparently, Maxine was caught trying to flog stolen goods – a ruby necklace belonging to that Russian oligarch, you know, the one with the waterbed.' I laugh. Trust Eddie to remember the embellishment. 'Can you believe it?' Oh my actual God. So she didn't even give the necklace back, she kept it for herself. No wonder she was so desperate to launch herself across the desk to grab her stuff before Camille had it all bagged up. It was probably in the drawer the whole time. 'Anyway enough of her, I want to hear about you. What are you wearing to the pre-wedding meal?'

'*Weell*, it's a one-off. A lovely floral maxi dress. And I made it myself,' I say, proudly.

'SHUT UUUP you did!' Eddie squeals, and I laugh out loud. 'Are you serious? I know you've been busy

380

executing your master plan, but hey, where did you learn to sew?'

'I taught myself, using Mum's old sewing machine,' I explain, smiling as I recall the many disasters at the start before I got the hang of it. He's right about my master plan. Oh, I forgot to say, that hefty 125 per cent mortgage? Well, the fixed rate ended, so with the rent from my new flatmate covering the now vastly reduced monthly payments, and my pay rise, of course, I was able to come to an agreement with my debtors to let me pay off the debts more slowly. And learning how to dramatically reduce my overheads has made a huge difference too. You know, they have magazines in libraries these days, and I cook with produce from a little allotment I managed to find up near Mulberry Common. I also sold some shoes and clothes on eBay and used the money to pay off the jeweller and clear the shortfall on the car loan, so I could return the car. Of course I had to keep the Gina sandals because they hold so many memories for me. I smile, as I glance down at them, twinkling like jewelled stars on my feet. I love to sunbathe in them because . . . well, just because I can.

'Good for you, honey. You really have set yourself free.'

'Thanks,' I reply, relishing how great it feels.

'Anyway, glad you're OK. Enjoy the meal. Give that cupcake queen a squeeze from me and tell her we can't wait to see her on Saturday. Our flight arrives on Friday and it's going to be fabulous standing on the Italian hillside in the glittering sun, witnessing her wedding ceremony, flooded with scent from the local lemon grove. Sooo romantic . . . Oh, hang on, Ciaran has just arrived home and is blowing you a kiss.'

'Ahh, blow one back from me,' I say, delighted they're still so happy together.

'Will do, sweetie. Chat more tomoz. Mwah, mwah, sending you cupcakes and puppies and all things lovely.' The line goes dead.

Shaking my head and smiling to myself, I flip over and lie on my front. Turning my face to the side, I close my eyes to soak up the last of the now setting sun. A magnificent smudge of orange and gold stretched across the horizon.

I can hear footsteps again – closer this time, much closer. They stop. I open my left eye and see the figure standing right beside me now. And then I realise who it is. And I can't believe it. I'm stunned. I open my mouth but words won't come out. I throw myself up into a sitting position. Balancing a cocktail tray in his right hand, he offers me a drink with the other. Parma Violet. Instantly I know Sam has had a hand in this guest appearance – as Queen of Hearts, she never could resist playing Cupid.

'Thanks. But, err, what are you doing here?' I manage, barely able to believe my own eyes.

'I came to see you. Sam invited me . . . you don't mind, do you, only I never did get an answer.'

Tom is standing over me, the sun dazzling like a giant halo all around him. He's wearing just a pair of aviator shades and fitted black Daniel Craig-style trunks. A little squeal of delight screams out inside me. His tanned body is magnificent, muscular and solid, and his chest hair is the darkest black, trickling down and underneath the waistband of his trunks.

'An answer to what?' I just about manage to squeak.

'Will you be my Valentine?'

But before I can respond he bends down, places the tray on the floor and brings his free hand around the back of my head and up under my hair, pulling my lips to his. My whole body tingles with desire. The feeling is incredible as the fireworks reignite and explode all over again. He pulls away, but I'm not letting him go this time, so I reach my hands around his back and down to his firm backside. 'One on each cheek', that's what Sam said.

Tom laughs and brings his hands up to tickle me.

'So you really are a cheeky cow,' he breathes into my ear before nuzzling the side of my neck.

'Hey, you were the one who went undercover. Now, I think that's very cheeky indeed. Tell me, why did you do that exactly?' I grin and raise an eyebrow. That little-boy look from the crazy golf course darts across his face, making my heart melt.

'Georgie, I wanted you right from the very first moment I saw you in the club. Laughing as you rolled around on the floor and then interrogating me at the bar. I couldn't get you out of my head after that . . . just like I said in your Valentine's card.'

Valentine's card? What's he going on about? And then I remember. The crimson envelope under my front door. Ahh, so it was from him. How romantic. I smile.

'But why did you keep your position a secret?'

'I had to. I started off wanting to see Carrington's from the inside, but that all went a bit pear-shaped when I met you.' He grins and shakes his head. 'Then all I wanted to do was to get to know you and see if you might be interested in the real me. Without everything else getting in the way. My family background,' he says quietly, and looks away. 'And then there was James, I thought there was something going on between you two . . .' His voice trails off.

I think of James. We met up, shortly after that day in Maxine's office, and he told me he'd had time to think and realised he was still in love with Rebecca. He asked if we could go back to being just friends. I'm so pleased things are back to normal between us. Lovely, kind James.

'It was nothing serious,' I say, gently pushing his chin back to see into his eyes.

'Where are those cheeky cow knickers? I think you need to put them on right now, Madam.' He tries to tickle me again, but I'm too quick for him.

'Come on. You might as well get it over with,' I say, trying to keep a straight face.

'OK,' he clears his throat. 'I deliberately seduced you over a game of crazy golf, which was totally shameless of me given my secret position.' We both burst out laughing. 'And I loved every minute of it,' he whispers suggestively into my ear, making my whole body burn with longing.

Of course, since Tom revealed his true position, we've seen each other at work and chatted over a cupcake or two on a few occasions, and every time, the sparks have been there and the connection so intense it's like nothing I've ever felt before. We even arranged a proper dinner date, but he had to cancel. Tom has to travel a lot, meeting suppliers and sourcing new lines, as he's determined to restore Carrington's to its former glory, so there never seems to have been the right moment for us. Sam has been badgering me for weeks now to make a proper move on him, but he's the boss. He owns Carrington's, and he's seriously wealthy, but really, I can't hold that against him now, can I? And he has come all this way to find me.

I pull away from his sexy embrace, to contemplate while I scan the view. The scene is fantastic. A gorgeous sunset. Tom. My secret Valentine. A perfect moment.

To be continued . . .

In Conversation With Alexandra Brown

What was the inspiration for Carrington's department store?

I've always loved department stores, there's just something so magical and euphoric about them, so when I met my husband and found out that his family used to own a department store in Ireland, I was beyond excited and my father-in-law was very generous in sharing his childhood memories of visiting the store. The other inspiration was Hannington's department store in Brighton where I grew up. I have fabulous memories of going there with my Nan, the smell of newness, the bright lights, the cage lift, the polite staff with their receipt pads – I loved everything about it, and of course, nothing bad ever happens inside a department store. Truefact.

Have you always wanted to become a writer?

Yes, as a child I loved reading and writing, it was an escape, a solace, and English Language and English Literature were the only subjects that interested me at school, which is probably why they were the only two exams I managed to pass. But I assumed writing was for other people – brainy, glamorous people who lived in London, which is probably why I ran away to London as soon as I left school. I soon realised this was a fantasy though, and quickly got myself a proper job. It took me twenty years to make my dream of writing all day, as well as all night, come true.

What was your worst job before becoming a writer?

Working in a bank, I was only nineteen – naïve and shy, and the manager would tap my bottom with his umbrella whenever I bent over to put the cash boxes into the safe. He was about a hundred years old and a total caricature with his pinstripe suit and bowler hat. I've had some fantastic jobs too though – switchboard operator in an old-fashioned telephone exchange where I got to listen in on famous people having conversations, a highpoint for a nosey writer like me. I loved being an usherette in a 1920s theatre and also working for a retired drag queen in his T-shirt printing kiosk on Brighton Pier.

What does your typical writing day look like?

I'm a complete routine addict, but also incredibly lucky in that my husband works from home too, so he takes our daughter to nursery, which means I can be at my desk by eight. I have a little ritual of lighting a candle and spraying the 'books' perfume* on my wrists, and then I write until she comes home, with a half-hour break for lunch and a catch up on Twitter, Facebook and the *Daily Mail* sidebar – I'm addicted to that too. If I'm nearing a deadline then I'll write at night, but never at weekends – that's thinking and family time. I also force myself to exercise regularly as sitting down for hours on end isn't good for my backside.

Do you put anything of yourself into Georgie?

Absolutely, especially the relationship with her dad, and her tendency to put two and two together and come up with five trillion. I'm a complete drama queen, but then there's part of me in Sam and Eddie too. Sam is my fun, Pollyanna side and a fantastic cheerleader, and Eddie – well, he's the naughty bit in me, the part that might think the outrageous things he says, but wouldn't dare say them out loud, unless I was chatting to my husband or very best friends.

Do you plan to write any more books about Carrington's?

Yes – there are currently three books planned in the Carrington's series, the second, *Christmas at Carrington's*,

---

* *Cupcakes at Carrington's* perfume is Jean Paul Gaultier Classique.

is coming soon and continues Georgie's story when she becomes a reluctant reality TV star.

What would be your desert island books?

Can I take a Kindle? There are so many books that I go back to time and time again, if I had to whittle it down, then it would be anything by Jackie Collins and Harold Robbins, *Valley of the Dolls* by Jacqueline Susann, the *Shopaholic* series by Sophie Kinsella, the *Malory Towers* series by Enid Blyton and the *Tales of the City* series by Armistead Maupin.

What is your guilty shopping pleasure?

Bags! Bags, bags and more bags – I'm addicted to them, hence Georgie works in Women's Accessories (my other dream job), even my husband has become a connoisseur of bags, he knows all the types, names, what's in, what isn't and for an ex-bodyguard from Belfast I'd say that's pretty impressive. Bags to me represent memories, the significant moments in my life – I have a beautiful rose pink Anya bag which my husband bought for me on my first Mother's Day after we adopted our daughter. I have a gorgeous emerald Dior top handle bag that I spotted in duty free at Hong Kong airport on the way home after our honeymoon six years ago, and I still use it every weekend. I have a gold beaded Fifties clutch from a charity shop that smells of nostalgia, lipstick and had a hand-written note inside from a man called Cyril – it holds glorious memories from my clubbing days, and there's even my old Ministry of Sound membership card still in it, circa 1993.